The Crucified Abbot

Where forbidden desires return to haunt you

Alan Brookes

Published by New Generation Publishing in 2021

Copyright © Alan Brookes 2021

First Edition

ISBN
      Paperback   978-1-80031-243-2
      Hardback   978-1-80031-242-5

www.newgeneration-publishing.com

New Generation Publishing

I couldn't help it. I can resist everything except temptation.

Lady Windermere's Fan (1891) Act 1

By Oscar Wilde 1854-1900

Prologue

Detective Sergeant Donald Lawrence and his new wife, Detective Constable Janet Lawrence, are two stalwarts of the Special Investigation Department at Scotland Yard. They begin their new life together staying at a mysterious hotel in the heart of England, *The Crucified Abbot,* on their honeymoon. Their exploits follow on from being integrally involved in one of the most gruesome cases the Metropolitan Police had ever confronted.

In the author's preceding novel, ***Mudlarks****,* Donald and Janet's romantic beginnings entwine with teenage amateur mudlarks, who continually find various body parts on the Thameside beaches at Rotherhithe. Along with their colleague, Detective Constable Lucy Barnes, they narrow the search for the source of multiple hideous murders to a lonely, riverside church, The Church of Secular Modern Saints at Deptford.

As Donald and Janet's marriage takes place in London, the evil, infamous church lies in ruins. Scotland Yard detectives Donald and Janet, encounter mysterious and supernatural experiences during their stay at *The Crucified Abbot* in rural Staffordshire. These experiences test their sanity and their burgeoning marriage.

Preface

Behind the old priory ruins at the summit of Brereton Hill, close by the village of Upper Slaughter and enclosed by two oak plantations, grows the Abbot Ibáñez yew tree. This living relic is not so much a landmark, but more well known by all who live nearby as a spooky feature embedded in the Triassic sandstone of Cannock Chase. Here turtle doves nest on the primaeval branches, looking down at the myriads of foxgloves, the vivid yellow kingcups, and the pungent wild garlic flowers. The tree indeed holds some gruesome features, like the iron nails that crucified the Abbot. However, few villagers will search for the nails in the shadows beneath those dark thickets where the sun seldom peeps through the trees. At ninety-three years of age, Ted Baxter, unofficial custodian of Upper Slaughter's archaic traditions, is indeed a man and a half, afraid of no one. Still, not even Ted would go near the eerie tree on moonlit nights.

One

Donald and his wife, Janet, breathed the fresh countryside aromas entering rural Staffordshire. With the car roof folded in the boot of the hired black Peugeot 307cc cabriolet convertible, they enjoyed the warm sunshine bathing their faces and the cooling breezes rippling their hair. 'Can you smell that scented air, darling? Take a deep breath. Unless I'm mistaken, that's the scent of wild hyacinth, the tang of pine forests and aromatic wild garlic flowers.'

'Yes, I can. The sweetness sure beats the choking diesel fumes of the Old Kent Road and the sickening stench of the dockland's breweries after fumigating the hops on a dismal Monday morning in London's east end.'

Donald and Janet's honeymoon had been idyllic, ambling through the rustic shire counties of England, casually selecting overnight stops at secluded hostelries and backwater pastoral hotels. They enjoyed passing through quaint villages with uncommon names that seemed cut off from the bustle and complications of modern life. Places where well-used stocks still adorned the village green, ancient ducking stools, augmented village ponds and horse and carts were still a favoured mode of transport.

'Here's a strange-sounding country hotel,' Janet commented to her new husband peering over the top of her sunglasses. 'Look at the thatched roof and the black and white half-timbered façade. It looks like a scene from Charles Dickens' Great Expectations.'

'Look at the unusual signboard. Wow, it's called *The Crucified Abbot;* shall we try it, darling?' Janet nodded as the car glided calmly along Gallows Lane. The tyres crunched noisily on the hotel's gravelled courtyard. Donald cut the engine, and he reached for his mobile telephone.

'Oh, that's odd, there's no phone signal here and the car's satnav display has disappeared from the screen.'

'Well, that doesn't matter, darling, we're on our honeymoon.'

'Well, you may wish to call for help in the middle of the night?' Donald added whimsically.

'What, from being attacked by you or the Abbot?'

'The way your sexiness is driving me crazy, you may be safer with the Abbot?'

'I don't know about that; I've read somewhere that these old-fashioned English Abbots used to have a rare old time when visiting the convents to receive the nuns' confessions.'

Their mutual laughter ceased immediately on entering the elaborate, old-fashioned hotel foyer. It seemed they'd entered a time warp and arrived in the midst of the Victorian era. A tall, stern, moustachioed man intensified their initial impressions. He dressed in an upturned, starched collar and buttoned pin-striped waistcoat spoke from behind the reception desk. He asked, 'Good afternoon, madam, and sir, how can I help you?' The man had one of those uncompromising stares symptomatic of photographs of the late nineteenth century where subjects had to keep a straight face for several minutes to capture the exposure. Extensive sideburns and greased, neat hair accentuated his long, gaunt face.

'My wife and I are thirsty, could we have a pot of tea, please, and we'd like to book a room for the night?' Donald asked.

'That's no problem, sir; follow me to the tea lounge,' the man answered with a dull monotone, devoid of emotion or enthusiasm. 'Please take a seat, and I'll call Mrs Strange to take your order.' He reached for a fob watch hanging on a silver chain across the front of his waistcoat to verify the time. Donald and Janet relaxed into bat-winged armchairs that swallowed them as the soft upholstery compressed under their weight. They looked around the room at old sepia-coloured photographs of groups of people dressed in Victorian clothes arranged in family groups. One fascinating framed document attracted Donald's attention. In olde-English calligraphy, a property deed conveyed *The Crucified Abbot's* title deed from the Crown Estates to a Mr Caleb Strange. Donald marvelled at the clarity of the document that revealed the date 31st October 1566. Donald at once imagined Halloween night in the reign of King Henry VIII, 'I bet that was a bundle of fun?' He mused.

'Ah, I can tell you're interested in the old title deed, young man.' A woman's voice interrupted his thoughts. Donald turned to look at a dark-haired woman dressed in a long brown dress overlaid with a white apron. She wore a white cotton bonnet tied with a loose knot under her chin. With a profuse smile displaying flawless white teeth, she placed a pot of tea on the low table where Donald and Janet sat.

'Hello madam, so the hostelry has existed since the Tudor period?' Donald asked, looking up at the ancient, gnarled, wooden oaken beams.

'The premises are much older than that. The Domesday Book of 1086 chronicles that King William the Conqueror appropriated *The Crucified Abbot* during his dastardly plunder of England.'

'That's even more interesting. To own and live in a property with a thousand years of history. Think of all the fascinating events that have occurred here over the years. May I introduce ourselves? I'm Donald Lawrence, and this is my wife, Janet. We're on our honeymoon.'

'My husband, Caleb, tells me you'd like to book a room for the night. It would be appropriate, as you're on a honeymoon, that you have the bridal suite. Reputedly, King Henry stayed in the room with his second wife, Anne Boleyn, while on a hunting trip for wild boar here in Cannock Chase. You seem a delightful couple, I'm sure your marriage will have a happier outcome than theirs?' She drew her fingers across her throat, alluding to the beheading of Queen Anne, and smiled. 'My name is Margareta Strange.'

'How did the hotel acquire the name *The Crucified Abbot*, Mrs Strange?' Janet asked.

'Well, Mrs Lawrence, the local legends explain the hotel rests on the site of a pagan temple going back to the mists of time. Although Christianity didn't take hold in England until the sixth century when Saint Augustine founded a mission in Northumberland. The first Christians wandered through here in the first century; known as the Kingdom of Mercia in those days. It's conceivable that the local Anglo-Saxon pagans didn't take kindly to being lectured to by some foreigner called Abbot Ibáñez. He told the local inhabitants they must repent evil and consider other ways of living. The locals crucified the Abbot on the yew tree in the rear garden of the hotel. The approaching dusk is causing the light to fade. Tomorrow you'll be able to look at the remains of the tree if you wish. The split trunk grows as several individual trees now, and some thick old, gnarled branches need propping up. Two of the original iron nails that held the Abbot pinned to the tree till his flesh eventually rotted away, still protrude from the bark. Caleb and I feel it would be sacrilege to get rid of the tree, knowing the relic's infamy and connection to the hotel.'

Donald and Janet were impressed by Mrs Strange's detailed knowledge relating to the property.

'What a coincidence that your husband, Caleb, has the same name as the person mentioned in the property deed from King Henry VIII?' Donald prompted.

'There's no coincidence, Mr Lawrence; the hotel has remained in the Strange family for all time. Sir Thomas Cromwell, the King's first minister, signed that document, not King Henry. I note you've finished the tea; I'll take you up to the King's bridal suite when you're ready.'

'Is there a chance my wife and I could dine here this evening?' Donald was tired and didn't feel like travelling any further.

'Yes, but unfortunately there is only a restricted menu today, with a speciality of braised loin of local wild boar with sautéed forest mushrooms and neighbourhood mead or local Abbot cider.'

'Why describe that as unfortunate? That sounds wonderful.' Donald enthused.

'Mead is produced from honey, isn't that correct, darling? I've never tasted that before...' Janet asked her enthusiastic husband.

Mrs Strange intervened before Donald could reply.

'The local mead is produced by two local farmers, Simon and Jasper, who have hives that have been producing honey for centuries. Of course, the secret of excellent mead starts with the bees and where the location is for harvesting the nectar. Caleb and I are fortunate on this part of Cannock Chase that there are dense patches of wild hyacinth and garlic flowers growing close to the hotel.'

Donald nodded to Janet in confirmation of the aromas that were apparent on their arrival.

'Two places will be set in the dining room at the rear for 7:30 pm. There's a pleasant outlook from there, looking out over the forest of Cannock Chase and, of course, Abbot Ibáñez's yew tree in the foreground.'

Two

Later that evening, a full moon illuminated the interior of the King's bridal room. Donald and Janet hugged each other, engulfed in the feather mattress on the four-poster bed. They marvelled at the innate carvings on the wooden framework of the bed's structure. Above the bolstered pillows, a wooden plaque displayed a monogram of the interwoven letters H and A. 'Do you think this was actually where King Henry VIII and Queen Anne Boleyn slept?' Janet surmised.

'Darling, imagine the King and Queen of England being on a honeymoon, sleep must have been an afterthought?' Donald laughed sarcastically. The room's brightness became dappled disturbances as fluttering shadows danced across the window.

'What's causing shadows at this time of the evening?' Donald wondered and moved to the window. Gazing through the dimpled mullion glazing, several bats flitted across the rear garden, gliding in and out of the trees. 'Janet, come here, there are loads of flying bats.' Janet joined her husband, both standing naked in the moon's glare. 'They're long-winged bats, like those vampire bats in natural history films of the Savannah in Africa that feed on the warm blood of wildebeest. I've only ever seen the short-winged pipistrelle bats in England. That's curious? These must be a localised species.'

'I presume that's the Abbot Ibáñez tree?' Janet pointed to the spreading yew tree with outer branches precariously supported by metal props.

'Ooh, Donald, I'm having tummy pains, do you mind if I get back into bed?'

'I hope those mushrooms were okay?' Donald questioned, recalling what they'd eaten at dinner.

'The mushrooms tasted bitter, but the mead was delicious.' Janet mumbled, holding her stomach.

Donald turned and watched Janet climb into bed. Within a few minutes, heavy breathing ensued from beneath the bedclothes. Upon looking closer, he verified her deep sleep. As shadows continued to trickle through the moonbeams, Donald returned to the window to gaze at the varied scenery of valleys and heathland spread across the hills of Cannock Chase. Drawing up a chair to the edge of the window, he made himself more comfortable. Shortly, a grey mist descended as the high temperature of the day eased away. Soon, cloying fog extended down to ground level in the hotel's garden and he could barely see the bats flying through the branches of the indistinct old yew tree. A faint yellow glare in the forest inflamed his imagination. First thoughts were that it was a giant firefly, but the blurred light soon multiplied. Donald saw two, and then four, until quickly losing count and estimated there must be about a dozen. The diffused glares formed a line that seemed to weave in and out of the yew tree's propped branches before forming a circle and then stopping.

Donald's breath faltered, triggered by his increasing confusion. The fog enveloped everything. Were there now figures moving around the tree? He wasn't entirely sure. Was he hallucinating as the faint yellow glares all merged into a brighter radiance? The soft, monotonous chanting brought on droopy, solemn eyes. Gradually, Donald slid from the chair onto the carpeted floor and slept.

Three

Donald's arms encircled Janet as he awoke to the garish dawn. Janet was still sleeping as puzzled recollections of the previous evening clouded his first thoughts. 'Did sleep overtake me as I sat by the window, or did Janet drag me into bed? Evidently, sleep overcame me after joining Janet during the night. This night's deep sleep is the best I've experienced in years.' After rubbing his eyes and looking towards Janet, he thought she looked radiant and noticed a twig entangled in her hair. Carefully, Donald detached it, as he also remembered his nocturnal adventures. 'It must have been those mushrooms; I've had the weirdest dreams. We were dancing around a maypole together in the nude. Or was it a tree?' he chuckled, 'oh my God, we danced with other naked people, and we were all singing and chanting poems, and Caleb was directing everybody. Bloody hell, the stuff we dream about when we're asleep? I can remember Mrs Strange holding my hand; she was naked and proud of it, shaking her tits at everybody. Oh, and that was funny when three naked old blokes dragged Janet into the middle of the ring, and they had their hands all over her as she danced for them. I hadn't better tell Janet about my thoughts. I'm sure she already thinks I'm sex mad?'

Janet slowly turned towards him. Although still asleep, she had a broad smile on her face. 'It looks as if she's having some nice dreams, too?' He bent towards her and gently kissed her forehead. 'Oh yes,' Janet sighed softly. He rested his head on his bent arm and watched her radiant beauty as she dozed. Her eyelids flickered as she placed her arm across his body. Her hand roamed and soon was holding his genitals. 'Oh yes,' she whispered again. Donald at once became aroused; Janet gradually opened her eyes.

'Oh, Donald, good morning, I've had a lovely night's sleep.'

'Good morning, darling, so have I.'

'It's so nice to wake up like this, lying next to you.' She closed her eyes again and was still dozing, half-asleep, half-awake. Then, as if startled by a loud bang, she suddenly sat up and looked around the room. 'Oh, Donald, oh my God, thank goodness that was a dream.' She rubbed her eyes and snuggled back down into his shape as they lay holding each other, submerged in the feather mattress. 'Darling, I've had such a peculiar dream. We went dancing together,' she mumbled in her slumbering state. 'We were dancing with other people, and we were all naked.' Donald looked in astonishment and was about to tell her of his dreams, but she carried on muttering. 'I realise I must watch you in the future, that Mrs Strange had the serious hots for you, and she couldn't keep her hands off you. The strangest bit of my dream was when three old farmers, one named Jasper, danced with me and kept holding me... ooh, Donald, the men were so rude, they kept touching me... It's your fault, darling; our lovemaking has stirred my subconscious to have many erotic dreams...'

'... Hang on, Janet...' Donald sat up, causing Janet to become fully awake. 'What are you saying to me?'

'Oh, Donald, I don't understand what I'm saying. It was such a weird dream. Come back down under the bedclothes with me.'

'This gets more bizarre every second. I've had the same dream.' Janet's eyes opened wide, and she sat up with him.

'What? That we were dancing naked with other people?'

'Yes, and especially the bit where three old codgers danced with you.'

'You saw that in your dream as well...?'

'Can you recall where we danced?'

'Oh, I can't think, oh yes around a tree...'

'... exactly and consider this, I pulled this from your hair as you were sleeping.' He showed her the twig. 'Unless I'm mistaken, it's from a yew tree. See the spiky green fronds attached to it?' Instantaneously, they both leapt out of bed and moved to the window. Peering down on Abbot Ibáñez's yew tree, they noticed a circular patch of grass that seemed trampled and flattened compared with the rest of the lawn. Then, despite both still being naked, they involuntarily returned a wave to Mrs Strange as she waved to them from the garden while she pegged some clothes on the washing line.

'Oh, sweet Jesus, she's seen us both starkers.' Donald instantly drew the curtains across the window.

'What's happening, Donald?' Janet asked as she sat back on the bed, holding her face.

'Let's not get carried away! It must have been those forest mushrooms we ate for dinner. They say some lesser-known varieties have hallucinogenic properties...'

'Can you remember what sort they were?'

'I'm no expert, but I think they were boletes and porcinis. The small crinkly black ones were morels.'

'... I appreciate today's youngsters are into many drugs, and they experiment with mushrooms, but how does that explain that we both experienced the same dream?'

'I don't understand either, perhaps because we're so close, so tuned in to each other? Mutually psychic even? Perhaps our pheromones interacted. I don't get it, Janet...'

'... and what about the piece of the yew tree in my hair?'

'Again, I'm not sure; perhaps you brushed against one of the yew bushes lining the entrance porch when we first walked into the hotel?'

'Oh, Donald, this gives me the creeps. It all seemed so real.'

'Let's have a shower and go down to breakfast. Perhaps we'll feel better after having some normal food?'

'Okay, but avoid any mushrooms.' They both laughed as they entered the shower together. What they didn't notice standing in the shower's cascading water were the dirty smudges and green grass stains being washed from their feet.

Four

'Good morning, Mr and Mrs Lawrence, your table is number three, over by the window,' Mrs Strange called to them as they reached the bottom of the staircase. 'Please help yourself to the cereals and fruit and I'll come and take your order for the cooked main course.' She hurried past them, carrying a tray of used plates and bowls.

They entered the dining room and were surprised to see so many people already seated. The hotel seemed quiet, and Donald knew their car was the only vehicle in the car park. 'Good morning', people called to them as they walked past their tables. Donald thought how friendly everyone seemed.

'Good morning,' they replied in unison. Janet sat at the table while Donald fetched their cereals and fruit juice. Standing at the hors d'oeuvres table, a small man with a large black moustache commented on what a pleasant evening it had been last night. 'Yes, it was a pleasant evening, wasn't it?' Donald answered politely. He recalled that he and Janet had got straight into bed, so he'd experienced little of it to verify whether or not it was pleasant. At the adjacent table to where Janet sat, she noticed three men were already tucking into their bacon, eggs, and mushrooms. As if being aware Janet was watching them, they all turned to face her and called, 'Good morning, Janet.' She also felt the friendliness and welcoming attitude. The total experience of entering the dining room was as if they were joining a sociable family gathering.

Janet smiled and involuntarily called back. 'Good morning, Jasper, good morning, Simon...' Her voice trailed off as astonishment inhibited her vocal cords. Her stare focussed on the third man. 'How did I know their names?' she reflected. 'Do I know them?' She swallowed. Then their smiles resonated with her subconscious. 'Oh, my word, they're the same men who were dancing naked with me in my dream.' Janet visibly sank back into her chair in embarrassment as the three men continued their knowing smiles in her direction. She remembered their intimacy with her in the dream as she enjoyed them touching her, as she'd relished fondling them. Janet fiddled with the tablecloth and shuddered as Donald returned with their cereals. Her self-consciousness and sense of insecurity manifested itself when she weakly called to her husband.

'Ahem! Um! Er! Donald...' She cleared her throat with a short dry cough. He wasn't paying her much attention as he placed the cereal bowls on the table.

'... wait a moment, darling, I'll get the fruit juice.'

'It's a beautiful morning, isn't it, Janet?' said the third man, whom she remembered was called David. She looked askance and eyed him suspiciously.

'Hmm!' she cleared her throat again. 'Yes, it is,' she called, hesitantly, not wanting to extend the conversation and brought the table napkin up to cover her mouth. Somewhere deep in her consciousness, she recalled that in her dream it had been David who kept fondling her breasts. 'Oh, my Lord,' she pondered, 'what am I thinking?'

Donald returned; she tugged his shirtsleeve as he sat down. 'Donald, don't look now, but in our dreams... you know we both said that I was dancing with three men...'

'... yes, three naked old farmers, one of them you called Jasper...'

'... and David and Simon...'

'... Oh, so you can remember the names of all three now...?' Donald immediately thought it was probably because, in her pornographic dream, the three men were naked. They were on honeymoon and following what she'd said to him in their bedroom earlier, perhaps their lovemaking had reinvigorated her interest in men.

'... yes, that's because... oh, Donald, this is so odd...'

'... What, darling...?'

'... Because all three men are sitting at the next table behind you, and they knew my name...'

Donald half-turned... 'No, don't glance at them now, they're still looking at me.'

'No, darling, if blokes are ogling my wife, I want to be aware of it.' He turned and addressed them. 'Good morning, gentlemen, do we know each other, only you seem to recognise my wife...? Have we met before?'

'I can't recall that we've met before, perhaps we have? The trouble is when you get to my age, my eyesight fails me in this bright sunshine, I can see better in the dark.' Jasper offered as he squinted at Donald.

The men resumed eating, and Donald turned back to Janet.

'Well?' Janet asked, 'are they the same men who you saw in your dream?'

'I'm not sure, darling; I must admit they appear familiar. We must have met them somewhere else?'

Donald started eating. He noticed Janet seemed preoccupied. 'Come on, darling, tuck in.'

'I've lost my appetite.'

'Nonsense! There must be a perfectly simple explanation for all this. Come on, darling. Don't let this spoil our honeymoon.' Janet lowered her voice, aware that others could hear them talking.

'Don't you see the irony of this? Only last week at our wedding ceremony, we pledged ourselves exclusively to each other. Here we are after only a few days of marriage, having dreams of being intimate with strangers...' Donald laughed.

'... Shh! I'm glad you think it's funny...'

Donald lowered his voice to appease Janet's desire for a private conversation. '... It was only a silly dream, probably brought on by those varieties of different mushrooms. Nothing more. Come on, tuck into your breakfast. You'll be starving later if you don't eat.'

'Alright,' she agreed, reluctantly and started nibbling her cereal.

Donald's attention returned to the old Victorian photographs hanging on the walls. Janet looked around at the people sitting at the other tables. Her unease grew when she realised they seemed to watch them. Janet particularly noticed one handsome young man staring at her. She held her hand to her mouth and swallowed hard. From deep within her subconscious reflections, Janet intuitively knew he had a sizeable, irregular, bluish scar across his stomach. 'How would I know that?' she remonstrated the contradiction with herself, as Donald had said it was in her dreams. Her anxieties resurfaced when she recalled she had enjoyed being close to such masculine attributes that his nakedness had displayed for all to ogle. As if sensing Janet was evoking their lewd dancing, he beamed at her. Without hesitation and reticence, she felt a tingle of pleasure of being able to return his smile and relaxed.

She looked around the dining room. Her unease developed again, when, in her dream, she remembered the other people had also been dancing in the nude. She continued staring in quiet contemplation, trying to make sense of her recollections when she heard Mrs Strange talking to Donald. 'What would you like, Donald? We've eggs, bacon, mushrooms and tomatoes followed by toast and local homemade preserves?'

'Yes, everything except the mushrooms, Mrs Strange, please.'

'Oh, don't you like our local varieties? They are all freshly picked from the forests of Cannock Chase, you know.'

'I'm sure they're excellent, Mrs Strange. We are city folk from London, and perhaps our stomachs aren't as fine-tuned to such freshness and delicacies as your other clients obviously are?'

'Oh, Donald, now we're getting to understand each other better, please call me Margareta.' She leaned forward, the open buttons of her dress revealing a liberal part of her breasts to him. His thoughts immediately recalled his dream when she'd kept brushing her naked breasts against his torso as she fondled him. She beamed a huge smile as if knowing what he was thinking. Janet also noticed Mrs Strange's overt flirtation with Donald and interrupted.

'... I'll have the same as my husband, please.'

'... Oh, yes, please forgive me for not asking you, Mrs Lawrence.' Janet was instantly aware of the difference in interacting pleasantries. She was on first-name terms with Donald, but she formally referred to her as Mrs Lawrence. Mrs Strange soon returned with the cooked breakfasts and left them eating. Other people moved away from their tables, nodding pleasantly to her and Donald, and soon they had the dining room to themselves.

'Donald, please don't encourage Mrs Strange, she's made it quite plain that she fancies you, and we both appreciate what she was doing to you in our dreams...'

Although they were now seated alone, he whispered. '... I'm sorry, darling, I was only being polite. I suppose its best that as soon as we've eaten, we check out of here and move on, don't you?'

'Yes, absolutely. The longer we're here, the more perturbed I become.'

After breakfast, they packed their overnight suitcases. While Janet took them to the car, Donald received the bill from Mr Strange. 'We only accept cash,' he said bleakly as Donald presented his debit card.

'Oh, I see, hang on; my wallet is in my suitcase.' Donald turned and retrieved his wallet. He told Janet what he was doing.

'It's peculiar that a hotel only accepts cash, isn't it? It's as if they don't want any official paperwork.' Janet mused. 'Perhaps it's a scam to avoid paying income tax?'

'No, I don't believe so, darling. Probably their debit card machine is out of order. I won't be a moment.' Donald returned and paid the bill. Janet sat patiently in the passenger seat, looking through the windscreen at the pristine hotel gardens.

'Right then, darling, we're resuming our journey going north towards a village called Stone.' He pointed out on the map she held the ancient village was built around a conglomeration of canals and the River Trent. He leaned over and kissed her before turning the ignition key. Janet looked across at him as he issued expletives. 'Bloody hell, nothing. Look, Janet, it appears the battery is dead. There are even no lights showing on the dashboard display. Hang on, I'll take a peek under the bonnet.' Donald pulled the release catch under the steering wheel and the bonnet sprung open a little. Donald got out and entirely lifted the hood. He peered at the battery and instantly identified the positive and negative terminals still rigidly attached. 'Oh, sod it!' he exclaimed. 'The battery indicator shows there's no power at all. It's as flat as last month's pizza.'

'What are you going to do?' Janet asked as she joined him, looking into the engine compartment, totally confused at the myriad of interlocking gadgets and electrical wires.

'I'll ask Caleb if he can phone a local garage for them to bring a battery out. It's a standard size amperage output, so any type of battery will do. You may as well go back inside the hotel and wait, darling, until it can be fixed.'

'Okay, it's such a lovely day, I'll have a wander around the gardens instead.'

Janet meandered to the rear of the hotel where the sun was shining overlooking the Abbot Ibáñez yew tree. She sat down on a wooden slatted bench and lifted her face to the warmth. Janet took off her short coat and let the sun penetrate her loose cotton blouse by undoing the top few buttons. As she dozed, she at once relived her previous night's dream, recalling the pleasurable sensations she'd experienced. Janet's fingers clutched the soft grasses that she felt tickling her naked body as she'd lain prostrate. She'd looked up at birds perched high in the uppermost branches of the yew tree. Two ring-necked turtle doves cooed at each other in synchronised rhythm with the handsome man she'd noticed at breakfast, making love to her as they'd writhed on the hotel lawn. Beyond his gorgeous smile and flowing black hair, she had been aware of other people gathering around watching them, including Donald, who was holding her hand. He was laughing and didn't seem to mind another man fornicating with his wife. Then in her peripheral vision, Mrs Strange had appeared, 'Hello Mrs Lawrence, this is my son, Ben. I'm so glad you're getting to know each other.' Margareta had her hand on his shoulder as he moved against

Janet's nakedness. Janet revelled in the convivial atmosphere where everyone seemed happy and agreeable. She imagined herself floating weightless on a cloud, watching an adorable Adonis named Ben enjoying her body.

'Hello, Janet,' he beamed.

'Hello, Ben,' she replied, looking up at him. 'I'm so glad to make your acquaintance so soon again. We had a good time last time, didn't we, but this is so special?'

Then she saw crinkly frown lines appear in his smooth brow. She sensed they were going to enjoy a mutual climax, but that faded as Ben's adorable nakedness seemed to float away from her. Annoyance and disappointment manifested itself in her scowl that such a pleasurable experience ended abruptly when Donald shook her and woke her up.

'Aw! Oh, no!' she muttered as her eyelids fluttered against the bright sunlight.

'I'm sorry to disturb you, darling; you seemed to have dozed off into such a deep sleep.'

'... er yes, I did.' Janet's senses gradually returned to the present. 'How did you get on with Mr Strange?' She queried her sanity that she was at once able to ask such a mundane question so soon after experiencing the most erotic sensations that previously only existed in her wildest fantasies.

'Caleb? He's sending for an engineer. However, it could take a few hours yet. I've been trying to fix it myself for the past half an hour, but with no luck.' He showed her his hands covered with black grease. 'You'd have thought a hotel like this would have a battery charger, wouldn't you? Shall we investigate this infamous yew tree?' Rubbing his hands on a cloth, they walked around the ancient tree. Janet looked guiltily down at the grass where she and Ben had been making love. She reached up to the thickest part of the trunk and felt one of the original iron nails still firmly embedded in the bark. Out of the corner of her eye she saw movement at the hotel and noticed that their bedroom window was being opened. It was Ben, and he waved before shaking a yellow duster out of the window. She returned his wave.

'Who's that?' Donald asked.

'Oh, I think it's Mrs Strange's son. It looks as if he's cleaning our room?' She turned back to face Donald.

'So, I suppose this is where they crucified Abbot Ibáñez on the tree?' She ran her hands over the rough, gnarled bark. 'Eerie, isn't it, to think the locals left him here until his flesh rotted away...?' She looked down to the ground, '... and that this very soil around the tree soaked up his blood... it gives me the creeps.'

'We can't appreciate how the vile demonic behaviour of people nearly two thousand years ago compares to our modern civilised standards, can we?' Donald added.

'Civilised? I imagine little has changed, what with all the recent wars where unthinkable atrocities keep recurring.' Janet offered, 'not to mention the recent case we were involved with at Rotherhithe with pieces of bodies turning up on the Thames beach.'

'Would you like to go for a walk? We may as well keep ourselves occupied while we're here. I asked Caleb where the best ramble routes are around here, and he suggested Castle Ring. It's about a six-mile circuit so by the time we return the mechanic should have fixed the car?'

'Oh yes, Donald, let's leave this place for a while. There seems to be an evil presence here that's gradually getting to me. I'm losing sight of where the actual world begins, and fantasy takes over.' She shook her shoulders, convinced she could still feel Ben's hands grasping her.

Standing on the ramparts of the prehistoric earth fort called Castle Ring, they looked over twelve counties of rural England. They lay down in the tall grasses and soft mosses and revelled in each other's rampant libido as they made love. Janet was happy and content to watch her handsome husband's exertions until sweat dripped from his brow. The idea of Ben performing the same acts with her seemed unnervingly erotic. Still, at that moment, he was precisely where he belonged, in a distant dream. In contrast, her husband's lovemaking was a reality. Their romantic idyll ended suddenly when Donald's mobile phone rang. 'Bloody hell, Janet, that startled me. It looks as if I've received a signal up here.' He reached into his knapsack and opened the phone without looking at the screen to verify who the caller was. 'Yes, Donald Lawrence here.' He listened.

'Hello, gov, how are you?' He covered the mouthpiece and told Janet it was Jack, their boss. She listened to him while lying naked, looking at the majestic scenery. The conversation lasted for ten minutes, by which time any further erotic thoughts disappeared with the fluttering skylark that hovered overhead. She put her clothes back on.

'Yes, not until next Tuesday. Don't you remember, you gave us ten days?' Donald listened to Jack's voice before replying.

'Okay, gov, we'll be with you next Tuesday, but before you go, I wonder if you could help. The battery on my hire car has packed up, and I've sent for a mechanic...' He listened to his boss.

'Yes, that's what I felt, thanks, gov. The address is *The Crucified Abbot*, Upper Slaughter, near Longdon, Staffordshire. It's the hotel in Gallows Lane. The village lies between the towns of Lichfield and Rugeley.' He folded away the phone.

'That's good of the gov, he's contacting the hire car company now to get them to send out another car, and then they'll collect the old one. That's brilliant. Unfortunately, the gov feels it'll be tomorrow morning before they can do the exchange.' He looked with regret at Janet. 'Oh, you've got dressed!'

She ogled his nakedness silhouetted against the bright sunshine and blue sky and sensed his disappointment. 'Yes, get dressed, darling; after all, we've another night in front of us...' she giggled. '... but that means staying another night at the hotel, doesn't it, unless Caleb can find an engineer?'

'Yes, but no mushrooms for dinner, so hopefully we can get a peaceful, dreamless sleep.'

Janet's thoughts fleetingly returned to Ben's ethereal lovemaking. A tingle of desire swept through her body, but she quickly admonished herself at committing virtual adultery.

Donald sat back down on the grass with Janet. She put her head on his shoulder, and they relaxed together.

Five

They ate a tasty dinner in an empty dining room and retired to their room without speaking to anyone other than Mrs Strange when she took their order. Janet's yawn quickly followed Donald's. 'Ooh, I'm so tired, darling, shall we get to bed?'

'Yes lets, I'm tired too, we've had a busy day. If we're going to dream, I'll start at Castle Ring...' Donald whispered to Janet as he lay beside her.

'... It was wonderful, darling, so romantic ...' Donald smiled, listening to Janet's voice trailing to a whisper, and then he listened to her heavy breathing. She was asleep.

In their dreams, they walked hand in hand out into the rear garden and watched the same people dancing around the yew tree as they held candle-lit lanterns. Their nakedness seemed inconsequential as the others were also naked, and the throng of people beckoned them to join their circle. Laughter echoed around Abbot Ibáñez's tree; everyone seemed happy. Then Margareta's harsh voice tempered the laughter. 'Ben, I told you Lizzie was no good, she has a baby in her belly. She still wears that damned cross around her neck, so the baby will be tainted by it too. The new life inside her will be no good for us. Your precious seed will have been wasted.' The circle parted as Ben and the naked blonde woman called Lizzie walked to the tree. They lay down in the grass and made love in the same place where, in Janet's earlier dream, he'd made love to her. Despite her jealousy, Janet took pleasure in ogling his manly features again. She felt grateful that earlier he'd bestowed those same extended attributes upon her. After writhing and satiating their lust for each other, Ben arose, joined the circle, and watched Lizzie as she sat by the trunk. The mood in the group turned sour and angry. Donald and Janet pulled away, stood on the patio by the dining room doors, and watched. Laughter became scowls, and shouts became threats. Lizzie started crying when someone yelled, 'Crucify her'. Janet clutched Donald in fearful apprehension.

Everyone joined in as the group engulfed Lizzie. Donald and Janet called out *'Stop!'* as they gripped each other. Amid Lizzie's screams, they watched her being lifted onto the trunk. At the same time, Caleb and Margareta hammered nails into her palms and ankles, crucifying her to the tree. While secured against the twisted bark, Ben reached up with a sharp serrated knife and slit Lizzie's throat. Instantly covered in her flowing blood, he turned to Janet, and they exchanged smiles. The circle reformed and everyone danced around as Lizzie's blood ran down the trunk into the ground.

Six

Next morning, heavy rain pelted the bridal suite's window. Donald woke first, instantly sensing his severe headache. He looked towards the window, surprised at the change in the weather. The forecast had shown unbroken sunshine for the rest of their honeymoon. The sound of a massive burst of rain and hailstones beating on the window panes woke Janet.

'Oh, Donald, it's raining!' she exclaimed.

'I know, darling. Hailstones were hitting the window. I've got a blinding headache.'

'Oh, that's funny, I do too.'

'Perhaps that local cider we drank at dinner last evening was more potent than we imagined.'

Janet sat up sharply, 'Oh my God, Donald, did you dream? I've had the most horrible dream. They crucified a lovely blonde woman on the yew tree...'

'... Yes, darling, I've experienced the same dream, Lizzie was her name ...'

'... and Caleb and Mrs Strange hammered nails into her.' Donald moved to the window to glance at the tree, but the heavy rain prevented a clear view. He moved back to Janet, '... and I've to mention something to you, darling. In my dream, you were ogling a chap called Ben as he made love to Lizzie. You asked him if you could be next. What's that all about?'

She remembered watching Ben and Lizzie but couldn't recall what else Donald was talking about. '... I can't remember that, Donald.'

'The sooner our new hire car is delivered, the better. Let's have a shower, have breakfast and, hopefully, we can leave?'

At breakfast, they again ate in an empty dining room. Dappled sunshine suddenly bathed the couple's faces as they waited for their cooked breakfasts to arrive. 'I feel we should take another glimpse at the yew tree before we leave, don't you...?'

'... Donald, there's someone at the reception desk for you,' Mrs Strange called, interrupting their conversation.

'... Ah, that will be the new car.' He got up from the table and walked to the reception. Janet listened and heard Donald go outside to collect the keys to the car. She heard footsteps and turned to find Ben smiling and carrying a tray holding their breakfasts.

'Here we are, Janet; I've brought your food while my mother's busy in the kitchen.'

'Hello, Ben,' she spoke quietly to him. He wore a tight-fitting pair of thin trousers and a short-sleeved shirt that tugged at the buttons emphasising his muscular torso and prominent manhood. Janet surprised herself by feeling entirely comfortable in Ben's presence, primarily that she hadn't previously spoken to him other than in her dreams.

'I apologise we couldn't find out more about each other last evening; I was rather busy.'

'Yes, you were remarkably busy, weren't you?' The thoughts of their mutual eroticism completely blanked out the horrors of watching him slit Lizzie's throat.

Janet's confusion wrestled her mind between dream and reality. 'I realise he wasn't in the dining room, but did he mean in the garden around the yew tree?' She hesitated as she answered him. She watched him place the food and utensils on the table, thinking how handsome and virile he looked as he brushed her arm with his hand. Tingles ran down her spine. Goosebumps came to her flesh, and she felt a flush come to her face and neck. He smiled, knowing she was ogling him.

'I hope we can see more of each other before you leave. You looked lovely last evening.' Janet's mind was in utter confusion. She heard Donald's voice as he re-entered the hotel foyer. Ben left the table holding his finger to his lips, whispering 'shh' to her. He and Donald passed each other on the four steps down into the dining room. 'Good morning, Mr Lawrence,' Ben said. Janet felt her stomach tighten and, with a heavy conscience, watched as Donald returned, passing Ben as he left.

Donald involuntarily replied, 'Good morning,' not being aware of who the man was. As he retook his seat at the breakfast table, he remembered and asked Janet. 'This is strange, darling, that man I passed looks like the guy you had the hots for in my dream last night. Ben was his name. You know, the one whom you asked if he could make love to you after he'd finished with Lizzie. These bloody weird mushrooms and cider have played havoc with my sleep. Anyway, our new car is here, and we can leave as soon as we finish breakfast.'

'Is the replacement car okay?'

'Yes, it's okay. There's a note here left with the keys by the delivery company. They've had difficulty finding *The Crucified Abbot*. They left the car in Gallows Lane.'

Janet's mind was still reeling from Ben's words and hadn't assimilated what Donald had said. Donald tucked into his bacon and eggs, unaware of Janet's mental dilemma. She absent-mindedly picked up her knife and fork while her thoughts revelled in the utter pleasure from being in Ben's company. As she robotically sliced her bacon and took a sip of tea, she reflected on having made love with Ben.

'Penny for your thoughts, darling, you seem extremely far away.' Donald sensed her cerebral detachment from him.

With a heavy conscience for her otherworldly infidelity, Janet looked at Donald. His handsome, smiling features pulled her into reality. 'Oh, I'm sorry, Donald, I understood what you said earlier when the car arrived. Before we leave, we should peek at that yew tree again...'

'... Yes, that dream I had felt too real, especially as we both experienced the same one again.'

'This all feels so creepy. Do you imagine Mrs Strange laces our food and drink with some drug that causes these strange dreams? Forgive the unintended pun.' They laughed.

'This sounds stupid but, after that dream, I'm half expecting to find blood around the yew tree. Mind you, that rain and hail earlier would've washed it away. I'm stupid, aren't I?'

'No, you're not, I've been contemplating along similar lines. For goodness' sake, let's leave now, Donald. We're on our honeymoon, and this is sounding like a nightmare.'

As the Ford Sierra's tyres crunched the hotel's gravelled forecourt, Janet turned for a last glance at *The Crucified Abbot*. She shuddered as she saw Ben standing naked, waving at her from the large bridal suite window. Without considering her actions, she waved back at him.

'Who are you waving at, darling?' Donald asked.

'I think it's Mrs Strange in our bedroom window, she must be cleaning the room now we've left.'

She silently berated herself for once again being disloyal to her husband by not being truthful about something so stupid and inconsequential.

Seven

The rest of their honeymoon returned to the idyllic times they'd experienced before they visited *The Crucified Abbot*. After staying at several other hotels and guesthouses, their route turned south, and they gradually made their way back to London.

Detective Sergeant Donald Lawrence and Detective Constable Janet Lawrence resumed their duties at New Scotland Yard. The staff at the incident room of The Metropolitan Police welcomed them back following their memorable honeymoon.

After joining the others over a cup of tea, amid laughter and the usual innuendos about honeymoons, Jack called them into his office. 'Careful as you go, Donald,' Tom called after him as he walked across the office, 'you appear unsteady on your feet. It must be because of those bandy legs you've acquired?' Hilarity erupted around the office, including from Donald and Janet themselves.

'I'm glad to find you both looking so fit and well. Loads of casework have piled up while you've been away,' Jack said as they entered his glass-sided office.

'Nothing as nasty as body parts on the beach again, I hope?'

'Well, Janet, there are two unpleasant murders, two teenagers stabbed and left lying in a back alley, but Tom has some leads on that case. Oh, before I forget, I must tell you the sad news that ex-Superintendent Blackshaw is seriously ill in hospital. He's had a massive stroke.'

'Oh, that's sad,' echoed Donald.

'I understand we had our differences with him. However, underneath all that nasty business where he supported Joseph Tomelty, I realise Stuart wasn't a bad apple. Anyway, I hope he recovers.'

'What do you want us to start with, gov?' Janet asked.

'Well, tomorrow the Deptford Public Works Department start clearing away the debris of what's left of the Church of Secular Saints. Do you remember in Charlotte Simpson's letter she said it might interest us to discover what's in the rubble...'

'... Gov, her exact words were, *I imagine it would prove remarkably interesting to you and your colleagues to discover what the rubble contains.*' Janet recited to him.

'Very impressive, Janet, how can you remember such detail?'

'The whole of that terrible case is imprinted on my brain.'

'Well, I hope, in time, you can let it go; it's the stuff of nightmares.'

Donald and Janet's eyes met, and they raised their eyebrows at each other. 'Yes, gov, there're too many incidences in this life that cause nightmares.' Donald offered as Janet smiled.

'Anyway, Janet, I'd like you to monitor the clearance of the church. I've already had a word with the director at Deptford's Public Works Department. They understand they need to be vigilant when the blades of those huge excavator buckets start digging into the rubble.'

'Donald, would you reconnect with the Rotherhithe case and the sources of drug money that kept Joseph Tomelty and his evil empire afloat? Tom's snitches in the East End have informed him money that previously used to end up at the Church of Secular Saints is being flashed around like confetti. I'd like you to investigate this. Liaise with Tom and keep me posted...' Jack's ringing telephone interrupted the conversation. He intimated for Donald and Janet to leave. He listened to the voice on the phone before knocking on the glass wall of his office and beckoning them to return as they walked back to their desks.

'That was one of the mudlarks, Jenny Jones. She and Simon have found a gun on Rotherhithe beach. Can you investigate, please? It may be a coincidence, but anything turning up on those beaches must have a connection with the case.'

'We'll go now, gov,' and they left the superintendent's office.

As they walked down to the carpool, Donald suggested they have lunch at the *Nautilus* café and examine the site of the church after going to Jenny Jones' home.'

'It'll be like old times, darling.' Janet smiled and held his hand.

Eight

'It was sticking out of the sand,' Jenny told them as they drank the tea that Jenny's mother had made for them. Donald examined the black metal gun.

'You have found nothing else, have you, Jenny?' Janet asked.

'No, only old coins and enamel brooches...'

'... Thank goodness there're no more body parts, sergeant.' Mrs Jones interrupted. 'It's enough to give anybody nightmares, isn't it?' Donald and Janet exchanged smiles at the mention of more nightmares.

Seated on the red, plastic-covered benches in the *Nautilus* café, they enjoyed their usual order of double cheeseburgers with a side order of potato chips. During the meal, Donald realised he was receiving stares from a man seated two benches further in the café. Janet also noticed and asked Donald, 'Do you know that nosey bloke over there? He has a fixation on you.'

'I've been sitting here considering who he is, and I've remembered. I came in here once with Lucy. Do you recall after you first came to my flat...'?

'... When I was drunk and stripped myself off while you were in the bath with Lucy...?'

'... yes, after that hilarious evening. Oh God, Janet, looking back at those days, that was so funny.'

Donald and Janet burst into laughter. 'Anyway, Lucy and I came here, and we sat and had a coffee. She was livid, and we started having a row. This guy, the one who is staring at us now, kept interrupting. Lucy and I raised our voices, and people here realised what had been happening, you know, that I had two naked women in my flat at the same time. This nosey bloke kept telling me he could solve my problems by taking you or Lucy off my hands...'

'... what an interfering git...' Janet guffawed. '... Oh-oh, he's coming over to us, Donald.'

'You don't remember me, do you...?'

'... yes, I remember you, sir. I was in here once, and you kept poking your nose in my business, as you're doing now.'

'No, I'm not poking my nose, I was going to comment that the last time you were in here, you got down on your knees and proposed to that blonde woman, yet here you are with another woman. I must hand it to you, and I don't understand how you do it. What's your secret that you're so successful with women?'

'Waiter, could I have the bill, please?' Donald shouted down the café. 'Old son. I'll not engage with your inane, stupid comments, so go back to your seat. We're leaving.'

'Could I ask is this the woman who came and stripped herself in your flat...?' Donald clenched his fist. Janet pulled him back as he was about to confront the man.

'Donald, I think he's drunk…?'

'... yes, I've had a few drinks, lady. Were you that other woman...?'

'... This woman is my wife...'

'... well, there you go, exactly as I said to you earlier. You sure are a fast worker... in the space of two months, you've proposed to one woman, and here you are married to another. Are you a bigamist? How many more...?'

'Waiter, I'm leaving twenty pounds on the table, keep the change.' Donald helped Janet to her feet, and they walked towards the door.

'... are you sure you don't want a hand with all your wives...?' His voice faded as Donald and Janet left the café.

'... you Casanova, Mr Lawrence. All these naked women complicating your life,' Janet scolded him in jest. They laughed as they ambled to the Thames quays. 'There's never a dull moment, is there?'

'You can talk. What about you dancing with the three naked old farmer codgers and that Arnold Schwarzenegger lookalike, Ben? I realise I've serious competition with that bloke.'

'Oh, Donald, I don't want reminding about *The Crucified Abbot*. At least that all happened in our dreams and wasn't real. Well, I believe it wasn't?' Janet shook her head and laughed.

At the Thames quays, they pushed their way through the temporary wicker fencing onto the site that was once the Church of Secular Saints. All thoughts of their earlier laughter deserted them.

'Although it's now a pile of debris and dust, this place still gives me the creeps...' Janet commented as they picked through the blackened timbers and piles of broken, carved stones.

'... as much as *The Crucified Abbot* gave you the creeps?'

'Yes, but this was actual people, real evil criminals. *The Crucified Abbot* is a fantasy.'

Nine

During the next few days Donald and Janet involved themselves in the respective cases assigned to them by Superintendent Jack Croaker. Janet visited the church clearance site every day, keeping watch as the heavy excavators carefully loaded debris onto lorries. Donald aided Inspector Tom Cropper in tracing the criminals who sold drugs and where they laundered the illegal proceeds. A quiet afternoon in the incident room was disturbed when Superintendent Croaker received a telephone call from Janet.

'Gov, can you arrange for the Scene of Crime Officers to get here fast? The excavators have uncovered the remains of two bodies; at least I assume they're bodies.'

'Okay, Janet. Well done, I'll be there soon along with Donald.'

When Jack and Donald arrived at the former church, the excavators were idle and parked off the site. Some machine drivers and their supervisor were standing with Janet, looking into the debris. 'What can you identify, Janet?' Jack asked.

'It looks a tangled mess to me. I suppose the Scene of Crime Officers will make sense of it.'

'How many bodies are there?'

'As far as I can tell, there are only two. One we can see here and another over there.' Janet pointed, and they hopped over rocks and pieces of brickwork to where Janet indicated.

'Oh see, here are the remains of the font.' Donald shouted. The wind blew dust around in circular wisps. They held handkerchiefs to their faces to keep the filth from their mouths.

'Unless I'm mistaken, this is all that remains of Joseph Tomelty.' Jack pointed. 'Can you tell what's left of his skull and his straggly grey hair?' As they looked down at the grisly remains, a Metropolitan van pulled up at the roadside. The Scene of Crime Officers, dressed in white overalls and masks, flooded the site.

'Let's leave the experts to do their job, shall we?' Jack mused as he looked at the spectacle of devastation.

Ten

Back at the office, Donald resumed his discussions with Tom Cropper about the chaotic drug scene in East London. At the other side of the office, over a warming cup of tea, Janet started reading the Police Gazette. The national newspaper is dedicated to officers from police forces across the country and the cases they were investigating. One headline on an inner page held her interest, that quickly turned to concern, disquiet and eventually confusion and horror the more she read. Staffordshire Constabulary was investigating a particularly gruesome murder. The parents of Miss Elizabeth Cartwright had reported their daughter missing over a week ago. From their home in Upper Slaughter, near Rugeley, they had given an interview to the press. Lizzie, her preferred name, was involved with a local man named Ebenezer Strange. Recently she'd discovered she was pregnant. The local constabulary, volunteers, friends, and neighbours had carried out an extensive search for her. It resulted in the discovery of her body concealed at a local beauty spot near Castle Ring on Cannock Chase.

Post-mortem examinations have revealed that she died a horrific death. Evidence of stigmata suggests she suffered crucifixion, with wounds to her wrists and feet. The police pathologist suggests her actual death was caused by a loss of blood through the severing of the jugular vein in her neck. Police are carrying out extensive investigations to find Mr Ebenezer Strange and appeal to anyone who may have information leading to his whereabouts. From the county police headquarters in Baswich, near Stafford, the Chief of Police, Sir Bartholomew Evans, appeals to members of the public who'd seen Lizzie during the past few weeks to come forward. The report revealed telephone numbers and personnel within the local constabulary to whom anyone should refer. At the bottom of the page, colour photographs showed Lizzie Cartwright smiling while on a recent holiday in Kinmel Bay, North Wales. Janet instantly recognised her, recalling her blonde hair falling around her shoulders as Ben made love to her under the yew tree at *The Crucified Abbot.* The gazette dropped from her hands, Janet closed her eyes and recalled, with horror, Lizzie's screams when her blood ran down Abbot Ibáñez's yew tree.

Janet sat transfixed, her mind reeling in utter confusion. She'd almost forgotten about her and Donald's troubling stay at the country hotel a month ago. Since then, whenever fleeting recollections came to her of what had happened there, she simply dismissed them as stupid dreams, induced by the unintentional and illegal consumption of drugs. The article in the Police Gazette threw those thoughts, and her life, in turmoil. 'Did she and Donald take part in some sexual ritual? Did she take part in sexual acts with Ben and the three farmers?' The implications were too bizarre to make sense of, and she felt her grip on reality deserting her. She felt the blood draining from her head and she fainted, sliding gradually and silently onto the carpet flooring at the rear of the incident room.

Rosemary Jennings, the filing clerk, was the first person to discover Janet's lifeless form as she lay prostrate on the floor. On route from the coffee machine, she quickly discarded her drink and called for help. 'Jack, Donald, anybody, help, it's Janet.' Jack was pinning some case details to the notice board when he overheard Rosemary shouting. He dashed across the office, and when he saw Janet, he reached for his mobile phone. 'Medics, please come at once to the incident room on the first floor we've got an officer unconscious.' Jack knelt by Janet and verified she was breathing okay. He gently placed his suit jacket under her head and straightened her left leg from underneath her. Meanwhile, Rosemary dashed to the adjoining office where Donald and Tom were in conference with a local constable. She opened the door and burst in.

'Donald, the incident room quick, it's Janet, she's unconscious.' Donald threw the papers he was holding onto the table and rushed from the room. By the time he reached Janet, two police medics had also entered the room.

'Oh my God, darling,' he gasped and knelt by her side.

'Move aside please, sergeant,' a medic dressed in a white gown asked him. He checked Janet's pulse and temperature and quickly made a diagnosis. 'It looks like she fainted. Donald, fetch your wife a cup of water, please.' Rosemary, an experienced civilian officer within the Metropolitan police, had already quietly assessed the matter and formulated her own opinion regarding Janet. She handed Donald a ready poured cup of water. The medic gently lifted Janet to a sitting position as she stirred. 'Here, Janet, take a sip of water.' At first, she couldn't focus her eyes properly, and her head lolled backwards and forwards as if it wasn't fixed to her neck. She drank a little. Everybody looked at her ashen face and gaunt expression.

'You'll be okay in a moment, darling,' Donald whispered gently as he rubbed her hands.

'Oh, Donald, what's happened?' she responded. The medic smiled and repeated what Donald had said.

'You'll be alright, Janet, you fainted.' He turned to his colleague, 'Susan, bring a wheelchair and we'll keep her under observation in the clinic for a while.' He looked at Superintendent Croaker. 'That will be okay, Jack, we'll take better care of her downstairs for a while.'

'You'd better go with her, Donald.'

Janet sat in a wheelchair in front of the window, looking over the embankment across the Thames. The colour returned to her cheeks as she tried to smile at Donald. He looked concerned at the saline drip the medics had rigged up attached to a vein in her hand.

'How do you feel now, darling?' he asked.

'I've got a blinding headache, but otherwise I'm okay. Oh, my leg hurts; I must have bent it under me as I fell.'

'What caused...?' James, the senior medic who came to check on Janet, cut Donald's words short.

'We're keeping you here for a couple of hours, Janet. A nurse will come to take a blood sample, to check for sugar levels and other causes for your fainting. We feel you may also be dehydrated; you're not drinking enough water.' He left Donald holding his wife's hands.

'You go back to work, Donald; I'll be okay here. You heard what the medic said, I'll be here until the afternoon.'

'I'm worried about you, Janet. What caused you to faint?'

'Oh, it's awful, I don't understand where we go from here?' Donald's concern increased when he saw her eyes darting from side to side.

'Calm yourself. What on earth are you talking about; you sound as if the world is ending?'

'I don't believe I can put my feelings into words right now. When you go back to the incident room, pick up a copy of the latest Police Gazette and read page seven. I'm sure your reaction will be the same as mine, but without the fainting part, I hope?'

Donald left Janet sitting staring at the sun glistening on the Thames. He knocked on the Chief Medic's door. 'Ah, Donald,' James said, 'I'm glad you're here, I was going to have a word with you.'

'How's Janet, I'm concerned...?'

'... Donald, can I ask have you had any upsets, or family traumas, or arguments lately? The reason I'm asking is that Janet seems very agitated. She's running a high pulse rate and blood pressure. For her age and excellent health, that's unusual. I've given her a slight sedative to calm her down.' Donald paused and reflected.

'Not as I'm aware of, James...'

'Okay, it was only an idea. Janet should be back with you later this afternoon.'

'Thank you for what you're doing for her.' Donald responded.

As soon as he entered the incident room, he turned to the publications rack to pick up a copy of the latest Police Gazette, but no issues were left. He asked Rosemary. 'Where've all the Gazettes gone?' he asked.

'Search me? I saw the last copy in the rack this morning. Hang on, Donald, I'll check with the main office.' She dialled a number on the internal telephone and spoke with a colleague.

'Okay, there're only two copies left, both in the fraud office apparently...'

'... Thanks, Rosemary' Donald was already leaving the office. In his urgency to read the gazette, he'd forgotten that his former fiancée, Constable Lucy Barnes, had transferred there. Donald walked straight past where Lucy was sitting at her desk, knowing the publications rack in that office was on the far wall. He reached for a copy and started walking back. Lucy had seen him walk past her, and although they had spoken little since their break-up and his later marriage to Janet, she didn't want them to become estranged. Because of his preoccupation, although he approached Lucy's desk, he still hadn't seen her.

'Hello, Donald,' she called, not wanting him to walk out of the office without even talking to him. Lucy's words pulled him out of his robotic thoughts.

'... oh, hello, Lucy. I'm sorry, I was miles away. I didn't see you. How are you?'

'I'm fine. How are you?'

'I'm okay, I suppose? Janet...'

'... oh yes, we learned. How's your wife? She fainted, apparently.'

Donald noted her informal, sarcastic tone.

'She's okay, thank you. She's in the clinic now. The medic is taking some blood samples and keeping her under observation.'

'That's good.' A pause developed between them as they looked at each other.

'... Lucy, I've been hoping we could have a chat sometime. Now that things have settled since our break-up... I was hoping we...?'

'... so was I. Events seem to have taken over so quickly since my accident, I never really had much chance to draw breath and then, hey presto, we split up and well, we all know the rest.'

Donald looked kindly at her, appreciating her radiant beauty that was so obvious to anyone.

'Janet will be in the clinic until later this afternoon; it's almost lunchtime. How do you feel about sharing a bite to eat together...?'

'Yes please, I'd like that, but taking your words at face value, are you only asking me to lunch because your wife is unavailable?'

'I didn't put that very well, did I? What I meant to say is that perhaps we could've met another time...?'

'... without telling Janet?' Donald looked askance at Lucy, knowing she was telling the truth.

'Shall we meet for lunch, or not?' Donald looked around the office, aware that others may listen to their conversation.

'Where? There's a charming little bistro in Horse Guards Avenue. *La Vista*, I believe it's called?'

'Is it Italian?'

'No, but does that matter?'

'No, of course not. Okay, I'll see you there at 1:00 pm.'

Donald returned to his desk and opened the copy of the Police Gazette, turning to page seven. With mounting trepidation, he read the article and now fully understood what had caused Janet's condition. Donald was deep in thought when Jack called to him. 'How's Janet?' he asked. He explained the medics were keeping her until later in the afternoon.

Rosemary overheard the exchange and had already formed her own opinion about Janet. While quietly sharing a cup of coffee with her colleague, Dorothy Jennings, they gossiped together.

'It stands to sense, doesn't it, Dorothy?' Rosemary whispered, 'they've been on honeymoon, haven't they?' Dorothy nodded and winked her eye, 'that's almost a month ago now. If they weren't at it before they got married, they must have been like a colony of frogs up a pump on their honeymoon, I should imagine...?'

'... so, you think Janet's, you know...' Miming as if Rosemary could lip-read, she silently mouthed, 'pregnant?'

'Stands to reason. We'll soon find out, won't we, Janet will turn up late for work soon with morning sickness...'

'... and we both understand how awful that can be, don't we?' Dorothy continued the speculation.

Donald continued reading the Police Gazette, unaware of the current gossip in the office. Still, he wouldn't have cared had he known. His thoughts returned to the troubling events at *The Crucified Abbot*. He knew that he and Janet had been material witnesses to a murder on a practical level. Consequently, they would be very much involved in the current investigation being carried out by the Staffordshire Constabulary. He and Janet needed to have an in-depth discussion about what they should do. Donald recognised it would be difficult and would involve much emotional turmoil between them and could even threaten their marriage. He was deep in thought when he listened to Rosemary call across the office. 'See you after lunch, Dorothy.' He looked at his watch. It was 1:05 pm.

'Oh God, I'm late for lunch with Lucy.' he realised. Donald dashed out of the office, trying to remember the bistro's name as he approached Horse Guards Avenue.

Eleven

He still couldn't recall the name, but he knew he had the correct place as he neared La Vista. People were going in and out of the main door. It seemed a popular choice for office workers to eat their lunch. He looked at his watch again. It was 1:12 pm. He saw Lucy sitting at a table at the rear of the restaurant. A young, tall, dark-haired man was sitting with her. Donald approached and offered his apologies. 'I'm so sorry, Lucy; Jack involved me with some stuff about the latest drug scene as I was leaving the office.' The fib rolled smoothly off his tongue.

'That's alright. I'd given up on you and doubted you were coming at all. This is Robbie. He saw I was sitting by myself and came over to join me. He's a stockbroker from the city.'

'... I'm a share valuer, Lucy.' Robbie corrected her.

'Hello, Donald,' Robbie offered to shake hands with Donald.

'Hello,' Donald replied, without even looking Robbie's way, ignoring his greeting. 'Well, if you're occupied then, Lucy, we'll lunch another time, shall we?' and he turned to go.

Robbie noticed Lucy's immediate discomfort and assumed he was playing gooseberry, interrupting her pre-arranged lunch with her boyfriend. 'No, don't go, Donald, I'm leaving anyway.' He got up to leave, but before he left, he apologised to Lucy. 'I'm sorry to be leaving so soon, Lucy, but I hope we can share another glass of wine soon?' He bent forward and kissed the back of her hand and left. Lucy enjoyed the flirtatious situation and was quietly thrilled that Donald was aware she was a free agent and attracted other men. Donald was annoyed with himself that he felt pangs of jealousy and cursed his stupidity by displaying it to Lucy. 'Well, it hasn't taken you long to get fixed up with another bloke, has it?' he sideswiped at her as he sat on the plastic-covered bench opposite.

'Excuse me! Do I need to remind you that you broke off our engagement, Donald, so I can't see what business it is of yours? I'll see any man I choose.' Donald recognised his foolishness and apologised.

'I'm sorry, Lucy; you're right, it's none of my business. Have you met him before?'

'I'm not answering you. You've already admitted it's not your business...'

Donald paused and smiled at her. 'What's so funny?' Lucy displayed her pique at his apparent crassness.

'Oh, I seem to recollect we always argue when we're seated in a café together. Remember the *Nautilus* in Deptford?' Lucy saw the parallel and smiled back at him. They shared a rare laugh, and Lucy relaxed a little.

'... for your information, no, I haven't met Robbie before today.'

'... okay, that's good. No, I mean it's nothing to do with me.' With awkward moments behind them, an impatient waitress asking for their order interrupted their attempts at any further small talk.

'A small jacket potato covered with coleslaw for me, please,' Lucy offered.

'I'll have the same, please,' Donald added.

'... and for drinks?' the waitress asked.

Donald looked at Lucy's glass of wine and then raised his eyebrow at her. She nodded.

'... and two glasses of whatever wine the lady is drinking, please?'

'... it's a Chianti' Lucy confirmed to the waitress who let out a deep sigh and left them.

'I should have known that, shouldn't I? Isn't that what we used to drink at *Ultima Puccini?*'

'You remembered that?' Lucy blushed, 'and when did you last call me a lady?'

'We had some wonderful times, didn't we?'

'Where did we go wrong, Donald?' He shrugged his shoulders and looked at her natural beauty. Her royal blue dress enhanced her blonde hair and ice-blue eyes.

'You are beautiful, Lucy.'

'Hey steady on. You're a married man with a sick wife, and here you are making a pass at your former fiancée.'

'... whether or not I'm married to someone else, I'm only stating the obvious. You *are* a beautiful woman. Even Roberto, the plumber, could see that...'

'... Robbie was his name, and he wasn't a plumber...'

'... oh, forgive me, Robbie bloody twinkle-toes, the stocks and shares wizard...'

'... if I didn't know you better, Donald, I'd assume you're jealous?'

'... maybe I am. What of it?' Their acknowledgement that they still had feelings for each other came to an abrupt halt when the waitress delivered their food and glasses of wine.

They ate their food in silence, staring at each other and smiling often. Clutching the glass of Chianti, Lucy stifled her remembrance of their former romance by starkly asking, 'Did you enjoy your honeymoon?' Donald's expression turned sombre.

'Oh, I'm sorry, didn't it go well then?' Lucy sensed his reticence to expand on the matter.

'With our recent history, I don't think it's appropriate that we should discuss such a subject. However, something troubling happened while Janet and I were away.' Lucy's ears pricked, sensing that all wasn't well with Donald and Janet's marriage. Secretly she was pleased but quickly contained her smugness by trying to sound constructive.

'How can I help?' Lucy asked, but quickly corrected her comment. 'What I mean to say is, that's a shame. We don't fully understand someone until after marriage, so the marriage guidance people say, anyway.' Lucy gulped her wine, trying to disguise her clumsiness.

Slowly, Donald explained about the troubling events that had happened at *The Crucified Abbot.* Despite concentrating intently on Donald's extended monologue, she ordered two more glasses of Chianti. By the time Donald had finished, those glasses were also empty.

He looked at Lucy, 'Would you like another glass of wine?' unaware that they'd already drunk two. She looked at her watch.

'It's already 2:00 pm; I should get back to the office.'

'Oh, is it? Can't the fraud squad muddle along without you for a while longer?'

'For your information, we don't muddle along in the fraud squad, as you so indelicately put it.'

'... I'm sorry, the incident room doesn't seem the same without you. I know the gov misses you.' Donald gestured to the waitress to bring two more glasses of wine.

'Do you miss me, Donald?' He looked into her eyes and paused before slowly answering.

'... Er... yes, I do.' Lucy felt like kissing him but resisted. She was surprised when he reached for her hand. 'I'm sorry how things have turned out between us, Lucy.' The waitress placed the glasses of wine on their table.

She pulled her hand back from Donald's and grasped her glass.

'What's going to happen about this awful business at *The Crucified Abbot?*'

'I honestly don't know. I'm at a loss to understand exactly what happened there.'

'Can I ask a question?'

'Of course, ask anything.'

'Notwithstanding the events were all drug-induced and you both experienced hallucinations, did Janet have sex with this chap, what was his name...?'

'... the chap's name was Ebenezer. Ben, a great hunk of a bloke he was. Handsome chap, at least that's what Janet and Lizzie felt, eagerly succumbing to his charms; in my dreams, anyway. Why do you ask?'

'... well, under some hypnotic fervour, so the experts say, a person's behaviour displays a true character.'

'Are you suggesting that Janet has been unfaithful?'

'Not in the practical sense of the word, but maybe metaphorically... I don't know?'

'Well, it could be misconstrued that the hotel owner, Mrs Margareta Strange, had the hots for me. I must admit I was sorely tempted, especially when her hands were everywhere while we were both naked...'

'... but you did nothing about it, did you? You didn't reciprocate her advances?'

'Well, no, not that I'm aware of.' Donald took a massive slurp of wine, trying to recall if he'd fondled her. The vision of Margareta's well-proportioned breasts came to his thoughts, and his honest assessment of himself was that he wouldn't have resisted. 'Anyway, I don't see how this will help?'

'I think I can assist you, Donald.'

'How?'

'When I return to the office, I'll do some research. I understand you'll be busy with Janet being ill...?'

'... Research?'

'Yes, research on *The Crucified Abbot*. There have to be some records about such an old place, especially being a public house and hotel.'

'Would you? Any information would prove useful to understand what happened there.' Lucy lifted her glass and drank the remaining wine in a single swallow.

'Anyway, I have to get back now. I'll keep you informed if I discover anything.' Lucy reached for her handbag.

'No, this lunch is on me, Lucy. Thank you for your company.' Donald stood and kissed her cheek. She looked intimately under her eyelashes before they simultaneously kissed each other on the lips.

Lucy turned, and he watched her saunter sexily out of the bistro. With a deep sigh, he paid the bill.

Twelve

'Ah, thank goodness, Donald, where have you been? Your mobile is switched off.' Rosemary berated him.

He reached for his mobile phone and at once switched the vocals back to live. 'Blast!' he exclaimed, remembering having switched the phone to silent mode; he didn't want his lunch with Lucy disturbed. 'Why, what's going on, Rosemary?'

'James, the medic, has been here looking for you. Would you go to the infirmary, please?' Donald instantly bounded down the stairs and knocked on James's door in the infirmary.

'Ah, Donald, I'm glad you've come. I've been trying to reach you. Now, don't get alarmed, but I've transferred Janet to Saint Thomas's Hospital around the corner in Westminster. I've got a good friend there, Doctor Giles Pritchard. He's a specialist in neurosurgical matters...'

'... why, has Janet taken a turn for the worst?'

'No, she's responded well. We determined that her blood sugars were low from the first blood samples, and dehydration was present. That would account for her fainting. However, her intense anxiety increased; that aggravated her condition, despite the mild sedative I'd given her. I considered it best to ask Doctor Pritchard for help. He's the best specialist there is in such complaints...'

'... can I see Janet?'

'Of course, you can. I explained to Giles that you are both on the staff here, so her admission comes under the private health care afforded by your ranks.'

'Thank you, James, for what you've done for her.'

'It's my pleasure, Donald; I hope Janet will return to full health soon.'

Donald's first stop at Saint Thomas's was at the general admissions desk, where he gave Janet's name. 'Your wife is in room 765 on the seventh floor, Sergeant Lawrence. I'll telephone Doctor Pritchard, who'll probably want to have a word with you?' The receptionist was clear and helpful.

Donald took the lift and tentatively pushed open the door to room 765 and was immediately relieved to see Janet sitting up in bed looking out of the window towards Saint James's Park.

'Oh, Donald, I've missed you,' she sobbed as he hugged her.

'I've missed you too.' He held Janet close, feeling massive guilt that he'd been with Lucy while Janet was being admitted to the hospital.

'Sergeant Lawrence, I presume?' Donald turned to see a tall, stooped man dressed in a green coverall, with a matching cloth hat.

'Doctor Pritchard? How's my wife, doctor?'

'She's responding well,' gesturing to Donald that he wanted to talk in private outside the room.

'I'll be back in a little while, darling.' He kissed Janet and joined Doctor Pritchard in the corridor outside her room. The doctor pulled the door closed so Janet wouldn't be able to overhear.

'We've already carried some tests out, sergeant...'

'... Call me Donald, please, doctor.'

'... Donald. I have to tell you that your wife is pregnant...'

'... What? How can you be sure? We've only been married a little over a month.'

'I agree it's a little early to be 100% certain. The estimation is three to four weeks, but your wife's condition contributed to the fainting episode. We've performed the HCG test on her urine, which is probably the most reliable indicator...'

'... HCG?'

'HCG stands for human chorionic gonadotrophin. It's a hormone that's only released and present in urine if the donor is pregnant. Are you aware if your wife has missed a period, or perhaps had stomach cramps?'

'I don't know, doctor. Oh, wait, she suffered stomach cramps a few weeks ago.' Donald remembered Janet complaining of tummy pain at *The Crucified Abbot*. 'Does my wife realise she's pregnant?'

'Not yet. Because of Mrs Lawrence's current anxiety, my colleagues and I felt it best to delay such information because of the possibility of worsening her condition. I would also advise you not to divulge the positive pregnancy test at present.'

'Very well. How long will Janet be in the hospital?'

'Ooh, perhaps two days. We'll monitor your wife and see how she responds.'

Donald spent the next few hours with Janet before deciding to return to their flat.

Thirteen

He soaked himself in the shower for fifteen minutes, reconciling the turbulent knowledge that Janet was pregnant, and he was going to be a father. He put on his dressing gown and went through to the kitchen to pour himself a glass of wine. As he reached for his mobile phone to order delivery of a Chinese takeaway, it rang. Donald returned to the lounge to take the call. 'Yes, Donald Lawrence here.'

'Donald, it's Lucy. I'm sorry to disturb you and Janet...' Donald didn't tell her he was alone. '... I've some news for you, and it's peculiarly exciting news about *The Crucified Abbot.* I've been doing some research, and I appreciate you'll be amazed at what I've discovered.'

'What is it, Lucy? Can't it wait until tomorrow? Can't you tell me over the phone?'

'I'd sooner see you face to face so I can explain it properly, particularly the sequence of my investigations. Because of your experiences, the results are utterly amazing.' Donald's curiosity was aroused and decided he didn't want to wait.

'Okay, Lucy, how do you feel about coming round to my flat?'

'Yes, okay, sure. When? I'm going to my parents' house tomorrow evening and then the following day...'

'... how about right now?'

'Now!? Yes, if you're sure. I don't want to be a burden to you both, especially as Janet is poorly?'

'You won't be a burden. I was about to order a Chinese takeaway. Would you like to eat too?'

'Well, I haven't eaten yet this evening, so yes, please. I'll bring a bottle of Chianti.'

Donald was about to get dressed when the doorbell rang, so he quickly put his dressing gown back on. He expected to be welcoming Lucy. Instead, a short, oriental looking, boyish man presented a white, plastic bag holding the Chinese takeaway. Leaving the man standing at the door, he walked to the bedroom to find some cash in his wallet. Back at the front door, he found Lucy standing there alone, holding the plastic bag. 'Hello, Lucy, I went to get some money. Where's the Chinese man?'

'No need, I've paid. Oh, I see you're ready to turn in as you're wearing your dressing gown.'

'I was getting dressed when the doorbell rang. Is that a problem?'

'Should it be? No, I don't suppose so.'

'Come in, please.' Lucy handed over the Chinese food and the bottle of Chianti.

'Make yourself at home while I prepare the meal. Here, let me take your coat.'

Lucy sat on the settee, holding a file of papers. Donald soon returned with two glasses filled with the wine. 'Cheers,' he offered, and they clinked their glasses.

'Where's Janet? Is she sleeping?'

'Janet's not here. She's been transferred to Saint Thomas's Hospital in Westminster today for a couple of days...'

'... oh dear, so you're alone. Will Janet be okay?'

'Yes, I'm sure the medics are only carrying out observations and tests.'

'You knew that when I telephoned and yet you asked me to come to your flat this evening?'

'Yes, what's wrong with that? I'm anxious to see what you've discovered.'

'Will you tell Janet that I've been here when she's home from the hospital?'

'I won't lie to you, Lucy, I probably won't tell her.'

A pause developed as they simultaneously considered the implications of Lucy's presence.

'Are you okay with that?' Donald asked. 'Perhaps you'd prefer to meet up some other time?'

'No, that's okay,' Lucy quickly answered.

'Well, while we're in the truth zone, I'll own up. I knew Janet was in the hospital. Nothing much happens at the Met without the grapevine broadcasting news and gossip between offices...'

'... And you still came, knowing that Janet wouldn't be here. Will you tell Roberto the plumber that you've been here?' Donald's attempted sarcasm didn't have the same resonance as Lucy's similar question.

'No, I probably won't, mainly because I'll almost certainly never see him again.' They laughed together.

'Make yourself comfortable while I prepare the food.'

'Does comfy include taking a bath, as I used to?' Lucy shouted through to the kitchen. Donald returned instantly and sat holding her hand, looking intently into her eyes.

'Lucy, as much as I'd love to say yes, at present I don't feel that's a good idea, do you?' He kissed her gently on the lips while she closed her eyes to hide her disappointment. As he stood up, he made sure he'd securely fastened his dressing gown. He didn't want Lucy to be aware of the physical effect her closeness was having upon him.

'Of course not! Can't you tell when I'm joking?' Donald returned to the kitchen. They both knew that she hadn't been kidding.

Seated at the dining table, they ate the delicious food and drank all the Chianti. Their conversation was mundane, stilted, and awkward. Without divulging the fact to each other, both were aroused in each other's presence. Both remembered the intimate times they'd happily spent in his flat. Still, despite both wanting that to happen again, it seemed inappropriate. They took the last of the wine to the settee and sat together.

'What did you discover about *The Crucified Abbot?'* Donald asked as he pressed a switch to light the flame-effect gas fire. Switching off the central ceiling lights and lighting the side lamps, created a cosier, intimate atmosphere. Lucy slipped off her soft shoes and drew her legs underneath herself on the settee.

'You won't believe what I discovered, Donald. First, I did a Register of Elector search for Upper Slaughter villages and extended it to the surrounding communities. I typed in the address *The Crucified Abbot,* Gallows Lane, and Upper Slaughter as you told me that was the address...'

'... and?'

'... Guess what the result was?'

'Tell me...'

'There's no such address. A Gallows Lane exists, but no address having *The Crucified Abbot.* There's a Red Lion hotel and pub in Gallows Lane, but that's all.'

'Wow, that's interesting...'

'... there's more, lots more.'

'Do you want a refill of wine, Lucy? I only have a bottle of rioja. Will that do?'

'Yeah, that will do, let's take a cruise across the Mediterranean Sea from Italy to Spain, recreating Emperor Augustus Caesar's journey to Cartagena in 78BC.'

45

'As usual, your knowledge of everything Italian is amazing. What did the Emperor go to Cartagena for?'

'Would you believe it was for romance, but he was out of luck. While in Murcia searching for an ideal mistress, he refocused his frustrations and libido from romance to more lasting ideals, by building the largest amphitheatre outside Rome.'

'Wow! That's some libido?'

'Well, the Emperor was Italian, of course.'

Donald continued the flirtatious conversation. 'Is that a serious suggestion, Italian men outscore the English where libido is concerned?'

'How would I know, Donald?' Lucy looked demurely sideways, suggesting a virginal innocence. 'Anyway, what have ancient Englishmen ever constructed? There's only Stonehenge that comes to mind, and that's only a haphazard pile of stones.'

'If we are still talking about libido and not ancient relics, I'm sure Englishmen directed romantic energies and rampant libido to the proper place.'

'Which is...'

'English women, of course, and not building irrelevant follies or other monuments?'

'I'm sure you are perfectly correct, darling.' Lucy purred seductively.

Donald moved to the kitchen for the bottle of rioja, as Lucy took off her cardigan, revealing a royal blue short-sleeved buttoned blouse. Resuming her place on the settee, Donald didn't comment but thought she looked beautiful. Her hair was tied with a black elastic toggle that she slipped through her fingers, letting her smooth, blonde locks fall to her shoulders.

'Now, the next search I did was for the Strange family. They're bloody strange because I couldn't find them. There was no Ebenezer, or Margareta, or Caleb Strange anywhere on any of the registers. Curious or what?' She lifted her arms to show how odd her findings were. Her loose-fitting sleeves allowed Donald a quick furtive glance at the outline of her breasts.

He swallowed and pulled his dressing gown belt tighter around his waist. 'Very curious, where did you go next?' Donald's voice seemed a little higher. Lucy knew what affect her closeness was having on him.

'With the advantage of being able to use police records, I gained access to genealogical records at the Staffordshire Records Office.' Donald sat back and listened. Lucy shuffled the pile of papers until she came to the genealogical printouts. 'There's so much paper. Here, have these sheets that refer to the Register of Electors.' She passed them to rest on his lap, but they slid to the floor as they wouldn't lie flat. 'Oh, sorry, Donald, wait for a second, and I'll pick them up.' Lucy bent forward to conceal her smirk. His complete sexual arousal was confirmed; as suspected, his erection had caused the paper to fall from his lap.

'It doesn't matter, leave them. Please carry on.'

'Well, I searched through the years from 1750 up to the present day. There are no open records of a birth, marriage, or death for either Ebenezer, Margareta, or Caleb Strange. The family could've been born, married, or died in adjacent parishes, so I extended the search. Still nothing.'

'You've been very thorough. Cheers,' they clinked their glasses again and took a large drink of the rioja. Mixing their drinks, they both began to feel the result of too much alcohol.

'I scratched my head then, wondering where I should go next...?'

'... I bet you did.' Lucy looked askance at Donald, wondering if he was concentrating.

'Are you following all this, Donald? You said you wanted to see what I'd found.'

'... yes, I did, and I'm following every word, and I want to know, but I'd like you to pause for a moment?'

'Why?'

'... Because I need to bloody kiss you, that's why.' Donald put his glass down and moved closer.

'... but the best piece is still to come...'

'... I bloody well hope so?' He held her shoulders as her arms enveloped him. The kiss was tender, becoming increasingly passionate. Holding their foreheads together paused the kisses. 'Ever since that bloody stockbroker pushed his big nose in, I've wanted to do that.'

'I could see that. Robbie would've stayed around if you hadn't arrived. Does he have a big nose?'

'It's a good job I turned up then.'

'That's a hugely presumptive remark considering Donald Lawrence is a married man, and I'm a free agent. I don't imagine Robbie was too pleased, either?'

'I've missed you, Lucy...'

'... even though you now have a wife who stole you from under my nose.'

'... yes. I realise I shouldn't be kissing you or that we shouldn't be here together, but...'

'... but? I agree we should face the truth.'

'Which is...?' mumbling between kisses prevented Lucy from giving a coherent answer.

'... I don't know anymore.' Lucy still had the file and other papers on her lap. They paused as Lucy looked at the sheets of paper.

'Let's finish all this stuff about *The Crucified Abbot*.'

'Yes, okay. You said the best was still to come...' Donald released the embrace. Lucy noticed Donald quickly check that his dressing gown was still in place. Lucy exuded a rosy complexion, while Donald was perspiring. She lifted the next sheet of paper as both attempted to focus on the typing.

'The next place to search was public records. Therefore, after typing the name, *The Crucified Abbot*, see what came up. This is a copy of the front page of the Staffordshire Newsletter dated 31st October 1866. Go on, have a read.' Donald read aloud.

'A tragedy has occurred at the village of Upper Slaughter, near Rugeley. Fire destroyed The Crucified Abbot, a hotel and public house situated in Gallows Lane. Twelve people died in the inferno that ripped through the thatched hotel, which has existed for two thousand years. The owners, Caleb and Margareta Strange and their son Ebenezer, perished as they tried to rescue nine local visitors trapped inside. The victims included three renowned local farmers, Jasper Clownes, David Thatcher, and Simon Stubbs and six other villagers from Upper Slaughter.'

'This is unbelievable, Lucy.'

'So now you understand this, does it explain the events you and Janet experienced? How can Lizzie Cartwright's death be explained, if *The Crucified Abbot* and Ebenezer Strange no longer exist?'

'It all seems like an incredible dream. Examine the date, Lucy. Halloween night. I also remember Mrs Strange being proud of the document that transferred the hotel's ownership from King Henry VIII to Caleb Strange. That date 31st October 1566 is exactly three hundred years before the place burned down and both events were occurring on Halloween.'

'... I don't understand how you can have witnessed the murder of Lizzie Cartwright, a woman from the present by a man who died in 1866?'

'It sends a shiver up my spine...'

'... the same here, and I haven't experienced what you and Janet did.'

'It's obvious that perhaps another visit to Upper Slaughter is necessary and to the Staffordshire Constabulary to explain what we saw.'

'The County officers will presume you've lost your marbles, especially if they ask you what case you're investigating in the Met. You must admit as it's about drugs in London, they'll assume you've succumbed to taking the weed. Come on, consider the facts, that's the first assumption officers at The Yard would make in such an interview?'

'Is that all the results of the research?' She nodded. 'Lucy, it's fantastic what's been accomplished. Thank you so much.'

'It's been a pleasure. The more information I've uncovered, the more I've become involved in it.' Donald poured another glass of wine, emptying the last dregs into a glass. 'Oh, the bottle's empty.'

'I don't feel I should have any more wine, Donald...'

'... why not?'

'Well, I drove my car from my flat to come here. There's a bloody strike on the underground. Haven't you tuned in to the news, and I didn't fancy travelling on the bus?' He shook his head.

'I've heard no headlines. What with Janet being admitted to hospital and then this troubling business with *The Crucified Abbot*, I've been preoccupied.' A loud clap of thunder preceded the rain pelting the lounge window. Donald got to the window and looked outside. 'It's turned into a foul evening, Lucy,' and returned to the settee, 'how do you feel about driving?'

'I suppose I'm capable. How much wine has been drunk?'

'Tallying these last glassfuls, about a bottle each.'

'Ooh, I suppose, technically, I've had too much alcohol. If one of the uniformed forces breathalyses me, I'd be for the high jump...'

'... and I'm in the same position, so I can't drive you home.'

'... also, there's a bloody tube strike...'

'... and the weather is awful. You'd get bloody soaked walking to the bus stop.'

That all other options had been eliminated, Lucy looked expectantly at Donald from under droopy eyelashes. 'What are we going to do, Donald?'

Donald gazed at Lucy's beauty and knew a line of fidelity to Janet had already been crossed. He desperately wanted to make love to his former fiancée.

'Well, there's only one bed in this flat...'

'... are you suggesting I stay the night, to sleep off the effects of the wine?'

'Who said anything about sleep?' Donald moved closer to her, and they kissed passionately.

'Donald, do you realise what you're suggesting? Your wife is in hospital...'

'... I've already told you I won't tell her about your visit...'

'... yes, but staying the night is something else...' Lucy reached to the table and finished the remaining glass of wine.

'... well, okay then, I'll sleep here on the settee, and you can have the bed.'

'Okay then, I'll stay, but can I have a bath, please? I always like a hot bath before settling down for the night?'

'Yes. You know where the bathroom is. Meanwhile, I'll make a cup of tea.' He drank the rest of his wine and carried the empty glasses into the kitchen. Donald listened to the water running into the bath. While the kettle was boiling, he reached for two cups and looked out of the kitchen window at the pouring rain. In the distance, the lights on Tower Bridge appeared diffused and distorted by the torrents of rain running down the windowpane. After making the tea, he shouted. 'Shall I bring the tea into the bathroom?'

At the same instant, Lucy's arms encircled him, and she whispered, 'Yes please, Donald.'

'Oh, I'm sorry I shouted, I didn't realise you'd come into the kitchen.'

Having dispensed with her clothes, Lucy hugged Donald; staring into his eyes, she undid his dressing gown and slipped it from his shoulders. Donald held her, pulling her close. Their naked bodies met, igniting sparks, and a thunderbolt of emotions that exceeded anything the raging storm could produce. Both knew that tonight, sleep would be an afterthought.

Fourteen

After undergoing various tests that proved inconclusive, besides showing she is in the early stages of pregnancy, Janet was discharged from Saint Thomas's Hospital. Doctor Pritchard recommended she take two weeks away from police work to recuperate fully. Donald requested compassionate leave to stay at home with her. Superintendent Croaker was compliant and agreed with his sergeant's request. As well as making sure Janet was okay, Donald had other motives in mind.

Over several evenings, Donald and Janet discussed the report's implications in the Staffordshire Newsletter. He produced the file showing Lucy's research, suggesting that he'd carried out the work, and omitted having met or collaborated with Lucy.

'What are we going to do about all this?' Janet asked, having read the research notes.

'We've two weeks away from Scotland Yard together. I suggest revisiting Staffordshire. Let's drive down Gallows Lane in Upper Slaughter, repeating our honeymoon visit, and take things from there. Evaluating all my research, *The Crucified Abbot* shouldn't exist.'

'... and what if we find otherwise...?'

'... We'll act upon what we find...'

'... and what are we going to do about Lizzie Cartwright?'

'... I've thought about that. Do you imagine the officers at Stafford Police Headquarters will have confidence in us? They'll think we are involved with taking drugs. Somehow more evidence is needed to gain credence...'

'... but you saw her being murdered the same as I did.' Janet was wringing her hands.

'Calm down please, darling. Doctor Pritchard told us you have to relax more.'

'How can we relax, with all this hanging over us?'

'Here's one of the sedative tablets prescribed at the hospital. I suggest we take things easy today and make plans to travel north tomorrow. I'll go now and arrange for a hire car.' Janet nodded in agreement.

'I'll have a nap before dinner. What do you fancy eating?'

'How about I call at the Chinese takeaway after going to Scotland Yard?'

'Hmm, that's what I fancy. Did you have a takeaway meal while I was in the hospital? I'm sure the flat smelled of curried chicken and bean sprouts when I came in?'

Janet's words caused Donald to swallow. 'Oh yes, I did, darling. I'm sorry I should have sprayed some air freshener around.'

'... Oh, also, can you call at the corner shop? There's no bath cleaner left, and there's a huge tidemark around the porcelain. I assume it's from those scented bath cubes you use. Are you still there, Donald?' Janet raised her voice, believing he'd already left. 'You'd better bring some more wine as well. The last remaining bottle of rioja has been drunk and there's none to have with the Chinese meal.' Donald swallowed again. 'Okay, darling, but is it wise to mix wine with your tablets?' he called as he left the flat.

Janet answered, 'Perhaps not?' but Donald was halfway down the stairs and didn't hear her reply.

Fifteen

Making use of the M1 motorway, the journey north took three hours from central London until reaching the city of Lichfield. 'We only have a few more miles to go. How about eating lunch here before carrying on?' They parked the car and ambled around the centre of the city before entering Cathedral Close. In a quiet corner of the courtyard, a delightful café served snacks. Afterwards, they toured the cathedral. The sombre atmosphere turned into amusement when upon leaving the eleventh-century Gothic edifice, they stopped to read the notice boards giving details of events, bulletins, and other information.

'Oh, read this announcement, Janet. *The sermon this morning is entitled - Jesus walks on water. The sermon this evening is - searching for Jesus.'* Loud laughter echoed across the courtyard before stifling their amusement. A perspiring, bespectacled vicar brushed past in a hurry, trying to fasten the stud keeping his dog collar in place.

'This one is even better,' Janet exclaimed. *'Weight Watchers will meet at 7 pm in the cathedral extension room. Please use the large double doors at the side entrance.'*

'What's with the person who writes these notices? See this one. *For the forthcoming jumble sale, the ladies of the cathedral have cast off clothing of every kind. They may be seen in the cloister basement on Friday afternoon.* Shame we won't be here on Friday, but where will the change be kept?' Janet playfully pushed Donald's arm.

They ambled through the city back to the car. 'The satnav says there are only four miles to Upper Slaughter.' Donald sensed Janet's apprehension. 'Try not to worry, darling, let's see what's in Upper Slaughter this time.'

After passing the sign for Upper Slaughter village, Donald slowly eased the Renault Megane into Gallows Lane. Inhaling deeply in expectation of arriving at the thatched *The Crucified Abbot* around the next bend. A collective sigh of relief manifested in Janet shouting, 'I don't believe it.'

Donald exclaimed, 'This is so weird!'

In front of the car, a large green and white sign displayed The Red Lion. The smooth, asphalted car park contained several cars as Donald chose a convenient parking space. After grabbing the overnight bags, they walked towards the front door of the hotel. The thatched roof of *The Crucified Abbot* had given way to interlocking rounded clay tiles on the smart rural hostelry. Modern red bricks with amber natural stone embellishments around the doors and windows replaced the half-timbered olde-worlde façade. 'We'd like to reserve a room for the night, please?' Donald asked the vivacious, attractive receptionist.

'Will you sign the register please, sir,' having to raise her voice a little because of the chatter of visiting diners in the adjacent room.

'Is there a room overlooking the rear garden, please?'

'Let's see,' the receptionist pondered, looking down the list of available rooms.

'Room number 103 is on the first floor. Would you like help with your baggage, sir?' she asked, as she handed Donald the room keys.

'No, we can manage our bags. Thank you. Could we also book an evening meal here in the hotel?'

'What time for?' Donald looked at Janet.

'Seven-thirty,' she suggested, 'and as with the room, is there a table looking over the rear garden?'

'That's not possible, madam. The restaurant only looks out over the front of the hotel.'

'Okay, that's no problem.' Janet looked curiously as Donald's mobile phone rang.

'That's your phone, Donald; at least there's a signal here this time.'

Ambling up the stairs, Donald flipped open the phone. It was a text from Lucy. He swallowed.

'Ah, it's a text from the gov. He's asking how you are. Here's the key to the room, darling, I'll sit down in the lounge and text a reply to him.' He read Lucy's message.

'Hello, Donald, I wanted to check with you that you were okay about the wonderful night we spent together. I thoroughly enjoyed your company. Love Lucy xx.'

He started pressing the screen and sent a reply. *Hi, Lucy, it was terrific. I enjoyed being with you too. Janet and I have arrived in Upper Slaughter in Staffordshire. When I'm back in London, can we meet, please? Love Donald xx.* He made sure the display showed that the message had been delivered; he then deleted the two responses.

The door to room 103 was wide open. Donald found Janet pressed up against the window, looking down on Abbot Ibáñez's yew tree.

'The tree is still here, Donald,' half-turning as he entered the room, gliding to the window to put his arm around her.

'What's happening, Donald? Why does the Red Lion stand where *The Crucified Abbot* used to be?'

'Let's unpack, make a cup of tea, and then have a walk around the grounds. Perhaps we can have a chat with the owner of the place?'

In the hotel foyer, Donald stopped the receptionist as she walked from behind her desk. 'Hello, my wife and I are interested in the area and wondered if perhaps the owner or anyone else could help us with details?'

'Well, the owner is Mrs Clara Downing, who lives in Stoke-on-Trent and isn't here today. She could've helped. She knows everything there is to know about the origins of The Red Lion.' She looked thoughtful before answering again. 'A guest at the hotel, Mr Ted Baxter, might help? Well, he's not staying, he's a daily visitor, and likes the draught cider here. Ted lives in Upper Slaughter and knows everything about the area. I'm sure he could tell you what you want to know. Ted's an old man and a little deaf, so you may have to speak up. I think you'll find him sitting around the back in the garden.'

'That's extremely helpful. Thank you.' Janet offered her thanks too, and they ambled to the rear garden. Donald and Janet fixed their sunglasses to shield their eyes from the bright sunshine and walked straight to the yew tree. Despite the heat, Janet couldn't help shivering a little. She reached up the tree and brushed her hand across a nail. 'It's still here, Donald. One of the original nails that crucified Abbot Ibáñez...'

'... are you sure it's not a nail that Mrs Strange hammered into... never mind?' They turned when a feeble voice called to them. 'I should mind what you're doing around that tree.'

Donald and Janet walked over to the old man who sat on a slatted bench. Janet was sure it was the same bench she'd sat on when experiencing the erotic dream about Ben.

'Hello,' Donald offered to shake the man's hand. 'Are you Mr Baxter; the receptionist said we might find you here?'

'Ted Baxter's my name. I sit here most days of the week in an afternoon. This is a delightful spot to soak up the sun and partake of the local Abbot cider. The nectar's made in a small brewery in Rugeley, a little way down Brereton hill, a few miles from here.'

'I'm Donald Lawrence, and this is my wife, Janet.' Ted shook hands.

'Can we join you on the bench?'

'Pardon, my young fella, my lad, you must speak up, I'm a little deaf, you see. It's not from my age. It's because of them blasted German howitzer's at Passchendale, on the Somme in 1917. Once their cannon shells thundered over your head, you couldn't listen to another thing for weeks. The loud bang also gave you the shits, but in the trenches, we were crawling in shit all the time, so a little more didn't make any difference. I was only a young sprig; in fact, I lied to the army recruiting people about my age. I remember mom and dad were so angry when I got home and told them I'd joined the forces. It was that army fella's fault, luring callow lads like me with tales that the French mademoiselles turned crazy for a bit of English rump steak, if you know what I mean.' Ted winked at Janet. 'The army stationed me at Armentiéres. Do you remember the old war song,' He started singing – 'Mademoiselle from Armentiéres, parlez-vous? Mademoiselle from Armentiéres, parlez-vous? Inky pinky parlez-vous. I can't remember all the words now, too many years have passed, but I never speak about the war.'

'I said, can we join you on the bench?' Donald reminded the old man.

'Dear lad, there's plenty of room. I often have an afternoon nap here. I'm ninety-three next birthday, so when I doze I dream of the old days. That's when the world was a much nicer place to live in. Today, the air abounds with computer gizmos, modems and mobile telephones. No one writes a letter anymore. God bless the good old days when flaxen-haired maidens danced around the village maypole and us young chaps watched. When we received a wink from one girl, we knew that would be our lucky day. Then there was old Capstick the thatcher. He used to come and tell a yarn or two. Do you see my young fella, my lad, Capstick used to weave peacocks out of excess thatch and put them on the top of cottages he'd just thatched? He told us he'd put them there because that's where he'd had a conquest with the lady of the house. When there were far more thatched cottages in Upper Slaughter than there is today, there'd be peacocks everywhere. Oh, I'm sorry what was I saying, my mind gets carried away. I don't see many people to have a chat with these days, especially as my two daughters have already passed on and my grandkids are living independent lives. Still, I'm okay as long as a drop of cider continues to lubricate my old tonsils.' Ted cackled an infectious laugh before pausing. Donald and Janet assumed the old man had dozed off. Donald coughed, and Ted roused again.

'Mr Baxter...?'

'... Call me, Ted. Silas Johnson, the old rector at Upper Slaughter Priory, christened me Edwin, not Edward, as you might imagine, but Edwin. The Priory isn't there anymore. A stray German Heinkel bomber in the 1940 blitz got lost en route to Coventry and dropped the blasted bombs willy-nilly. Bang, wallop, the old place exploded. A direct hit... Oh, I'm sorry, where was I?'

'... okay, Ted, the young lady in reception...'

'... who?' Ted took a considerable slurp of cider and emptied the glass before wiping droplets of foaming orange cider from his whiskers with the back of his hand. 'Oh, now see that... the glass is empty. Chatting always makes me thirsty.' He looked optimistically at Donald.

'Alright, I'll get another. What are you drinking?' Donald smiled at Janet.

'... ah, that's exceedingly kind of you, young fella, my lad. Tell that lovely young receptionist the cider for old Ted, she knows what I like. Tessa's a lovely young lady...'

'What about you, darling?' he gestured to Janet.

'I think I'll have half a pint of what Ted's drinking, please.' Donald left them soaking up the sun.

'Well, well, young lady, you're going to have a drop of cider. That's what I like, a woman with a bit of spirit. This cider is much tastier than these new gassy beers from abroad. The foreign vapours give me the wind and make me fart. Have a mind though, you must be careful because some old lady friends tell me after they've had a couple or three, they go all randy like. I understand when they've had a few cos they wolf-whistle as I pass their cottages. This local cider beats these new-fangled oysters and fancy magic mushrooms that are supposed to make bedtime more interesting. Tell that young fella with you he'd better watch his step tonight?'

'I'll make sure and tell my husband.' Janet laughed. 'Perhaps I should have ordered a whole pint instead of only a half?'

'In your condition has the doctor told you it's okay to drink strong alcohol-laden drinks?'

'In my condition, what do you mean? How did you know I've seen a doctor?'

'Well, dearie, I'm no expert, but I've seen enough women in my time who're blooming in health and seem to have a natural glow as you do. That's a sure sign that you're pregnant.'

'What? I'm not pregnant, Ted. Donald and I haven't been married long.'

Ted laughed. 'I wish I had a pound for every young lady that says what you've said. If you are newlyweds, it's a sign that you probably are pregnant. Anyway, don't listen to me, it's only my opinion and none of my business. In my time, I've seen my mother and my sisters, then my girlfriends, wives, and daughters, have all been pregnant, and I was the first to tell. Not as they're all my doing, you understand.' He tapped the side of his nose and winked. 'There's nothing as lovely as a pretty young lady who has that natural pregnant glow.'

'Well, I believe you're mistaken this time, Ted.'

'... Oh, you seem like a lovely young lady, I wish I were fifty years younger, that nice young fella of yours would've had a fight on his hands for your favours... ah... if only...?' Ted turned quiet again but seemed to rouse up when Donald returned with the drinks.

'Ah, thank you kindly,' he gushed at receiving a new sparkling pint of cider. He tapped the side of his nose at Janet as she took a sip. 'Now remember what I said, young lady, that's potent stuff. Now, young fella, what were we talking about?'

'The lady in reception...'

'... oh, you mean Tessa, she's no lady, every young buck in Upper Slaughter who's acquainted with the birds and the bees knows what she and her arse are like between the sheets if you know what I mean... and if they didn't, Tessa would soon explain how things work... Oh, I'm sorry milady, I didn't mean to offend you...'

'That's alright, Ted, no offence taken. Please go on...' Janet smiled at the white-whiskered man. She liked him and considered him a fascinating character as she took another drink.

'... Where was I...?' He looked towards Donald for clarification before slurping from his glass.

'Tessa in reception tells us you know everything about these parts, and particularly Upper Slaughter.' Donald raised his voice as Ted put his hand to his ear, trying to gather the sound of his voice, as if he were using an ear trumpet.

'There isn't a mouse farts in Upper Slaughter without me knowing about it.' The second glass of cider was loosening Ted's tongue.

Donald shouted again. 'So, you could tell us a thing or two about this old yew tree?' Ted's expression changed. He squinted and looked under his eyelids at the tree.

'Keep away from that tree, its unwelcome news. I was going to tell a young woman to be careful this morning. I watched her feel around the bark, but I may have dropped off and dreamt it instead?'

'That was probably me, Ted, as we arrived at the hotel.' Janet explained.

'... Oh, that was you, was it? Well, all the same, be careful. What were you feeling the bark for if you don't mind me asking?'

'To see if the nails were still there that had crucified Abbot Ibáñez?'

Ted's voice changed, and he became sober. 'What do you understand about Abbot Ibáñez?'

'Oh, not much, only what I've read...'

'My advice is to keep away from that tree...'

'Why, Ted? Please tell us why.' Janet pleaded.

'... okay, if I must. I was only a young lad. I used to sit here on this very bench with my mom, dad, and sisters, and we'd listen to the story of *The Crucified Abbot.*' He digressed again by lifting himself off the bench and looking at the wooden slats. 'Wait a minute, it can't be the same bloody bench because my older sister, Caroline, was courting a young bloke called Jacob Marlywood. She used to complain about a knot in the wood that used to stick in her bum. I remember she wore no knickers. Jacob used to call on her, so he could pull out the splinters, but that's another story. Now, where was I...?'

'... You were telling us about *The Crucified Abbot.*' Ted's face turned serious again after Janet reminded him.

'... ah, yes. Mom and dad told us youngsters that when they were young sprigs in the village, an old, thatched hotel and pub stood here, well before the time of the Red Lion, of course. Since the dawn of time, everyone called it *The Crucified Abbot.* Anyway, one Halloween night, the place burnt down and everyone burnt to death.'

'Did they realise how it happened?'

'Well, it's rumoured that many evil goings-on used to take place here, orgies and magical ceremonies and such like. A few of the villagers used to dance around the old yew tree. Yes, dancing around the tree in the nude; it takes some crediting, doesn't it? There were also some old codgers. When I think of some old folks that I see, they will do well to keep their bits to themselves. Not a pretty sight.'

'I could ask you how you know that.' Janet laughed.

Ted laughed. 'You're a lucky man, young fella. Your wife has a mischievous nature.'

'I'm aware of that.' Donald and Janet shared a knowing expression.

'Anyway, do you know they were all naked, and they carried lanterns to ward away the evil spirits. Or in this case, to attract them? On this Halloween night, they'd had a special orgy. Mass fornication under the yew tree happened. Then they came inside the hotel after prancing around in the buff again, and things got out of hand. Someone new in the village took a fancy to the owner's son's girlfriend, and they had a punch up. Ben was his name. Someone knocked over one of the paraffin lanterns, and before anyone could piss on the flames, the old thatch caught fire and well... that was that. Next morning a dozen people were dead, including nine villagers, with blackened bodies. Nobody could tell a bloke from a gel; their bodies were so burned. Imagine having all your dangly bits burnt off?'

'You say your parents knew about this...?'

'Yes, they were only youngsters when that happened...'

'I'm told it took place in 1866.'

'... yes, I believe it did. It was before my time, of course. It happened on All Hallows' Eve 1866. Listen, I must go soon, but if you're here tomorrow, I'll tell you about the owners of *The Crucified Abbot.* Caleb and Margareta Strange and their son, Ben; were evil devil worshippers. We can share another pint of cider if you like?'

A voice diverted Donald and Janet's attention. Someone called, 'Pops, are you ready?' They looked to see another elderly man walking towards them.

'Ah, it's my son-in-law, Tommy, come to collect me. I saw his car coming down Gallows Lane.'

'Hello, Tommy, I'm talking to this nice young couple...'

'... good afternoon,' gestured Tommy as he tried to take Ted's arm.

'Hi,' Donald and Janet called as Ted became unsteady on his feet and started wobbling.

'Bloody hell, Ted, how much have you had to drink today?'

'... aw stop moaning, Tommy, you're aware that I like my cider...'

'It may be my fault,' Donald confessed. 'I bought him another pint.'

'There's no problem. When the old sod's had too much to drink, Ted becomes boisterous.'

'Boisterous?' Donald and Janet questioned.

'Yes, well, my elder sister, Aggie, who lives with us, says whenever Ted drinks too much, she never feels safe when it comes to bedtime if you know what I mean.'

As they started laughing, Ted berated Tommy as he helped him towards his car. 'That bloody sister of yours doesn't appreciate what's good for her. I could give her a better night's sleep if I had the chance. I listen to her farting and belching in the night. What she needs is a good...'

'... Pops, neither I nor anyone else wants to get to know your vulgar language; I hope you've not been swearing in front of these nice young folks...?' Their voices faded as they walked further away.

Then suddenly, Ted reappeared, and he shouted back to Janet. 'Don't forget what I told you, young lady.' Ted tapped the side of his nose and winked.

'For goodness' sake, Pops, come on, Aggie's got your dinner ready. It's your favourite today, tripe and onions...'

'... but we had tripe and onions the other day, Aggie said we'd have sausage and mash today...'

'... well, we're having the same again, so be thankful...'

Donald and Janet sat on the bench, looking at the yew tree. 'Well, well, so it looks as if it's true, *The Crucified Abbot* burned down in 1866.' Donald reflected on what Ted had told them.

'That makes things worse, doesn't it?'

'How, darling?'

'How can the old pub have burned down over a hundred years ago, if we spent two nights here a few weeks ago? It still doesn't explain what we experienced...'

'Well, I've been thinking about this. Listen to me and then tell me what you feel. You know, in ghost stories and movies, there's this theory about the fourth dimension; time travelling or entering a time warp and all that...'

'... You sound like old Ted; it must be the cider...'

'... no, I'm still sober, listen to me.'

'Well, in the absence of any other theories coming forward, I suppose I must.'

'Somehow, we crossed an invisible demarcation line, and we ended up back in the nineteenth century for a while...?'

'... that still doesn't explain what we saw, Donald. That young woman, Lizzie, murdered back in your 1800s theory. Except that it's now that young woman is the subject of a current murder being investigated by the Staffordshire police.'

'Imagining Ted Baxter, if he knows everything that goes on in Upper Slaughter, why didn't he say anything about that?' Donald questioned.

'Well, we never gave him a chance, and he's ninety-three next birthday. You must admit he's a fascinating character.'

'Yes, he certainly is. When he left, he shouted for you to remember what he said to you. I suppose that was something he said while I was fetching the drinks?'

'Yes, I couldn't shut him up. He said that you'd better watch your step tonight, as this cider is potent stuff and makes women randy...' Donald laughed.

'I don't suppose Ted's women need cider to make them randy. He'd charm a bird off a tree. Oh, and he said I was pregnant.' Donald's silence was deafening before staring at Janet.

'Oh, that's not the reaction I expected...'

'... I'm sorry, darling. I'm delighted you're pregnant...'

'... so, you believe I may be pregnant too? It definitely must be the cider.'

'... I know you are. I should have told you before. Doctor Pritchard at Saint Thomas's Hospital deemed it best not to tell you yet because of the state of your anxiety.'

'... but I've only missed one period, and you understand me: I'm never regular anyway...'

'During some tests they've carried out at Saint Thomas's one was an HCG test, and it proved positive...'

'Oh my God, Donald, *am* I pregnant?' Donald nodded.

'... I'm *actually* pregnant!' Donald smiled.

'... I can't believe it. *Am* I pregnant?' Donald nodded and smiled again.

'... I *am* pregnant then?'

'Yes!' Donald laughed in mock exasperation.

'... wheeeee! We're going to become parents.'

'It's wonderful, darling.' They hugged and kissed each other, celebrating the news.

'Wow! This will take some getting used to. This puts a whole new viewpoint on life, doesn't it?' Janet's hands felt her stomach and looked again at Donald. They laughed and hugged each other in a close embrace. With her head resting on his shoulder, Janet opened her eyes and looked at the yew tree. Her thoughts reverted to the erotic dream she'd had about Ben. They were making love together under the tree. A shudder rippled through her body when she recalled that in the reverie he'd climaxed during their copulation. 'Don't be so ridiculous.' She reprimanded her stupidity in imagining such a scenario that Ben could be the father of her foetus.

Sixteen

They were preparing to go down to the restaurant for their evening meal. As Janet waited for Donald to finish his shower, she sat at their bedroom window looking out at the yew tree. She tried to make sense of their earlier visit to *The Crucified Abbot.* 'How was it possible to watch a murder in a place that hadn't existed for over one hundred years? Yet the case was being investigated by the County Police?'

She thought more about what Donald had said about needing more evidence before discussing their predicament with the local constabulary. 'Of course,' she smacked her forehead. 'That's it! We watched the murder. We saw Lizzie's blood running down the yew tree. If it happened, there must be some remnants of that blood, perhaps lying at the base of the tree within the soil?' She continued to stare at the tree and wondered why they hadn't considered that before. 'Donald,' she shouted.

'I'll be out in a minute, darling.'

'Donald, I think I may have solved our dilemma?'

Donald appeared, rubbing his hair with the towel. She smiled at his nakedness. 'Oh, darling, you're such a stallion.'

'I'm so pleased you think so. I know you're only saying that because we've celebrated our good news in the best way we can.'

'Well, I'm always impressed with your performance, darling, but now you've proved there's some lead in your pencil.'

'Pardon me; I haven't heard that saying before.'

'Your virility, your potency, you aren't firing blanks.'

'Ah, I see. I'm glad to be of service, my love.' He sealed his comment with a passionate kiss.

'Now, what did you want? You shouted while I was in the shower.' Janet explained what she'd deduced.

'Well done.' He moved to the window and looked at the yew tree. He didn't notice Tessa, the receptionist, out in the garden picking some fresh mint leaves to flavour the roast potatoes. He remained at the window, evaluating how they should continue. Tessa forgot all about the mint leaves as she sat down on the grass and ogled Donald's masculine nakedness.

'Oh my,' she whispered. 'Mr Lawrence doesn't realise I'm here, or perhaps he does and he's deliberately letting me have a full view of his manhood. I must get out more, there's currently no one I see in Upper Slaughter who can match what he has. It must be the London air that produces specimens like that?' Tessa continued to watch as Donald finished drying himself. 'Ooh, I'd be pleased to do that for him.' she muttered.

Donald's prolonged stance at the window cemented his thoughts on what his next actions would be. He called to Janet, who was in the bathroom. 'There has to be a garden spade and a pot or a box out in the garden somewhere. After dinner, I'll dig up a sample of the soil.' He moved from the window to get dressed. Tessa reluctantly finished selecting the juicier mint leaves and returned to the kitchen.

'Hello, Mr and Mrs Lawrence, your table is number three, over by the front window.' Tessa ushered them through to the restaurant. She smiled demurely at Donald as he walked past her.

He recalled what Ted had told them about her. 'What did he say? Ah yes, *there isn't a young buck in the village who doesn't know what she and her arse are like between the sheets.*' Donald almost laughed aloud at Ted's vivid description of her. He soon had another closer glance at her when she came to ask them if they wanted a drink before they ate.

'Yes, we'll have two half-pints of the local cider Tessa, please' Donald asked. 'Ted Baxter told us how good it is.' She returned with the glasses, exchanging smiles with Donald before she returned to the bar.

'What are you smiling at?' Janet smirked at him.

'I've remembered what Ted told us about Tessa,' he whispered. 'You know that all the young bucks in the village understand her if you get my polite meaning?'

'I know what you mean. I'm getting to understand you, Donald Lawrence. I'm sure it can't have escaped your attention that she possesses an extremely curvaceous figure...'

'Does she...?'

'... You bloody well know she does. Make sure that she doesn't add your name to her list of conquests, as Ted indelicately described the parallel with Capstick the thatcher yesterday.' Janet displayed a smirk and a grin, but the implication resonated with Donald's guilty conscience about his recent episode with Lucy.

Tessa returned carrying a tray holding the pints of draught cider. She bent forward in front of Donald. Had he been looking, he would have seen her navel, such was Tessa's extremely low-cut tee shirt. She sashayed away.

'I'm impressed. I was watching you. Not once did your eyes deviate to Tessa's nether regions?'

'I only have eyes for you, darling.' He mentally berated himself for imagining Lucy's gorgeous figure as he spoke. They took a sip of cider and studied the menu.

'I'll have the pears and prawn to start, followed by the roast beef.'

'That sounds good to me. I'll have the same.' Tessa returned and took their order. As she finished writing on her notepad, she asked if Ted had helped them with information about the area.

'Yes, he did, thank you. As you know him, you'll also realise that once he starts, you can't shut him up, but he was extremely accommodating,' Donald answered. This time, as he looked directly at her, he couldn't avoid allowing his eyes to stray to her voluptuous figure.

'Do you live locally?' Janet asked. Donald assessed Tessa's figure thoroughly without being attributed as a voyeur with the attention diverted from him.

'Yes, I live in Gentleshaw Avenue in Upper Slaughter, down Gallows Lane a few hundred yards from here. Why do you ask?'

'We wondered if you could tell us anything about the murder of Miss Elizabeth Cartwright, I understand she lived in the village?'

'Well, of course, I know a lot about Lizzie. She was my friend, but I'm afraid I can't talk about it right now, as you can see, I'm busy, but later after dinner. We could share a drink in the lounge together. Again, could I ask why you want to know?'

'Yes, okay, we'll see you later this evening. Thank you. We're police officers.'

'Oh, I see, but I've already given plenty of statements to the Staffordshire Police...'

'... we're from the Metropolitan Police in London.' Donald added.

After eating their dinner, they relaxed in the lounge with another drink, waiting for Tessa to join them. Donald noted that various pictures and photographs of the local area decorated the room. He studied them with interest before calling Janet to examine one particular artist's painting. He pointed it out to her.

'Oh, my word, it's *The Crucified Abbot*,' she held her hand to her mouth. 'It looks exactly as I remember it. See the half-timbered façade and the thatched roof. It's a brilliant painting. It's in oils, I imagine?'

'That's not the best bit, darling. Notice the signature of the artist.'

Janet clutched her throat and peered closely. 'I can't make it out, Donald; it's such a scrawling hand.'

'You know him.'

She looked closely again. 'Ebenezer Strange 31st October 1865. That's exactly one year to the very day before it burnt down. It was created on another Halloween night. Why does everything concerned with *The Crucified Abbot* happen on Halloween?' She ran her fingers over the montage of irregular layers of oil paint. 'To think Ben applied this paint with his own hand?'

Tessa's arrival in the lounge disturbed their observations of the picture. 'Oh, you like my painting of *The Crucified Abbot,* do you?'

'This is *your* painting?' Donald asked.

'Yes, it is. I hung it here for safekeeping. If I kept it at home, my younger hooligan brothers would destroy it or scribble all over it. Of course, as you'll no doubt have learned from Ted, the old pub used to stand on this very spot, before it burnt down. So, I considered it very apt to display it here.'

'Could I ask how you came by it?' asked Janet.

'This is so odd that I'm here to talk to you about my friend, Lizzie. I received the painting from her as a gift, two months before she disappeared. Now she's gone, the painting is more valuable to me as a reminder of her.'

'Do you know why she gave the painting to you?'

'Well, I like to feel it was because we were friends, but she mentioned that she no longer wanted it. Her boyfriend painted it, and she'd fallen out with him. She said it brought back terrible memories every time she looked at it...'

'... did she say who her boyfriend was?' Donald interrupted with a question.

'All she ever called him was Ben. That's what I told the Staffordshire Police when they interviewed me.'

'Did you meet him?'

'No, I wanted to. Lizzie kept telling me how handsome and virile Ben was, but she kept him to herself.'

'Okay, thank you, Tessa. This isn't a formal interview. As we said, we're only tourists to Staffordshire, and interested in the local case.'

'You're welcome...'

'... oh, and I almost forgot. Could we book for another night at The Red Lion, please?' Donald asked.

'No problem, could you come to the reception desk with me and I'll take the number of your debit card, please? I should have done this when you first checked in. It's only standard procedure. There'll be no money debited from your account until you leave.'

Donald walked out of the lounge with Tessa, leaving Janet still looking at Ben's painting.

'Well, you won't find that we've done a bunk in the middle of the night and left without paying.' Donald laughed. 'You understand we're from the Metropolitan Police, so you could find us at Scotland Yard.'

'I'm sure about that. I sleep here in a second-floor bedroom, so I wouldn't hear you if you did. I'm immediately above your room, actually.' Tessa looked under eyebrows at Donald as he handed over his debit card.

'Thank you for such a wonderful dinner. It was delicious.'

'Oh, I'm so glad you enjoyed it. The local herbs make all the difference to the taste. I was out picking some earlier in the rear garden. It's a wonder you didn't see me. I noticed you were looking out of your bedroom window.'

'Oh, when?' Donald looked wide-eyed at Tessa, remembering he'd stood naked at the window.

'A couple of hours ago, before dinner.' She smiled at him and winked her eye. Donald gulped.

'Tessa, I've got a question. In your rear garden, do you have a spade and a box or a pot I can use please?'

'Whatever for?'

'In connection with our investigations, we'd like to take a soil sample from under the yew tree.'

'Be my guest. Help yourself.'

Donald and Janet proceeded into the rear garden. He found a sharp spade and a terra-cotta pot; they carefully took small soil samples from around the tree. 'We'll get this analysed back at the Met,' Donald suggested.

'Presuming the soil contains some of Lizzie's blood, they can extract her DNA. However, we need something to correlate it with. Something personal of Lizzie's, like a hairbrush,' Janet added. 'I wonder if Tessa could help us with that.'

'Or what do you think about us going to her home, to explain what we want her hairbrush for?'

'We could also have a chat with her parents about Lizzie and her relationship with Ben,' Janet prompted. 'We could go there in the morning. I'll ask Tessa for their address.'

'We need to tread carefully, Janet. We're trespassing on Staffordshire Constabulary's patch, and here unofficially; their Chief would surely contact our gov if he found out?'

Seventeen

Donald and Janet walked down a shingle pathway to a quaint cottage door surrounded by tall, multi-coloured hollyhocks. 'Hello. Are you Mrs Cartwright?' Donald asked of a small, elderly woman dressed in a white apron with a red scarf turban keeping her long, greying hair in place.

'Yes, I'm Dolly Cartwright. Who are you come knocking on my door on this dull morning?'

'I'm Sergeant Donald Lawrence, and this is my wife, Constable Janet Lawrence. We're police officers with the Metropolitan Police in London.'

'You've come from London to speak with me...?'

'Well, we're in Staffordshire as tourists, and I stress this isn't an official police call...'

'My husband, Dandy, and I have only ever spoken to the Staffordshire police before. Is it about my daughter, Lizzie, you've come to speak to me?'

'Yes, we're staying at The Red Lion, and we spoke to Tessa. She said to come to see you. Is your husband in? You said his name is Dandy.'

'Dandy is his nickname. His proper name is Dandridge, but that sounds so posh, doesn't it? He prefers everyone calls him Dandy. No, he's not in the house, he's down at gooseberry field where our pigsties are. He's feeding the drove and cleaning the sties. Our Tamworth Old Spot sow, Jemima, has given birth to a new litter of eighteen piglets. They're Dandy's pride and joy, so I won't see him again today. Please come in. Would you like a cup of tea?'

'Thank you, Mrs Cartwright. Oh, that's a lovely smell. What are you cooking?' Janet asked.

'Oh, that's the pig feed. I've not long finished cooking it in the boiler. It's a mixture of oatmeal, cob nuts and potatoes, flavoured with a good dose of curry powder. It looks similar to porridge when it's cooked. Our drove goes crazy for it. They almost sit up and beg for it when Dandy gets near the pigsties with the buckets of boiling food.'

'Go through to the living room, I've got a lovely coal fire roaring in there.'

'Oh, Donald, isn't this a cosy room?' Janet enthused as they sat in two fireside armchairs.

Mrs Cartwright brought a tray of cups of tea, and she pulled up a pouffe towards the fire between them.

'We'd like to offer you our sincere condolences regarding your daughter, Lizzie.' Donald offered. 'What's the latest situation regarding police investigations?'

'Well, it seems to have gone cold. The police have requested anyone with information to contact police headquarters regarding Lizzie's boyfriend, that horrible Ben...' She took a slurp of tea and stared at the flames.

'... Ben? Did you meet her boyfriend, then?' Janet asked in surprise.

'Oh, yes, many times. Lizzie brought him here for tea, but Dandy and I detested him. We tried to tell Lizzie, but the youngsters are so headstrong. She wouldn't listen to us and see where we are now...'

'... Why didn't you like him?' Janet asked, keen to learn more about him. She interlocked her fingers around her cup of tea.

'He seemed a lot older than Lizzie and a proper man of the world, if you understand what I mean. Cocksure of himself, as Dandy used to say. He was a real charmer. I'm sure he tried to chat me up twice, but I suppose he was sweetening me up to get to Lizzie?'

'Did you ever notice that he threatened Lizzie, or perhaps expressed any violence towards her?' Donald asked.

'No, never, and Lizzie thought the sun shone out of his big backside. Oh, he was an enormous man, with lots of muscles in the right places. I believe Lizzie saw him as her protector and shining light to guide her through life. How wrong she was.'

'What troubled us was that he used to take her away from us for days on end sometimes. Then when she never came back at all...' Mrs Cartwright held her handkerchief to her mouth.

'We're sorry to cause you upset asking these questions.' Janet looked at Donald. 'Perhaps we should leave?'

'No, don't go on account of my snuffles, dearie. I'm okay.'

'Are you sure?' She nodded.

'... you can imagine the day was awful when the police came and told us they'd found Lizzie's body near Castle Ring. I'll never forget. It got worse a few days later when the police asked us to go with them to identify her body in Stafford morgue.'

'That must have been a dreadful ordeal for you both.' Janet sympathised.

'When we looked at her injuries, we couldn't have imagined it. How could somebody be so cruel? Do you realise she had wrought iron nails through her hands and ankles? Someone had nailed her to a tree! Crucified, like our Lord Jesus.' Donald's thoughts returned to the vision they'd seen in their dreams. 'And then someone had cut her throat, as sure as my Dandridge cuts the throats of chickens out back. The same as if she'd been a chicken ready to be prepared for the oven. All the time I stood by her side in that cold morgue, I kept believing Lizzie was only asleep and would wake up if I shook her. Then the doctor, the police pathologist fella, told us she'd been pregnant. So, as she lay there, she was carrying our grandchild. Dandy swore on his life that if they ever found out who did our Lizzie to death, he'd be prepared to go to his own death by killing them. I hope he never finds out; I can't lose my husband, and he meant what he said. I understand my Dandy and when he says something in the manner he did, woe betides the culprits.' Donald and Janet reflected in silence, knowing that it was Ben who had slit Lizzie's throat. They all looked to the front door of the cottage as they listened to the latch being lifted.

'Oh, hello. You've got company, then?' Mr Cartwright walked through the door in his stockinged feet. 'I've left my wellies outside, Mary; I haven't finished mucking the pigs out yet. Would you like these?' He held out two small, dead, pink piglets. 'These were the runts of the litter. I suppose Jemima must have laid on them and smothered them? Anyway, there's nothing else wrong with them, so we'll have them for dinner.'

'Dandy, I've two police officers here from London...'

'... from the smoke, eh? What do they want?' Mr Cartwright called from the kitchen as he put the piglets in a large metal oven tray. Donald walked into the kitchen and offered to shake his hand.

'Hello, Mr Cartwright, I'm Sergeant Donald Lawrence from the Metropolitan Police at Scotland Yard. I'm here with my wife, Constable Janet Lawrence...'

'... why have the County Police brought in Scotland Yard.? Have you found out yet who murdered my Lizzie?' Mr Cartwright looked as he arched his long, greying eyebrows at Donald's outstretched arm. '... you won't want to shake my hand, young fella, my clothes are smelly, and I've been handling dead piglets.'

'As I've been explaining to your wife, we aren't here on an official visit. We're visiting the area, and your daughter's case has attracted our attention. If we could help, we'd be glad to do so.'

'I see. Well, if you catch the bastard who's done away with my Lizzie, could you do me a favour, please, and give him to me for thirty minutes first? I'd save the taxpayer a lot of unnecessary expense by the government keeping him in prison for thirty years. She brought her boyfriend, Ben, home a few times. He was a big, strange bloke, but no matter how big he is, that wouldn't stop me. If he was responsible for my Lizzie's horrible injuries, then I'd make sure he pays for it.'

'I'm sure I'd feel like that if Lizzie was my daughter.'

While Donald was talking to Mr Cartwright, Janet asked if she could see Lizzie's room. Mrs Cartwright showed her upstairs, and they entered Lizzie's bedroom. 'Mrs Cartwright, I've another favour to ask you, please, and remember this isn't official. Could you let me borrow a hairbrush or toothbrush of Lizzie's?'

'Whatever for...?'

'To obtain a sample of your daughter's DNA from perhaps a stray hair that's still on her hairbrush or something similar? It could prove useful in discovering where and how Lizzie met her death.'

'By all means. Anything that helps to find her killer is alright by me.' She reached for a hairbrush sitting on Lizzie's dressing table. 'She used to use this every day. See, there are still lots of her blonde hairs still between the bristles.' Once again, Mrs Cartwright snuffled and grasped her handkerchief. As they left the bedroom, she gave the hairbrush to Janet. Soon afterwards, Donald and Janet drove back along Gallows Lane to The Red Lion.

'What a tragedy, Janet. They're such a lovely couple. I feel so sorry for them. They've lost their only child.'

'To assume that we hold the answer to Lizzie's killer, and it's such a heavy burden to bear. We must try our best to bring closure for Mr and Mrs Cartwright. I've Lizzie's hairbrush here. She pulled it from her pocket and held it up for Donald.' He glanced at it as he drove. 'It has lots of her blonde hair still in the brush, so the scientists at the yard will compare the soil and the hairbrush for matching DNA.'

Eighteen

Tessa brought the lunch menu to Donald and Janet as they sat in the Red Lion's dining room.

'Thank you for giving us Lizzie's parents' address. We visited them this morning.'

'That's okay, Mrs Lawrence,' Tessa replied. 'They're a lovely couple; I can't imagine how they're coping without Lizzie around.'

Donald asked for two tomato salads. They ate their lunch in a quiet room. Donald and Janet were the only diners, so their voices echoed around the oak wood panelling that lined the walls as they spoke. 'After lunch, we'll relax in the garden and wait for Ted to arrive, shall we?' Donald suggested.

They sat on the bench and lifted their faces to the intermittent sunshine. Donald relaxed and smiled when, after a few minutes, he listened to Janet's soft breathing. He looked towards her and saw she was asleep. Donald looked at his watch. It was 13:15; he knew Lucy would have her lunch break. Carefully, he got up and sauntered to their bedroom, where he phoned Lucy.

'When are you returning to London?' she asked him.

'Soon, when we've gathered evidence that will shed some light on Lizzie Cartwright's murder. I hope the pathology lab will correlate her DNA?'

'Guess who came and sat by me again in *La Vista* yesterday?'

'Not Robbie, the plumber?' Lucy laughed. 'Yeah, very same; he explained what he did at the London Stock Exchange...'

'Don't tell me, let me guess. He wants to visit your flat to explain some investment possibilities for you?'

'... something like that.'

'... are you telling me about Robbie to make me jealous?'

'... *are* you jealous?'

'... do I *need* to be jealous?'

'... and what of *my* jealousy?'

'... are *you* jealous?'

'... jealousy isn't only a male preserve, you know.'

'I'll be back as soon as I can.'

While Donald and Lucy had their telephone conversation, Janet's impromptu sleep once again produced weird dreams of Ben and *The Crucified Abbot.*

Under the glare of a full moon, naked and hand in hand, smiling at each other, they walked around the Abbot Ibáñez yew tree. Her slight bulge suggested she was at least four months into her pregnancy. Ben stopped and raised his hands aloft and recited a poem to the moon. Positioning himself with outstretched legs, he called louder. Within seconds, three naked women appeared and suggestively ran their hands over his body. Janet noticed that the three other women also displayed bulges, indicative of different stages of their pregnancies. Other naked people joined them and, holding hands in a circle, they danced around the yew tree. Then the circle parted. Caleb and Margareta, partially dressed in cloaks of loose strips of flowing pink lace, led a young, dark-haired, naked girl into the middle of the circle. She lay down on the grass and waited for Ben to join her. His parents stood by the trunk of the old tree reciting chants, inviting Lucifer to appear and witness the creation of another incubus into their group. The women prepared Ben for the mating ritual by ensuring his maximum arousal. As he copulated with the dark-haired girl, everyone stood around watching them as they writhed in the grass, shouting encouragement to him...

Ted's voice disturbed Janet's explicit reverie. She opened her eyes to see him sitting next to her on the bench. 'Hello, my dearie, I'm so sorry to disturb you.'

'Oh, hello, Ted. I was dreaming.' Janet gasped and rubbed her eyes as the sun shone brightly into her face.

'I'm glad you're still here. My son-in-law, Tom, has dropped me at The Red Lion, while he and his sister have gone shopping.'

'Did you enjoy your tripe and onions yesterday?'

'I certainly did, my dearie. That's what Aggie's gone shopping for, amongst other things...'

'I understand you've been visiting Dandy and Mary Cartwright. I told you, not much gets past my noticing what goes on in Upper Slaughter...'

'... yes, we have. Why didn't you talk to us about their daughter Lizzie's murder?'

'Why? Because its bad news. Awful news. I don't enjoy talking of such things, especially here at The Red Lion, where *The Crucified Abbot* used to be.'

'Why not? Why is it bad to talk here...?'

'... for fear of reincarnation of the devil.'

'... do you believe in such things then?'

'... my dearie, it's not a case of whether or not I deem it to be true. The devil exists and is amongst us today, here and now, especially in such proximity to Abbot Ibáñez's yew tree.' Janet looked across to the yew tree.

'You were telling my husband and me about the orgies here and devil worshippers that used to dance around the tree...'

'... that's right, I was telling you, wasn't I? That's only a fraction of what used to go on...'

'... you said you were going to tell us about Caleb, Margareta Strange, and their son, Ben.'

'... did I?' Janet saw Ted's face expand into a smile as he looked along the pathway. Janet turned to see Donald approaching, holding a tray holding three pints of Abbot cider.

'Hello, Ted, I saw you arrive with your son-in-law, so I thought I'd get you a drink. It's the Abbot cider, that's what you prefer, isn't it?'

'I wouldn't drink anything else, young fella.' Ted took a pint from the tray and guzzled a huge swallow. 'Cheers, and good health to you both,' he said cheerily. 'Now, where was I, young lady?'

'My name's Janet. Had you forgotten? My husband's name is Donald.'

'Pardon, my dearie, you must speak up. I believe the battery is on the blink in my hearing aids. Did you say your name was Janice? Now, Janice, these devil worshippers...'

'Ted, my wife's name is Janet...'

'Yes, that's right, Janet. You mustn't go forgetting your wife's name, especially in her delicate situation.' Donald raised his eyebrows at Janet.

'... particularly Caleb and Margareta Strange.' Janet reminded Ted.

'... and their son, Ebenezer. Don't forget him, he's the biggest devil worshipper of the lot.'

'Why do you say that?'

'Well, I understand you and your husband visited the Cartwright cottage yesterday to enquire about Lizzie. I know for a fact that Ebenezer Strange was Lizzie's boyfriend....'

Donald looked intently at him and then at Janet. '... How do you know that, Ted? It's not possible. Ebenezer Strange died in the fire that burnt down *The Crucified Abbot* in 1866. You told us that yourself. Lizzie Cartwright is the here and now and until a few months ago lived in Upper Slaughter.'

After taking another huge guzzle of cider, Ted tapped the side of his nose. 'Because Ebenezer Strange is an incubus.' Janet at once held her hand to her mouth, recalling from her latest dream that Caleb and Margareta Strange had uttered this word.

'What's an incubus?' Donald asked with mounting interest, as he pulled up a patio chair directly in front of Ted. He rested his glass on a metal filigree table alongside Janet's untouched pint glass. Ted replaced his pint on the table and took a sharp intake of breath. He looked to the left and right as if making sure no one else was present to overhear.

'I'm sure you could do some research for a more educated reply than I can give you, but an incubus is a devil himself, or at least one of his disciples.'

'Come on, Ted, in today's technological age, the devil in living human form is hard to suppose as a credible entity.'

'Young fella my lad, now, or in any other age, the devil exists. I've seen him and he's occupied my mind in waking dreams. Here in Upper Slaughter, and particularly right here at *The Crucified Abbot*, oh sorry, I mean The Red Lion.'

The mention of waking dreams caused Donald to glance at Janet. They hesitated about whether to tell Ted about their own experiences.

'I mentioned yesterday, I want to tell you about the Strange family, Caleb, Margareta, and Ebenezer. You may not assume what I'm about to tell you is the gospel truth, but that's up to you. I know what I know. I realise my hearing isn't so good and I forget things, particularly names. I'm nearly ninety-three years old and folks around here, and also my family, will tell you I'm past it and a farthing short of a shilling. Still, my mind and my memory are as sharp as when I was a young sprig...'

'... I think you're remarkable for your age, Ted...' Janet encouraged him.

'... and as I told you yesterday if I were fifty years younger, this husband of yours would have got a problem in keeping me away from you. Now, where was I? See what I mean, I've forgotten already. Oh yes, the Strange family in name and deed.' He took another slurp of cider. 'Only to lubricate the old tonsils, you understand,' he winked.

Ted's face took on a grim expression as he looked towards the yew tree. 'When I was a young sprig, fifteen or sixteen years old I'd be, I sat here on this very bench with my dear old dad and he told me all about *The Crucified Abbot* and the Strange family. He told me about his own experiences. It was a few years later, I came to experience the same things myself.' He took another swallow of cider.

'... What experiences?' Janet asked impatiently.

'Both my dad and I have drunk this same cider in the old hotel and met the Strange clan and...'

'... but *The Crucified Abbot* burned down in 1866 and that was before your father was born.' Donald prompted him.

'... aye, that's as maybe, but it's a fact. Caleb Strange was an Arch Incubus, an evil devil worshipper. He met Margareta, and she became his mistress, and he indoctrinated her into his evil ways. She converted into a succubus. Together they conceived Ebenezer. So, from the first time he drew breath he inherited the malevolent genes from an incubus and succubus. Legend and countryside traditions tell us that this is a momentous combination that's rare and toxic. It's a perversion of nature that he grew into an Adonis capable of seducing any woman that looked upon him. Of course, those evil genes have been passed down the years to his descendants.' He almost emptied his glass by taking another colossal swallow. He looked expectantly towards Donald.

'I'll gladly fetch you another pint, Ted, but I'm remembering what Tom, your son-in-law, said about you drinking too much.'

'That's all my eye and Betty Martin. I'm as sober as any judge in any court. Another pint of Abbot cider is what my old digestive bits need on a sunny day like this.' Donald smiled, nodded, and took Ted's glass for a refill at the hotel bar.

'Hello, Mr Lawrence,' Tessa chirped from behind the ale pumps.

'Tessa, please call me Donald. A refill of cider for old Ted, please. Are you not picking herbs today, Tessa?' Donald asked as his eyes feasted upon her low-necked tee-shirt that strained to withhold her feminine form devoid of a bra. She noticed him ogling her.

'Perhaps I'll go into the garden later? I'll make sure I do, especially if I think you'll be standing at your bedroom window again, Donald.' She smiled, and they shared a laugh as she pulled the draught bar handle to fill Ted's glass. 'I usually pick the herbs about an hour before dinner.'

'Maybe I'll stand at the window after I've had a shower, but only to admire the view over Cannock Chase, of course,' he winked.

'That's all I'll go into the garden for, to appreciate the spectacles of natural life.' Their intense glares into each other's eyes replaced the earlier laughter. She handed the drink to him and their fingers lingered on each other's hand, grasping the glass.

'I'll bear it in mind then.' Donald offered as he glanced at her and left the bar.

Janet took the opportunity of Donald's temporary absence to tell Ted that she'd also met Ebenezer Strange.

'... oh, my dearie, I'm so sorry to learn that. If you know Ebenezer Strange, I don't need to ask what happened...' He looked askance at her from under his eyelids. Janet blushed and looked to the floor.

'Where did he lie on you, under yon yew tree?' Janet nodded. 'Please don't let my husband know?'

'Your secret is safe with me, my dearie, but as far as I'm aware, from the experience of other women he's laid with, he'll know soon enough cos your belly will swell. I suppose your husband imagines he's the father, does he?'

'Are you telling me that Ebenezer Strange could be the father of my unborn child!?'

'It's uncertain, but I'd consider the possibility if I were you.' They looked up as Donald returned with Ted's refilled glass.

Ted was as good as his word and quickly returned to his narrative about Ebenezer Strange.

'My old dad told me incubi have the power to slip in and out of time. He met Ebenezer when he was a teenager himself. Of course, that was after the fire had destroyed *The Crucified Abbot.* I've also met him three times during my lifetime. So, what my dad told me about is true. Ebenezer also possesses the capability of taking people with him backwards and forwards as if there's a door that he can pass through.' Ted took another drink. Afterwards, he licked his lips and wiped his whiskers with the sleeve of his coat.

'I understand you'll find this hard to believe, but a few years ago when I could walk here under my own steam, I called for my usual afternoon tipple. I approached the front of The Red Lion without looking up. Can you imagine my astonishment when I stood inside *The Crucified Abbot?* Caleb Strange was serving ale and cider, and he knew my name. The usual Abbot cider is it, Mr Baxter,' he said to me in a deep, odd voice. 'The place had wispy thatch all dropping from around the eaves. Had old Capstick been around, I'm sure he could've tidied the roof and been able to place a straw peacock on the ridge. I came around the back to this very bench and sat and had my pint, as we're doing now. I became drowsy, not my usual nap, you understand, but a deeper, more intense sleep. Before I knew what was happening, I was dancing around yon yew tree stark naked with a lot more unclothed folk, including Caleb and Margareta Strange. Then Ebenezer appeared with a young nubile girl. We all started chanting and singing while Ben gave her a right seeing to, if you know what I mean. Not meaning to cause any offence, my dearie.' He nodded to Janet. 'Right there on the grass under the yew tree.' He pointed with his walking stick. 'After that, I assume I woke up cos I remember finishing the cider. Then, blow me down with a feather, Ben appeared dressed as a waiter asking me if I wanted another drink. I couldn't appreciate whether or not I was still in a dream? I remember I left without waiting for him to bring me another pint. My skin was sweaty with fright, I can tell you. I must have been scared, mustn't I, to leave a whole pint of Abbot cider behind? I rarely do things like that...'

'... we've noticed that' Janet whispered. 'Carry on.' She smiled at Donald.

'The next time I saw Ebenezer was a few months ago, here in Gallows Lane.' He nodded to the hedgerow lined thoroughfare. 'It was such a beautiful day. Tom, my son-in-law, fancied a pint of cider himself, so he pushed me here in my wheelchair from the village. Halfway along the lane, Ebenezer came walking towards us with Lizzie Cartwright. They were holding hands and laughing. They didn't see us until the last moment when Ben turned and asked me if I was going for another drink. 'Your cider is still waiting for you, Mr Baxter,' he said. Just like that, no hello, or goodbye, or kiss my arse. Of course, Tom asked me who he was, but I ignored him. I pretended I didn't understand him. I was frightened all over again. While Tom was pushing me, I half expected to arrive at *The Crucified Abbot* but, thankfully, we walked into The Red Lion. I hope I never get to see him again. Then, of course, we learnt poor Lizzie had been found dead at Castle Ring. I'd bet every guinea I've ever had in my pocket that Ben Strange did it, but how can that be proved?' Ted sighed and turned quiet. In a few moments, Donald and Janet walked towards the yew tree, knowing that Ted had dropped asleep.

'How about that then, Donald, we've experienced the same dreams as Ted?'

'I need to understand more about this incubus and succubus nonsense before I can bring any sort of reality and understanding to all this...'

'... It can't be nonsense, Donald. What about Lizzie Cartwright?'

'Well, when we get back to Scotland Yard, perhaps then it will make sense.'

'I wonder where we can find out more information about local traditions here?' Janet surmised.

'As we're in Staffordshire, I'd have thought the county library in the county town, Stafford, is the best place to explore. Surely they must have old books in there probably going back as far as Caxton's first printing press in 1470?'

'Let's go tomorrow morning and do some research.'

They heard Ted mumble.

'Oh, my dearies, thank goodness you're both real. I dropped off to sleep for a moment and when I awoke, I felt I was still dreaming.' Ted reached to drink the last dregs of his cider.

'Are you ready, Pops?' Tom scurried down the path towards them.

'That's good timing, Tom, I've just finished my cider.' Tom exchanged pleasantries with Donald and Janet before escorting Ted back to the waiting car. 'Hope to see you tomorrow,' Ted called back to them.

'He's already imagining drinking more cider,' Donald chuckled and called to Janet. She was already walking along the pathway to return to their bedroom.

Later in the day, Janet had dressed for dinner and sauntered down to the hotel lounge to read her book. Donald stepped out of the shower and remembered the earlier suggestive conversation with Tessa. Eyeing his mobile telephone, he saw it was 18:30, an hour to go before dinner. Donald carefully moved towards the window and peered around the curtains. He saw Tessa's basket resting on the grass half-filled with herbs, then she came into view and knelt on the lawn. She looked up expectantly towards the bedroom window. Donald tried to hide, but he realised she'd already seen him when she waved. He held the full-length curtain against his nakedness and waved back. Tessa expressed her disappointment by placing her hands on her hips in a defiant stance and pouted her lips.

'Oh God,' Donald thought. 'Now the bravado is over, I'm not so sure about this?' He peered down into the garden. Tessa was still looking anticipating a better view of him.

'Oh well, here goes.' He resigned himself but was also excited by the erotic notion of deliberately revealing himself to her. 'What harm can it do? If it pleases her.' Slowly he released the curtain and moved into the centre of the window. His hair was still wet, so he rubbed it with a towel. He stood with his legs apart, watching for Tessa's reaction. She held her hands to her cheeks and smiled.

'Oh my, this gets better and better,' she whispered. She leisurely clapped her hands while her smile broadened. She teased Donald by running her hands around her breasts. Donald responded by bowing, then holding out his arms and flexing his biceps.

'Donald, what on earth are you doing?' Janet barked as she opened the bedroom door.

'... What! Oh my God!' he panicked. '... Oh, only doing my exercises, I have to keep toned up...'

'... well, I should keep away from the window if I was you. You never know who can see you from the garden. I've returned to collect my other reading glasses.' Janet closed the door behind her, and he heeded her retreating footsteps along the landing. Donald looked back to the garden. Tessa was still watching him. He blew her a kiss that she returned. He waved to her and got dressed.

Tessa served Donald and Janet at the dinner table. Several times he and Tessa surreptitiously exchanged knowing looks as she brought the food and collected the empty plates. At the end of the meal, she asked them if they'd like drinks in the hotel lounge.

'Yes, please,' Janet replied.

'Two half-pints of Abbot cider please,' Donald added.

'Will you be staying another night?' Tessa asked.

'Yes, one more night at least. We're visiting the county library in Stafford tomorrow.' Donald and Janet sat for an hour in the lounge drinking and absorbing themselves in books from the hotel library on local history and folklore. Janet found a book entitled, *The Demons of South Staffordshire*. 'Oh, this looks interesting. I'm tired, darling, I'll take this to bed and read.'

'Okay, darling. I'll finish my drink first.' Donald sat on the comfy settee facing the cosy log fire. Within a few minutes, Tessa came and sat beside him in the peace and quietness of the dimly lit room. He looked towards her and then back to the leaping flames.

'I'm glad you haven't gone to bed,' she whispered. 'Thank you for this afternoon. Could I ask if everything was okay? I had the impression you finished your exercise routine a little abruptly?'

'Yes, you could put it like that. My wife came into the bedroom, but there's no problem.' She leaned towards him. 'You've got a very sexy body, Donald...'

'... have I?' He noticed she was wearing another revealing tee shirt, leaving nothing to his imagination.

'It's such a lovely evening, I'm going for a walk into The Chase later. If you fancy a stroll, I'd love some company.' She reached forward and rested her hand on his knee.

'Don't you have a boyfriend who would like a walk with you?'

'None that I'd like to be with me this evening. What do you think?'

'I'm not sure it would be a good idea? My wife is only upstairs. She'll wonder where I've gone.'

'That's a shame. If you change your mind, I'll be going down the path that leads from the rear garden at ten o'clock. I'll glance up at your window. If you decide not to join me, perhaps we could take a stroll together another time?' She left Donald gazing into the flames. He lifted his eyes and watched her go. His eager eyes never strayed from her alluring figure. She looked back for an instant and noticed him ogling her. Her smirk was a symptom of the understanding she had for men. She'd planted a seed of desire that she knew would be difficult for him to resist.

Donald climbed the stairs to his room. Janet was fast asleep. Laying on her chest was the book she'd been reading; her fingers held the pages open. He lifted the book and read.

'An incubus is a demon in male form who, according to mythological and legendary traditions, lies upon sleeping women to engage in sexual activity with them.'

'Well, well,' he imagined. 'Perhaps there's something in all that's been happening here after all?' He placed the book on her bedside table and sat by the window. A full moon illuminated the rear garden. The green-tinted fluorescent lamps highlighted the yew tree. It was, as Tessa described, a beautiful evening. He sat watching small bats and moths flit across the garden as if ensnared in the beam of the lamps. Donald heard the chimes of the grandfather clock in the hotel lounge strike ten. With the bedroom window slightly open, he also listened to cicadas fixed to the pine trees' bark chirping as they searched for a mate. If he closed his eyes, he could've imagined he was on a Mediterranean shoreline, such was the balm of the evening. As if she was reacting to a director's cue on a theatre stage, Tessa started walking along the pathway. She looked up and noticed him before carrying on to the end of the garden where it reached the edge of the forest. She turned and looked up again. He stood in the centre of the window, illuminated by the moon's glare. Slowly she beckoned him by crooking her forefinger. Positioning herself under overhanging conifer fronds, she slowly undressed. Raising her skimpy tee shirt over her head and then unbuttoning her skirt and dropping it to the floor, she was naked. The moon illuminated her like a spotlight as she beckoned to him again. Donald looked at Janet and noticed her deep slumber, emphasised by her heavy breathing bordering upon snoring. Carefully, he tiptoed past her and joined Tessa. By the time he caught up with her, she'd ventured further into the woodland carrying her garments and walking barefoot on the grassy pathway.

'I'm so glad you've come with me,' She reached for his hand and they walked further. They stopped and kissed passionately.

'Where are we going?' he asked nervously, totally entranced by her naked beauty.

'A little further where only the creatures of the forest will see what we're doing. It's my secret little hideaway, a green copse under the shade of oak and aspen trees.'

Vivid dreams overwhelmed Janet's deep sleep. She sensed she received a knock on the bedroom door and opened it to find Ben summoning her to join him outside. They held hands, walking out to the garden. It didn't matter to her about them both being naked and soon joined the other unclothed group as they encircled the yew tree. Caleb stood by the knurled tree trunk and encouraged their singing and chanting. He invited his son Ebenezer to select one woman to mate with and produce another incubus. Janet, along with other nubile women, begged Ben to choose them. Their pleading extended to fondling and kissing him. He stretched out his arms and held his hands out to Janet. 'Janet first,' he called. Amid cries of disappointment from the other women, Janet lay down on the soft grass and gestured for Ben to enter her. As Ben copulated with her, the gathering turned into a mass orgy as other couples copied Ben and Janet. Other unaccompanied women massaged Ben's body as he attended to Janet. They fondled and kissed him, but his concentration was solely to achieve the maximum pleasure for Janet. Her gasps turned to mild screams when he climaxed. She eventually relaxed and enjoyed watching Ben as he turned his attentions to other women who lay on the grass awaiting his pleasure.

Donald gasped his surprise as the grandfather clock in the hotel lounge accusingly chimed three-thirty as they entered the hotel foyer. They reached the first floor landing and released hands. Tessa climbed a further staircase; he silently unlocked his bedroom door. To his relief, Janet was still asleep. After undressing, he entered the bathroom and washed away all traces of his lovemaking and writhing in the forest undergrowth with Tessa. The flushing toilet caused Janet to wake. 'Are you okay, Donald?' she called.

He joined her in bed. 'I've drunk too much of that bloody Abbot cider, darling,' he whispered, but Janet had already gone back to sleep.

Nineteen

Donald yawned as they walked down another aisle in the county library's reference section. The librarian had directed them to a small area with comfortable chairs and desks where readers could write and study books in comfort. While Janet perused the top racks of ancient and modern texts, Donald rested in one row of chairs aligned against the windows, looking out into the town. Presently she brought a book to him.

'Here, take a peek at this, Donald. It's like the one I was reading in bed last night but goes much further in the explanation of the phenomena.' They read together the text she'd selected.

'An incubus is a demon in male form who, according to mythological and legendary traditions, lies upon sleeping women to engage in erotic activity with them.'

'They're reputed to have abnormally large genitals. Its female counterpart is a succubus. Salacious tales of incubi and succubae have been told for many centuries in traditional societies. Some traditions hold that repeated sexual activity with an incubus may result in the deterioration of health, mental health, or death. According to the Malleus Maleficarium, exorcism is one of the five ways to overcome the attacks of incubi, the others being Sacramental Confession, the Sign of the Cross (or recital of the Angelic Salutation), moving the afflicted to another location, and by ex-communication of the attacking entity. On the other hand, the Franciscan Friar Ludovico Sinistrari said that incubi don't obey exorcists, have no dread of exorcisms, show no reverence of holy things, at the approach of which they aren't in the least overawed.'

'A scientific explanation

Victims of incubi experience waking dreams or sleep paralysis. Motor sensors in the brain are inhibited, producing sleep paralysis, and acting out one's thoughts in the real world. Additional to sleep paralysis is hypnagogic. In a near dream state, it's common to experience auditory and visual hallucinations. The combination of sleep paralysis and hypnagogic hallucination could easily cause someone to believe that a demon was holding them down and carrying out sexual deviations with them. Nocturnal arousal can be explained away by creatures causing guilt-producing behaviour. Add to this the common phenomena of nocturnal arousal and nocturnal emissions result in the belief that an incubus is present. Some victims of incubi have been the victims of real sexual assault. Some authors speculate that rapists may have attributed the rapes of sleeping women to demons to escape punishment.'

'Bloody hell, Janet, where's that leave us? I'm as confused as ever.' He yawned again.

'Not necessarily, Donald. Now we understand that if we ever met Ebenezer Strange again, we could try exorcism to counter him. You appear to be tired, darling; didn't you get much sleep last night?'

'I drank too much of that Abbot cider, it kept me awake for ages. The Franciscan Friar says exorcism doesn't work, though.' He hastened the conversation away from the events of the previous evening.

'I'm taking this book to the librarian to get a photocopy of this. I agree we've accomplished all we can do in Staffordshire for the time being, Donald, don't you think?'

'Yes, I believe we have, darling. Let's check out of The Red Lion and we'll take a leisurely ride south back to the smoke.'

'I hope to see you again soon,' Tessa smiled at Donald as he handed over his debit card.

'We must return at some point.' Janet intervened. 'We need to get back to work for a while.'

'I hope you've enjoyed your stay at our hostelry?' Tessa asked.

'We have, especially the local scenery. The forest and isolated glades around these parts seem remarkably interesting,' Donald replied with a wry smile amidst another yawn. As if his yawn was infectious, Tessa stretched too.

'It looks as if you both need to get a good night's sleep. Come on, Donald,' Janet commented as she slung her overnight bag across her shoulders and walked towards the door.

Twenty

'It's good to see you both back at the Yard again,' Jack beamed at Donald and Janet.

'It's good to be back, gov,' Donald responded.

'How are you, Janet? Fit enough to return to police work, I presume?'

'I'm fine, gov, thank you.' She looked towards Donald, and they nodded to each other. Earlier that morning they'd taken the superintendent into their confidence and ask his advice on how to continue with the Lizzie Cartwright murder. 'Could we have a chat with you, please, gov, when you can spare the time?'

Donald cleared his throat. Jack sensed they wanted to talk urgently with him. 'Get us all a cup of tea, Janet, please, and then both of you come into my office. I'll tell Rosemary to hold my calls for a while.'

Jack and Donald sat on the low, comfortable chairs next to the coffee table and waited for Janet. 'Is it police business you want to chat about or something private?'

'It's a bit of both.'

'It sounds intriguing!'

Janet brought the mugs of tea and placed them on the coffee table. Jack emptied a sachet of his artificial sweetener into his drink and asked. 'How can I help?'

Donald tried to describe their experiences over the past few months. 'If you'd have mentioned anything about devils and such like to me a few months ago, I'd have laughed in your face, but now I'm not so sure.' Jack looked to the floor. 'I've never encountered such things in my life, but from what you've told me, I believe it's best to stick with the facts.' Donald and Janet held their mugs of tea and looked expectantly at him.

'Whatever the dubious circumstances you found yourselves in, you witnessed a girl being murdered. You then discover her body was found and now there's a murder investigation being carried out by the Staffordshire Constabulary. Imagine if we were carrying out such an investigation, and it came to our attention that there are material witnesses who decide to keep the information to themselves. One, we'd be furious and two, it's an offence to withhold information that obstructs the police carrying out their duties.' Donald looked to Janet; they hunched their shoulders.

'What can we do, gov?'

'First, get the hairbrush and samples of soil to the lab. The sooner we see if your suspicions hold any credibility, the better. Whether the DNA analysis results prove or disprove your allegations, you must contact the Staffordshire chief constable and explain everything you've told me. It'll take two days for the results to come back from the pathology lab. When it does, come and have another chat with me. From attending police conferences, I know the chief of police at Stafford. Sir Bartholomew Evans is a respected colleague. Bart, I understand, would give due consideration to the predicament you've found yourselves in. You've done the right thing in coming to talk to me about this. In the meantime, I'll have a private chat with him while you two get back to routine business here. There's been a big development in busting the drug ring leftover from the Church of Secular Saints case, which will require input from both of you. Liaise with Tom Cropper on that. He's been interacting with other officers over the hoard of cash that has been discovered.'

'Hi, Tom, it's good to be back. The gov has asked us to liaise with you regarding the drugs ring in East London.'

'Hello, you two. We can do with all the help we can get right now. We're coordinating with the fraud squad on this.'

'Yea, so we understood from the gov. Before we left, you were getting close to the peddlers and how the drugs and the money get transported about. Any further progress on that?'

'Some progress, but not enough. We're trying to keep it under wraps. We understand there's a long chain of delivery guys and collectors. A few have been found but, of course, if we pounce on one or two, that will alert the entire gang. We'd like to nab the lot, that's why I was waiting for you to return. I'd like us to go undercover together and try to infiltrate the organisation...'

'The gov said I was to be involved too.' Janet interrupted.

'Yes, Janet. I'd like you to be our liaison officer with the fraud squad. You'll be on a day to day working relationship with our old colleague, Detective Constable Lucy Barnes...'

Donald and Janet's eyes met. His expressed apprehension, hers displayed disappointment and trepidation.

'... we've uncovered respectable people who deliver and transport drugs and money across the capital. Can you imagine some are

National Health Service ambulance drivers, others drive taxis? We've even uncovered an undertaker who shifts money in coffins holding the dead. I can't imagine where the malevolent, dishonest actions of people will lead next?'

'Have you looked at midwives on their way to deliver babies?' Donald joked.

'Many a true word is spoken in jest, Donald. Perhaps we should investigate midwives? Anyway, after lunch, we'll have a chat about the next move. Janet, perhaps you could contact Lucy Barnes and get her to update you on the current investigations regarding the mules.'

'... Mules?'

'That's what we call these delivery drivers who peddle the filth.'

After lunch, Janet tentatively dialled the number for Lucy in the fraud office. 'Hello, Lucy, it's Janet here. This morning, the gov asked me to contact you about the current investigations into the East London drugs scene. I've been designated to liaise daily with you.'

'Yes, I understand. My gov, Superintendent Allan Bailey, told me. How are you, anyway? I learned about you being taken ill in the incident room the other week...'

'... oh, I'm fine now, thank you, and glad to be back at work. Can I come over and have a chat with you?'

'Well, I've got to come and talk to Jack Croaker this afternoon. After I've seen him, why don't I come to your desk and we'll have a chat over a cup of tea? It'll be good to catch up with all the others too.'

'Fine, I'll put the kettle on ready. See you later.' Janet replaced the telephone with trepidation already pervading her mind. 'I wonder if she included Donald in that statement?' she wondered.

Donald was deep in conversation with Inspector Tom Cropper when Lucy left Superintendent Jack Croaker's glass-sided office. He didn't see her cross the office en route to Janet's desk. 'Hello, Janet, how are you? You look well,' Lucy commented politely, but was surprised to see how tired Janet appeared to be.

'Hello, Lucy,' Janet responded and rose from her desk and greeted her former colleague with a peck on the cheek. 'You always look amazing.' Janet's reply was also polite but understated. She thought Lucy looked more attractive than ever. Lucy nervously took a seat beside Janet's desk and commented about the drugs issue. Still, Janet's intervention caused her to hesitate.

'Lucy, before we begin official business, I feel we need to clear the air about Donald...'

'... oh, bloody hell! How did she find out so soon about the other week at their flat?' Lucy's guilty conscience at once came to the wrong assumption.

'... since Donald and I married, I've had the most awful sense of what's right and wrong gnawing away at me over you. We used to be excellent mates here in this office...'

'... hey, kiddo, what's happened is over. It's in the past. I don't bear any grudges, disappointment maybe, but...'

'... I'll tell you what. We were going to share a cup of tea here in the office, but why don't we go somewhere a little more private and we can have a catch up without being disturbed?'

Lucy smiled, 'Good idea, I know just the place; it's only a short walk. Come on.'

They got up and walked across the office. Janet shouted to Jack. 'Hi, gov, I'm going with Lucy over to the fraud office.'

Her loud voice alerted Tom and Donald from their conversation. Donald looked towards the women as they left the incident room. 'Bloody hell, I wish I were a fly on the wall,' he brooded.

'Where are we going, Lucy?'

'I know a lovely, charming bistro around the corner in Horse Guards Avenue called La Vista.'

Twenty-one

The waitress smiled at Lucy as they entered the bistro. 'Hello, Conchita,'

'Your usual, madam?'

'What do you want to drink, Janet?'

'Oh, the same as you, please?'

'A bottle of Chianti and two glasses, please, Conchita.'

Lucy and Janet moved towards the rear of the cosy, dimly lit premises, hoping for a quiet corner. Lucy's expectancy was dashed when she saw Robbie. He was sitting opposite an attractive, smartly dressed woman with auburn hair. As they leaned towards each other, holding glasses of wine, the couple's body language suggested that their rendezvous wasn't solely about business. Janet and Lucy took their seats. Lucy made sure she could make eye contact with Robbie. He looked across. Lucy responded. 'Hello, Robbie. I didn't expect to see you here during the afternoon; you usually have to leave to return to your office at two o'clock.'

'... er... Hello, Lucy. This is my colleague, Annabel,' he responded, hesitatingly. Lucy and Annabel nodded and glared at each other as the waitress came with the bottle of Chianti. Janet looked on, sensing a possible embarrassing confrontation was about to happen.

'Shall we move to another table, Lucy,' she whispered. Lucy spoke louder.

'No, there's no problem. Robbie's only an acquaintance. He keeps trying to give me financial advice. He wants to come to my flat, but I've kept him at arm's length so far.' Lucy made sure her voice was loud enough for Robbie and Annabel to hear. She turned to Janet and asked, 'Dare I ask about the honeymoon? You motored on a tour of England, didn't you?'

Before Janet could answer, they overheard Annabel's Scottish lilt pierce the normally sedate ambience of La Vista. 'Who the fuck is that? Are you two-timing me, Robbie Bainbridge?'

'Oh, oh,' Janet thought, 'I'm playing gooseberry here.' Lucy smiled as she filled the two glasses with Chianti. They listened to Robbie vainly trying to explain.

'Cheers, Janet,' Lucy offered. 'Here's to men and the complications they bring into our lives.' Janet looked from the red-faced Annabel towards Lucy and reciprocated the toast.

'I'll certainly drink to that.'

'So, you want to go to this nice lady's flat, do you? Is that where you go every Friday evening? And don't tell me it's only to advise on investments...'

'Oh, oh,' Janet whispered. 'I get the impression that Annabel isn't a colleague, do you, kiddo...?'

'... and don't bother calling me again.' Along with other customers of La Vista, they were aware of Annabel's icy tongue as she stormed out of the bistro, leaving an embarrassed Robbie looking deflated. Lucy spoke across the aisle between the tables.

'Oh, Robbie, this is my colleague, Janet. Would you like to join us?'

'What! Lucy, I believed we were going to have a chat?' Janet sighed as Robbie joined her side of the table.

'Hello, Janet, I'm pleased to meet you. My name's Robbie.' He offered his hand, and their fingers touched briefly.

'... I'm sorry about that, Lucy, I was...'

'You don't have to explain anything to me, Robbie, we're only friends...'

'... yes, I know, but I don't want you to get the wrong impression of me.'

'... and what impression would you like me to have of you?'

'... well, that I'm a sincere bloke that doesn't pick up girls in bistros...'

Lucy teased him and extended the charade with an ulterior motive in mind that extended beyond the three of them sitting at the table. She gambled Janet would relate the embarrassing episode to Donald.

'Don't you suppose I know that? I'm sorry if I interrupted your rendezvous with... Annabel, was it? Was that your girlfriend's name?'

'Annabel is not my girlfriend, she's a colleague...'

'I believe you, Robbie. I tell you what, why don't we postpone our chat today and I'll see you here at our usual time, one o'clock tomorrow? I need to discuss work matters with Janet now, so let's leave things until tomorrow.' Lucy's tone expertly dismissed Robbie. All he could do was give his goodbyes, and he left.

'So, you're going to keep seeing him? What about Annabel?'

'It's nothing serious with Robbie. I enjoy his company over a glass of wine, but that's about all. It amuses me how he wants to explore my knickers and the crass way he goes about trying to achieve that. I can see through him a mile away. It gives my feminine instincts a boost of adrenaline that a nice handsome bloke still fancies me, especially...'

'... especially after all that happened with you and Donald?'

'I wouldn't say that...'

'... but that's what you meant, wasn't it?'

'I suppose so, but I wasn't being sarcastic, Janet. What's happened is history as I told you in the office. He's your husband now...'

'... I'm glad we can be grown-up about this. I still want us to be friends and work colleagues.'

'So do I,' Lucy echoed, and they leaned forward and pecked each other's cheeks.

'We used to be wonderful mates, didn't we? Remember all the high jinks we got involved in?'

'... and we were always honest and open with each other. So, what I'm going to say now I hope won't upset you...?'

'... Go on, out with it.'

'In the office, I said you looked well but, if I'm candid, you appear tired and anxious. Are you alright? Is anything troubling you?'

Janet pulled her handkerchief out of her coat pocket and held it to her mouth.

'Oh, I'm sorry, Janet, I didn't mean to pry.'

'No, that's alright. I suppose I'm glad I've got a friend whom I can chat to. So much has happened over the past months that I find it hard to know where to begin?'

'Are things with Donald not as you hoped?' Lucy was expecting a different response from the one she received.

'With our marriage?' Lucy nodded. 'Donald and I are fine. I'm hoping you can keep this to yourself, but I've only recently found out I'm pregnant.'

Lucy was stunned. She opened her mouth to answer, but her voice cracked. Lucy took a large slurp of wine.

'I can see you're stunned. That was my reaction, I couldn't consider it was happening to me.'

'Wow! Pregnant! How do you feel? Oh, I see now, is that why you were poorly in the incident room?'

'Probably, but I feel fine now...'

'... how far gone are you?'

'Only about a month.'

'That's early in a pregnancy, to be sure, isn't it?'

'Yes, that's what the doctor said.'

'Well, that answers my first point about you looking tired... I offer you and Donald my congratulations.' She swallowed as the words seemed to have stuck in her throat.

'Thank you, Lucy. You said I was looking anxious too and there's a particular reason for that.'

'... oh?'

'Would you be a dear friend and listen to my story...' Janet started her monologue where she and Donald came upon *The Crucified Abbot.* Lucy did her best to feign surprise and astonishment at various points and pauses as Janet took sips of her wine between the salient points.

Lucy picked up on Janet's ethereal lovemaking with Ben. 'How do you feel about that, Janet?'

'Weird. At one point, I imagined Ben may be responsible for my pregnancy.'

'What was this Ben like?'

'Oh, a complete Adonis. Donald calls him an Arnold Schwarzenegger lookalike. Incredibly handsome and virile and an absolute stud. One glance from him and I defy any woman not to want him. He's hypnotic, and it's mesmerising how he instils desire and yearning for his amazing body...'

'... Bloody hell, Janet, can you get me an introduction...?'

'... there's also the downside, Lucy. He scares the shit out of me. Don't forget, Donald and I witnessed him committing murder.'

'What are you going to do about this?' Lucy refilled their glasses with Chianti.

'The DNA test results should be back tomorrow so, after that, the gov has smoothed the way smoother for us to go to the Staffordshire chief of police. Hopefully, we can get some closure?'

'Surely this can only be closed when Ben is brought to justice for Lizzie Cartwright's murder?'

'How can a man who burnt to death in 1866 be indicted for murder in the twenty-first century?'

'Shall we turn to police business?' Lucy prompted, realising she desperately needed to talk to Donald, and further conversation with Janet made her feel more frustrated.

'What stage are you at with the drugs investigations?'

'We've identified several mules. That's what we call the people who're delivering drugs and money across London. Men *and* women. We're resisting arresting them until we can close in on the organisers and nab the entire operation. One such example is Brian Daley. He's an ambulance driver for the East London Health Authority. Brian's also a mule, using a public vehicle for his own private gain. He lives in a dingy rented apartment in Dagenham with his wife and four young children. The family is always in debt, and they barely survive on his meagre wages from his employers. So, can you blame him when an opportunity arose to earn extra cash, Brian didn't hesitate to take part. He received his mule status when local drug dealers approached him and offered him money for delivering parcels and envelopes. We've been observing Brian for weeks, the routes his ambulance takes between hospitals and health centres, where he stops for lunch, where he lives, which pub he frequents and who are his friends. These characteristics of his life were all considerations before the mob bosses contacted him. The dealers considered him an ideal, trusted individual who can maintain confidentiality about what he does. The dealers are ingenious. What's more innocuous than an ambulance stopping and starting at various locations around the area and the driver carrying parcels and envelopes?'

'So, you're letting him carry on as normal, hoping that he'll lead you to the bosses?'

'Exactly, and Brian is only one small link in a complicated system. Another mule is Jack Weston, a taxi driver who works in the borough of Lewisham. Another target for the drug dealers is self-employed delivery riders who distribute pizzas and take away meals. Tom Cropper is currently keeping tabs on an undertaker who carries drugs and illicit money inside coffins that hold dead people en route to a funeral. Would you believe that Tom has witnessed these undertakers passing sealed brown envelopes to vicars and priests at various churches in that stakeout? The one common factor that keeps this illicit system running efficiently is the threat of violence. Occasionally, for a myriad of reasons, a mule decides they've earned enough cash and want out of the dubious business. The dealers don't hesitate to remind them they know all about them, who their families are and where they work or where their kids go to school. A mule who inadvertently opens his or her mouth about what they do soon realises the consequences. Cars are vandalised, windows smashed in their homes and even their limbs are broken by thugs as they walk back from the local pub in an evening. The dealers' tentacles also extend to compromising local police officers who walk the beat. When their suspicions are aroused and ask questions, the dealers instinctively know who is susceptible to accepting a bribe. Afterwards, those dealers and mules operate with impunity because they've identified an individual police officer is on the take and will look the other way.'

'Are you currently keeping tabs on these mules?'

'Yes, we are, but could do with more help. That's why you've been assigned to this, too. I suggest tomorrow morning we take a ride to Dagenham and take another peek at this Brian Daley. The work is very demanding in terms of available police time, so your help will be very welcome...'

'... he's the ambulance driver.'

'Yes, we can follow him at a distance and note what he's doing, what he carries and delivers and the rest of the investigation, who he contacts.'

Twenty-two

'What did you two get to talk about in the fraud office? You were absent for a long time?' Donald asked Janet as they sat together eating their evening meal.

'Two? Who do you mean, Donald?'

'You and Lucy, of course. Who else did you suppose I meant? I saw you both leave the incident room...'

'... We went to a bistro in Horse Guards Avenue. We felt we could have a good chat there. There are too many prying eyes and eager ears in these offices.'

'Oh, what's the bistro called?' Donald's conscience clouded his thoughts. He knew the name of the premises, having already been there with Lucy. His evasive question gave him time to contemplate the implications of Janet and Lucy having an intimate conversation.

'La Vista. It's genuinely nice and cosy. I sensed Lucy was hoping for it to be quieter than it was because she met her boyfriend in there...'

'... boyfriend. She has a boyfriend?'

'Yes, don't sound so surprised. Lucy is a free, single woman.'

'No, I wasn't surprised, and I'm glad.' Donald's evasiveness extended into lies.

'I'm pleased she has new acquaintances. At least that's what he looked like to me, but Lucy perhaps feels otherwise.'

'Oh, why's that?'

Janet smiled. 'Lucy is stunning, and she's enjoying having male admirers. She told me she knows Robbie...'

'... Robbie?'

'Yes, that's his name, Robbie. Robbie Bainbridge, but it was only a girl he was with that called him by his surname. I'm not sure that before then Lucy knew his full name.' Janet broke from eating and burst into laughter.

'What's so funny?'

'Oh, only Lucy. She's a canny lady. This Robbie won't know what's hit him. She knows Robbie only wants to get into her knickers, as she indelicately put it. Still, she's only playing him along.'

'I see. Poor man. You say Robbie was with another woman?'

'Yes, Annabel. She soon left after she realised Robbie was also friends with Lucy.'

'It all sounds like a complicated mess to me. What else did you talk about? Us by any chance?'

'I told her I was pregnant if that's what you mean?' Donald had swallowed a lump of chicken and he coughed hard to dislodge it.

'Are you okay?'

'Yes, I'm fine,' Donald replied, but was silently anxious about Lucy knowing Janet is pregnant.

'You told her that. Darling, I thought we were going to keep it private until you're certain...'

'... yes, we were, but, well, we're good mates, or used to be. Anyway, I took her into my confidence. I told her all about our experiences at *The Crucified Abbot*.'

'How did Lucy react when you told her you're pregnant?'

'Very well. Lucy gave us her congratulations.' Donald gulped and wondered what her actual feelings were and what she'd say to him when they met.

'Enough of Lucy and her romantic adventures. We also discussed this drugs case we're both now involved with. In the morning, she and I are going to Dagenham to check out an ambulance driver who delivers drugs and money. What will you be doing?'

Donald was silent. He hadn't been listening to her last statements. He was still pondering about how Lucy would react to him being a prospective father.

'... Donald?'

'... I'm sorry, darling. What did you say?'

'What are you up to tomorrow?'

'Oh, Tom Cropper and I are checking on drugs barons in North London, who he believes have muscled in on the territory once controlled by Joseph Tomelty at the Church. Why do you ask?'

'You haven't been listening to me, have you? I told you what Lucy and I will do in the morning. She's picking me up here, so I don't need to go directly to the office. We're starting early as this ambulance driver starts work at 08:00. We want to trail him the minute he leaves his home.'

'Lucy's coming *here* tomorrow?'

'Yes. Oh, Donald, this is as painful as having a tooth extracted. You aren't listening to me.'

'I'm sorry, darling. I'm only tired. I'll have an early night; are you coming to bed?'

'I'll tidy up the flat first. Have you forgotten that we should get the results from the pathology lab tomorrow on Lizzie Cartwright's DNA?'

'Oh yes, thanks for reminding me. I'd forgotten.'

Twenty-three

Donald and Janet listened to a car horn honking repeatedly as they sat finishing their breakfast. 'That'll be Lucy,' Janet uttered and rose from the table to grab her bag and coat. 'Bye, darling, I hope you have a good day. See you this evening, or perhaps sooner if Lucy and I get back from Dagenham early.'

Donald moved nervously to the window, deliberately held the curtains aside, and exchanged glances with Lucy as she glowered up through the misted windscreen of her car. Donald's wave wasn't returned. Lucy stopped glaring upwards when Janet opened the car door and the car sped down the street, leaving clouds of bluish smoke hanging in the still, fresh air from its diesel engine. Straight away, Donald reached for his mobile phone and sent Lucy a text.

'Can we talk? How about meeting in La Vista this afternoon? See you at 4:00 pm.'

He looked at the screen and waited. At once he received a standard message automatically sent if a recipient had their phone switched off. *'Sorry, I can't talk right now, I'll return your message later.'*

'Damn!' Donald cursed and prepared to get ready for work.

'Slow down, kiddo,' Janet said to Lucy. 'Are you practising for the British Grand Prix? You seem all steamed up. Look at the windscreen, can you see properly?'

'Am I speeding? Sorry, Janet, I feel wound up this morning. She reached for a box of tissues to wipe away the mist from the windscreen. I had bloody Robbie ringing me at half-past three this morning. Once I'm awake, I take hours to get back to sleep.'

'He's still trying, is he?'

'More like striving...?'

'... What you said yesterday, to get into your knickers?'

'He'll never get there, not if I have anything to do with it.'

Janet laughed. 'Well, who else will give him access? They're your knickers.'

Lucy laughed too. 'Anyway, I said I'd meet him in La Vista this afternoon, so do you mind if we perhaps cut short our trip to Dagenham?'

'No problem. Once we return to the office, I can check if the DNA results about Lizzie Cartwright are back from the path lab.'

After driving across the London suburbs following the Thames, Lucy's black, unmarked Ford Mondeo arrived on Dagenham's outskirts. Such was the complete urbanisation of Essex, north of the river. It was unclear where Barking ended, and Dagenham began, and before giving way to the district of Rainham. Lucy parked across the road from an untidy block of six-storey flats in Piddock Mews. Once neat, white, plastic cladding now despoiled by successive years of air pollution hung in splintered tatters, revealing the cheap unjointed brickwork beneath.

Lucy looked up, 'Brian Daley and family live at number 309 on the third floor. It's alright for some; his bloody curtains are still closed, and his ambulance is parked over there.' Lucy pointed to the bottom of the Mews where cars were parked under spreading plane trees.

'Where does Brian usually go with his ambulance?' Janet asked.

'His normal journey takes him first to Dagenham General Hospital and then out to the district clinics. When we've been following him before, we've only been able to note the address that he visits. What would be useful is for one of us to tail him when he gets to his first stop; notice who he meets, what contacts Brian makes, and if he collects or delivers anything.'

'How about if you drop me off at his first stop after the hospital? You carry on tailing him in his ambulance while I go inside the clinic?'

'Sounds good to me. I can pick you up later. Oh, here's Brian now. Do you see him, black hair, about forty, tall and slim?' He climbed into the ambulance and pulled off the private driveway.

'Yes, I've got him in my sights.'

Lucy started the diesel engine and pulled unnoticed behind Brian's ambulance as it journeyed towards the city. They waited in the hospital car park for Brian to collect an elderly patient in a wheelchair before it pulled back out onto the main road and took the signs for Romford. Trailing behind at a short distance, Lucy started rambling on about Robbie. 'What would you do, Janet? I believe it's going to be crunch time this afternoon. Either I'm going to ask him to come to my flat or I'll give him the heave-ho?'

Janet wasn't listening intently; she was concentrating on the ambulance. She answered mundanely, 'It'll come to you, kiddo, either you want him, or you don't...? Oh, here we go, Brian's pulling off the road.' She read the notice board, *Romford and District Care Homes, Dagenham Road Clinic.*

'Drop me off here on the main road and I'll follow him. See you later, Lucy.'

Janet slung her handbag over her shoulder, crossed the road, and waited outside the busy clinic for Brian to push the wheelchair carrying his patient through the automatic opening doors. She walked immediately behind him, gaining access at the same time before the doors closed behind them. She hung back as Brian approached the reception desk. A bespectacled, grey-haired woman spoke, 'Oh hello, Brian, is that Mr Peter Clark?' Brian smiled and nodded. 'Take him to room 126, come back to the waiting room while the doc examines him.' Janet sat down and watched Brian go down the corridor and then return and sit a few rows from her. She noticed the signs indicating other rooms with numbers extending to 566, which she noted was for bath water therapy treatment. Brian picked up a newspaper from a low table and started humming to himself. After a few minutes, a man in a brown coat approached Brian and, with no words passing between them, he handed him a brown, unmarked envelope. Seamlessly, without stopping humming or reading the newspaper, Brian put the envelope inside his NHS dark blue woollen cardigan and pulled up the zipper. Janet transferred her observations to the man in the brown coat as he walked down another corridor. Janet got up and followed him. After turning two corners, she watched him enter a room and close the door. She reached for her notebook and scribbled the name from the nameplate on the door: *Mr Colin Harmsworth, Maintenance Supervisor.*

Janet thought for a moment and wondered if the man she'd seen passing the envelope was indeed Colin Harmsworth. It could be someone else who used that office. She quickly concocted a pretext to speak with the man and knocked on the door. 'Come in,' she received the man's gruff voice. Janet entered.

'Hello, yes, can I help you?' he asked with a smile, eyeing Janet's shapely figure.

'Hello, I've been told to ask for Mr Colin Harmsworth...' Janet returned his smile.

'... yes, that's me...'

'Oh, I'm a health visitor. I'm currently seeing a patient in room 566, the bathwater therapy room. The attendant there asked me to find you and ask you to come straight away. One of the taps there has jammed and the water's running everywhere.'

Colin immediately rose from his chair and started cursing. 'Damn and blast, those idiots in there have turned the tap off too tightly again. I bet they've stripped the rubber washers like they did last time. Thanks for finding me, darling, I'd better turn off the main stopcock or water will soon seep into the circuit room and then we'll have a bloody power cut again! This is an antiquated building; there's never any thought given to maintenance and us poor sods who have to deal with these crises.'

Janet followed him along the corridor back to the reception area, past where Brian still sat waiting, and walked outside. She dialled Lucy's number on her mobile phone. 'Lucy, can you come and pick me up? I've identified a contact of Brian's in the clinic.' She watched Colin charge down the corridor towards the water therapy department, still moaning and cursing.

'I'll be there in five minutes.' As Lucy pulled into the car park, they watched Brian leave the clinic pushing his patient.

'Let's follow him, Lucy. I watched him take delivery of a brown envelope. It would be interesting to see what he does with it.'

After following the ambulance along Dagenham Road for about four miles, it stopped outside a line of small shops. It pulled onto the service road that fronted the shops. Brian scurried from the ambulance, holding the brown envelope. He entered a bicycle repair shop. Janet quickly followed him and walked into the shop. Brian stood at a counter waiting for a young man to pay for a cycle tyre, which he held over his shoulder. Brian looked back at Janet as she stood behind, casually glancing at the new bicycles for sale. The young man brushed past her. Brian ambled casually to the counter. 'Here's the order for those new bikes, Stan,' he muttered to a small, balding man standing behind the plate glass counter.

'Thanks, Brian, see you again sometime,' the man replied, and Brian walked down the shop and past Janet back to the ambulance. Janet thought quickly again.

'Yes, can I help you?' the man asked.

'I hope so, I'm Mary Noone, from Dagenham Borough Council, trading standards...'

'... not you lot again...' The man puffed out his cheeks. 'I've only lately finished paying the fucking fine you imposed on me the last time...'

Janet held her notebook in front of her and pretended to read from it. She turned a page. 'Let me see, are you the proprietor?'

'You lot bloody well know I am...' Janet watched the man put the brown envelope in the drawer of his till under the banknotes and cheques.

'... oh dear, my pen has smudged, I can't quite read your name here in my notebook...'

'You lot need to get into the real world. Are you blind and stupid? Reg Stainbrook, I'm the owner, trying to make a living and all I get is aggravation from the council. You should be grateful for the outrageous rates I pay to your corrupt department. Anyway, what do you want, can't you see I'm busy?'

'It's only routine; I'm checking all the shops in the row to verify that you've paid the current rates. You know I do that the new rateable year starts soon and we need to check whether we have to add any arrears to your new bill?'

'More bloody money, that's all you people want. You're like fucking blood-sucking vampires, never content until I'm broke. Perhaps you'll be satisfied then?'

'I don't have to stand here and take all your rude innuendos and foul language, you know. You are vulgar, Mr Stainbrook, that's no way to talk to an officer of the council. I'll come back another time then.' Janet made an excuse to leave.

She left the shop with Reg still ranting and raving and returned to Lucy's car.

'Oh, Janet, thank goodness you've come. Brian has gone, but I can still see his ambulance down the bottom of the road...'

'... we don't need to follow him, Lucy. He's made the drop to the owner of the bicycle repair shop. I saw him put the envelope into the cash till.'

'Well done, kiddo. You've accomplished more this morning than the whole of the fraud office has over the past week. That's two accomplices you've identified. We can watch these blokes next time. Do you fancy a bite to eat for lunch? I'm not seeing Robbie until about 3:30?'

'Why not, I'm sure we'll find a nice café along the Dagenham Road somewhere en route back to the city?' As they ate their lunch of fish and chips, they recapped what they'd discovered. Janet wrote in her notebook and repeated it to Lucy, as she wrote.

'Mr Reg Stainbrook, the proprietor of Stainbrook Cycles of 778 Dagenham Road, Romford, received a brown envelope from Mr Brian Daley, the ambulance driver. He'd received the envelope from Mr

Colin Harmsworth, the maintenance supervisor at Romford and District Care Homes, Dagenham Road Clinic.'

'What do you suppose is in the envelopes, Janet?'

'It has to be money; the envelopes are flexible. If they had contained drugs, they would've been bulkier.'

'So, are these two guys selling drugs and receiving money, or only intermediaries in the delivery chain?'

'We need to consider an undercover strategy to observe them more closely. Shall we take one each?'

'Yeah, I'll take the care home and maintenance supervisor. He's already met you.'

'So has the bike shop man.'

'Can't you continue the pretext with him about his rates?'

'Yes, I could. Do you consider it possible that I could get a fake ID card printed? It would give me more credence. I'm surprised he didn't ask for one when I annoyed him.'

'Why don't we ask Rosemary back at the office. She's brilliant at duplicating official documents and badges.'

'Those fish and chips were delicious. I don't know what Donald will have for dinner. I don't feel I could eat another thing today?' Janet grinned as she wiped the grease from her mouth with a paper towel.

'Do you usually eat separately?' Lucy asked.

'Sometimes, and when we do, he usually telephones for a takeaway. He did that while I spent two days in the hospital and the little toe rag drank all the wine. It must be a male thing. I can imagine him stretched out on the settee, watching *Match of the Day* on television. All around him are Chinese takeaway cartons and empty wine bottles. Mind you, if he did, he cleared everything away before I returned, apart from the smell! The whiff of Chinese food seems to linger in the air, doesn't it?'

Lucy gulped and smiled at her. 'I know what you mean. It hangs around in a room. Mind you, at least you'd know if he was unfaithful to you by having another woman in your flat; you'd smell her perfume.' Lucy laughed nervously, trying to provoke Janet into disclosing if she had discovered anything else about her and Donald's night in the flat.

Janet laughed too. 'I've no worries there. Donald talks in his sleep, so I know he'd give himself away if he was seeing someone else. Men, Eh! They're naïve, aren't they?'

Lucy tried to conceal her trepidation, wondering what Donald could disclose in a nocturnal reverie. She made a mental note to ask him to be more streetwise about his transgressions, but then checked her thoughts. She had to confront him about Janet's pregnancy.

Back at the office, Lucy checked her telephone and saw Donald's early morning message. She smirked. 'This will be an interesting afternoon, what with Donald and Robbie being in the bistro at the same time.'

Twenty-four

Lucy checked her black-faced Rolex wristwatch, it was 3:30. She left the office and walked purposefully into La Vista. Conchita, the receptionist, looked up and anticipated Lucy's tipple by holding up a bottle of Chianti. Lucy smiled, nodded, and walked down the bistro to where Robbie was already waiting for her. He smiled when he saw her approaching and rose to greet her. He kissed her outstretched hand and flatteringly offered, 'You are beautiful, Lucy.' They sat facing each other as Conchita placed a glass of wine in front of her. Robbie already had a bottle opened, expecting what she'd drink. 'Oh, you've ordered yourself some wine; I've got this bottle ready for us.'

'Oh, thank you, but perhaps this one glass will be enough for me. I'm officially still on duty, so I shouldn't be drinking at all.'

'Lucy, before anything else, may I offer my apologies for the upsetting scene the other day. My colleague, Annabel, was quite embarrassing...'

'... for you, Robbie, but not for me. We aren't an item, so you're free to see whoever you want, as I am. You still maintain she's a colleague, do you? She seemed to be more intimately involved with you than having a working relationship?'

'Well, to be frank, I'd sold her some investments. I suppose she somehow had the impression that I wanted more than that.'

'Are you sure it's not the other way around? She was a beautiful woman.' Lucy smiled. 'I noticed her stunning figure and how she was looking into your eyes.'

'Does she have a good figure? I can't say I'd really noticed that, but then that's what you beguiling women notice about each other, isn't it?'

'Don't try to soft-soap me. What I know of men is that a woman with a good figure will always attract their attention.'

Robbie smiled too. 'Well, maybe, perhaps, but Annabel is history, it's you that interests me more.'

'To sell me some investments, as you did with Annabel?'

'If you like, but I imagined more...' He reached to the seat beside him and produced a bunch of white freesias and red roses. 'This is to reinforce how sorry I am and hoping...'

'... Oh, thank you, Robbie, they're lovely. It's been a long time since anyone bought me a bunch of flowers. Perhaps you could explain more about investment possibilities that I could benefit from? Are we talking long term here or a quick injection of cash that gives immediate benefit?' Lucy suggestively raised her eyebrow, pouted her lips and smiled.

Robbie smiled at the innuendos and indecent correlation that Lucy had asked.

'That's entirely up to you, darling, either way, whichever option you decide that suits your current needs, I'll do my utmost to provide complete satisfaction.' Lucy issued a chuckle at Robbie's witty and equally evocative reply.

Because of Donald's situation becoming an expectant father, she'd already encouraged the budding relationship with Robbie. Her feelings towards Donald hadn't changed, she loved him dearly, but right now she needed to have something less complicated in her life. If, in the meantime, this something else, meaning Robbie, caused Donald anguish and jealousy, then all to the good. She looked at her watch again and expected him to walk into La Vista at any moment.

'Shall I come to your flat...?' Robbie asked as Lucy saw Donald walking towards them.

'Oh, hello, Donald, you know each other, don't you? Hold on a second I'm writing my address down for Robbie.' While Lucy scribbled her address, Donald stood uneasily at the side of the table, exchanging glares with Robbie. 'Here you are, Robbie, call me before you come to make sure I'm decent and properly dressed. Once I get home from work, I relish casting off my working togs and spending the rest of the evening as nature intended.' Lucy smiled. 'I'm sure I'll find your financial proposals beneficial to my immediate and long term future.'

Lucy's continued innuendos, were mainly for Donald's benefit to enrage the jealousy she knew he was enduring.

Robbie reached forward and kissed her hand. 'Ciao, bellissima una donna.'

'Hmm, che romantico, par li Italiano. Bye, Robbie, see you soon.'

Robbie left the bistro glaring daggers at Donald.

'Are you going to sit down then or perhaps you've developed piles or maybe the cat's got your tongue?' Lucy snapped at Donald.

He sat opposite Lucy, looking at her through the foliage of the flowers. He reached forward and brushed them to one side.

'These are so lovely. It was genuinely nice of Robbie to...'

'... So, he *is* your boyfriend, then?'

'Whatever do you mean?'

'Well, that was how Janet described Robbie to me when she met him in here the other day.' Lucy smirked. She knew Janet would've told him about Robbie. Donald hung his head in silence.

Lucy looked from under her eyelids at him, enjoying seeing his discomfort and jealousy. 'Why didn't you tell me about Janet's pregnancy?' she asked quietly. 'You knew she was pregnant when I came to your flat, didn't you? Yet you concealed that from me during the entire night we spent together. We made love; you expressed your love for me, and yet you've only recently made your wife pregnant.' Donald hung his head further.

She stayed silent before twisting the knife further. 'How do you think that news made me feel, Donald? To learn it from your wife made me feel six inches tall and worthless.' Donald didn't know what to say.

'Hmm, perhaps the cat has got your tongue, after all?' She looked askance at him, wondering how much more agony to put him through. 'Well? What do you have to say for yourself?'

He broke his silence in a quiet, faltering voice. 'I'm so sorry that I didn't tell you, Lucy. Janet may not be pregnant; it's only a few weeks...? I feel so desolate that I've caused you hurt.'

Lucy felt triumphant, but equally sorry for him, seeing him squirm and desperately unhappy. Her regard for him as a decent and resolute man increased. He looked her in the face, sitting up erect, straightening his posture and jutting out his jawline. He spoke firmly and purposefully.

'I realise I've lost you to this chap, Robbie, and, in the circumstances, I've no reason to complain about that...' However, his bravado was short-lived. He hung his head again and retreated into his shell. Lucy was about to reach for his hand, but he rose from the table and turned away. She watched him slink down the restaurant and back towards the reception desk. Conchita's polite 'goodbye sir, thank you for your visit' went unheeded. Lucy expected him to stop and order a drink or some food, but he carried on past the reception desk and left the bistro. Lucy held her hands to her face, her emotions were in turmoil. She hadn't wanted to cause Donald anguish to the extent that he had shown. Her planned ruse to cause him discomfort and jealousy had backfired upon her. She recalled the common proverb her mom, Lucia, used to recite to her. *Don't cut off your nose to spite your face.* Her mom was Italian, and Lucy recounted the exact words imprinted on her brain her mom used in her native tongue. '*Non tagliarti il naso per far dispetto alla tua faccia.*' People sitting at other tables looked around to see who was speaking Italian but turned away when they saw Lucy, sitting by herself with her head in her hands.

Lucy finished her glass of wine and walked down to the counter to settle her bill. She left the flowers and Robbie's unfinished bottle of Chianti on the table. Strolling back to Scotland Yard, she realised, with complete discomfort, she'd achieved a Pyrrhic victory that gave her no satisfaction at all.

Twenty-five

Rosemary Bird placed an envelope on Donald's desk. He was busy working with Inspector Tom Cropper and was unavailable to open his mail. From her desk, Janet watched as Rosemary delivered the letter. She got up, strode over to Donald's desk and noticed the gold-coloured logo of the Metropolitan Police Pathology Laboratory emblazoned in the top right hand corner of the envelope. Janet sat down reached for his paper knife, and slit open the sealed, gummed strip. Nervously, she lolled back in the rocking, swivelling office chair and opened the letter. She felt faint the further her eyes travelled down the two-page exposé on Lizzie Cartwright's DNA.

'Oh my God!' she exclaimed loudly. She didn't finish reading the second page, her body slid effortlessly and smoothly to the carpeted floor. Rosemary was standing at the kitchenette, making a cup of tea. She turned when she heard Janet cry out.

'There, that's better, Janet, drink some water.' Janet vaguely discerned Jack's voice and tried hard to focus on his face. 'You've fainted,' she heard him say. Rosemary took over and held her head while coaxing her to drink more water.

Janet listened to Jack speaking again. 'Thank goodness you've come, Donald; Janet has fainted.' Donald at once reached for the internal telephone. 'James, it's Donald Lawrence here, can you come to the incident room, please? Janet has fainted again.' He replaced the receiver and dashed to her side. Janet, ashen-faced and feeling weak and woozy, tried to smile at him.

'You've fainted, darling. I've phoned James, the medic. He'll soon put you right.' In less than a minute, James came into the room pushing an empty wheelchair. Together with Donald, they helped her into the wheelchair and pushed her down to the clinic.

'Leave her with us for a while, Donald; I'll call you after we've examined her.' Donald kissed her and left. As he walked back into the incident room, Jack called him over.

'Donald, I'm worried about Janet. She still doesn't seem to be in the best of health. Perhaps an extended period of sick leave might be the best outcome for her?'

'Thank you for offering that, gov, but can we wait and see how she responds? Until today, she's been fine. It's puzzling why she should suddenly faint again.'

'She was sitting in your chair when Rosemary found her...'

'... My chair? I wonder why Janet wasn't sitting at her own desk?' Donald walked towards his desk and passed Rosemary.

'How's Janet?' She asked.

'Okay, thanks, I can't understand why she fainted?'

'She seemed fine earlier. I watched her open your mail...'

'... She opened my mail?' He looked on his desk, 'but there's no mail here...'

'That's funny, I placed a letter on your desk earlier.'

'Well, it's not here now...'

'... Oh, there it is, Donald, on the floor under your desk.' Rosemary pointed. Donald knelt to the floor and retrieved the letter. He saw the logo, sat in his chair, and realised why Janet had the reaction she did. Clasping the sheets of paper, Donald walked back to Jack's office. Swinging the door open, he apologised for barging in.

'Here's the reason Janet fainted, gov.' He handed the letter over and sat down. Jack read aloud.

'Utilizing the Kerogen Mi-Seq Forensics Genomics Solution, the following results are as follows.' He silently read down the rest of the detailed technical specification before coming to the conclusion paragraphs that he read aloud to Donald.

'It's 98.8% conclusively proven that the DNA extracted from the follicles present in the hairbrush match the DNA distilled from blood samples extracted from the soil. Therefore, the matching DNA is concluded to be from the same person.' He looked towards Donald.

'The implications of this are profound, Donald. Before receiving this, I've been thinking about what we should do. These DNA results reinforce my decision. I'm going to ask Sir Bartholomew Evans and his deputy down to Scotland Yard for a meeting. You and Janet will be needed to attend. In the meantime, I hope Janet recovers as quickly as possible?'

Donald returned to his desk and considered the consequences of the path lab results. He looked out of his window, but his thoughts freewheeled with the implications of the pathology laboratory results. 'It proves that Lizzie was murdered at the yew tree, and Janet and I witnessed her death and know who the culprits are. Understanding how police procedures and the justice system worked would be impossible for the authorities to accept that the perpetrators lived in the past. They'll conclude they're real and living today. Where were they? Who are they? He thought of Janet and fully understood why she reacted as she did and accepted that they needed an in-depth chat with each other.' He rose from his desk and wandered down to see James in the clinic.

'Hello, Donald, I'm glad you've come. I was going to ring you.'

'How is she, James?'

'Well, as before, she needs a stronger sedative than I can give her. She's quite agitated. So, I've already asked Doctor Giles Pritchard at Saint Thomas's Hospital if he'll keep her under observation again. As we speak, he's arranging for an ambulance to collect her. I've told Janet what's happening. This is only a precaution, you understand. This is the second time this has happened. I'm also concerned about your unborn child.'

'Thank you, James, can I...' He beckoned towards the room where Janet was resting.

'Go through, she's sitting by the window in the main clinic.' Janet smiled when she saw Donald approaching.

'You've done it again then. I can't leave you for a second,' he joked. 'James has told me you're going to Saint Thomas's again for more tests.'

'Looks like it. I've told James I'm fine, but you know what these medics are like. It's as if they have to be carrying out some action to justify their job.'

'I'm sure that's not how James operates. He's concerned for you, as we all are.'

'Okay, I was only trying to be facetious. It's so inconvenient. Lucy and I have uncovered some more leads on the drugs situation. I was looking forward to getting stuck in...'

'... well, you can't go for a little while.' She smiled at him, comforted by the concern he was showing for her.

'I assume you read the path lab report?'

'Yes, I did...'

'... What are we going to do, Donald?' He told her about his conversation with Jack.

'Well, at least the official part of the investigation can be sorted out, but what disturbs me more is the personal implications for us.'

'I know what you're feeling and why you fainted. It's because of Ebenezer Strange, isn't it?'

She looked him directly in the face and gasped. 'Donald, the path lab results have proven that Lizzie's murder happened as we witnessed it. What does that tell us about everything else that we dreamt about? Did that happen too?'

'I know, the same thoughts have troubled me.'

Janet lowered her voice and looked furtively around the room before speaking. 'Donald, I haven't told you before, but I've had other dreams where Ben has been making love to me...'

'... What?'

'... I'm sorry, darling. It was nothing I wanted, and anyway I had no control over my dreams. As you'd had the same peculiar dreams too.'

'... What else happened in these dreams with Ben?' Janet's eyes moved away from his gaze.

'Face me, Janet. Please tell me.' With a crinkled brow and heavy eyes, she replied.

'... oh, Donald. He climaxed inside me several times.' He felt the blood drain from his head. He sat down in the seat next to her wheelchair as she silently sobbed into her handkerchief.

'... so, what you're saying is that Ben could be responsible for your pregnancy, not me?'

'That's my greatest fear. Now Lizzie's murder has been proven to be real, common sense logic suggests everything else could be real too. That includes Ben having sex with me.'

'... I don't know where this will lead, darling. I can't think straight. If you can recall him climaxing inside you, does that mean you derived pleasure from his lovemaking?' He watched her closely for a response. She hesitated and stammered, but Donald saved her embarrassment by trying to manufacture a plausible answer to satisfy his anguish.

'... no, don't answer that. I think I know already. What do we do now?'

Janet recognised her recent marriage to Donald was at a critical tipping point, and he needed some assurance from her. 'Well, I've already imagined the main implication affecting us, darling. If Ben is responsible for my pregnancy, I want an immediate termination.' Donald looked shocked. They turned towards the door as a paramedic officer came into the room. 'Are you Constable Janet Lawrence?' Janet nodded. 'I'm from Saint Thomas's Hospital.'

Donald kissed her. 'I'll see you later in hospital, darling.' The medic wheeled Janet away.

Twenty-six

Lucy reached her flat suffering from a headache, having not had a good day. She still felt an enormous conscience about how she'd treated Donald. One minute remonstrating with herself for her stupidity; Donald was married to Janet and what she did with her life was not his business. Then the love she felt for him clouded every other consideration. The mental conflict had been with her all day. She poured herself a glass of Chianti and turned the taps to run her bath. From the effects of alcohol and immersing herself in hot water, she relaxed. After relishing the soothing moisture for a while, she listened to the doorbell ringing. She opened her eyes and immediately wondered if it might be Donald. She discounted the possibility after recalling from the office grapevine that Janet had been admitted to hospital again. 'It won't be him, especially after our encounter in La Vista, and anyway, he'll be visiting Janet. Whoever else it can be, they can wait.' She ignored it. She heard the bell a few more times but immersed herself fully under the water to obliterate the noise. She surfaced and exhaled a sigh of relief at the silence and concluded that whoever it was had gone away.

Clad only in her loose-fitting dressing gown, she prepared a sandwich and sat in the lounge watching the day's news on television. Her annoyance resurfaced when the doorbell sounded again. 'Oh, bloody hell, whoever it is isn't going away, I must answer.' She moved to the door and pulled the safety chain across the threshold before opening the door slightly.

'Hi, Lucy, it's me, Robbie,' he whispered in answer to her enquiring expression, partly visible through the three-inch-wide opening the security chain allowed.

'Robbie! I told you to text me first before coming to my flat.'

'I know. I'm sorry, I was passing your street, and I felt I'd surprise you.'

'Well, I've had my bath and I'm ready to go to bed. I've had a busy day today. It's not convenient right now.'

'Oh, okay. It was merely a long shot. I thought I'd call for a cuppa and then be on my way, but if it's inconvenient, I'll call another time. Perhaps I'll see you in La Vista, but I'll be out of town for the next few weeks. Never mind, I hoped to see you before I disappeared for a while.' His voice trailed off, and she noticed him edging backwards away from her door.

Lucy sensed his disappointment and thought of the lovely flowers he'd left for her. She recalled how romantic he was and had even spoken to her in Italian. 'Oh, alright then if it's only for a cuppa, come in.' Lucy raised her voice and released the safety chain considering no scenario other than sharing a cuppa with him.

Robbie entered. She closed the door behind him, leaving him standing on her doormat. 'Hi, I'll make us a cuppa then,' she called back to him as she walked to the kitchen. He followed her and noticed the settee. Without being asked, he sat down.

'You've got a lovely flat,' he replied, but she couldn't understand him for the sound of the kettle boiling. She returned with two cups of steaming coffee and noticed he'd made himself at home. He'd left his shoes by the door and he'd removed his coat and sweater. The top three buttons of his shirt were open. She felt slightly uneasy that he looked comfortable and ready to spend much longer than merely having a quick cup of coffee with her. He'd already gazed upon Lucy's alluring beauty, covered only by her dressing gown.

'There, I hope you like coffee, it's the instant variety, that's all I have. I've had a gruelling day today…'

'… well, I'm hoping my presence will help you relax and drive your anxiety away.'

'Anxiety…?'

'… Well, because of my unannounced call on you, of course. I realise I'm out of order dropping in on you.' He looked at what she was wearing and laughed.

'… Pardon me?' Lucy tried to return the laugh. 'What's so funny?'

'Do you remember what you said in La Vista?'

'Remind me, as I said I've had a few busy days at work,' she prompted.

'You told me when you get home after a hard day in the office, you strip off the way nature intended or something like that.' Lucy pulled the collar of her dressing gown tighter around her neck. 'So, you can see I'm a little disappointed to see you clothed.' He laughed again, but Lucy didn't. Her unease grew, realising that he expected her to be naked.

'You expected me to be wearing nothing? And even if I was, do you seriously imagine I'd have opened my door to you?'

He rested his hand upon her knee. 'I was only joking.' She took a slurp of coffee and eyed him suspiciously, questioning her stupidity in letting him into her flat. Robbie sensed her discomfort as she pulled her leg away from him.

'Oh, I'm sorry. Please don't get the wrong impression of me. I'm slightly nervous and only making conversation. I'll have this cuppa and be on my way. Perhaps we can have a date another time?' His words caused her to relax a little.

'Please don't misinterpret my actions either. I rarely open my door to any Tom, Dick or Harry, especially in an evening,' Lucy laughed.

'Especially Dick, eh?' His laughter and words caused her short-lived jocularity to evaporate instantly. She realised any careless talk from her, however slight and inconsequential would be immediately seized upon by Robbie as a pretext to develop it into a sexual motive. He looked around the room and saw her photograph standing on the mantelpiece. He rose and picked it up.

'This is a lovely photograph. You look wonderful in your uniform, smart and very official.'

'Oh, thank you. My mom took that photo when I graduated from the police academy.'

He replaced the photo and complimented her on the flat again. 'You've lots of room, haven't you? Is this a two-bedroom flat?' He took a few steps and peered into the bedroom.

'No, only the one. Have you finished your drink, Robbie; I'm feeling rather tired?'

'Yes, of course. You are lovely, Lucy. I bet you get lonely here, all by yourself. I could help you with that if we become friends?' He sat down and finished his coffee. He noticed Lucy had drunk hers, and he took both cups into the kitchen. Lucy followed him with a growing sense of unease at how he wandered around her home as if they were close friends.

'Robbie, I'm jaded and…'

'Yes, I can see that. I don't want to cause you extra work on my account, I'll wash the cups. Where's the washing up liquid? Is it here…?' he opened the cupboard under the sink. 'Where's the tea-towel? Oh, yes, over there.' He brushed past her to get the towel hanging by the door. As he did so, he gently tugged the belt holding her dressing gown together. She didn't sense the tension of the belt slacken as the two lapels opened. In an instant, he had a full-length view of her nakedness.

'Oh, my bloody God!' she exclaimed.

'Ah! That's better. That's how I imagined you'd be walking around your flat. Wow! You weren't at the back of the queue when they gave those out, were you?' He motioned towards her generous breasts. 'You have a gorgeous figure, darling.' His instant ogling had absorbed the whole of her nudity. 'Is that a birthmark on the top of your thigh?' he commented.

'Aargh!' Lucy howled in exasperation, grasped her belt, and refastened her dressing gown.

'Robbie, I'm asking you to leave now. Please go.'

He looked at her and smiled. 'That's a shame, just as we were getting to know each other better. I don't mean you any harm, Lucy. You're such a sexy girl; you can see how much I'm besotted with you, can't you?' Lucy didn't follow his eyes as he looked down at his trousers. She started walking towards the door.

'Robbie, if you don't leave now, I'll call a colleague of mine…'

'… not that dozy Donald?'

'He's a police sergeant at Scotland Yard.'

'That's as maybe, but he's still a drip, leaving such a gorgeous woman as you are all alone.'

He'd walked behind her and tugged again on the belt. In one pull, the dressing gown slipped from her shoulders again and fell to the floor. Disregarding her nudity, she dashed towards the front door and tried to open it. Robbie was too quick and powerful and grasped her hand. He pulled her back towards the settee and pushed her down. 'If you know what's good for you, you'll not resist and play along with me, darling.' His leering smile caused Lucy to feel nauseous as yellowish saliva oozed from his mouth and dripped onto her breast. 'As I said, I won't hurt you.'

Lucy's anxiety had multiplied into terror. Criss-crossing her hands over her breasts, she tried to stay calm and reasoned how she could extricate herself from the foolish situation she'd caused for herself. She figured the more she antagonised him, the more aggressive he'd become. Recollecting her police training, she knew she needed to stall him, giving her time to call for help. Her hands felt down the back cushion of the settee and felt the hard outline of her mobile phone, where she'd left it when she'd spoken to her parents earlier. In her anxious state, she tried to recall how to use speed dialling to call Donald. Perhaps if I could press his number, he could listen in to what's happening? She swallowed and tried to disguise her feeling of panic, all the time aware that her complete nudity was emboldening him.

'Oh, yes, I can see what you mean now, Robbie.' She beckoned to his distended trousers and smiled. 'You have got the hots for me, haven't you?' Her false encouragement caused him to pause his advance towards her and smile. Behind her back, her fingers fumbled with her phone's keypad.

'There, that's better. I knew you'd come round to my way of thinking. It's such a shame to let an opportunity like this pass by. Get you, naked and as sexy as can be, and here's me wanting you like crazy.' He slipped off his shirt, revealing his muscular upper body.

'You frightened me at first, but now I can see you only want to please me. That's very considerate of you, Robbie, to call on me when you know I haven't been able to get you out of my mind… You are such a stallion…'

'Oh, darling, that's such a nice thing for you to say. I work out at the gym most days. Can you see my muscles…'? He flexed his biceps and puffed out his chest.

His narcissistic reaction reinforced her strategy on how to deal with him.

'… We'll have such a fantastic night together, darling.' She tried not to express her distaste or recoil as he reached forward and fondled her breasts with greasy, rough hands. She flinched, gritted her teeth, and whispered. Detesting his invasion of her body, she released the phone and reached for his hand. 'Ooh, that's lovely, but your fingers are cold…'

'… We'll soon warm each other up in bed.'

'I need the bathroom first though, Robbie, I've only recently finished having my period, and I'm dirty down there. You get into bed, and I'll be straight with you.'

'Okay, darling if you must, you are adorable to me, but don't take too long though. You won't imagine what I've got waiting for you.'

Lucy felt Robbie's piercing eyes like daggers ogling her figure as she rose and walked to the bathroom. He put two fingers into his mouth, slobbering with saliva and wolf whistled. His eyes were everywhere except for her hand, where she clutched her phone. Lucy watched him walk into the bedroom before closing the bathroom door. Once inside, she closed the door and pressed number two on her phone, the shorthand, speed dialling code for Donald's phone number.

She turned on the showerhead and shouted to Robbie. 'I'm taking a quick shower, Robbie; I want to be at my best for you.'

'Okay,' she listened to him shout. 'I'm in your bed waiting...' He took complete advantage of his intrusion into Lucy's bedroom and peered into her bedside drawers. 'It's as I thought,' he whispered. Fumbling quickly through her personal items of bra and panties, he found a packet of condoms and a flattened tube of lubricant gel, entitled *Cream Erotica. '*... yeah, this bird knows where it's at and how to get it.' He lay on the bed studying the room but soon became impatient. 'Hey, what is this?' he concluded with irritation. 'This bird is giving me the run-around. Robbie Bainbridge decides the agenda here, not some floozy, Marilyn Monroe lookalike.' He stopped talking to himself and shouted. 'Ready or not, I'm coming for you baby.'

'Hello,' Lucy fixed upon Donald's voice. The sound of the falling water drowned out her voice. She turned the flow to its maximum amount to make sure Robbie couldn't hear her speaking.

'Oh, thank God, Donald. Please come to my flat straight away...' Relaxing in his apartment, Donald nearly choked on his nightcap cup of cocoa, recognising the terror in her voice.

'... Lucy! Are you okay? What's going on?'

'... it's Robbie, I believe he's going to rape me!'

'What? The bastard! Stall him for as long as you can; I'll be there in five minutes.' The line went dead. She hid the phone in the airing cupboard under some towels and stood under the water. She lingered in the steaming cascade, wondering how much longer she could delay Robbie. Her thoughts proved groundless, as he appeared standing before her naked sporting a massive erection. Her shrieking gasp exhibited a combination of surprise and fear.

'Ooh, Robbie, you frightened me, I *can* see now what you've got waiting for me. Why don't you come into the shower as well?' Lucy surmised she'd be safer standing in the shower with him than lying in bed about to be raped.

'Oh, yes. That sounds perfect. I couldn't wait around any longer, babe.' He stepped forward and put his arms around her as the water tumbled over them. He bent his head to kiss her. He pressed his body against hers and it quickly became clear to her she wasn't as safe as she imagined. She felt his erection pressing in her groin, his kisses becoming more passionate as the hot water poured over them. He pinned her against the tiled wall, fondled her breasts, and then reached down with his hand. She was powerless and knew he was going to penetrate her. She endured the lesser of two evils to placate him.

'Here let me do that, darling,' she whispered, breaking from his grip, and trying to sound as passionate as he was, but detesting the entire experience. She reached down and grasped him.

'Ahh!' he panted. Lucy expertly brought him to a climax within a few seconds as the hot water continued to pour over his genitals. He threw his head back and leaned against the tiled wall. Robbie shouted and wheezed in ecstasy. They both looked down as she directed the flow of semen into the drain hole and paused until he'd finished. It seemed an eternity before the flowing water flushed away his remaining ejaculation, and she released him.

'Oh, that was amazing,' she whispered and almost choked on her own bile, believing she was going to vomit.

'Oh, baby, that was something else. You sure know how to do that.' He kissed her again, holding her breasts and pressing his stubbly chin against her face. Despite the hot water falling over their faces, she was able to detect his odious breath, resisting the urge to flinch and turn away from him.

'Perhaps we could repeat that another night, baby?' he sighed. She switched off the water, towelled herself, and lurched from the bathroom. Lucy was pleased to put her dressing gown back on and slump onto a comfortable chair. She glowered at Robbie as he sauntered into the lounge naked, soaking wet and flopped onto the settee.

'Well, baby, I didn't have that outcome in mind when I came here, but the night is early…?'

The implication that Robbie wouldn't leave horrified her. She realised that her earlier strategy of placating him wouldn't work. Lucy was shaken and trembling with fear.

'… I want you to leave now, Robbie. If you don't, you are going to be arrested. Before I got into the shower, I phoned Donald. He's on his way here, now, together with backup police officers…'

Robbie's previous arrogant expression turned into a grimace. '… You're only saying that…'

'… am I? Wait around for a while longer and you'll soon find out…'

Robbie focussed upon Lucy's steely eyed, resolute face. '… you bitch. I knew I shouldn't have bothered with the likes of you. Women police officers, you think you are God's gift to men. I've a good mind to…' Lucy's fear increased when Robbie quickly approached her and slapped her twice across her face and kicked her legs.

'Stop it, you're hurting me,' she yelled. She held her face and cowered before Robbie got dressed. 'Fucking bitch,' muttered. 'Next time, I won't mess about. I know what your sort needs.' Demonstrating a further glimpse of his sadistic temper, he lashed out with his foot. He kicked the coffee table sending it tumbling across the lounge as the glass top split in two against the wall with a deafening crack. Magazines, pens, and table mats flew in all directions.

Still mumbling obscenities, he put on his clothes and shoes and walked towards the door. Lucy tried to hide her feeling of terror and wanted him to go but tried to keep composed and to keep him calm.

She opened the door, gritted her teeth, and imagined the future. '*I'll never let you in here again, you pervert'* she decided resolutely.

Robbie glared and threatened her. 'Alright, Lucy, I'm going. This has been a waste of my time. You fucking bitch. Watch your back, because if I catch up with you again, there'll be a different outcome.'

'Bye,' she uttered through clenched teeth, trying until the last moment to keep sociable to get rid of him.

Then he was gone. Lucy replaced the slide bolt, turned the key in the lock, collapsed to the floor, and cried. Her body shook and trembled, but the sound of the doorbell disturbed her extended sobs. 'Oh, not again,' she cried out then she heard Donald's voice.

'Lucy, Lucy, are you, alright? Let me in.'

'Donald!' She opened the door, fell into his arms, and cried with red hot tears stinging her reddened face.

'Where is the bastard?' He gently pushed her aside and strode purposefully into the bedroom and then the kitchen, noticing the untidy room and the smashed table lying against the wall.

'Robbie's gone.' Lucy called to him. Donald moved to her, and they hugged again. He could see she was shaking, so they sat together on the settee.

'Did he hit you? What're those marks across your cheeks? How long has he been gone, perhaps I can catch up with him?'

'Let him go, please. Don't leave me.' She hugged Donald as closely as she could and sobbed into his shoulder. Tears ran down her face as she told him everything that had happened. 'You shouldn't have let him in, Lucy. That was stupid.'

'I know that now, I knew that within two minutes of opening the door to him. Oh, Donald, it was horrible. I knew he was going to rape me, he's a sexual predator. He needs to be investigated. That's the only reason I did what I did, darling. I didn't know what else to do.'

'I would've got here sooner, but there's still that unofficial wild-cat tube strike going on. I jumped on the number twenty-two bus and ran the rest of the way. See, feel.' He reached for her hand and placed it on his neck.

'… Ooh, you're sweating. Perhaps you'd like a shower?'

'Yes please, if I could, in a little while. Shall I make you a cuppa, or something stronger? You look very shaken up.'

'There's a bottle of Jack Daniels whiskey on the sideboard…'

'… I'll pour us both a double helping.'

She rested her head back on the upholstered padding and sighed. She looked across at Donald and realised how much she still loved him. He saw her looking at him as he poured.

'… With ice, lemon, and soda?' She nodded. He rummaged in the fridge and returned with their drinks. They sat sipping the bitter bourbon, he with his arm around her shoulders, she with her hand resting upon his knee. 'In the circumstances, you did well by keeping him at bay.'

'It was horrendous. Thank you for coming, darling…'

'… I wish I could've got here a little sooner. You wouldn't have had to… you know what…'

'… I honestly didn't know any other way of preventing him from raping me, Donald; he was terrifying. I'll never speak to him again. If I see him in La Vista, I'll arrest him for sexual assault and harassment.' They managed a weak smile and tenuous laugh.

'What's that laugh for?' she asked.

'You've had an interesting evening, haven't you?'

'… Are you referring to…?' Lucy couldn't resist teasing him, but kindlier than she did the last time they were together. She raised her eyebrows. 'Yes, his erection made for an interesting sight when it ...! When we were in the shower together, it crossed my mind that perhaps I shouldn't have been so quick to get rid of him?' She saw the wrinkles appear in Donald's brow and quickly qualified her words. '… but he didn't come anywhere close to what you have, darling.' Donald eyed her closely. She was shaking and knew she was nearly breaking down totally and merely putting a brave face on her ordeal for his benefit.

She saw his concern. 'I'm sorry, if I didn't make a joke of it, I think I'll lose my mind. It shows what flirting and idle, innocent chat can lead to when you don't really know someone. I feel so naïve, being taken in by him. In my job, I'm thinking of the number of times I've interviewed women at The Yard. They come in dishevelled and distraught, saying they've been raped and how foolish they've been. I'll be more sympathetic and understanding with them in the future.' She reached in her dressing gown pocket for a tissue and blew her nose. He stretched to her, and they kissed.

Despite still trembling, she felt stronger. 'Why don't you have that shower and I'll telephone for a Chinese takeaway. It's my turn to repay you for the last one we shared.'

'Are you sure you're up to it, darling?'

'I learned about Janet's admission to Saint Thomas's Hospital again. I hope she's okay?' Donald nodded. 'As you're alone again tonight, why don't you stay? It'll be my pleasure to make amends for how badly I treated you in La Vista.'

'There's no need, Lucy. I deserved everything you dished out…' She put her finger across his lips as she keyed the Chinese takeaway's number.

'Two number thirty-two and two fried rice, please,' She gave her address and hung up but then started quivering and felt faint. 'Oh, Donald, I feel woozy.'

Donald saw how distressed she was and guessed she was suffering a delayed reaction because of her ordeal. 'I can see you're trying to be brave about all this but forget the meal and everything else.' Carefully, he picked her up, carried her into the bedroom and tucked her into bed.

'There, rest now. I'll tidy up the flat and sort out the Chinese meal, we'll have it later after you've had a sleep.'

As she looked up at Donald, she whispered. 'Please say nothing about this evening. Not to Janet, or anyone else at The Yard. I don't want anyone to know how absolutely foolish and naïve I've been.' Donald smiled his reassurance, nodded, turned off the light and closed the bedroom door.

Twenty-seven

'Janet, I'm concerned about you. Are you sure you're fit enough to return to work?' Jack asked.

'I'm fine, gov. One day and night in Saint Thomas's were enough for me. I'm keen to get back on this fraud case. I've come straight from the hospital. James offered to collect me after Doctor Pritchard discharged me on his early morning rounds.'

'That's good to know. I've heard about the excellent results on the drugs case you had with Lucy in Dagenham. You've always made an excellent team. You both know instinctively what's important.' Jack hesitated. '… oh, I didn't mean…'

'… that's alright, gov. I know exactly what you mean, we've got the same tastes in men too, if that's what you referred to?'

'… yeah, that's a pity. Anyway, before you get back to some work, has Donald told you about the forthcoming meeting?'

'The one with the Chief of Police from Stafford?' He nodded.

'It's scheduled for tomorrow at 2:00 pm in the Commissioner's office. He's away for the time being, so I felt we should impress our colleagues from the country how we work down here. I've asked the catering section to prepare us a light buffet.'

'Who'll be at the meeting?'

'You, Donald, me, Tom Cropper, and the Staffordshire Chief and his deputy. Although Tom isn't directly involved, he's your immediate superior. Plus, I always value his common sense in police matters. He may point a way forward. I imagine I already know what tack the country boys will take?'

Janet looked through Jack's glass-sided office and saw Lucy enter the incident room and walk over to Donald's desk. 'Oh! Oh, gov, Lucy's here to collect me. We're off to Dagenham again. I rang her from the hospital.'

'Good morning, Donald, how are you? It's a lovely morning, isn't it?' Lucy purred through her beaming smile.

'It sure is, Lucy; you seem well. It's been a while…' Their formal conversation benefited anyone within earshot. They'd spent the night wrapped in each other's arms.

'I love you,' she whispered.

'I love you too,' Donald answered quietly. 'What're you doing here? I thought you'd gone straight to the fraud office?'

'I did, but Janet rang me and asked me to be ready to go to work.'

'What?'

'Didn't you know, she's been discharged from Saint Thomas's?' He then saw Janet walking towards him.

'Janet, what are you doing? Why didn't you tell me you'd been discharged?'

'Well, I bloody tried several times, but your mobile phone's switched off…' He reached in his pocket for his phone.

'Blast, I switched it off. I've had several nuisance calls. I'm sorry, darling.' He looked sheepishly towards Lucy, remembering he'd turned it off before they'd stood in the shower together. Lucy smirked and looked away before turning to Janet.

'You seem well, kiddo; are you ready to face the villains in Dagenham?' Donald pushed past her and embraced his wife, not giving her the time to answer.

'I'm sorry, darling. I'd have collected you if I'd known,' he uttered between kissing her.

'That's what I tried to ring you for, but Doctor Pritchard phoned James and he called for me.'

'I see.'

'I hope you haven't left the flat in a mess like you did the last time I was in the hospital?' Donald hesitated and mumbled.

'… Pardon, darling?'

'… have you left the flat tidy?'

'Oh, that! I've tried to clean up this morning. You won't even know I've been there.'

Lucy looked away again and tried to disguise her smirk but couldn't help being amused by Donald's witty response. She was about to laugh, so she walked to the kitchenette. 'Looks like you two need a moment alone before we start work. Shall I make us all a cuppa?'

'… er… er. Yes, that's a good idea, Lucy. I bet you could do with a nice cuppa after that hospital grub, darling?'

'Yes, okay, let's have a cuppa.' She lowered her voice, 'What were you talking to Lucy about when I came out of Jack's office? I saw her walk straight to your desk.'

'… er… er… did she? Oh, yes, she did. We said we hadn't seen each other for a while, that's all.'

'It looked to me like you were whispering together?'

Donald thought quickly. 'Yes, we did. Lucy asked me about *The Crucified Abbot* business. We don't want it common knowledge and idle talk around the office, do we? Not yet anyway.'

'No, of course not. There's still a lot to sort out. Has the gov told you about the meeting tomorrow?'

'What meeting tomorrow?' Donald raised his voice.

Janet's irksome response was just as loud. 'The meeting with the Chief of Staffordshire Police. Bloody hell, Donald, where've you been while I've been in the hospital?'

'Nowhere, busy, that's all. I knew about a meeting but didn't know it was tomorrow.' At the kitchenette, waiting for the kettle to boil, Lucy feigned sneezing into her handkerchief, preventing her from laughing again.

'Bless you.' Janet offered.

Twenty-eight

'Now we both have pukka Ids, we shouldn't have any problems with these guys we're going to interview. I hope not, anyway. So, you've decided you'd fare better with the maintenance man, after all?' Lucy commented as she drove towards Dagenham.

'That's alright with you, is it? You haven't met either of them yet. Still, I felt as he fell completely for my ruse as a health visitor last time, I stand a better chance of gaining more sympathy and acceptance with him. He's already halfway there, anyway; he thinks he's on a promise with me. Bloody hell, kiddo, the situations we females must put ourselves in. I wouldn't mind if he was good looking, but he's detestable, and his breath smells like Brixton sewage works on a wet Monday morning. You'll find the bicycle repairman very tetchy, so I suggest you play to his gripes about the council rates. I think it's a brilliant idea of yours to say you're from the council ombudsman investigating the low business rates subsidy. You'll get his cooperation straight away.'

Lucy dropped off Janet at the Romford and District Care Homes' Dagenham Road Clinic; she then continued to keep an unannounced rendezvous with Reg Stainbrook, the proprietor of Stainbrook Cycles at 778 Dagenham Road, Romford.

At the clinic, Janet walked directly to the receptionist's desk. She showed her laminated identity badge hanging on a broad yellow ribbon around her neck. The bespectacled, middle-aged woman had difficulty focusing upon the identification. Her eyes narrowed as she peered through her thick convex lenses mounted in crooked, black-rimmed spectacles. She asked Janet what she wanted.

'I'd like to see Mr Colin Harmsworth, the maintenance supervisor, please.'

'Who shall I say wants him?' She reached for her telephone.

'Miss June Landy from the Care Home Administration Department.'

'Mr Harmsworth, there's a Miss June Landy here to see you. Shall I send her down?'

'Okay.' She replaced the receiver. 'Take the third corridor marked…'

'… that's alright, I know where it is, thank you.' Janet strolled down the corridor and knocked on the familiar door. She straightened her collar and undid two buttons on her blouse, revealing a hint of cleavage.

'Come,' she recognised Mr Harmsworth's voice.

'Hello again, Mr Harmsworth. It's June Landy; I don't think we were properly introduced the last time we met?' Colin initially looked puzzled, and then he recalled their previous meeting.

Janet thrust her neck forward and held out her identity badge to him.

'… but you were the…?'

'… oh, I know, that's why I called in on you while I'm here. May I offer my apologies for the total mix-up when I was here last. My head gets so bewildered with technical issues, like taps, circuits, and plumbing. I obviously interpreted the message completely the wrong way. I hope I didn't cause you any inconvenience. You maintenance men are so clever how you know what to do with all the various equipment here. My befuddled woman's brain expects the water to run by itself in my bath; I don't know which tap is which?' Janet laughed and touched her cheek, trying to express embarrassment.

He laughed, 'I wondered when I got to the bathwater therapy room why there wasn't a problem, but no, you didn't cause me any inconvenience. It's genuinely nice of you to come and apologise, but there was no need.' Janet noticed the customary male ogles of her figure that she'd become used to. This time she welcomed Colin's attention and intended to use it to her advantage. 'Please sit down, anyway; you don't have to rush off, do you?'

'Oh, thank you. It's so good to receive such a friendly welcome for a change. The people in the admin office here are so stuffy and unfriendly, you'd be forgiven for believing they suffer from piles; they never smile, do they?'

'I know exactly what you mean, Miss… um oh?'

'Miss Landy, but please call me June.'

'Oh, hello again, June, I'm Colin.'

'It's lovely to take the weight off my feet.' She lifted her leg and bent her knee, making sure he received a generous view of her thighs. 'Colin, do you mind if I slip my shoes off for a moment? These new shoes are killing me. The fashion these days; I tell you, why do they make such ridiculously shaped shoes? See my toes are all scrunched up together.' She held up her leg so he could get a better view of her feet but noticed that his eyes had travelled up her leg and to her thighs.

'Help yourself, June. It's lovely to have some nice female company for a change.' His obsequious smile made her feel nauseous.

'You seem such a friendly man, Colin. Do you know what, I'm dying for a fag, but never mind, I know it's not allowed…?'

Colin looked furtively from side to side before answering her with a whisper. '… June, I know what you mean, I can't go more than half an hour before I need a puff…'

'… well, how do you manage, Colin; this is an office…'

'… tell me about it. If we smoked in here, darling, the bloody sprinklers would soon activate.' He pointed and looked upward at the ceiling. Janet's eyes followed his gaze to the small star-shaped wheel.

'Oh, is that what a sprinkler looks like? I've often wondered about those things. Stupid me, I thought it was a camera?' She laughed. 'You maintenance men are so clever and worldly wise knowing about such complicated things.'

Colin laughed too and looked up again. 'I hope it's not a camera, June, or else I could be in trouble knowing someone is watching what I get up to here?'

'Ooh, my mind boggles Colin. I bet you can get up to many things down here in this remote office?' Colin's reply was a disparaging snigger.

'Ah well, I suppose I must wait until I get home to have a smoke…'

'… Where's that, June?'

'I've got a lovely cosy flat down the Romford Road. It's small, but as I'm by myself, it's adequate, I suppose. Are you married, Colin?' Janet fluttered her eyelids, trying to show she was interested in his situation.

'Yes, does it show? I've been married for fifteen years now and have two teenage kids.'

'Oh, I assumed you were a bachelor? You seem such a friendly man. I don't get to meet many nice handsome men like you in my boring work.'

'I shouldn't be telling you this, June, but I've got a little room behind my office. I disconnected the sprinkler system in there, and there's a fresh air extractor fan. I go in there for a crafty smoke. You're welcome to share a fag in there with me if you like?'

'Ooh, you crafty so and so. I don't know, Colin; you could be a rapist for all I know.' Janet laughed. 'I bet you've taken lots of young women in there, haven't you?'

'Oh yes, loads. Pigs might fly, and the moon is made from green cheese, June. I promise you'll be safe with me.'

'Oh, alright then. I must admit I'm dying for a fag.' Colin reached into his desk drawer and pulled out a packet of king size cigarettes and a lighter.

'Follow me.' He opened a door at the rear of the office and flicked a switch. The light and the extractor fan came on simultaneously. He closed the door and offered Janet a cigarette. She wasn't a smoker and wasn't looking forward to the experience but intended not to take the smoke into her lungs. They stood facing each other. 'Oh, isn't this brand to your liking?' he asked, noticing that she wasn't inhaling?

'It's passable, but I prefer something a little stronger.'

'I see,' he said, looking more closely at her. She cringed as she noticed his eyes looking down into her cleavage but continued the charade and encouraged him further by fluttering her eyelids and smiling.

'Colin, can I take you into my confidence?' She held his bicep with her left hand. 'Ooh, you are such a powerful man.'

'Go on,' he asked eagerly as he put his arm around her and inhaled the generous application of Chanel perfume she'd applied earlier. She noticed some beads of sweat appear on his forehead. Her plan of encouragement and appealing to his male instincts was working.

'I live in my small flat in Dagenham, but I haven't been there long. I used to have a flat in the West End, but I couldn't afford the rent any longer. Anyway, to cut a long story short, I had a regular supplier up west, didn't I…?'

'… and…'

'… well, Dagenham is too far for him to deliver to my new address, so I'm bloody desperate for a decent…'

'… a decent spliff?'

'How did you know?'

'I can tell who's on the take, darling?'

'How?'

'Trust me, it's down to my experience of dealing with people.' Janet held her hand to her mouth and gasped.

'Oh, Colin, whatever do you think of me? I think I may have overstepped the mark here. If anyone knew in my office, my superiors and such like, I'd get dismissed in no time…'

'Your secret is safe with me, June.' He ran his hand across her shoulder as if smoothing her clothing. 'The trouble is, the stuffy folks in authority who run places like this, don't know how the other half live, do they? They haven't a clue what drives ordinary folk like you and me, what's important to them and what their needs are, if you know what I mean.'

'I knew the minute I spoke to you; I knew we're on a similar wavelength.' He edged closer to her, and she felt like retching, but choked it back, as she smelled his foul breath.

'It takes one to know one, darling. I can help you if you like?'

'Oh, Colin, I'd be ever so grateful if you could…?'

'… how grateful can you be, June?' He deliberately looked down at her breasts.

'Oh, I get it, you men are all alike. Well, let me put it like this, my previous supplier up west used to call with the stuff, and he never left my flat with any cash.' Janet winked. 'Oh, I miss Jerry, he was such a dear man.' Emboldened by her reply, Colin reached forward and softly ran his hand around her breasts.

'It sounds as if you're having a tough time in Dagenham. How long have you been in your new flat?'

'It's four months now…'

'Bloody hell, you must be desperate! That's a long time to go without… you know what.'

'The stuff…'

'... Yes, of course, and anything else that Jerry brought with him.'

'… especially the other things that Jerry supplied, and you know what young foreign men are renowned for. Mind you, he was athletic and very gung ho. It never lasted awfully long. Give me an experienced, sympathetic Englishman any day of the week ...'

'... Or night, darling, eh?'

She smiled and gave him a sultry stare. Colin puffed out some smoke and moved even closer to her. Repressing an urge to puke, Janet reached for his stubbly, pock-marked face and kissed him. She almost vomited when he pulled away, leaving the stench of stale sweat and tobacco behind.

'… do you ever have a desire for something stronger?' Colin asked quietly.

'Like this, do you mean?' Janet rolled up the sleeve of her blouse. She showed him her arm, gambling that he couldn't distinguish between hospital saline and antibiotic drip puncture marks and the illegal injecting of street drugs.

He saw the needle marks and small blue scars. 'Wow, darling, it looks as if you've had some recently.'

'Yes, I have, I was lucky. I looked through my window the other night. A couple of hoodies stood under the streetlight having a puff, so I walked over and approached them. I managed to get a quick fix, as you can see.' She pointed to the latest saline drip mark that was still red and inflamed.

'Bloody hell! You must be careful with dirty needles, darling, and what stuff you're ingesting. Casual street fixes are dangerous. In the future, there'll be no need for you to endanger yourself like that again.'

'I had no other choice, did I?'

'Well you do now, darling, search no further than yours truly…'

'Can you supply me…?'

'… Whatever you want I can get you, and I mean *whatever* you want.' He winked.

'Come on, Colin, you're putting me on, you're a maintenance engineer in a care home, how can you get supplies…?' She flinched as his fondling of her breasts became rougher.

'This job is useful for a bit of bread-and-butter cash, but my primary income is from being a dealer…'

'Straight up…?'

'… on the level, anything. For the right rewards, of course?' Janet flinched again as he lowered his hand. He stroked her thigh and slipped his fingers under the hem of her panties.

'Ooh, Colin.' She feigned a gasp and asked. 'I'd never have imagined there were any dealers this far out of the city and especially where I can get anything you can offer me.' She gulped and then panted as if what he was doing excited her.

'You'd be surprised, there are loads of opportunities now that the big boss in Deptford isn't around anymore. You wouldn't know about that, would you? A bloke south of the river used to control everything, a real highflyer. But he got careless, and I heard that one of his ex-partners caught up with him. Anyway, a mate of mine, Jake Turner, lives in Cain Street, Romford; he has a handle on some old territory controlled from Deptford. He runs a fruit and veg stall on Dagenham street market, but that's only a front. Of course, he's been around the block a few times; he's been inside a few times too, but he's in the big league now. He controls a stable operation and doesn't take any prisoners, if you know what I mean?'

'... Oh, yes, Colin,' she flinched again as his hand lingered in her groin.

'… Jake passes the stuff to me, and I pass it on. Same route with the payments. The more middlemen there are, the less the fuzz can trace us.' His hands were rough and uncaring.

'Is it kosher stuff?' Janet clenched her teeth as she let his fingers wander while she placed her arms around his neck. His distinct pleasure in what he was doing seemed to loosen his tongue even more. She detested his evil grins as he looked into her eyes, watching her reaction to what he was doing. 'I should have been an actress,' the idea crossed her mind. 'Here I am smiling, and I'm doing my utmost to avoid vomiting in his face.' She moved her hand down to his groin and felt the bulge through his trousers' thin material to encourage him.

'I can sense we're going to get on fine and develop a genuine friendship.' He leered and wheezed a slight intake of breath.

'Is it genuine, though? I don't want any old second-hand rubbish.' She squeezed her fingers against his growing erection. His tongue loosened some more. His voice raised higher.

'Only the best, darling. Our circle only deals in the best. The goods come straight from Ernesto Cortez, the top drugs baron in Santa Cruz, Columbia, to here in old Blighty, to fruity Jake no less. Every three weeks on the Esmeralda container ship, the shipments come directly to dock 56 in aisle sixty-one in Tilbury Docks.' He gave Janet a kiss but needed to gasp again as Janet stroked him.

'… yes, Colin! Go on, but I can see I'm stopping you talking ...' She laughed, enjoying the apparent dilemma he was in.

'… yes, but please don't stop, June. We need to make ourselves more comfortable, don't we?'

'… yes, we do, but finish what you were saying first. I don't want to distract you anymore. Can you lock this room?'

'… yes, I can' He moved from her to reach for a key, but Janet held him tightly.

'… Finish telling me first…' Colin nodded as more sweat formed on his brow, and he slackened his tie.

'Of course, the customs blind idiots imagine it's only bananas that are being imported. It's amazing how much you can stuff in a banana when the middle is taken out...' A buzzing noise interrupted his narrative.

'... blast, that's my office phone. I'd better see who wants me. I'm sorry, darling: if I don't answer, someone will be down here, and we don't want that, do we?' He withdrew his hand. Janet breathed a sigh of relief, straightened her panties and dress, and walked back into Colin's office. He put the telephone down. 'Bloody hell, talk about sod's law. There's a serious problem over at the geriatric block with the heating, I must go. How about you come and see me tomorrow, June, same time? I'll be ready for you, and I'll make sure you have what you want, if you get my meaning?' He tapped the side of his nose. Janet smiled. They walked out of his office together but took separate paths after he locked the door. He strode to the geriatric block, and Janet to the adjacent ladies toilet, where she heaved and vomited into the closest washbasin. Quietly sobbing, she staggered into a cubicle to sit and compose herself.

After a while, she texted Lucy. She received a standard reply, saying she was busy and would return the message later. Janet walked down the street to a small café and ordered herself a strong black coffee. After relaxing in the café, she reached for her notebook and wrote down everything Colin had told her. Janet smiled, envisaging the riot squad hiding in wait at Tilbury docks for the Esmerelda to arrive from Columbia. Shivers ran down her spine as she recalled how she'd suffered being fingered by the foul-smelling Colin Harmsworth. 'I'll make sure I'm in court the day he gets sent down,' she thought with determination.

Twenty-nine

Lucy parked in the service area outside Stainbrook Cycles. She crossed the pavement and opened the door to the shop as a young hoodie barged past and knocked her, causing her to drop the car keys. 'Hey, who do you think you are?' she shouted after him as he nonchalantly carried on, ignoring her cry. She picked up her keys and entered.

'Bloody hoodlums.' Reg called to her from behind the counter. 'You're lucky he's only barged into you, darling; we had a young woman stabbed by a hoodie walking the street the other night.'

'Are you the proprietor here?' Lucy asked with a smile. She straightened her dress and smoothed her hair.

'Yes, I am. Reg Stainbrook the name. How can I help you? You don't seem to be the cycling sort if I may say so, madam, so I assume this is a business call.'

Lucy showed him her identity badge hanging around her neck. 'Hello, Mr Stainbrook, I'm Linda Boughton, I'm an investigating officer with the city ombudsman's office…'

'… investigating officer? Am I in trouble then?' Reg joked with her.

'No, not at all. I'm hoping I can be of help to you?' Lucy smiled at him.

'I'm always glad to meet anyone that's offering help. It makes a pleasant change from the continuous parade of blood-suckers who keep demanding more money.'

'I'm here about your business rates…'

'… exactly as I was saying to you. The bloody council rates for my little bicycle shop are outrageous. It was only the other day a bloody snotty woman from the council came here, demanding more money.'

'Your shop is only one of many I'm visiting in the area. In the ombudsman's office we make periodic checks now and again to determine that shop owners, like yourself, aren't being over-charged for their rates. We recognise how important it is for small shop keepers, to keep local commerce wheels ticking along. Why, this street would be yet another ordinary roadway devoid of interest without such sporting ideals you promote. Is it possible we could sit down together for a moment and talk about the level of rates you pay?'

'Yes, of course, darling. Wait a moment, I'll put the closed sign on the door, and we can go through to my living room.' Lucy was pleased that the flattery of his business had gained his confidence.

Reg showed Lucy into the living room. She inwardly gagged at the smelly, untidy room. Spare parts of bicycles littered the small room. Every wall and surface seemed to be cluttered with tools and rubber tyres and metal frames. 'Oh, this looks an interesting room,' Lucy lied while continuing her smile.

'Let me clear some stuff away, and we'll take a seat.'

'I don't suppose you have your current rates bills to hand, do you?'

'They're here in this drawer somewhere.' He rummaged through the untidy drawer, discarding small cans of grease and packets of screws, before lifting an oil-stained envelope.

'Here we are. Hold on a sec, while I clean the mess away.' He reached for a tea-towel, wiped the envelope, and passed Lucy the rates bill before sitting opposite her. She read the statement before speaking.

'See, it says here…' She reread the bill. 'As I suspected, I believe you're paying far too much for this year's rates. Phew, £4,653, that's excessive!'

'… that's what I've been telling those idiots down at Dagenham Council office for bloody years, and the new bill is due again soon.'

'Oh, Mr Stainbrook, do you mind, I'm desperate for a cigarette. Can I pop outside…?'

'… There's no need, darling. I could do with one myself. Here, have one of mine.' He handed her a cigarette, placed one in his mouth, and lit them both. 'Oh, and please call me Reg.'

'Oh, thank you…. Reg… that's nice of you. There are very few premises I can go to that allow me to have a fag. My name's Linda.' She took a puff from the cigarette. 'Ah, that's better. Of course, when I get home, I have something stronger… oh, I apologise, I shouldn't have said that. Ignore what I said, Reg, please. I shouldn't let a stranger know about my habits, should I? It's only that I feel at home here and comfortable in your presence.'

'Well, I'm that sort of guy, aren't I? Live and let live is my motto. I like a joint myself in the evening.'

'Now, Reg, these rates of yours…'

'… hold on a sec, Linda. Could I ask where you get your supplies from?'

'Oh! Well, I live in Hammersmith. Can you imagine how expensive it is to get stuff in the city…?'

'… Tell me about it…?'

'Anyway, I believe I can get a reduction in rates for you. I'd say, hmm, let me see, at least £1500 for this year alone. Then there's the previous years to examine… there'll be refunds due for those years too. Can I ask how many people live here in this house?'

'… there's only me and my wife, Esme.'

'… only the two of you? Well, that's why your rates are so much higher than they should be. By default, the council always assumes a minimum of four people living in one household unit. It's up to you to inform the council if you have less than that. Have you informed the council, Reg?'

'… ooh, I don't know, Linda. I must ask Esme. She deals with all of those complicated matters.'

'… well, by my rough calculations, I'd say you could claim back another… ooh!… another £2000 at least.'

'That's fantastic, Linda. You've made my day. If I can help you, I'd be glad to.'

'I don't suppose you'd be able to help me with anything, Reg, we live in different towns, different social circles…'

'… yes, but we have one thing in common, don't we?'

'Do we…?'

'… we do. We both like a joint in the evening, don't we?'

'… Reg, I'd be grateful if you'd keep that to yourself. I feel awful for letting that slip… I'm embarrassed about that.' Lucy smiled and tried to appear ashamed. She reached for her handkerchief and dabbed her nose.

'… There, there, darling, don't upset yourself. Nobody will know from me about your habits.'

'… Reg, this job with the ombudsman doesn't pay very much. I only became a civil servant because it has such an excellent pension scheme, but that's years away yet. I struggle, financially I mean, to afford a decent joint now and again…' She crossed her legs, revealing a large area of her thighs. She noticed Reg was looking.

'… well, you can stop worrying about affording a joint from now on. Think of me as your Uncle Reg.'

'I still don't understand how you can help me.'

'… Because I can supply you from now on.'

'... Can you? But how? I live in Hammersmith. I probably won't be coming out to Dagenham for a while after I've finished visiting these other shops today.'

'I'm merely a minor cog, in a bigger wheel, if you'll pardon the pun.' He looked around the room at the spare wheels and tyres. They both laughed.

'If you let me have your address, I'll add your name to the ever-expanding list of places we deliver to…'

'… but how will I pay you, or even afford to?'

'Linda, you've helped me with this rate reduction, so I'll help you. The woman who'll deliver to you is Amanda Samuels. She works as a cosmetic consultant. Shall we say every other Saturday evening? Hammersmith is on her route. I'll make sure you only pay the rate I get it for.'

'A woman? I wouldn't have imagined…?'

'We have all sorts in our small organisation, Linda. Give me your mobile number, and I'll get her to ring you to sort out delivery arrangements and where she can collect payment. When she can't make it, there'll be a taxi driver, Michael Rennie is his name.'

Lucy wrote her mobile telephone number on the rates bill.

'… This all seems amazing. We've both helped each other today. I'm so glad I found you. Reg, could I ask you something…'

'… fire away, darling.'

'… don't you ever get concerned about the police authorities finding out? What I mean to say is, you obviously must have the stuff delivered here. We must all be careful, mustn't we? We live in such an old-fashioned uneducated country. Holland, now that's the place for someone like you and me to live. We could enjoy a spliff over there to our heart's content, knowing that nobody is going to come knocking on our door.'

'… that's where our organisation is at its best. See those cardboard boxes over there by the corner?' He pointed; Lucy turned her head.

'What, the ones marked *Miletto, Gearing for Bicycles?*'

'Yes, the very ones. Of course, you won't find bits and pieces for bikes in there, only the best cocaine and heroin that's available in London today.'

'What?! That's amazing.'

'We have a warehouse next to Tilbury docks where boxes of stuff get repackaged for delivery to most places in the south-east. I'm only a one stop-off for the delivery company.'

'Anyway, Reg, I'd love to stay longer, but I've got these other shops to visit. I hope we can meet again?'

'It's been lovely to meet you, Linda. Don't forget to keep your eyes out for Amanda Samuels peddling lipstick, or the taxi driver, Michael Rennie, offering you a ride up west.'

Once back in her car, Lucy noticed the missed call from Janet. She called her number.

'Hi, kiddo, sorry I missed your call, I was busy. Is everything okay?'

'Hi, Lucy, yes, I'm fine now. I'll tell you all about it later. Can you pick me up, I'll be waiting in the health centre car park?'

Thirty

'Bart, can I introduce my colleagues, Detective Sergeant Donald Lawrence and Detective Constable Janet Lawrence. You know they're husband and wife and form a vital part of my team here in Scotland Yard. Their experiences in Staffordshire, while on their honeymoon, is why we're all here. I've also asked their gov, Inspector Tom Cropper, to attend. Could I also introduce the department secretary, Rosemary Jennings? As the proceedings are part of an active investigation, she'll record all our conversations verbatim.'

'Thank you for asking us down to London, Jack, and many thanks for your chauffeur meeting us at Euston Station. May I present my deputy, Roger Naismith.' The assembled personnel all acknowledged each other's presence.

'Donald and Janet, I'm going to let you explain what you saw and experienced in Staffordshire. I've already briefly outlined why I wanted Bart and Roger to attend today. Still, I feel it pertinent that our Staffordshire colleagues listen to the evidence from both of you directly.'

'Can I say a few words before you start please, Donald!' Sir Bartholomew exclaimed. 'Perhaps I can put the case into context of where we, at the Staffordshire Constabulary, became involved.'

'I apologise, Bart, I should have asked you to begin instead of Donald.'

'No problem, Jack. The local coppers at Rugeley patrol the village of Upper Slaughter. They received a report from a Mr and Mrs Dandridge Cartwright that their daughter, Elizabeth, had gone missing. The sergeant at the Rugeley nick, who interviewed them, wasn't too concerned at that stage. Their daughter, Lizzie, as they call her, regularly went absent without leave for days at a time, mainly because she'd taken up with a new boyfriend named Ebenezer Strange. He asked Lizzie's parents to be patient and to get in touch again if, after a week, she still hadn't come home. After ten days, the Cartwright's contacted Rugeley force again, and a local search of the area was instigated. Posters were printed and posted throughout Cannock Chase, but still there was no Lizzie. Then the local coppers brought in the local council rangers. Their job is to manage the fifty square miles of forest and heathland known as Cannock Chase. One of their rangers found Lizzie's body concealed in the undergrowth at the local beauty spot called Castle Ring. The five-sided monument is an ancient motte and bailey earthen fort that historians tell us dates to 1000 years BC.'

'Can you explain what you mean by motte and bailey, please, chief?' Tom Cropper asked.

Sir Bartholomew nodded to his deputy for him to explain. 'Sure, inspector. Over two thousand years ago, the local people at that time, the Iceni tribe, were constantly being invaded by the Celts. The locals chose the highest point of Cannock Chase to build a fort. It is one thousand feet above sea level. Their choice of the fort's location offered them protection against the invaders. The Iceni dug a circular ditch that, as I've said, is five-sided and not a perfect circle. Historians estimate it took them about ten years to complete this ditch. The soil from the twenty feet deep ditch was placed outside and inside this ditch to form two concentric soil mounds or walls. The ditch is called the motte and the earthen mounds are the bailey.'

'Excellent, Roger, thank you.' His gov complimented him, eager to shut him up and get onto the reason they were there. 'Anyway, Lizzie's mutilated, naked body was discovered in one ditch, concealed under leaves and branches and partly submerged in brackish water. The local ranger told us he was alerted to where Lizzie's body lay by wild animals, foxes, pine martens, and weasels foraging in the shallow water. Luckily, the animals hadn't yet nibbled away at much of Lizzie's body. Two fingers and the tips of several toes were all that were missing. It was at that stage that Rugeley Police called us in on the case. An extra bit of information is, the local ranger is so severely traumatised by his discovery, he's currently under sedation. We did, of course, initially investigate him as a suspect. Still, no evidence links him to ever touching Lizzie's body.'

'Pardon me, Bart, interrupting for a second, as you can see there are refreshments and a light buffet on the table if anyone wants a bite to eat.'

'Thank you, Jack, I'll finish my preamble, and then we'll take a brief break before we listen to Donald and Janet. My homicide team at county HQ created a closed crime scene and called our Scene Of Crime Officer boys to investigate. One of the first facts to emerge was that Lizzie was not murdered at the place she was found, but elsewhere. Anyone who has visited Castle Ring will testify to the remoteness of the ancient fortress. There are no adjacent roads or tracks that link the earthen ramparts to the outside villages. Therefore, whoever killed her had to have carried her there. Lizzie weighed eleven stone six pounds, so carrying her for such a considerable distance would have required great strength and stamina…'

'… So, we're looking for a well-built person as her likely killer?' Tom interrupted.

'That assumption has to be considered first. The crime pathologists proved Lizzie died from a loss of blood and that she was five months pregnant. The post-mortem examination revealed that her throat had been severed. Both her windpipe and oesophagus were separated. Thankfully, she would have succumbed very quickly to unconsciousness through lack of oxygen. Coincident to that, both her carotid arteries were also severed. The internal carotid artery supplies blood to the brain, so her immediate state of unconsciousness was doubly ensured. The pathologists also discovered stigmata marks. Wrought iron nails had penetrated her feet and hands. Samples of flakes of the iron were revealed under a microscope.'

'Stigmata suggests crucifixion, Bart?'

'Exactly, Jack. This poor girl was crucified in a vertical position when her throat was cut. The place of crucifixion suggests a wooden post, or a tree, or extending the Christianity correlation, a wooden cross. The only item found on Lizzie's body was a silver crucifix hanging on a chain around her neck. Slivers of wood remained in Lizzie's wounds when she was detached from the nails, so her body could be transported to where she was found. My path lab boys have been comprehensive; they've even named the genus of the wood or tree. The wood belongs to the Taxus genus, more commonly known as the yew tree.' Sir Bartholomew hesitated, as if trying to picture Lizzie being crucified.

Seizing advantage of the lull, Roger Naismith intervened. 'Here are photographs of Lizzic Cartwright taken at the scene where her body was found and again in the pathology lab. The last photos are close-ups of her horrific injuries.' He described the photos as he passed them around the table. Sir Bartholomew looked briefly at the pictures before continuing.

'Since then we've carried out extensive search operations for her boyfriend, Ebenezer Strange, but without success. That's about as far as our investigations have gone. Roger and I are eager for any help that Sergeant and Constable Lawrence can give us. Everyone will understand this case is too awful to comprehend and mysterious as to the lack of leads we've yet uncovered.' The Staffordshire Chief of Police paused. 'Phew, I don't know about the rest of you, but I'm ready for that cup of tea now.'

'Let's all take a quick break.' Jack reflected sombrely.

Donald and Janet stood together, drinking their cups of tea. 'I feel very anxious about the next part of this meeting, darling,' Janet whispered.

'I am too. I'm not sure how the Staffordshire Chiefs will react to what we're about to tell them. Thank goodness we've Jack and Tom here to support us.'

Jack stood at the window with Sir Bartholomew gazing out at the Thames as they drank their tea. 'It's a beautiful outlook you have here, Jack.'

'Yes, it's wonderful, but I imagine your HQ in Stafford is equally pleasant?'

Bart laughed. 'What can surpass the momentous River Thames, but we have something similar as historic.'

'Oh, that sounds interesting…'

'The county headquarters is at Baswich, a small hamlet on the outskirts of Stafford. Positioned immediately outside our sprawling offices is a crossroads that still contains an ancient yew tree, coinciding with my earlier reference of Lizzie's yew tree. For centuries, the tree was used as a location for hanging malefactors in the area. Later executions were transferred to Stafford gaol in the town. So, no, Jack, not as pleasant as the view you have here.' They both laughed. Donald and Janet listened and looked on anxiously, hoping that the rest of the meeting's mood could continue in a similar vein, but Donald was exceedingly pessimistic.

'Now, Donald, over to you.' Jack resumed the meeting.

Donald eyed everyone seated around the table. For what he was going to say, he didn't need notes or an *aide-memoire*. The recent events were implanted in his brain. Jack was quietly impressed with his younger colleague's demeanour.

'Ahem!' Donald cleared his throat. He reached for Janet's hand. They smiled. 'My wife, Detective Constable Janet Lawrence, and I enjoyed an idyllic honeymoon until we entered Gallows Lane, near the village of Upper Slaughter, in Staffordshire. After that, it gradually turned into a nightmare. What my wife and I are about to tell you, actually happened. I stress that neither of us has ever taken drugs of any sort in our lives. We only drink alcohol in moderation when we partake of a special meal. So, our experiences were real and uninfluenced by substance abuse or stimulants of any kind that we know of. I know you will question our sanity at some point in my narrative, but that's your prerogative. As serving police officers in the Metropolitan Police we're dedicated to truth, complete honesty, and the pursuit of justice.'

'Well said, Donald,' Tom Cropper interceded. Donald turned towards Tom and resumed. Jack pursed his lips, feeling pride for the staff under his control. Sir Bartholomew noticed Jack's evident satisfaction and smiled at him.

'In Gallows Lane we stopped our car up outside a quaint hotel and public house called *The Crucified Abbot.'* A questioning stare passed between Roger Naismith and Sir Bartholomew.

'I already notice that our colleagues from Staffordshire may find that dubious?'

'Please excuse me for interrupting, Donald, but I know the environs of Upper Slaughter very well. No such place exists...'

'... Please bear with me, Roger, I hope you'll come to understand? We stayed at the hotel for two nights, three days, leaving as soon as we were able. After the first night there, the battery on our car became dead. My guvnor, Superintendent Croaker, arranged for another car and we left the following morning. During our stay, we experienced events and visions that I'd never have believed possible or credible.' Donald looked towards Janet to continue as he sat, and Janet stood.

'Gentlemen, we ate a meal in the hotel's restaurant that evening. Afterwards, both my husband and I experienced vivid dreams. What's unusual about that, you may wonder. We both visualised and took part in the same dreams. As part of the evening meal we had eaten the local mushrooms. We suspected that perhaps they'd caused our collective hallucinations.'

'What happened in your dreams?' Sir Bartholomew asked unsympathetically, lifting one eyebrow in a quizzical expression.

'We'd been dancing with the local villagers around a yew tree in the hotel's rear garden. We were all naked and took part in some ritual presided over by the hotel's proprietors, Caleb and Margareta Strange. The dancers became promiscuous and…'

Roger exhaled a raspberry, guffawed and slapped his hands on the table.

'… Detective Constable Lawrence, come on, we all know you've both recently got married. Are you sure you weren't engaged in some private sexual deviancy? We are all aware of what constitutes a successful honeymoon…?'

'… I resent the implication, Roger. I'd appreciate your silence while my wife continues.' Donald forcibly intervened, looking sternly at him.

'My sergeant's right, Roger, we should consider the full account before passing judgement.' Jack said.

'Very well, I apologise. Please continue, Constable Lawrence.' Roger conceded with a forceful sigh.

'The abnormality of the collective dreams was compounded at breakfast the following morning when all the participants of the previous night's dancing were seated in the dining room. They were strangers to us, but they knew us, and we knew them by first names…'

'But…' Roger intervened again, but his superior held up his hand, indicating for Janet to continue.

'After breakfast we were going to leave the hotel, but discovered the flat battery on the car.' Janet turned to Donald to continue, and they changed places again.

'Marooned at the hotel, until we could get another car, we walked over Cannock Chase until we arrived at Castle Ring, the location described by Sir Bartholomew.'

'I suppose you met members of the Iceni tribe, did you?' Roger added derisively. Donald ignored his sarcasm and continued, albeit staring menacingly at him.

'Later in the afternoon, we relaxed in the hotel grounds and fell asleep on the garden bench. More dreams occurred, but this time far more explicit, involved, and with devastating conclusions.'

'Don't tell me you involved yourselves in orgies dancing around the tree again?' Roger guffawed and blew another raspberry.

'Bart, Sir Bartholomew, I must protest at your colleague's behaviour…'

'I have to agree with you, Jack.' Bart turned to Roger. 'Please keep any further comments like your last remark to yourself. As Donald said earlier, we can pass judgement when he's finished. Please continue, Donald.'

Donald smiled at Roger and directed his comments at him. 'Roger, thank you for that educated observation, but you are actually correct.' Donald's blasé witty riposte deflated Roger and stole his thunder. Jack smiled.

'The devastating conclusion to our dreams that afternoon was witnessing the murder of Lizzie Cartwright.' Sir Bart and Roger's faces dropped in disbelief. Donald paused dramatically, letting the impact of his statement resonate in the Staffordshire policemen's minds.

'We pulled away from the crowd and witnessed pregnant Lizzie Cartwright copulating with her boyfriend, Ebenezer Strange. That was before the mob of people, turning violent, lifted her onto the tree trunk. Caleb and Margareta Strange hammered nails into her feet and hands before crucifying her on the old yew tree. Ebenezer then appeared with a long, sword-like knife and slit her throat. We watched Lizzie die at once as her blood ran down the tree into the surrounding soil. I don't have to explain how terrible that was to witness and then to come to terms with.' Donald held his head down before looking to Janet to continue, but Roger intervened again.

'This gets more and more unbelievable, Sergeant Lawrence. May I point out, you and your wife committed a serious crime from that moment onwards by withholding evidence from us. In your positions, you should have known better…' Donald's patience at last evaporated.

'… and I'm getting sick and tired of your inane comments, Mr Naismith. Not even yourself, ensconced in your rural bloody ivory tower, picking your bloody nose in Stafford, knew that Lizzie existed. So, she wasn't the subject of a murder inquiry then. So, no, we had not committed a crime as you so indelicately put it. And in our esteemed, respected positions as detective officers at the Metropolitan Police, we concluded there had to be some rational explanation. On a later visit to Upper Slaughter, we.gathered that physical evidence. We will submit this shortly as part of our presentation. Superintendent Croaker, I'm respectfully, formally suggesting it's futile carrying on with this charade. We're delivering our account to a hostile audience who aren't prepared to listen. Come on, Janet, we're leaving.' IIe beckoned for Janet to stand.

'Sit down, Sergeant Lawrence. You'll both only leave when I end this meeting, is that clear?' Jack admonished him severely. Donald sat down as Janet reached for his hand and smiled.

'Sir Bartholomew, despite my sergeant's outburst, I have to admit he has a point. If anyone is leaving this meeting, it will be your deputy, Roger Naismith, not my officers. They are doing a fantastic job explaining what took place, and until now, they have only received derision. I leave the decision, whether it is worthwhile carrying on in your capable and respected hands.' Jack faced his counterpart with gusto. Janet squeezed Donald's hand, feeling the utmost pride for his brilliant put down of the Staffordshire deputy. They both felt encouraged by Jack's support and Tom's distinct pleasure at their performance.

'Jack, can you give me a moment, please?' He turned to his deputy. 'Roger, can we have a chat outside, please?' Sir Bartholomew and Roger Naismith rose and left the room.

Jack turned to Donald. 'I had to correct you there, Donald. You were out of order but, off the record, I applaud you. I couldn't have put it better myself. The guy is an utter shit. Please don't record my last few words, Rosemary.' He turned to his secretary, and they exchanged smiles.

As Jack finished speaking, the two Staffordshire policemen returned. 'Jack, Roger has a few words to say before I'd like this meeting to carry on and then conclude; Roger.' Sir Bart nodded to his deputy.

'Donald, please accept my apologies for my remarks. Despite my gov instructing me to apologise, I have to say I'm still extremely sceptical. Still, I promise I won't interrupt again.'

'Good, I'm glad we've cleared the air. Donald, where were you?' Jack said.

'Janet will describe how we gained concrete evidence on Lizzie Cartwright's murder on a subsequent visit to Upper Slaughter.'

'As Donald said, we visited Upper Slaughter a second time. Remarkably, there was no trace of *The Crucified Abbot.* It's the Red Lion that now occupies the same space. We revisited Upper Slaughter after we'd read in the Police Gazette about Lizzie's murder and your subsequent investigation, Sir Bartholomew. It was, of course, at that point that we needed to divest ourselves of the evidence we were aware of. Without concrete evidence, we knew you would have laughed in our faces or, at the very least, received the comments we have this afternoon.' Janet looked towards Roger.

'Donald and I visited Lizzie's parents, not officially you understand. We were merely tourists and visited the village only in that capacity. I obtained a hairbrush of Lizzie's, given to us by her mother. Donald obtained soil samples from around the yew tree in the garden of The Red Lion.'

'So, the same yew tree is still there, the same one that existed in *The Crucified Abbot's* rear garden?' Tom asked.

'Yes, it's the same tree. We verified nails that had crucified Lizzie Cartwright are still embedded in the tree. We brought the hairbrush and the soil samples back here to Scotland Yard with us. Donald is now passing out the results of a DNA examination on both articles carried out by Scotland Yard pathological laboratory. If you turn to the report's final page, you'll see that there's a 98.8% match on both articles. This proves conclusively that what we witnessed happened where we saw it. Lizzie Cartwright was murdered on that yew tree in the rear garden of The Red Lion or, as we experienced, at *The Crucified Abbot.*' Janet nodded to Donald, and he resumed.

'We later tried to make sense of our experiences there. We found no records that prove the existence of Caleb, Margareta, Ebenezer Strange, or *The Crucified Abbot* in any tax records, the local Register of Electors, or genealogical records. The Staffordshire Newsletter of 31st October 1866, however, comprehensively details the account of a fire. Donald is passing around a verbatim record of that editorial. May I read it to you?'

'A tragedy has occurred at the village of Upper Slaughter, near Rugeley. The Crucified Abbot, a hotel and public house, situated in Gallows Lane, was destroyed by fire. Twelve people died in the inferno that ripped through the thatched hotel, which has reputedly existed for two thousand years. The owners, Caleb and Margareta Strange and their son Ebenezer, perished as they tried to rescue nine local visitors trapped inside. The victims included three renowned local farmers, Jasper Clownes, David Thatcher, and Simon Stubbs and six other villagers from Upper Slaughter.'

Janet passed back to Donald. 'That concludes our presentation to you. We have to say we're still as perplexed as you all may be. We would be glad to answer your questions.'

'Before you take any questions, can I pass on my approval for the professional way you've handled the issues. As I said to you, I can't explain away some extremely unusual events you've seen. However, I'm sure there's a rational explanation.' Jack offered his congratulations to them.

Tom was the first to ask a question. 'Donald, Janet, you've both met this Ebenezer Strange…'

'… yes, we have, Tom, both in the visions we experienced and physically at *The Crucified Abbot* in the dining room….'

'… yes, but you aren't the only people to have met him, are you?'

'The only other people we're aware of are Mr and Mrs Cartwright, Lizzie's parents. Also, a ninety-three-year-old gentleman from Upper Slaughter named Ted Baxter. We've spoken to him, and he maintains he's met him several times.'

'Exactly, and that information counters Roger's arguments. Other people are aware of him. Were they in a hallucination or dreamlike state when they met him? I'd say not. To me, that points to definite evidence that Ebenezer Strange is an actual person. To the Staffordshire officers I'd say, he's out there somewhere; find him. More pertinently, why have you not found him already?'

Jack, as always, appreciated Tom's practical assessment of many situations.

Roger, however, came up with a different viewpoint. 'That's as may be, inspector, but there are far more serious questions here relating to the conduct of these two officers of the Metropolitan Police. With respect, Superintendent Croaker, I feel you've overlooked these issues and have been too lenient with your junior colleagues.' Jack opened his mouth but was stopped by Roger.

'It's your turn to listen to me, superintendent. Sergeant Lawrence and Constable Lawrence are material witnesses to a foul murder. As far as we in Stafford County Police are aware, the only witnesses. In any other murder enquiry, we, as a matter of normal procedure, would immediately suspect them of being more involved…'

'… please don't tell me you are seriously considering my officers are more involved…?'

'… that's exactly what I'm saying…'

'… but…'

'… but nothing, superintendent. I'm formally stating, these two young officers of yours are considered *the* prime suspects in the murder of Lizzie Cartwright.'

Sir Bartholomew looked questioningly at his deputy. 'I'm sorry, gov. I'm responsible for the day to day running of the county incident room. I know my subordinate detective officers would consider me remiss if I didn't take this action. We have to face facts.'

Donald and Janet looked at each other. This was the scenario they'd previously feared and privately discussed.

'Personally, Roger, I think you're mistaken, and you'll be seriously wasting police officer's time in pursuing this line of enquiry. How you'll explain to the ratepayers of Staffordshire the way in which you wasted their hard-earned money is your concern. Please know that I'll be supporting my officers for as long as it takes. I'll stake my career that Sergeant Lawrence and Constable Lawrence are 100% innocent.'

'I note your allegiance and comments, superintendent. I think your loyalty is misplaced. Sergeant Lawrence, Constable Lawrence, I'll require you both to attend County Police Headquarters at some stage in Baswich, Stafford, to aid our enquiries further.' He turned to Jack. 'I assume you'll be keeping your officers here at Scotland Yard and not giving them leave so that they can disappear to the continent somewhere.'

'Superintendent Naismith, I've previously followed the behaviour expected of my rank, in responding to you with diplomacy and courtesy. Rosemary, I allow you to record what I'm about to say to our Staffordshire colleagues. Whether I give extended leave to my officers is my business entirely. I called this meeting intending to provide support to the Staffordshire Police in this matter. I note, with disappointment, that you have flouted my hospitality at every turn. So, Superintendent Naismith, go to hell. This discussion is now closed, everybody. Thank you for attending. Donald, Janet, I'd like a chat with you in my office, please?'

'Jack, please don't end the meeting there…' Sir Bartholomew pleaded.

'The meeting is over, Bart. I noted your silence while letting your deputy speak. You could have stopped him but said nothing. Your silence says everything about how you choose to run your county authority. I expected more from you having seen how you perform at constabulary seminars. Still, now I consider that to be a front and window dressing. Rosemary, will you please show the Staffordshire officers the way out, please? I trust you can find your way back to Euston Station by yourselves, gentlemen. Goodbye.'

In Jack's office, Donald, Janet, and Tom sat facing Jack, holding a cup of tea. 'Thank you for your support in the conference room, gov,' Janet offered.

'Both of you will always have that. I know you haven't any motive other than wanting this to end and the culprits brought to justice. It seems our friends from Staffordshire have other intentions in mind. I'm urging you to watch your backs and keep me informed of any and every development. Tom, I'm asking for your support in this matter. When you have a spare moment, I'd like you to visit Staffordshire with Donald. I'd value your opinion on this horrible murder. See what you can both find out. I won't be requesting any permission from the

Staffordshire county lot to intrude on their patch. Quite the opposite. After this meeting, I'll be drafting a letter to Sir Bartholomew informing him we here at Scotland Yard will be officially involved from now on. From this moment onwards, this is also a Metropolitan Police matter and I'll be informing the Commissioner formally of what's happening.'

'Will do, Jack', Tom replied, and he got up to leave.

'Janet, can you spare a minute, please?'

Donald joined Tom in the incident room.

'Yes, gov, how can I help?'

'Well, I'm helping you, I hope. Firstly, well done on your excellent work at Dagenham with Lucy. Your discoveries have paved the way to nab this drugs gang in the bud. We know it won't stop others from carrying on the illicit trade in drugs, but it'll be a major dent in illegal usage in East London. Second, how are you? I'm mindful not to overtax you…'

'… I'm grateful for your concern, gov, but I'd prefer to be treated like everyone else. If you knew what personal indignities I withstood with that prized piece of shit, Colin Harmsworth, I know you wouldn't be saying what you just said.'

He smiled at Janet. 'That's exactly the reaction I expected. I'm always amazed and full of respect for women police officers, knowing you're more vulnerable to the perverts out there.'

'I can take care of myself, gov. I had to endure a little embarrassment to get the maximum information from Harmsworth. I'd like to be in court on the day he gets his sentence, so I can look him straight in the eye.'

'I'll make sure of that, and perhaps I'll be sitting alongside you in solidarity?'

In the incident room, Tom and Donald sat together. 'When do you want to go to Staffordshire, Tom? Do you have a spare couple of days?'

'How about tomorrow? Because of Janet and Lucy's excellent work, we're ahead of the curve on the drugs investigation. We're closer to when we can make a coordinated arrest of all the individual participants. That'll require collaboration with the riot squad. So, we could leave tomorrow for two days? I'll clear it with the gov, but I'm sure he'll agree.'

'As it's official police business, I'll book a pool car and ask Rosemary to reserve two rooms at The Red Lion.' Donald added.

Thirty-one

Tom and Donald shared the drive from London to Staffordshire. Tom relinquished driving for the last few miles as his sergeant was more acquainted with the route and the local roads. Donald was relieved to see The Red Lion and not *The Crucified Abbot* standing in Gallows Lane as he pulled into the car park. Walking into the reception foyer, he expected to see Tessa, but was disappointed. Behind the desk was a plump, elderly woman with greying hair, leaning forward with a considerable stoop. He noticed a walking stick propped next to the counter.

'Hello, I'm Sergeant Donald Lawrence from Scotland Yard. This is my colleague, Inspector Tom Cropper. We have a reservation for two rooms with en-suite bathrooms.'

'Hello, Sergeant Lawrence, your rooms are ready for you. My name is Mrs Clara Downing. I'm the proprietor of The Red Lion. Would you sign the visitor's book, please? Could I ask you for a credit or debit card number for our records? You understand this isn't for payment now, but when you leave. Your reservation is for two nights in rooms 103 and 105 on the first floor.'

'Mrs Downing, I stayed here a few weeks ago with my wife. The receptionist on that occasion was a young woman named Tessa. We became friends with her. Could you tell her I'm here, please?'

'I wish I could, but she's not here. I've not seen Tessa Jackson for five days. I've sent Tony, the gardener cum handyman, to her house in Upper Slaughter, but her parents haven't seen her either. We're getting rather worried about her.'

'Does she usually go missing?' Tom asked. 'Are the police involved?'

'Not our Tessa, she's like clockwork. She runs the hotel for me when I'm not here. I live in Tunstall, Stoke-on-Trent. I find it difficult to get out and about these days. My rheumatoid arthritis is gradually taking its toll. Thank goodness for my staff, but Tessa usually coordinates everything. I've not learned that she's been officially reported missing yet.'

She turned to Donald. 'Did you want to see Tessa about anything in particular?'

'No, not really. Tessa said she'd show me more of Cannock Chase if ever I came here again, that's all.'

'Oh, she's an expert on Cannock Chase, alright, she knows all the best rambles and where the best viewpoints are. The week before she became missing, she was showing her new boyfriend all over the neighbourhood.'

'She has a new boyfriend?'

'Yes, a great big strapping bloke named Ben. A real charmer he is. No wonder she's fallen for him. I would've too if I'd have been forty years younger.'

Donald looked concerned at Tom. 'Can you describe him?'

'Well, he's a big bloke broad shoulders, black, swept-back hair. Very handsome with a charming smile…'

'Thank you, Mrs Downing.'

'Would you like a hand with your bags…?'

'No thanks, we can manage, we only have these overnight bags. Oh, one more thing, can you let me have Tessa's address in Upper Slaughter, please?' Mrs Downing wrote the address on Donald's reservation letter. She described the address at the same time.

'You can't miss it, go down Gallows Lane, then you'll see Gentleshaw Avenue on the left. About fifty yards on the right is Tessa's house. A lovely bungalow with dormer windows and a thatched roof; Dingle cottage, I think it's called? She lives there with her parents and younger brothers.'

Donald and Tom unpacked and sauntered down to the lounge. The first thing they discussed was Tessa's disappearance. 'It sounds as if you and Janet got close to this Tessa when you were here last?'

Donald's guilt immediately surfaced. He didn't want Tom to know of his intimacy with her. 'Yes, we did, she's a lovely girl and extremely helpful.'

'I wonder why she hasn't been officially reported missing?'

'It all sounds very suspicious, especially as she's tied up with this Ben.'

'Do you think he's the same Ben that murdered Lizzie?'

'I'd stake my pension on it, Tom.'

'Well, if it is, that all adds credence that he's an actual person and not some devil or phantom. In the meantime, I'd like to examine the murder scene, this infamous yew tree.'

'Hello young fella, my lad. How nice to see you again. Where's that lovely wife of yours?'

'Hello, Ted, I'm so glad to find you well. I've left Janet in London. May I introduce my colleague, Inspector Tom Cropper. Tom, this is Ted Baxter.'

'Hello, Mr Baxter, I've heard a lot about you.'

'Please call me Ted, and I hope my lovely young friends haven't been exaggerating about me? Folks I know say I like my cider too much, but I only like a small tipple now and again. Oh, but Inspector Tom, if you've only just arrived you won't know about the locally brewed cider, Abbot cider it's called. It's named after *The Crucified Abbot*, an old, thatched pub that used to stand on this very spot. Haven't you told Tom about the Abbot cider yet, Donald?'

'No, I haven't got around to that yet, but we may as well start now. I can see you're ready for another…? A pint for you, Tom?' He nodded with a smile.

'… am I? Do you know, my young fella, I hadn't noticed that my glass was nearly empty, but if you're offering, I wouldn't say no.' Donald strolled along the patio to fetch three pints of cider while Tom sat on the bench with Ted.

'Donald tells me you're nearly ninety-three…'

'Yes, I am, Tom. I sometimes think I've lived too long. I don't like what the world has turned into. Give me the olden days when everybody knew what was happening and everybody knew their place.'

'I know what you mean, Ted. Life today seems overly complicated sometimes.'

'I suppose you're here to investigate Lizzie Cartwright's murder, are you?'

'I can't tell you that; it's confidential police business, but I can't see what harm it could do if you knew. Yes, Donald and I want to check a few things out.'

'This murder is a nasty business.'

'I'd like a peek at this infamous yew tree…' Ted turned and looked at the tree.

'Ah, the old tree. Has Donald told you it's history?' Donald returned with the cider.

'Yes, he has, and lots more about what occurred around the tree…'

'I'm telling your friend, Donald; the yew tree is an unpleasant business. When the old pagan English folk crucified Abbot Ibáñez, they started something evil that exists until this very day. Oh, here's my cider, thank you, Donald. I was getting carried away with your colleague about the old tree. It's not like me to leave a brand-new pint of cider standing neglected, not even for a second.' He picked up the glass and looked at the effervescence in the amber coloured liquid. 'See that, young fella my lad. There's nothing as pleasing as seeing the bubbles rising in a pint of Abbot's cider. The old-timers around here used to say every bubble contains one more day of life…'

'… Old-timers, Ted? You're nearly ninety-three, are there any left in the village who are older than you?' He looked wistfully at Donald.

'No, sadly, there aren't. All my old mates have passed on now. Old Joseph was one hundred and nine when he took his last sip of Abbots, then Arnold was ninety-six…'

'… Perhaps you're right then, Ted. If there's a day's life in every bubble, they must have drunk a few pints then?' Tom laughed.

Ted's loud laugh echoed around the rear garden. 'Oh, I like this friend of yours, Donald. He knows what's important in life.' They all took a big slurp and looked at the yew tree. Tom put his glass down and walked across for a closer examination.

'If you feel around the bark, young fella, you'll feel the original nails that done the poor Abbot to death.' Ted shouted. Tom looked more closely and captured the images on his mobile phone.

While Tom walked around the tree, Donald asked Ted about Tessa. 'I understand Tessa's gone missing.' Ted's face saddened, and he looked towards Donald with a tear in the corner of his eye.

'Lovely girl Tessa is, she'd do anything for anybody. Nobody's seen her for a few days. You know why she's gone missing, don't you?' Donald looked bemused as Tom joined them.

'Because of that incubus, Ebenezer. Oh, my God, Donald, I've seen him again. I never wanted to see him again, not in this life or any other life that I'm going to. I saw him walking along Gallows Lane with poor Lizzie, I noticed Ben calling here at The Red Lion for Tessa. Then off they wandered, strolling down the garden, past yon yew tree into The Chase. I haven't seen hide nor hair of them since. He sent a shiver down my spine. Do you know what he said to me as he ducked under the tree, He turned to me as I sat here on this very bench, *still drinking the Abbot cider are you, Edwin?* That's my proper name you see. Most folks think my actual name is Edward, but it's Edwin.' They saw him close his eyes and his breathing become heavy.

'I think he's having a doze, Tom,' Donald commented.

'What a lovely old man.' Tom whispered. 'What's the plan of action, Donald?'

'It's 3:30 pm, I suggest, as it's such a lovely day, we have a stroll across The Chase to Castle Ring. We can see where Lizzie's body was found and see some of Tessa's favourite beauty spots. Tomorrow morning, we'll go to her home and interview her parents.'

Thirty-two

'Good morning, are you Mr and Mrs Jackson?' Donald asked as he and Tom stood at the threshold of the cottage.

'Yes, I'm Doreen Jackson, my husband Albert is inside, who are you, and how can I help?'

'We're police officers from Scotland Yard…'

'… Scotland Yard in London? Whatever brings you here to my doorstep in Upper Slaughter?'

'I'm Sergeant Donald Lawrence, and this is Inspector Tom Cropper. We're here about your daughter, Tessa…' Mrs Jackson started fiddling with her hair, trying to smarten her appearance. She noticed scuff marks on her cardigan sleeve. She licked her fingers and tried to erase the marks.

'… what do you want to know about Tessa?'

'Only what Mrs Downing at The Red Lion told us, that she's missing. My wife and I stayed at the hotel a few weeks ago. Tessa and I became friends, so to learn that she's missing causes me some concern, especially as we're here to investigate Lizzie Cartwright's murder.'

Doreen held her hands to her face and yelled. 'Oh my God, are you suggesting she's been murdered like poor Lizzie? Albert!' She bellowed towards the living room. 'Albert, where are you? Albert!'

'No, of course not, Mrs Jackson…' Donald raised his eyebrows at Tom in frustration.

'… What's the problem, Doreen?' A tall, balding man with a black smudge moustache came to the door. He was wearing a white vest overlain with elastic braces that held up his baggy trousers.

'These are police officers from Scotland Yard, London, and they think our poor Tessa's been murdered?'

'What? Have you found her…?' Mr Downing added to his wife's frenzy. Tom moved forward.

'Mr Jackson, I'm Inspector Tom Cropper. Your wife has misunderstood. We don't know what's happened to your daughter. We're here in Staffordshire to investigate Lizzie Cartwright, not your daughter. My colleague is Tessa's friend.' Albert looked at Donald.

'You're her friend, are you? She's never mentioned you to us.' Albert eyed Donald suspiciously.

'We only met at The Red Lion a few weeks ago.'

'Well, how can we help you? Be quick about it because I'm feeding my pigeons.'

'We understand from Mrs Downing that recently Tessa had a new boyfriend named Ben.'

'Yes, that's right. Ben seems a genuinely nice bloke. Why are you asking?'

'They're both missing, aren't they? Aren't you concerned?' As they spoke, Tessa's two younger brothers pushed their way past their father.

'Hey you two, I hope you've fastened the door to the pigeon coop, I haven't finished feeding them yet.' Albert remonstrated with his sons. 'Bloody kids, they do my head in ...'

'Are you real policemen from Scotland Yard, mister?' Donald smiled and nodded to Michael, the older brother who was thirteen.

'You don't seem to be policemen,' the smaller boy commented. Danny was ten. 'You aren't wearing uniforms or those funny, tall, black hats.'

'No, we aren't, we're detectives.' Tom added.

'So, do you still carry police whistles?' Danny asked.

'Blasted nosy kids, always nattering and wasting folks' time, aren't they?' Mrs Jackson scolded them and escorted them back into the house.

'Tessa will turn up, eventually.' Mr Jackson added. 'If I'm honest, I'm more concerned that detectives from Scotland Yard have travelled one hundred miles from London merely to ask stupid questions about my daughter. How much has that cost the taxpayer?'

'I can see we've had a wasted journey then. Thank you for your time, Mr Jackson.' Tom added. 'Come on, Donald.'

As Tom and Donald walked back to their car, Albert Jackson reached for his mobile phone. He dialled the number for the County Constabulary. 'Hello, could I speak to someone in charge of the Lizzie Cartwright investigation?'

'Yes, this is Superintendent Roger Naismith, how can I help you?'

He explained who he was and why he'd telephoned.

'You're telling me that two Scotland Yard detectives have interviewed you?'

'That's what I've explained. Are you stupid or deaf? What is it with Mr Plods these days, I thought you lot needed an education before becoming police officers?' He was frustrated and shouted down the telephone. 'The astronomical cost of the bloody rates we pay in Upper Slaughter these days…'

'… What is it, Albert, why are you shouting?' Doreen came into the hall.

'It's these bloody policemen; they're as thick as pig shit.'

Roger tried to ignore Albert's insults. 'Mr Jackson, why have the London detectives called at your house?'

'Well, my daughter Tessa is missing, and they asked about her, that's all.'

'Why haven't you reported her missing? You said you live in Upper Slaughter?'

'You know what young women are like when they have a new boyfriend. She'll be back.'

'Mr Jackson, my sergeant and I will come to interview you…'

'… More bloody policemen, more bloody wasted money.' He cut the phone off. 'Bloody coppers, wasting my time and preventing the feeding of my pigeons ...'

'Well, Donald, that didn't go well.' Tom chided him as they returned to The Red Lion.

Over lunch, they talked about Lizzie Cartwright's murder. 'This bloke, Ebenezer Strange, has to be a local chap. I suggest we take the rest of the afternoon asking around the village if anyone knows him or has seen him lately,' Tom said as he pushed his empty plate away.

Suddenly loud voices boomed from the hotel foyer. 'That's Mrs Downing telling someone that we're in here.' Tom said.

'There you are. What the fucking hell do you two think you're doing trespassing on our patch?' Superintendent Roger Naismith yelled at Tom and Donald.

Behind Roger, Sergeant Davies looked bewildered at his gov's outburst. Further behind, Mrs Downing came into the dining room. 'I don't care if you are a superintendent or the Pope; this is a private, respectable hotel, and I'm the proprietor. If there's one more word of that nature spoken on my premises, I'll get the gardener to boot your backside and kick you out. I don't allow any foul language of that sort in here.'

Roger turned to face her. 'I apologise most sincerely, madam.'

'I should think so indeed, a man of your age.' She returned to the hotel foyer.

Tom laughed. 'Everywhere you go, Roger, you have a knack of upsetting people.'

'I asked, what are you doing here?'

'So, you haven't read the communiqué Superintendent Croaker sent to Sir Bartholomew Evans, stating that the metropolitan police are now officially involved with the Lizzie Cartwright murder?'

'What? Over my dead body.'

'This pathetic man tempts fate, doesn't he, Donald?' Tom's sarcasm even caused Sergeant Davies to suppress a smirk. Roger pulled a chair up to the dining table where Tom and Donald sat.

'I understand from Mr Albert Jackson that his daughter is missing…'

'… Ah, that's how you knew we were here!' Tom exclaimed.

'Also, Sergeant Lawrence, you're involved with yet another missing woman here in Upper Slaughter. It seems every time you come here, someone else goes missing. Mark my words, sergeant, if I find the slightest item that connects you further, I'll be arresting you as a suspect. Come on, sergeant, I need to have a chat with Sir Bartholomew back at HQ.'

'Phew!' Donald exclaimed.

'He's a nasty piece of work, Donald. We shouldn't underestimate him. Anyway, let's have a stroll into the village and see what we can find out about Ben Strange.'

Thirty-three

They walked past Tessa's home and sensed the ire and derision of Albert Jackson as he watched them from his living room window. They stopped at the bottom of Gentleshaw Lane. 'There's a post office here,' Donald said. 'Do you think it would be more efficient if we split up, Tom? That way we can maximise the rest of our time here.'

'Good idea, Donald. You go to the post office, and I'll carry on into the centre of the village.'

'Hello, I'm a police officer.' Donald showed his identity badge to the postmistress.

'How can I help, sergeant?' Miss Brenda Hastings asked.

'My colleague and I are trying to trace a Mr Ebenezer Strange, better known as Ben. We understand he was a friend of Lizzie Cartwright and currently a boyfriend of Tessa Jackson. Has he ever been to your post office?'

'Yes, he has, but I only knew him as Ben because that's what Lizzie, and then Tessa, called him. I didn't know his surname…'

'… he has? When?'

'Two weeks ago, he came in here with Tessa…'

'Had you seen him before then? What I'm trying to establish is whether he lives around here or even in the village?'

'He doesn't live in Upper Slaughter, I'm certain of that. I know every name and address who receives mail from here, and his name's not on that list. I've seen him before, though. You mentioned poor Lizzie. He used to come in here with her occasionally.'

'Can you tell me anything else about him? Or his family? Did he buy anything?'

'No, I'm sorry, sergeant. I'd never met him before the two village girls brought him with them. I never saw him buy anything either. Lizzie and Tessa both only came in here to post their mail.'

'Thank you, Miss Hastings, you've been immensely helpful. Would you take my card? If you think of anything else, please contact me. My email address and telephone numbers are on the card.'

'Could I suggest you try Williams' grocery store, across Windmill Square? I remember I watched Tessa and Ben leave the post office the other week and go directly into the grocery store.'

'Why did you watch them leave?' Donald looked to where she was pointing. 'Square? I can't see a square?'

'We call it a square. It's the village green, I suppose.'

'So, you watched Ben and Tessa walk into the shop over there.' Donald verified where Williams grocery store was. 'What made you notice them?'

'Sergeant Lawrence, Ben is an extremely handsome man. I'm fairly sure I wasn't the only young woman in Upper Slaughter who swooned over him?'

'I see. Thank you again.' Donald remembered what Janet had said from her encounters with him. 'Hmm! Perhaps his masculine good looks may lead to his downfall if other women remember him too?' he thought.

Donald stood outside the grocery store and looked back across the tree-lined village green to the post office and thought how beautiful and typically English the rural scene was. He entered the shop and heard the bell clanging above his head. He reached for his warrant card and showed it to the young, blonde-haired woman who stood behind the counter.

'I'm searching for a man called Ebenezer Strange. He's been friendly with Tessa Jackson. Have you seen either of them lately?'

The woman rested her elbows on the glass counter and looked upwards in thought. 'Let me see. I haven't seen them for a couple of weeks. They came in here for some snacks for a picnic. I remember they said they were going for a ramble up to Castle Ring.'

'This Ben Strange. Do you know him? Does he live in the village?'

'No, he doesn't. I remember hearing Tessa and him talking about them visiting his aunty in Hazelslade village as they discussed what to buy for their picnic.'

'Hazelslade? Where's that?'

'It's a village across The Chase, about four miles from here.'

'I don't suppose you have an address for her?'

'Not a clue, sorry.'

'Other than that, can you think where either of them would have gone?'

'The only other place I can think of is Tessa's Uncle Silas's. He lives on the other side of the village in a small cottage. Now, what's it called? She told me. Oh, yes, Brooklands, it's called that because there's a stream flowing through his big back garden.'

'So, is his name Jackson, the same as Tessa's?'

'Yes, Silas Jackson. He's her dad's elder brother.'

'You've been extremely helpful, thank you, Miss…?'

'Jacqueline Bailey's my name, but everyone calls me Jackie.'

'Oh, so you aren't related to the proprietor of the shop then… Williams, isn't it?'

'Yes, I am. Williams is my mom's maiden name. This was my grandparent's shop going back before the war.'

Donald came out of the shop and saw Tom walking into a bungalow fifty yards away. He waited for him to come out of their driveway. 'How've you got on, Tom?'

'No luck. I've only asked at five houses. They're all elderly pensioners. They don't get out much, so they don't seem to know anything. One chap commented he knew Tessa was a flighty girl, so he wasn't surprised she'd gone missing. Other than that, nothing. How did you fare?'

'I've got a couple of leads.' He told Tom about the conversation with Jackie Bailey.

'Where are we going first, then?'

'Well, we'll need the car to visit Ben's aunty, it's four miles away, so let's have a stroll to see Tessa's uncle now.'

Thirty-four

'Here it is. Jackie told me it was called Brooklands. This looks quaint.' Donald noticed the thatched roof with a peacock made of straw perched on the apex. He thought of Ted's tales about Capstick, the thatcher.

Donald lifted the iron knocker and let it fall on the rapping plate. An old man with a stoop opened the door; he squinted against the daylight pervading his dim hallway.

'Yes, who is it? Pardon! You must speak up as I'm a little hard of hearing.' Tom and Donald hadn't spoken, but Donald offered their greetings with a loud voice. 'We're trying to find Tessa; I understand you're her Uncle Silas.'

'Guess what? I haven't got time to play games, young fella…'

'… Tessa, your niece, not guess.'

'… Tessa, well, why didn't you say so instead of trying to be a smart arse?'

'Have you seen her lately?' Tom shouted.

'There's no need to shout so much, you'll wake the departed around the corner in the cemetery. That wouldn't include my old granddad though because he died of head rot with cauliflower ears. You'd better come in, and I'll put in my hearing aid. Come in, come in, you're letting the cold air in.'

Silas led Donald and Tom into his lounge. 'Wait here, I'll find my hearing aid. Blast! I haven't worn it for a while, I bet it'll need a new battery?'

They looked around the cosy room. Low oaken beams ran either side of a more massive block beam split with age that supported the entire ceiling. An enormous coal fire roared in the brick-built grate. Tom looked through the leaded, dimpled windows at a gurgling stream meandering through the extensive garden. Silas reappeared and asked Donald if he could help him fix a new circular battery in each of his hearing aids.

'There, that's better, I can hear the flames flickering in the fire. Ooh, it's whistling now, though. Here young chap can you turn them down a bit for me, I think they need adjusting.' Donald turned the dials towards the minus sign.

'Ah! That's better. Sit you down, both of you. Now, you want to know about Tessa. She's my niece, you know. My younger brother, Albert's eldest child.'

'Yes, we understand that…'

'… how did you know that? I'm asking because you can't be too careful these days…'

'… Jackie Bailey at Williams' shop told me. Anyway, we're policemen from Scotland Yard.'

They both showed their warrant cards to Silas. 'Ah! I see. Well, how can I help you?'

'Have you seen Tessa lately?'

'… oh, I'm not sure; I may have done. My memory isn't as sharp as it used to be.' Tom heard a noise from above them and looked up.

'Don't take any notice of that noise, young fella, I think I've got pine martens in the loft. Yes, come to think about it, I saw Tessa the other week.'

'… and you've not seen her *since*?' Tom asked, pointedly. Donald looked curiously at him.

'No, I don't think so.'

'Was she with anybody, a boyfriend perhaps?'

'No, she came by herself.'

'Does she usually come to visit you?'

'Why wouldn't she? I'm her uncle.'

'It must be a lonely existence here all by yourself?'

'Yes, it is sometimes. My dear Molly passed on a few years ago now.'

'Anyway, it's been a pleasure to meet you, Mr Jackson. Don't bother seeing us out. Thank you.'

Donald followed Tom as he strode through the village. 'Wait on a bit, Tom, you seem preoccupied with something?'

'Well, if we're going to the village of Hazelslade to see this aunty of Ben's we need to get a move on.'

'Why? What's the rush, all of a sudden?'

'My copper's nose, Donald, that's all.'

'I don't understand.' Tom stopped and faced Donald.

'If that old man, Silas Jackson, is alone in that cottage, I'll give you my pension…'

'… Do you think there's someone with him? Who?'

'I guess that it's Tessa.'

'What? How do you know that?'

'You were aware of the movement from upstairs…'

'… Silas said he'd got pine martens…'

'… since when do pine martens make noises like footsteps? They make scratching noises. Then I verified Silas lived alone…'

'… yes, well? He said his wife died a few years ago…'

'… so, why is there a woman's cardigan draped over the chair by the window? Why is there a pair of women's shoes pushed under the dresser in the hall?'

'Was there? You noticed all those things, Tom?'

'I didn't go to the window only to admire the view, Donald, and I didn't say we'd let ourselves out because of politeness. I had a closer peek at the pair of shoes that I'd noticed when we first entered. They were modern, high-heeled shoes, not a typical flat-heeled shoe that a pensioner would wear.'

'Wow! Tom, I can see I've got a lot to learn. I noticed none of that.'

'You let the old scoundrel side-track you about his deafness. If he's as deaf as he made out, his hearing aids would've been on hand and fully charged. That was a smokescreen to put us off the scent.'

'It's easily done, Donald. Always remember, never take things at face value. There's always a motive for most things that present themselves to police officers, especially when people have things to hide.'

'What are we going to do about it? Tessa being at Silas's cottage, I mean. Why do you think she's there?'

'Going into hiding is my best bet.'

'Hiding, why and from whom?'

'She's concealing herself from this bloke, Ben.'

'I hope you're right, Tom, because it means she's safe. I imagined he'd done her in, like Lizzie. I wonder why she's chosen her uncle's cottage.'

'Well, let's face facts, he's an old man. I bet he leads quite a solitary life, so I'd imagine his cottage is the last place anyone would think of looking for her. Second, Donald, I remembered something you and Janet told me about from your experiences at *The Crucified Abbot*.' They reached a bench on the village green and sat down.

'We said such a lot, there was so much that had happened.'

'You told me about Ben's mother's reaction to the crucifix around Lizzie's neck…'

'… Margareta.'

'Yes. Did you notice the brass crucifix above Silas's front door and again a free-standing brass cross on his mantelpiece?' Donald shook his head.

'It seems old Silas is a God-fearing Christian of the old school. Tessa must know something by now about Ben that he wouldn't go to a place that's protected by a crucifix. That's conjecture, but it fits in with what you and Janet told me.' They arose from the bench and carried on walking back to The Red Lion.

Entering the hotel foyer, Mrs Downing greeted them. 'Ah, you're back. There's a message for you, inspector.' She passed a piece of paper to him. He unfolded it and read aloud.

'It's from Jack. He wants to know when we're returning to the Yard. I've left my mobile in my room; I'll ring him.'

'Also, I've had Superintendent Naismith here again from the county police.'

'What did he want, Mrs Downing?'

'Well, he didn't leave a message. He said he wanted you, sergeant.' Donald looked at Tom and raised his eyebrows.

'Yes, gov, okay. I was going to ring you. We've had some developments that may need our presence here for one more night…?' Tom listened as Donald watched his reactions to the telephone call with Jack Croaker. 'Yes, gov, we'll be back tomorrow at the latest.' Tom closed his mobile phone.

'The gov wants us back at the Yard as soon as we can. That sting on the drugs gang is all ready to go. You listened to what I told him; we need to tie things up here as quick as we can.'

'Are we going to Hazelslade, then?'

'Yes, now, and then I think we'll call on old Silas Jackson again.'

Thirty-five

As Donald drove towards the village of Hazelslade, Tom marvelled at the majestic forest scenery. 'We don't have forests like this in London, do we?'

'There's Green Park, and Hyde Park is even bigger.' Donald suggested.

'Oh yes, a few plane trees and half a dozen oaks compare very well to this,' he added sarcastically.

'We don't have an address for Ben's aunt, Tom. I suggest we call at the post office in Hazelslade. We can study their copy of the register of electors.'

'Good thinking, Donald, that'll save us some legwork.'

Tom waited in the car outside. At once, a group of young children came running down the street chasing a football. A boy kicked the ball, and it landed directly on the windscreen of the car. A startled Tom got out and retrieved the ball; it had nestled by the front bumper of the vehicle. He held it out for the boy to collect. 'Be more careful where you kick that in future, son. It could have hit somebody.'

'I'm sorry, mister,' the boy shouted, and he resumed kicking it down the road the same as he had before. Tom shook his head in frustration.

Donald was in a queue in the post office and smiled as he watched Tom's confrontation with the local children through the window. 'Yes, can I help you?' the postmaster asked. Donald had been concentrating on Tom and hadn't noticed the queue had dwindled.

'Hello, I'm Sergeant Donald Lawrence from Scotland Yard in London.' He showed his warrant card to the postmaster. 'Can I have a peek at the register of electors for Hazelslade, please?'

'Certainly, hang on a moment, I'll get it from the back of the office. There are a few people who ask for it. I don't think many people know we have a copy here, though. Here it is. Is there a person or family you're looking for? Perhaps I can help to save you the bother of having to trawl through the complete document?'

'The person my colleague and I are trying to trace is a Mr Ebenezer Strange, but I'm led to believe he has an aunt who lives here in Hazelslade.'

'Ebenezer Strange, hmm! I can't think that he has an address in this village. There's an Agnes Strange who lives in Rawnsley Road and a

Michael Strange in Paget Row. Michael is Agnes's son. Here let me help you.' Donald handed the register back to the postmaster. 'The streets are listed in alphabetical order. Here we are, Rawnsley Road.' He ran his finger down the page. 'Yes, Agnes Strange, number twenty-four. There's only Agnes registered at the address for voting purposes but, of course, that doesn't mean that she lives alone. Not everybody wants their names to appear on the register. Michael lives with his wife, Esme, at number fifty-nine Paget Row.'

'You've been extremely helpful… Mr…?'

'Frank James, postmaster, at your service. You'll find Rawnsley Road about a mile down this road. Carry on down the dip, then up the hill. Go down again, and that brings you to where the rows of houses start. I think number twenty-four is in the middle of a row of townhouses. Paget Row is about two hundred yards further on.'

'Carry on this road for about a mile, Tom, and we should come to number twenty-four Rawnsley Road.' As they were pulling away, the football hit the car again and rolled away.

'Bloody hooligans. The local kids here are as bad as in the East End of London.'

'Yes? Can I help you?'

'Are you Agnes Strange?'

'Who wants her?' she asked before committing herself, as she opened the door to Donald and Tom.

'We're police officers from Scotland Yard in London.'

'Have you some identification? You could be con men or rapists for all I know?' They showed their warrant cards to Agnes.

'You are Mrs Agnes Strange, then?'

'Yes, I am, but I can't imagine why policemen from London would want to talk to me?'

'We're here about your nephew, Ebenezer?'

'What's Ben been up to now? My late husband, Hubert, always said he was no good. You'd better come in.' Donald and Tom entered the low ceiling terraced house. They stood against a blank wall as Agnes sat next to her coal fire. 'Well sit yourselves down, there's no charge for making yourselves comfortable.'

'As you can see, I'm knitting my son, Michael, a new cardigan. His new wife, Esme, is hopeless at knitting or providing for any of his creature comforts. Still, he seems happy enough, so why should I complain.' Tom and Donald sat on a threadbare settee opposite the fire. Agnes reached for a twisted metal poker and prodded the dormant ashes, making the flames leap higher.

'We've come about your nephew…'

'… yes, you said. He's a bad lot, our Ben. Always was, always will be. Ben never listened to anything his mom and dad tried to tell him. He's so headstrong and wilful because he's good looking and has the gift of the gab, he thinks he can muddle through life with no discipline or conscience.' Agnes looked wistfully through her sitting-room window at a tumbled down old wooden shed and rusted greenhouse, devoid of a single piece of unbroken glass. 'Once upon a time he was in and out of our house like a fiddler's elbow. He used to come to play with our son, Michael. They would play football in the street with the other lads.' Tom looked at Donald and raised his eyebrows.

'So, you don't particularly like your nephew, then?' Donald suggested.

'Well, he's not my flesh and blood, is he? He's Hubert's nephew.'

'Have you seen him lately?' Tom asked.

'Now you mention it, yes I have. Ben came here a few weeks ago with his new girlfriend. I want you to meet my new girlfriend, Tessa, he said. Mind you, over the years he's been here with so many girlfriends I've lost track of who he's with and who've fallen out with him. What I know is, whoever he comes here with, he'll never be tied down into marriage because the girls get fed up with him. He has a one-track mind, always has had; he's girl and sex mad.' She paused and swallowed before resuming.

'Do you know my Hubert caught him once, making love to a young girl in our shed? Hubert thought we had a fox after our fowl. We used to keep hens in the shed. He noticed this banging and walked into the shed and there they were stark naked, rolling in the straw and the mess left behind by the fowl. Well, you can imagine, Hubert lost his cool. He took a stiff-bristled broom to their backsides and sent them on their way. We had a merry laugh about that afterwards.'

'Are Ben's parents still alive?' Tom asked.

'No, his dad, Caleb, and mom, Margareta, have both passed on now,' Donald sat forward.

'Caleb and Margareta, that's interesting. There used to be two of the same name who used to keep an old pub in Upper Slaughter.'

'I know nothing about that. They're my late husband's family, you see. I know who could help you with the Strange family tree though if you're interested. That's my son, Michael. He's always been interested in genealogy.'

'He lives in Paget Row, around the corner, if you want to meet him?'

'Number fifty-nine, I believe?'

'How did you know that?'

'The postmaster, Frank James…'

'… oh him, the nosey old so and so.'

'Anyway, thanks for your help, Mrs Strange.' Tom said. They shook hands and left.

'Number fifty-nine Paget Row, I presume, Donald?'

'Yes, any information on the Strange family will help to complete the picture of who's who?'

Donald and Tom knocked on the door. After explaining to Michael Strange why they were calling on him, he discussed his interest in genealogy and produced an outline family tree.

Michael explained the intricacies of the tree. 'Of course, I've only given you the Strange family as far back as 1761. Did you know that King Henry VIII gave a pub called *The Crucified Abbot* to my ancestor, another Caleb Strange, in 1566? The pub used to stand where The Red Lion stands today in Gallows Lane, Upper Slaughter.'

Donald nodded in interest, not revealing to him he'd seen the actual deed.

'Don't you think it's a little odd that all the wives in the Strange family have the same name, Margareta or Margaret?' Tom asked.

'Yes, except my father, who broke with family tradition and married Agnes, my mom. I understand the Margareta or Margaret thing is like Australian men who call their wives Sheila?'

Strange family tree

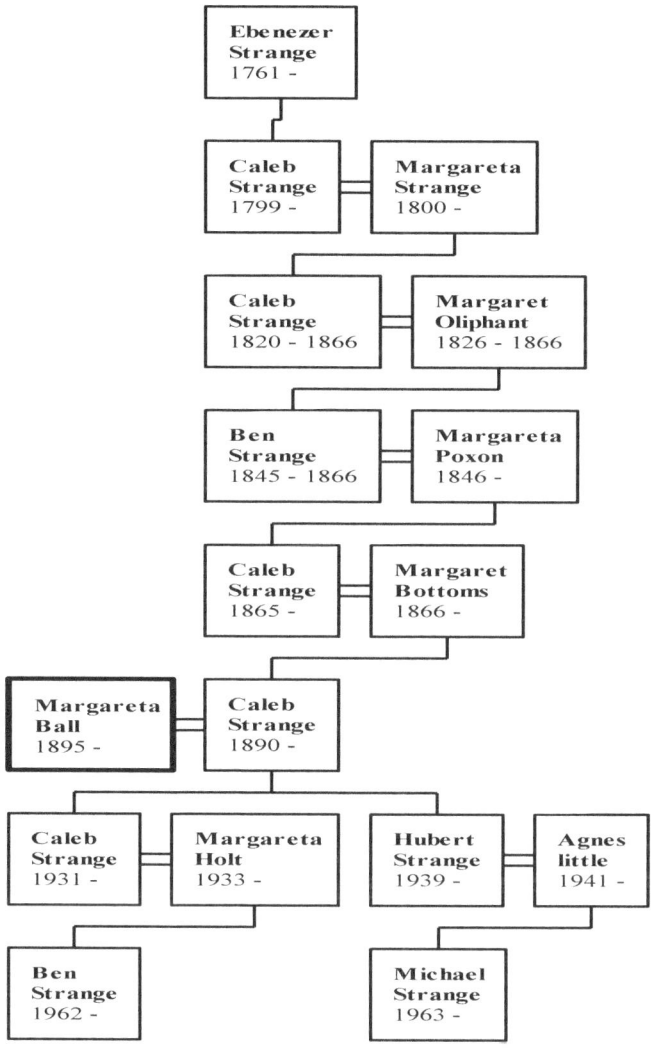

'Here's the interesting point, Tom,' Donald pointed out. 'Consider the dates of the death of Ben, Caleb, and Margareta Strange 1866...'

'... that was in the fire that burnt down *The Crucified Abbot,* of course,' interjected Michael. 'You're welcome to take this copy of my family history with you. Of course, if you want to know more, my cousin Ben is the one to talk to. He's always been more connected to the Strange family than I ever have. I remember as a lad, my dad having a blazing row with his brother…'

'… That would have been Ben's father?'

'… yes, my Uncle Ben. After the argument, my parents and Ben's parents never spoke again. My dad never agreed with the haphazard way they used to lead their lives. I remember my dad telling me once never to get involved with my cousin Ben and his family. My dad reckoned they were evil.'

After leaving Michael's house and while travelling back to Upper Slaughter, Tom commented to Donald. 'At least this visit to Michael's house has proved one unalterable fact.'

'What's that, Tom?'

'That an actual person named Ben Strange is living today. So, whatever you and Janet witnessed at *The Crucified Abbot,* the facts point to the murder of Lizzie Strange being carried out by today's Ben Strange and not the Ben Strange who lived and died in 1866. How else can her DNA be found in the soil you gathered from around the tree, and that also matches the DNA in her hair? This visit of ours also shows another obvious fact to me.'

Donald swerved to avoid a stray dog wandering across the road in Hazelslade. 'Go on, Tom, I'm listening.'

'We've been here, what, for only two days and think of the appreciable amount of information we've found out. Staffordshire's pride and joy, Superintendent Roger Naismith lives and works on this patch of his territory and what has he to show for his investigations? Only hot air and expletives. He's pathetic!' Donald laughed.

'Next stop, Silas Jackson's cottage.' Donald said, feeling pleased with the day's work so far. 'Saying that, Tom, my mobile phone needs charging. Let's have a break and a cuppa at The Red Lion before we go to see Silas.'

Donald relaxed in his room after switching on his phone charger. Someone knocked on his door. 'I'll be right down, Tom, you carry on.' The door opened.

'This is the Staffordshire police. Arrest that man, constable.' Superintendent Naismith read Donald his statutory rights, while the constable placed handcuffs around Donald's wrists.

'Tom!' Donald shouted.

'I'm right here, Donald, I'm aware of the intrusion. What's the meaning of this, Roger?'

'I'm arresting you, Sergeant Donald Lawrence, on the suspected murders of Lizzie Cartwright and Tessa Jackson. Take him away, constable.' Roger barked, ignoring Tom's question.

'You're making a terrible mistake, Roger…'

'… save it, inspector…'

'Donald has killed nobody…' Tom shouted down the stairs as Donald was led to the waiting police car.

'… go back to London, Inspector Cropper.'

'Find Tessa,' Donald shouted back. 'then get on to the gov and ask him to tell Janet, will you?'

Tom reached for his mobile as the car sped out of the hotel car park into Gallows Lane. 'Gov, is that you? Listen, Superintendent Roger Naismith of the Staffordshire lot has arrested Donald on two counts of murder…'

'… What!' Jack responded loudly down the phone.

'They've taken him to county headquarters at Stafford…'

'… thanks for letting me know, Tom. I'll get straight on to Sir Bart.'

'Despite Donald being out of action for a while, there are still things to be tied up here, gov…'

'… do what you can, Tom. I'd still like you back at Scotland Yard tomorrow, if you can?'

'Okay, gov. Can you keep Janet in the loop about Donald, please? I'll keep my mobile switched on if you can let me know what Sir Bart says about Donald.'

Tom left The Red Lion and walked determinedly to Silas Jackson's cottage.

He rapped the door knocker at Brooklands Cottage. 'Hello, it's you again.' Silas held the door partly open, as if trying to prevent Tom from looking inside the hall. 'What do you want this time?'

'I've lost my warrant card. I've looked everywhere for it. I think I must have dropped it inside your cottage…'

'… I don't think you have; I would've seen it…' Tom was aware of footsteps coming from inside.

'… oh, Silas, there it is, behind you on the floor.' Silas turned to peer at the carpet and left the door open a little more, enabling Tom to step inside. He shouted, 'You can come down now, Tessa. I know you're in there.'

'You can't come barging into my house…'

Tom continued shouting. 'Tessa, remember you met sergeant Donald Lawrence at The Red Lion.'

Silas put his hands over his ears. 'Please stop shouting,' he pleaded.

'I'm his friend and colleague,' Tom called again.

'You'd better go into the lounge…' Silas said, resigned to Tom's presence. Tom stood by the window and looked back at Silas as he followed him into the room.

'How did you know Tessa is here?' he asked sheepishly.

'This is her cardigan, isn't it?' Tom picked up the garment, 'and her shoes are in the hall. That noise we heard on our last visit, you know as well as I do that a pine marten scratches and rummages for food and shelter and doesn't walk about making a noise like heavy footsteps.' As Tom finished speaking, Tessa sauntered into the room.

'Ah! Thank goodness you're safe!' Tom exclaimed.

'I'm sorry I hid from you when you were last here. I didn't know whether Ben was with you.'

'I'll make us a cup of tea,' Silas said. 'I can see you've got some explaining to do to the policeman, Tessa.'

'Why are you hiding? Everyone is worried to death about you.'

'I had to hide. Ben is going to kill me. I'm frightened.'

'How do you know that?'

'He threatened that unless I did what he asked, he'd kill me; just like Lizzie. Where's Donald?'

'Donald has been arrested by the Staffordshire police.'

'Why?'

'For murdering you and Lizzie.'

'What! The local coppers are stupid.' Silas brought cups of tea.

'You and I know that but, in the circumstances, you need to come with me to Stafford. Your presence will make sure he's released.' Tom's phone interrupted him.

'Yes, gov.' Tom listened before replying. 'Ah! That's good. I'll get there straight away. In connection with his charge, I've found Tessa Jackson, so she'll be coming with me to county headquarters. It looks like we'll be back at the Yard tomorrow after all.'

'Right, Tessa, my guvnor has arranged Donald's bail, but I'll need you to come with me to refute and disprove the charge of your murder.'

'Yes, of course, stupid police. How ridiculous the Superintendent is going to appear when I present myself at their headquarters.'

'It's laughable, Tessa.' Tom added.

Tessa laughed. 'Imagine when I tell them, oh, here I am Mr Plod, Mr policeman. I'm the woman who has been murdered by the man you are holding, accused of murdering me. I think you'd better release him before he murders anyone else. I wonder what people would say if this ridiculous situation found its way into the local newspapers?'

Thirty-six

'Hello, my name is Detective Inspector Tom Cropper from the Metropolitan Police. I'd be grateful if you would let Sir Bartholomew Evans know that I'm here, please?' The receptionist spoke into her uncomfortable looking headphones and mouthpiece, that perched untidily upon her head.

'Yes, sir, right away.' She turned back to Tom.

'He's sending a constable to escort you to his room. Would you take a seat for a moment, please?' Tom and Tessa sat down in the plush waiting room surrounded by an abundance of tropical palms and ferns.

Outside the waiting room window, the dog handling unit put Alsatian police dogs through their paces, walking them through hoops of fire and running up and down balancing see-saws. Tessa moved closer to the window to get a better view. 'Arrgh!' She suddenly screamed. A fierce looking dog with saliva running from its mouth ran into the glass as if trying to get at her. Blood and saliva ran down the outside of the window.

'I wouldn't get too close if I were you?' a voice shouted. It was the constable who came to escort them. 'The handlers train them to be fierce like that, so they react with menace to anyone who would threaten them or their handlers.'

'Nasty dogs!' Tessa commented.

'Inspector Cropper and Miss Tessa Jackson,' the constable announced to Sir Bartholomew as he beckoned them to enter his chief's office. Sir Bart stood and welcomed them.

'You know Superintendent Naismith, of course,' he said. Tom noticed Roger didn't stand or offer a greeting, so Tom ignored him.

'I've had a telephone call from your Superintendent Croaker from Scotland Yard. He's *demanded* that I release Sergeant Lawrence to you. I don't emphasise that word too lightly. Frankly, I don't appreciate being spoken to in the manner that Superintendent Jack Croaker did to me. However, in the circumstances, I bow to the seniority of The Metropolitan Police in this matter.'

'I have to tell you, Sir Bartholomew, that I too resent the action of your deputy against a detective sergeant of Scotland Yard. There is no evidence for justifying his actions. I have with me Miss Tessa

Jackson, who Donald was accused of murdering. This is laughable in any police force in any part of the country and in any age where police forces have operated. If you consider the behaviour of your deputy has enhanced the reputation of Staffordshire county police, then you are to be pitied...'

'... That's enough, inspector...'

Tom rose from his seat. 'Where can I collect my colleague from? I don't wish to stay here a moment longer than necessary.'

'I was hoping we could have a conversation regarding the murder of Lizzie Cartwright and collaborate?' Sir Bartholomew asked.

'Over the past few days, Sergeant Lawrence and I have investigated this case and have unearthed substantial amounts of pertinent information pointing to the culprit. My superintendent has informed you this matter is now also the edict of The Metropolitan Police. Whether we are to collaborate our facts with you will be a matter for my superior and not me. So, what we have discovered stays with me for the time being. Good day to you, chief constable.'

Sir Bartholomew asked his constable to escort Tom to collect Donald.

'Thank goodness you've come for me, Tom,' Donald exhaled. 'That Roger Naismith is a clown. He said he was going to find evidence to put me away for murder. How can somebody be so stupid and be in the position of deputy chief constable?'

'I think it points to the weak leadership of the entire force.' Tom concluded. Donald turned to Tessa.

'I'm so pleased to see you.' They hugged. 'We were all worried about you.'

As they walked back to the car, Donald asked what she was going to do?

'Please drop me back at my Uncle Silas's cottage. If I return to The Red Lion, I know Ben will find me.'

'Why did you befriend him in the first place?' Donald asked.

'He turned up at the hotel. He's very charming and persuasive and extremely handsome. I was flattered that he wanted to go out with me. I asked him straight out what happened with Lizzie. He assured me he had nothing to do with her death. He said he was devastated. I remember what Lizzie told me about him, how passionate and loving he was. It was fun to begin with, but he soon became violent. He wanted me to take part in some sort of devil worship ritual and go to an orgy with him. I refused, of course. I like a good time, but that's taking things too far. Then he threatened me. He said I'd end up like the other girls, with my throat cut. I was terrified. That's when I came to Uncle Silas.'

'Okay. We have to return to London, so please keep your mobile phone turned on so we can keep in contact.' They exchanged numbers while Tom drove back to Upper Slaughter. 'What's especially important is that if you see Ben, or know where he is, you must let me know.'

Thirty-seven

'Oh, Donald, thank goodness you're back home.' Janet hugged him as he joined her at their flat.

'I'm glad too, that Superintendent Naismith is so stupid…'

'… and it looks as if he intends to implicate you in Lizzie's murder…'

'… and Tessa's, but she's fine and hiding at her uncle's house, so Ben can't find her.'

Donald explained all that he and Tom had been doing in Staffordshire and showed her the Strange family tree.

'Oh, this is interesting, darling. See here, there's a Ben Strange born in 1962. I wonder if this is the same Ben that we saw at *The Crucified Abbot*?'

'It has to be. It certainly can't be the Ben that died in a fire in 1866. He's hiding somewhere, and he's a lot of explaining to do, preferably under interrogation when he's arrested for Lizzie's murder.'

'Well, before we can return to that, we have some busy days ahead of us at the Met. The gov has been coordinating the imminent sting on the massive drugs cartel in East London. Here's the report he's prepared on how the operation should go.' Janet passed him a file bearing the Metropolitan Police logo, stamped as confidential and only for detective officers' attention.

'Wow! This looks comprehensive.'

'Yes, it is. It details who we are going after and who is carrying out each raid.'

'Where are we?'

'I'm going for Colin Harmsworth at the Dagenham Health Clinic. I want to see his face when I clap the handcuffs on his wrists. After the ignominy he subjected me to, I'll enjoy watching him squirm for a change.'

'I hope you'll have some back-up with you…?'

'… It's all detailed in the file. I have two uniformed constables from the fraud office, Adrian Jones, and Morris Hope. We'll be travelling with Lucy in a black Maria. She's calling in on Reg Stainbrook at the bike shop first before we go on to the health centre.'

Donald opened the file and read. Janet brought him a glass of rioja.

'Oh, I see I'm going to Tilbury docks with Tom and a few squaddies from the riot team. Oh, and some River Police Authority guys. This should be interesting watching the Esmerelda from Columbia berth in the Thames bringing special bananas.'

'Remind me where the gov is going?'

Donald put his glass down and thumbed through the pages. 'He's off to Romford market with three riot regulars to catch up with the boss of the cartel, Jake Turner.' He continued reading through the file. 'I never realised there were so many contacts identified…'

'Lucy and I discovered a few…'

'The boss has even got two constables keeping tabs on the taxi drivers, Jack Weston and Michael Rennie. I bet they get to see quite a lot of the city.'

'Have you read about the cosmetic seller, Amanda Samuels…?'

Donald flipped the pages to where she received a mention. 'Oh yes, that should be an interesting arrest…' he laughed. 'Detective Christine Walters is having some cosmetics delivered to her home in Battersea. I'd love to be a fly on the wall and watch Amanda's reaction as she gets a pair of handcuffs in return for delivering some bath salts?'

'Have you read what the gov has assigned to Sergeant Jimmy Groves…?'

'… Hang on. Oh, yes, following the ambulance driver, Brian Daley. He's going to be arrested when he returns to his home in Piddock Mews, Dagenham, and then his flat will be searched.'

Janet took another drink of wine and added, 'the gov has certainly been comprehensive in this sting. He wants the arrests to take place simultaneously so that each person won't warn their immediate contact. If you read further, you'll see several other cogs in the network. Lesser minions who act as go-betweens on a smaller scale…'

'… it's these types of people who perpetuate the whole insidious business, though. These minions are as guilty as the boss, Jake Turner.'

'The sting is set for 14:00 tomorrow afternoon, but first thing tomorrow morning Lucy and I have been assigned to another sting. We are scheduled to attend a funeral…'

'… oh, is it anybody I know?'

'I don't think so, Donald. It's a Mrs Emilia Follows, an eighty-one-year-old woman from Beckenham. The firm of funeral directors from Lewisham, JC Manglers, and Associates have the funeral scheduled for 10:30 in the morning. Lucy and I will mingle with the mourners to nab not only the funeral officials but also the priest that'll be carrying out the service…'

'… what will you do, show your warrant cards as everyone sings *Abide with Me*…?'

'… there's no need to be so flippant about it. It's going to take some delicate handling.'

'… sorry!'

'We've been tipped off the funeral company transport drugs and money in coffins, whether or not they are holding bodies. What we don't know is who the recipients are. We know that the priests at Saint Cuthbert's in Lewisham receive envelopes, but do they pass drugs on as well? Also, we'll follow the hearse and the mourners to Lewisham's crematorium. We suspect that prior to the coffin being placed in the crematoria chamber, the staff open the coffin and take out the goods and the money. We're not aware that the coffin is opened at any other location en route.'

'This sounds intriguing and ghoulish.'

'It can't be any worse than the Church of Secular Saints case, can it?'

'Are there any more receivers or peddlers?'

'The only other one I'm aware of is Constable Harvey Dewsnap in the traffic division. He's been under suspicion for a long time for being on the take. Harvey is due to receive a takeaway pizza at 17:00 this evening at his home in Bromley. He regularly has pizzas delivered from a small company on the town's High Street. It's proved puzzling in the traffic division why, despite having vans and motorcycles parked on double yellow lines, the company never receives traffic violations….'

'… don't tell me their pizza boxes contain more than tomato and olives…?'

'Yeah, for the right price their pizza boxes contain extra additives.'

'So, both Constable Dewsnap and the pizza delivery boy will receive a surprise.'

'Hopefully, and the major premises on the High Street.'

Thirty-eight

Donald and Tom sat in an unmarked, black, Ford Transit police van with twelve other officers from the riot squad. Parked on the dockside away from other vehicular traffic, they peered through the darkened windows at the depressing, rain-soaked vista of Tilbury's commercial port. It was 08:30 am, and they awaited the Esmerelda container ship, from Columbia due to dock within thirty minutes. Sergeant Williams of the riot squad pressed the short-wave radio receiver to his ear and listened. 'The ship has passed under the Queen Elizabeth Bridge at Dartford,' he barked to his companions, 'in about another ten minutes it will edge onto the dockside.'

Donald looked anxiously at Tom as he checked his firearm pistol was fully loaded and ready to fire. 'You'd better check your gun too, Donald,' he said.

'Can I confess something?' Donald whispered.

'What is it…?'

'… apart from in the practice range, I've never fired a gun in anger. The thought of actually killing someone with it horrifies me…'

Sergeant Williams, sitting behind Donald and Tom, listened to the exchange and noticed Donald's nervousness.

'… Don't worry about it, son. To be honest, my colleagues and I would prefer that you two detectives didn't get involved in the live fire, anyway.'

Tom responded. 'I understand that, sergeant, but I'm sure you appreciate we have to protect ourselves.'

'Of course you do but, with respect, inspector, our riot procedures work better without hindrance from untrained officers.'

'Point taken, sergeant, we'll do our best to stay out of the rough stuff.'

'Good man,' the sergeant said.

The officers looked out on the dreary scene as they waited and kept checking their watches.

Tilbury dock was a hive of activity. Six dockers clad in bright yellow waterproof overalls awaited the Esmeralda. Their jobs entailed tying up the mooring ropes that would be thrown from the ship onto the dockside's cast-iron capstans. Donald looked through the side window at the myriad of stacked crates and cargo containers to be loaded on board by the portable overhead gantry cranes. Cars and lorries crisscrossed along the concrete roadway that extended for hundreds of yards down the port.

Further along, Donald could see other ships being loaded and vehicles gliding on the flyovers boarding the ferries. His concerns about being involved in a major police raid in such a busy public environment were allayed. He saw other police officers cordon off the immediate area with blue and white tape where they were parked. The inside windows of the van were steaming up. He opened the nearest sliding glass. Cold air and raindrops immediately blew into the interior and he breathed the crisp, salty air. The clamour of the marine environment recharged everyone's nervous anticipation. This heightened further when they heard Esmerelda's siren announcing its arrival. They looked in awe as the massive 45,000-tonne container ship slowly edged closer to the green, algae-stained dockside. The onshore breeze discharged blackish diesel smoke from the two funnels.

'Are we ready, everyone?' Sergeant Williams primed his team. 'You all know what to do. To recap, John, and Colin, you and your men, take the bow gangplank and secure it. Derek and James, your job is to storm the central entrance. Albert and I will take the stern and make our way to the bridge. Brian and Richard, your task is to ensure that nothing, that means personnel or goods, gets moved off the ship. Inspector Cropper and you, sergeant, can move onto the ship once we have it safe. We are all tuned in to frequency code 316 on our short-wave radios, so I want to know from anyone who has a problem as soon as it happens. For any of the ship's crew that jumps ship, be assured that our pals from the Thames River Police are waiting further down the docks. They'll be watching and ready to apprehend any escapees.'

Everyone nodded their approval and understanding of the sergeant's commands.

Donald eyed the comprehensive body protective equipment the riot squad officers wore. He felt reassured with the bulletproof vests that he and Tom wore at the insistence of Sergeant Williams.

'Here come the mooring rope leaders,' the sergeant commented. They watched the dockside workers pull the lightweight ropes until they reached the main, thick, plaid, spun nylon cables that they looped onto the massive cast-iron capstans. The waiting officers listened to the dockers yell into their radios that the mooring cables were locked. The ship's electric motors took effect, pulling on the tensioned cables drawing the vessel closer to the harbour wall. Sensors in the harbour side's compressed air fenders automatically stopped the ship's capstan motors when the required stress in the cables had been accomplished. The ship had docked. The instant the three gangplanks were slid onto the dockside, the police operation began. Donald and Tom watched in admiration as the riot squad quickly and quietly proceeded to their respective tasks. After five minutes had elapsed, Tom's radio burst into life with a faint crackling before a clear voice came through.

'Ok, inspector, we have the bridge secured. Come aboard now. Out!' Sergeant Williams's call was abrupt and efficient.

'Come on, Donald, let's have a gander at what's on this ship.'

They picked their way along a maze of corridors, metal stairways, and sealed doors, following the signs for the bridge on the eighth deck.

'Here's the cargo manifest, inspector,' said Sergeant Williams.

'Christ almighty!' exclaimed Donald. 'What's happened here?' He followed a trail of blood to two ships officers sitting on the floor, holding bloodied towels to their faces. Their white shirts were spattered red.

'Oh them!' The sergeant replied. 'That's what they get for trying to resist the riot squad,' he hissed down at the wounded men. 'Here's what they brandished at us,' he beckoned for Donald to examine the firearms. 'Two Kalashnikov K157 automatic repeating short-barrelled rifles; two of the deadliest guns in the world. All credit to my men for quickly putting them out of action.'

'*Malditos cerdos Ingleses*,' one of the wounded men shouted.

'If you want to say something, buddy, speak English, not that Spanish-Columbian crap,' Sergeant Williams shouted back.

'He said you are fucking English peegs,' the other officer mumbled as he dabbed his stiff, bloodied moustache with a handkerchief.

'Oh, I see, and who are you?'

'My name is Jose Ramires, I am the Capitán of the Esmeralda. You're no better than pirates, illegally boarding my vessel...'

'... well, take up your grievance with the Director of Public Prosecutions. I'm not sure he'll have much sympathy for you, especially when we show him what you have packaged in your hold.'

'Where are your men now, sergeant?' asked Donald.

'Down in the cargo hold with the nineteen crew they've rounded up...'

'... bloody hell!' exclaimed Tom. 'Examine this manifest, fifteen thousand tonnes of bananas and five thousand tonnes of pineapples.' He flipped the pages on the clipboard.

'That's a lot of fruit salad,' quipped Donald.

Sergeant Williams turned to one of his officers. 'David, keep an eye on these two reprobates while I go with the detectives down to the cargo hold. You have my permission to restrain them if they decide to cut up rough.' He directed his last sentence menacingly towards the two Columbian men sitting on the floor.

'Hi, sergeant,' one of the riot squad constables named Stephen greeted his superior. 'As you can see, we've cut open this first crate to verify what's inside.' He pointed to a pallet loaded with bananas wrapped in clingfilm.

Tom and Donald looked around the cargo hold at the surly looking Columbian crew held at gunpoint by other squad members. Sergeant Williams opened his pocket-knife and cut three bananas from the first bunch that fell from the crate. He passed two to Tom. He parted them and gave one to Donald. 'Go on, Donald, try it?'

Donald carefully peeled the banana and eyed the flesh suspiciously. 'It looks kosher to me, gov?' he questioned. He smelled the ripe flesh and took a tentative bite. 'Wow! It's delicious, go on, gov, you try one.'

Tom took a bite and agreed with Donald. Sergeant Williams also ate his banana and exclaimed. 'These outer ones are bound to be kosher. It's the hidden ones that will contain heroin.' He chomped the succulent flesh before turning to the constable.

'Stephen, dislodge a few more hands of bananas to get inside the crate.' The constable pulled out a few large bunches of the fruit before exclaiming, 'Gov, these inner bananas are all separated, not still attached to a complete bunch like the outer ones. They're packed tightly, one on top of the other.' He passed one to the sergeant.

Sergeant Williams carefully peeled the banana as Tom and Donald gathered more closely.

'Here we are, chaps!' the sergeant exclaimed. 'This is full of heroin.'

Donald eyed the white powder, carefully sealed in cellophane packed inside the banana in place of the soft flesh.

Tom held open the banana, 'Here, Donald, take a photo of this while I hold it.'

'My guess is every crate on this boat will contain the same. The natural outer fruit conceals the real cargo, that of tonnes of heroin and cocaine.' Sergeant Williams eyed the hundreds of crates that stretched down the entire length of the cargo hold, stacked from the deck up to the ceiling.

Thirty-nine

Simultaneously, as Donald was chomping on another banana on the Esmerelda, his wife, Janet, and ex-fiancée, Lucy, sauntered together up the ten steps into Saint Cuthbert's Church, Lewisham. Their seamed, black tights coordinated with the black skirts and coats they wore to attend Mrs Emilia Follows' funeral. They, along with other mourners, paused before entering the thirteenth century church. They turned to watch the gleaming, black limousine hearse with JC Manglers and Associates, Funeral Directors, emblazoned along the side of the vehicle, pull slowly to a halt behind them. In the old clock tower seventy feet above them, the Victorian clock, despite being covered in several layers of pigeon droppings, clanged a single chime. It was 10:30. Four perpetually glum-faced funeral operatives carried the coffin bearing the eighty-one-year-old deceased woman from Beckenham on their shoulders up the steps. Suitably attired in a black top hat and starched, upturned, white collar, the Maître d of the undertakers, placed his hand on the back of the coffin. This was to prevent the coffin from sliding backwards. He synchronised his steps to match those of his subordinates.

As she sat on the uncomfortable, austere pews, Janet's nose scrunched in reaction to the old church's unpleasant fusty air. Despite the procession bearing the pine coffin passing where she sat, her attention focussed upon the bearded vicar standing in front of the altar. She held her hand to her mouth and spoke quietly to Lucy. 'That's him, Lucy, Father O'Flaherty.' Lucy's attention diverted from the coffin that now rested on the bier before the altar. 'He's one of the church officials who reputedly takes drugs.' Janet assured her.

Lucy also covered her mouth and replied softly, 'He looks a right weirdo, a throwback to the '60s with his long beard and permed hair. I can imagine him taking a quick spliff as he lounges in his vestry after giving a sermon on piety and righteous living, can't you? Hypocrites the lot of them.'

The service ended and with a bowed head, Father O'Flaherty followed the coffin as it was borne back down the aisle. Janet and Lucy followed closely behind the priest. The harsh, metallic sound of the church door's bolts being opened contrasted with the wind organ playing soft, sympathetic music. Everyone's eyes narrowed as they left; they walked out into the bright sunshine leaving behind the dimness of the church. Janet and Lucy stood to one side and watched Father O'Flaherty shake hands with the congregation as he bade them goodbye. John Mangler, the Maître d of the undertakers, was the last to leave the church. Janet watched closely at his deliberate handshake with Father O'Flaherty. He surreptitiously placed a brown envelope in the priest's hand, which he then concealed by letting the long sleeves of his white surplice extend beyond his grasp. Barely any eye contact was made between the two. It suggested to Janet that the act of passing goods and money between them was an everyday occurrence. Janet reached for her radio and spoke quietly. She looked across the street to where Constable Jones stood watching.

'Constable Jones, Detective Barnes and I will accompany the funeral cortege to the crematorium. I've seen the boss of the undertakers pass an envelope to Father O'Flaherty. I want you and Constable Hope to come into the church and see what he has received. I suspect it's drugs. If it is, arrest him and then come to the crematorium where I expect more detentions will take place.'

At Lewisham crematorium, Janet and Lucy waited until the end of the service. They stepped inside the curtains that had been drawn in front of the coffin. They noticed a click and a slight whirring noise as the coffin started rolling forward on the conveyor belt. Janet held Lucy back as voices came up ahead. They watched the coffin go through some more draped curtains. 'Listen!' Janet said.

A deep, rough voice sounded. 'Yep! This is it, Fred! The nameplate says Emilia Follows. That's the stiff from Manglers, isn't it?'

'Right, bring her through then, Jerry. We'll examine the coffin before putting her into the crematoria.'

Janet peered carefully around the curtains and watched Fred and Jerry wheel a bier holding Emilia's coffin into a room that resembled a workshop.

'Pass us that electric screwdriver, Jerry.' Fred uttered.

Janet held her radio phone close to her mouth and whispered. 'PC Jones, have you reached the crematorium yet?'

'Yes, ma'am, I'm right outside. PC Hope is in the Maria with Father O'Flaherty.'

'Good man! Detective Barnes and I are about to make an arrest. Please keep on standby.'

'Will do!'

'Janet, they've taken the lid off the coffin...' Lucy whispered.

'… and there's the evidence, six brown envelopes. Come on, kiddo!'

'Gotcha! You're both under arrest. We're police detectives from New Scotland Yard…'

'… what…'! Fred grasped the envelopes and tried to avoid arrest by dashing towards the rear door. Unfortunately, where they had propped the coffin lid barred his exit. He kicked at the cover, trying to move it aside. It slipped down the wall and took Fred's legs from under him. He fell prostrate on top of the lid as it clattered to the tiled, ceramic floor. The envelopes dispersed in the melee and landed on the floor. Lucy pounced on him, kneeing him in his groin and pulling his arms behind him. As he groaned from the sickening pain and gasping for breath, Lucy expertly clasped handcuffs on both wrists.

Jerry, seeing the plight of his colleague, held his arms up in surrender. 'Put your hands behind your back.' Janet quickly fixed handcuffs to his wrists and reached for her telephone. 'PC Jones, get in here quick, we're in the rear room.'

'What the dickens is going on here?' yelled an elderly, balding man who rushed into the room.

'Who are you?' Janet shouted.

'I'm Michael Berryman, the manager here. Who are you? Why is this coffin open?'

'We are police detectives from the Metropolitan Police. We're arresting your colleagues on suspicion of dealing in illegal drugs.'

Behind the incredulous manager, PC Jones appeared, flushed and in a hurry. 'Are you both alright, ma'am?'

'Here's two more for your collection, constable.'

'What's going on, Fred, Jerry?' Michael asked. His subordinates stayed silent as PC Jones pushed the two men past their superior. They eyed with unease the sight of the deceased Emilia Follows. She looked serenely unconcerned at the drama unfolding around her.

'Are you connected with this?' Lucy asked.

'With what…?'

'… This!' Lucy tore the flap from one envelope and showed him the packet stuffed with smaller cellophane parcels full of white powdered heroin.

'This has nothing to do with me, and I've totally unaware of what's been going on. You'll pardon me saying so, detective, but this is a crematorium. Regarding the deceased woman on display, I'm going to replace the coffin lid. We have another funeral due soon, and I have to get prepared…'

'… Alright, that's all for now, but I'll need you to make a statement at Scotland Yard. A colleague will contact you to make the arrangements.' Janet watched as Mr Berryman fixed the coffin lid over Emilia Follows. Lucy collected the remaining envelopes from the floor.

Janet turned and looked at the arrested men in the police Maria, as two uniformed constables secured their handcuffs to adjacent vertical poles where they sat.

'What a sorry sight you lot are!' she exclaimed.

Lucy was in the driving seat and started the engine. 'Dagenham, here we come.'

Forty

'Here we are, Stainbrook's bike shop,' Lucy said as she pulled to a halt.

'Can you manage this one by yourself, kiddo?'

'No problem, Janet. I won't be too long.'

Lucy slammed the door of the Maria, straightened her crumpled overcoat, and entered Reg Stainbrook's bicycle repair shop.

Automatically reacting to the clanging doorbell, Reg appeared behind his cluttered counter.

'Hello, Linda, how nice to see you again. Didn't you get your stuff from Amanda Samuels, together with your cosmetics? I told her where…'

'… Reg Stainbrook, I'm arresting you on the charge of dealing in illegal drugs.' Lucy held up her warrant identity card. 'My real name is Detective Constable Lucy Barnes. You do not have to say anything, but it may harm your defence if you do not mention when questioned something which you later rely on in court. Anything you say may be given in evidence.'

'Esme! Esme!' Reg shouted.

From the interior of the Reg's backroom, Lucy listened to his wife's indistinct voice coming from the back room. 'Bloody hell, Reg, what do you want now, I've only just got the hoover out…'

'… sod the hoovering, Esme. You'd better come quick, I'm being arrested.'

In a bluster, with loose hair hanging over her eyes, Esme charged into the shop.

'What do you mean, arrested…?'

'… I'm arresting your husband, Mrs Stainbrook, for dealing in illegal drugs.' She turned to Reg. 'Come here and hold your hands behind your back.' Lucy clasped handcuffs on his wrists as he looked forlornly to his wife.

'Make sure you are okay, Esme, and look after the business. Give our George a ring to come and help in the shop.' he called as Lucy led him away.

From the black Maria, Lucy called her boss in the fraud squad. 'Gov, can you send two officers to Reg Stainbrook's bicycle shop, straight away? There are several boxes full of illegal drugs on his premises that are pertinent evidence and will need to be collected.'

Forty-one

Elaine Brindley, the receptionist at the Dagenham Road Health Centre, pressed her index finger on the intercom machine. 'I have a Miss June Landy here at reception, Colin. She said you'd told her before that she didn't need to book an appointment to see you?'

Colin Harmsworth momentarily looked to the ceiling and scratched his head before remembering who June Landy was. 'Oh yes, Jenny, send her down, please,' he replied with added gusto, recalling their previous encounter in his secret room. Colin unlocked a drawer in a tall filing cabinet, pulled out a brown envelope and placed it on his desk as a knock sounded on his office door. 'Come,' he shouted. Janet entered and immediately smiled at him.

'June,' he said as he greeted her enthusiastically, 'how lovely to see you again. You appear very sombre, have you been to a funeral?' he joked but stopped when Janet told him she had. 'Oh, I'm sorry, but I've got a little something ready for you, as I promised. It will put a glow on your cheeks again. Would you like a cup of tea or something stronger…?' Before Janet could answer, his telephone rang. 'Blast! Excuse me, June, I'll answer the damned thing first before we get down to business.' He beckoned for her to sit down.

From the other side of his desk, Janet watched and listened to him giving an opinion on the electrical circuit problem in a Doctor Harris's consulting room. 'You should know how these new diodes work, Claude. All you need to do is tweak the resistors ...' Colin then listened to his subordinate speak. Janet could faintly hear complicated technical details being described by Claude. Colin covered the mouthpiece with his hand, smiled at Janet and ceased listening. 'You are lovely today, June, black suits you. I won't be a moment… Yes, yes, Claude. Dammit, do I have to come and show you how it works?' Janet returned his smile and waited for him to finish, mentally rehearsing the standard arrest caution she would soon be explaining.

'Alright, hang on, Claude, I'll be there in a jiffy.' He replaced the receiver. 'I'm sorry about this, June. Make yourself at home, I'll be back in two minutes.' Before Janet could react, he left his room, leaving her looking around the empty office. She noticed the drawer on the filing cabinet that Colin had left open. Her interest was aroused, seeing it was full of large, brown envelopes stuffed untidily in a haphazard fashion bulging down the side of the metal drawer slides. She felt one of the soft, pliable envelopes and carefully slid her fingernail along the gummed edge. Janet wasn't surprised to see it was full of smaller, bright, plastic wrappers full of cocaine. She reached into her handbag and spoke into her radio.

'PC Jones, I'll need you to come in here when I've made the arrest. I've discovered where Harmsworth keeps the drugs. Keep alert, I'll get back to you.' The uniformed constable she'd left standing outside the health clinic walked backwards and forwards in front of the main reception windows, speaking into his radio.

Coincidentally, Colin walked through the reception area en route to Doctor Harris's room and straight away his senses recoiled seeing the uniformed policeman through the window, waiting outside. He stopped and strolled to the receptionist.

'Elaine, what's that copper doing outside?' She stopped peering at her computer screen and looked first to Colin and then to the window.

'Oh, I haven't got a clue, Colin. Do you think I should ask him?'

'No, it's alright, I'll have a word with him.'

Colin walked through the automatic opening sliding door and approached PC Jones. 'Hello, officer, I'm Colin Harmsworth, the chief maintenance officer here. Is there a problem?'

PC Jones thought quickly and replied nonchalantly, knowing that Janet was there to arrest him.

'No sir, no problem. We had reports that some hoodlums were seen near here harassing some old folks near the bus stop. I'm hanging about in case they show their faces again.'

Colin's guilty thoughts were at once calmed. He was always over-cautious where the authorities were concerned and quickly reasserted his usual confidence that the police's presence was nothing to do with his drug dealings. After sorting out the electrical problem, he returned to his office where he found Janet waiting patiently.

'Now, June, I'm sorry to have kept you waiting. I don't know about you, I'm dying for a smoke and getting to know you better; shall we go into my inner room?'

Janet smiled and answered, 'Why not? I'm looking forward to this.'

'So am I, darling. I've thought of nothing else since you were last here.' Colin pressed the switch that opened the door to his private room. 'After you, my darling.' He stood aside, beckoning Janet to enter. Once inside, he moved to her side and placed his arm around her shoulder. She reached down to her handbag to grasp her warrant card.

'We don't need any of those, do we? I assume you're getting a condom?' He was already undoing his belt and the flies on his trousers.

'No, not a condom. This is my warrant card. Mr Colin Harmsworth, I'm Detective Constable Lawrence of the metropolitan police.' She held the card before his bewildered eyes. 'I'm arresting you on the charge of actively soliciting illegal class I drugs. You do not have to say anything, but it may harm your defence if you do not mention when questioned something which you later rely on in court. Anything you say may be given in evidence.'

Colin's face twisted in an evil leer. 'You fucking bitch,' he seethed at her. Sputum frothed from the corners of his mouth. He violently pushed Janet backwards. Her knees buckled as she stumbled over a low coffee table and she fell to the floor, smashing the glass-topped table to pieces. Colin saw his opportunity to flee. He ran from the private room through his outer office and down the corridor. Despite blood running down her hand from having cut her wrist on the broken glass, Janet switched her radio to full volume.

'PC Jones, Harmsworth is doing a runner. Keep your eyes peeled and detain him as he leaves the health centre. I'll be along in a minute.' She entered the outer office and saw a first aid point. She reached for the handle of a cupboard hanging on the wall marked with a green cross and immediately spattered it with her blood. It was clear to Janet that the broken glass had cut a vein in her left wrist as she fell. Quickly rummaging through the three shelves, she found a broad pressure bandage pad and applied it to her wrist. With her right hand and gripping a reel of band-aid in her teeth, she wrapped several layers of the adhesive tape to secure the pad.

As PC Jones put his phone back in his shoulder harness, Colin Harmsworth dashed past him running hard and panting for breath. Within ten yards, the younger and more athletic constable caught up with Colin and pulled him to the ground. Exploiting his considerable weight, he knelt on his back, clasped his hands behind him, and applied handcuffs. Colin's cheeks and forehead scraped on the gravel, causing blood to ooze from the abrasions. PC Jones looked up as Janet dashed from the building.

'Outstanding work, constable.' Janet yelled as other curious people gathered around.

'Are you alright, ma'am, you're bleeding?' he asked, concerned to see the blood dripping from her bandaged arm. 'Please stand back everyone, this is a police operation.' PC Jones shouted.

'Yes, I'm ok, thank you, but as I'm at a health centre, I'll go back inside and get this cut treated properly. Take this miserable wretch back to the van. I've already cautioned him, so he's officially under arrest and in your charge for now. Secure him with the others.'

Colin Harmsworth was seated along with the other miscreants. Lucy had seen the confrontation and asked PC Jones where Janet was. After he explained, she dashed into the health centre and enquired about Janet.

'She's in the first door on the left, Doctor Harris's room,' the receptionist explained.

'I'll be okay, kiddo,' Janet told her as the doctor applied sutures across the deep cut on her wrist. 'You go ahead, I'll get a taxi.'

'No way, Janet, we're waiting for you. Had you forgotten? We've another call to make. Mangler's the undertakers in Albury Street, Lewisham.'

Doctor Harris spoke to Janet. 'There, you'll be fine, but you must be careful, no more rough stuff for you for a few days or the cut will open up again.'

'Thank you, doctor, I'll be fine…'

'… I'll make sure she is, doctor, thank you.' Lucy added.

'Oh, before you go, to make certain, here's a prescription for some blood clotting tablets. These are only in case you get compromised in your next encounter with Dagenham's criminal fraternity. You're not pregnant, are you? This…'

'… yes, she is pregnant, doctor,' Lucy interrupted before Janet could respond.

Doctor Harris looked at Janet. 'Only about two months.' Janet prompted.

'Ah, well! No coagulation medicine for you. You'll have to be careful, as I said.'

Forty-two

'It's in Corporation Street,' PC Jones replied to Lucy's question as she drove the Maria van through Lewisham.

'Thanks, Adrian, I thought it was on the west side of town…' Lucy mumbled.

'… What the fuck's going on, are you keeping us in this bleeding van all day…?' Colin Harmsworth shouted from the back of the van.

'… and I'm dying for a piss.' echoed Reg Stainbrook.

'Shut up, scum bags,' PC Hope shouted, sitting behind Lucy. 'You'll have to wet your pants.'

Fred and Jerry exchanged looks with Father O'Flaherty, who then hung his head looking to the van's floor.

'Here we are then, Manglers funeral directors!' Lucy exclaimed as she pulled the handbrake on the van. 'Janet, I'm taking charge of this. You must watch that wound. PC Jones and PC Hope, come with me and we'll round up a few more of this gang.'

Left by herself with the handcuffed men in the van, Janet looked back at them. Colin Harmsworth caught her eye. 'June, oh sorry, that's not your real name, is it…?'

'… Detective Constable Janet Lawrence is my name…'

'… Yes, well, Janet, you know this is all a mistake, I meant you no harm, you know. I was only trying to be friendly…'

'… Save your breath.' Janet cut him off abruptly.

John Mangler watched Lucy and the two uniformed policemen walk down the open workshop from his glass-sided office. Lucy's blonde hair fluttered in the brisk breeze from the air conditioning, her determined gait, taking her past several coffins, some empty, some openly displaying corpses.

'Adrian and Morris, both of you stay outside the office and keep an eye on the other blokes in the workshop. If they try to bolt, detain them. I'm seeing the boss man by myself,' Lucy barked assuredly to the two PCs.

Lucy entered the office and was immediately addressed by Mr Mangler. 'Oh, hello. I saw you in the service at Saint Cuthbert's earlier, didn't I…?'

'… John Mangler, I'm Detective Constable Lucy Barnes from the Metropolitan Police at New Scotland Yard…' She held up her warrant identity card.

'… what…'

'… I'm arresting you on the charge of dealing in illegal class 1 drugs. You do not have to say anything, but it may harm your defence if you do not mention when questioned something which you later rely on in court. Anything you say may be given in evidence.'

John Mangler calmly reached for his telephone.

'*Now*, Mr Mangler, you're under arrest.'

He dialled a number and spoke to Lucy before he shouted down the phone. 'I know my rights, darling. I'm ringing my solicitor… yes, Tim, it's John here. I'm being arrested…'

'… put the phone down…!' Lucy yapped.

'… can you hear that, Tim? Some blonde bitch from Scotland Yard is in my office ordering me about…'

'Adrian, get in here.' Lucy shouted towards PC Jones as he stood outside the office.

'Yes, ma'am.' PC Jones answered as he burst through the door.

'Take this man away, Adrian. Handcuff him and put him with the others.'

PC Jones took the phone from John's grasp and slammed it on the desk. 'Stand and put your arms behind your back, sir, please.'

'Like hell I will! You can't barge your way in here and…'

PC Jones's massive frame dwarfed that of the funeral director as he pulled his hands behind his back and applied the cuffs.

'… What's going on, John?' They were aware of a voice coming from the receiver as it lay on the desk.

'Tim, they've cuffed me and are taking me to Scotland Yard…' John shouted forlornly back to the phone as PC Jones frogmarched him across the office.

Lucy reached forward, replaced the receiver, and followed PC Jones. She spoke to PC Hope as he waited outside. 'Any movement from the others, Morris?'

'No, ma'am, there are three over there, watching what's happening. I heard a noise from the back, so I think there's another one as well.'

'Wait for a moment and then arrest all four. That will be the four pallbearers that came to the church. I'll make sure John Mangler is in the van okay and send Adrian back to help you.'

'Bloody hell!' PC Jones commented to PC Hope as he looked around the van as it sped through the city. 'We have ten suspects. I've never arrested so many before in one go.'

'Yes, we have Ade. Remember that sting at Tottenham football club last September. We had twelve drunken louts who had charged onto the pitch, thirteen if you count the wife of one of them, who kept hitting me with her brolly…'

'Oh, yes, I forgot about them.'

Lucy swung the steering wheel and manoeuvred the Maria van through the bustling London traffic. She smiled and looked across at Janet, nursing her cut wrist, holding it against her chest and supported by the seat belt. 'Are you alright, kiddo?'

'I'm fine, Lucy. This has been a good day, hasn't it? It's gone exactly as we hoped and planned it would.'

Forty-three

Superintendent Jack Croaker portrayed an ordinary shopper as he ambled through Romford open-air street market. He carried a plastic shopping bag and eyed the fresh produce on the market stalls with interest. He wore a light jacket over an open-necked shirt. Each Tuesday and Friday Marble Street and Porthaven Road were closed to through traffic. The thoroughfares were given over to market traders who set up their canvas-covered stalls to hold and display their wares. Jack was the focus of the police raid operation that was in the market to detain the central lynchpin and controller of the illegal drugs scene of East London. At various points throughout the market, four members of the drugs squad from Scotland Yard stationed themselves to help Jack, should he need it. They kept in constant touch by using their lapel phones. They too were in plain clothes and blended into the ambient background of the bustling market scene.

Since Janet had discovered that Jake Turner is the controller of the illegal drugs empire, other investigating officers from Scotland Yard had been watching him. They found he had four assistants who carried out the dirty work for him. The criminals put pressure on receivers of drugs who were tardy in their payments. They controlled the mules who distributed the drugs and used threats and violence to cement a smooth-running business. Jack and the other Scotland Yard officers ambling through the market had already verified that Jake's henchmen were also present. The plan was to arrest them at the same time as their boss.

Jack approached Jake Turner's stall in a steady saunter. He smiled a little at the painted business sign above his booth that proclaimed *Jake Turner of Romford. Importer of high-quality fruit and vegetables.* 'Yes, and we know what else you import, don't we?' Jack thought. He held back and waited his turn while Jake served other shoppers, eager to buy his plump bananas. He observed Jake's ebullient personality, vociferously promoting his product with rosy cheeks and a smiling, cheery manner.

'Get your bananas here, ladies, fifty pence a kilo, or twenty pence per pound in old money. Fresh bananas straight from the plantations of Columbia.' Jake shouted. He looked at one smart, attractive lady standing in front of his stall. 'Here, missus, I can tell you like a nice straight banana most evenings.' She blushed and sniggered at Jake's saucy suggestion and the unwarranted attention she was receiving. 'Here, missus, have a bite and try one.' Jake offered her the banana, so she bit off some flesh and chewed. 'See, I was right; ladies and gentlemen, see how much this nice young woman is enjoying my banana.' He winked at her, causing her to blush some more. 'Beautiful, isn't it, my lovely, and I've got a lot more where that came from.'

'Go on then, I'll have a pound's worth,' the woman shouted back. Jake turned to his wife, who was helping in his stall.

'A pound's worth for the young miss, please, Gladys, while I serve this gentleman. Yes sir, what can I get you?' Jake asked Jack.

'I'll take two kilos of bananas, please. How do you know they're from Columbia?' Jack asked.

'Because I pick them up directly from the ship at Tilbury docks, sir. That way I know they're always as fresh as they can be. Some bananas, sir…?' he shouted to a man standing behind Jack.

'They certainly appear genuinely nice. My junior colleague recommended I try one. He sampled one as it arrived on the Esmeralda.'

With no change in his cheery demeanour, Jake served Jack before turning to his wife and muttered. 'Gladys, I've got to go somewhere; I won't be long away. Carry on, and I'll see you later.'

Jake suspected he'd been rumbled. Anyone who knew about bananas on the Esmerelda also knew they held drugs. Jake thought quickly. His car was parked in Triumph Street that ran parallel to Porthaven Road. He dodged a few people who were mingling at the rear of his stall and turned a corner, barging straight into two drug squad officers. One held his chin in his massive grip while the other pinned Jake's arms behind him and applied some handcuffs. Jack appeared on the scene and spoke to him.

'Your bananas are very nice, Jake. I didn't get around to telling you that my colleague also found some that tasted very bitter, but I'm sure you'd know that those were the ones containing heroin. In case you're wondering about my assistant, he's a detective sergeant at Scotland Yard, and I am Superintendent Jack Croaker. Jake Turner, I'm arresting you on the charge of dealing in illegal class 1 drugs.' Jack read him the standard arrest clause. 'Get him into the Maria, gentlemen.'

Meanwhile, the other drug squad officers had apprehended Jake's unsuspecting associates without fuss or struggle.

Forty-four

At Scotland Yard, the incident room became raucous with busy police officers preparing charge sheets and assembling evidence connected with the largest illegal drug syndicate handled by the metropolitan police. The input from Detective Constables Janet Lawrence and Lucy Barnes were pivotal in compiling testimonies and support data. Superintendent Jack Croaker coordinated the complicated operation and recognised the excellent work of the two young detectives. He regularly held meetings with the commissioners of Scotland Yard. He took pleasure in commending his protégées to the hierarchical officers who sat in their plush offices overlooking the Thames. Janet and Lucy's work and accomplishments had far exceeded responsibilities associated with their lowly rank. Their promotion to the position of sergeant became a formality.

On a rare quiet afternoon in the incident room, Jack telephoned the fraud office and invited Lucy to join the other assembled officers. Donald sat quietly with a smile on his face, watching the team go about their work. Jack had previously briefed him on the upcoming promotion of their unsuspecting female colleagues. Everyone else thought the meeting's sole purpose was to receive an update on the drugs operation. Janet and Lucy helped Rosemary prepare and distribute mugs of tea to the enthusiastic team as Jack entered the room.

'Hi, everybody, I see you all have some tea.'

'Yours is on Tom's desk, gov.' Janet called.

'Thanks, Janet.' He picked up the mug and asked her to join him. 'Can you come here for a second, and you, Lucy?'

'Oh, haven't I put your sweetener in? I'm sorry,' Janet replied as she walked to the front with Lucy, both holding their own mugs of tea. Janet noticed she'd spilt some of her drink on the clean, white bandage covering her wrist.

'Are we in trouble, kiddo?' Lucy whispered to her.

'What's new?' she whispered back.

Jack was aware of Lucy's surreptitious comment. 'Yes, you are both in deep trouble,' he called loudly, so everyone could listen, while keeping a stern expression on his face.

Lucy and Janet looked at each other with a grimace. Tom looked back at Donald and saw him suppressing a smile. Donald nodded furtively to him, and at once realised what was about to happen. He turned around to the front to see the concerned stare on the women's faces. They felt conspicuous standing alongside Jack in full view of everybody.

'Ladies and gentlemen because Janet and Lucy have been pivotal throughout this recent drug operation, I've had to resort to bringing the chief commissioner of Scotland Yard here to have a word with them.' On a pre-arranged cue, the commissioner, resplendent in his black uniform bristling with gold epaulettes and silver trimmings, entered and stood beside Jack. 'Attention everybody, it's my pleasure to present the Chief Commissioner of the Metropolitan Police at Scotland Yard, Andrew Benn, OBE.' Janet involuntarily bit her lip and looked concerned across at Donald. Lucy too looked apprehensively at Donald, and behind their backs she reached for Janet's hand. With perspiring fingers, they gripped each other as the commissioner spoke.

'Superintendent Croaker has kept me informed about the drugs operation you have all been involved in. He has brought to my attention the conduct of the two officers standing in front of you.' Janet and Lucy fidgeted nervously.

'I can see they are completely unaware of why I am here.' The commissioner exchanged glances with them as Jack passed two stiff paper scrolls to him. 'Constable Janet Lawrence, here is one for you and another one for you, Constable Lucy Barnes.' He passed the manuscripts to them. 'Or should I now say, Detective Sergeant Janet Lawrence and Detective Sergeant Lucy Barnes. Congratulations to you both.' He smiled and shook their hands.

Janet and Lucy stared at each other open-mouthed before breaking into broad smiles. Donald and Tom whistled and shouted, while everyone else applauded and cheered. Jack kissed each new sergeant on their cheeks. 'Well done, both of you,' he added.

The commissioner held up his hand to quell the noise. 'It's been a pleasure for me to accept Superintendent Croaker's invitation to present the well-deserved promotions to these splendid young officers. They are a credit to the metropolitan police force in how they conduct themselves. It's come to my attention how, with no thought for their own safety, they have diligently applied themselves to apprehending the criminals who ply their disgusting trade on

London's streets.' He shook their hands and added his congratulations again.

He turned to Jack and spoke quietly. 'I'm off now, Superintendent. Please keep me informed how the rest of this operation progresses.' He turned to face the office. 'Good luck, everybody,' he called as the officers applauded.

As the commissioner left, the noise within the incident room increased as everyone crowded around Janet and Lucy to add their congratulations. Jack calmly walked to sit in his glass-sided office to watch the merriment of his officers. Flashing a broad grin, Donald approached Janet and Lucy, expecting a hug and a kiss. He saw the corner of Lucy's mouth dip in disappointment as he approached Janet first. 'You knew about this, didn't you?' his wife chided him with a laugh. He nodded before going to hug Lucy. Janet eyed them carefully before Tom diverted her attention by coming to give her a hug.

'Congratulations, sergeant,' Donald called loudly to Lucy before he held his face close to hers and whispered, 'We must celebrate.'

'Thank you, Donald,' she called out, before whispering, 'call me later.' Donald returned to Janet and hugged her again.

Jack's enjoyment in watching his subordinates celebrate was cut short when his telephone rang. The first sound he listened to when he picked up the receiver was a high-pitched woman's voice, panting for breath. 'Hello, hello, is that Scotland Yard…?' Before Jack could answer, the line disconnected. He looked at the earpiece and wondered who it was that had sounded so anxious. He took a slurp of tea and opened a file marked Colin Harmsworth, but the telephone rang again.

'Please can somebody hear me? I want to be put through to Scotland Yard?' Jack recognised it was the same caller, so he sputtered quickly.

'Yes, this is the Metropolitan Police, Superintendent Jack Croaker here. How can I help you?'

'Can I speak to Sergeant Donald Lawrence…?' The woman's voice started panting again.

'… hang on a moment,' Jack called into the phone before laying it on his desk. He knocked on the glass surrounding his office and waved his arm to attract attention. Tom was the first to notice Jack's gesture and by lip-reading understood what he wanted.

'Donald,' he shouted across the office. 'It's the gov, he wants you.' Donald looked across and saw Jack waving and pointing to the telephone. The peace in Jack's quiet office was suffocated by the din as Donald opened the door.

'It's a woman for you, Donald. She sounds very agitated,' Jack said as he passed him the phone.

'Hello, Sergeant Donald Lawrence…'

'… oh, thank God I've reached you, Donald. It's Tessa here. I lost your mobile number, so that's why I've rung the main number for Scotland yard…'

'… what's the matter, you sound very distressed; is everything okay?'

'… not really. You asked me to get in touch with you if I saw Ben Strange again. Well, I have…'

'… where? Stay away from him, Tessa....'

'… I'm trying to Donald. I'm frightened.'

Donald explained to Jack who he was speaking to, before resuming.

'Where have you seen him, Tessa?'

'He's walked past my uncle's house four times now. He's searching for me. I was watching from behind the curtains yesterday afternoon as he walked by. Then he turned and looked straight at the window as if he knew I was here…'

'Does he know Brooklands belongs to your uncle?'

'Not that I know of, but I suppose he could ask about, as you did.'

'Tessa, stay put. Make sure all the windows and doors are secure. I'll try to get to Staffordshire as quickly as I can.' He looked hopefully towards Jack, who nodded. 'My gov tells me that's okay. We need to talk to Ben Strange, anyway. He holds the key to everything that has happened. Hello, hello…' he looked to the telephone before replacing the receiver. 'The line's gone dead, gov.'

'Get to Staffordshire, Donald. Take Tom with you. See if you can find this Ben Strange and arrest him. There arc sufficient officers here to wrap up the paperwork involved in the drugs operation.'

'… is it okay if Janet comes along too, gov? She's been as much involved with this as I have. Discovering Ben will answer such a lot of questions that are still troubling her.'

'No problem. Watch out for her. The women involved in all of this seem to be very vulnerable. Donald, please get back in touch should you need more back-up. We could have more officers with you in a couple of hours.'

'Okay, thanks, gov.' Donald left Jack's office to find Janet. He found her chatting to Lucy.

'Who'd have thought it, kiddo, both of us are sergeants now,' Lucy spoke quietly to Janet as Donald sidled up to them.

'… and who knows where you'll be in ten years. You could be the new Chief Commissioner of Scotland Yard.' Donald offered. 'There's never been a woman commissioner as far as I'm aware.'

'Oh, yes! Why not? Then you could all look out.' Lucy laughed at him. He turned to Janet, making sure that Lucy could hear too.

'Janet, I've had a phone call from Tessa at Upper Slaughter. She's seen Ben …'

'… oh God! What with everything happening here, I'd forgotten all about *The Crucified Abbot*.' She held her hand to her mouth.

'The gov has asked Tom and me to find him and detain him. I suggested you come along too. I'm sure you'd find some peace of mind if you could see him in handcuffs.' Janet nodded.

'When…?'

'… we'll go first thing tomorrow morning. The gov also offered back-up should we need it,' He turned to Lucy. 'If we do need back-up, perhaps you could come too?' He turned back to Janet. 'You wouldn't mind that, darling, would you? Another feminine perspective on the unique events in Staffordshire would help you make sense of all this, Janet?'

Before Janet could answer Lucy stepped in. 'Well, if nothing else, it would make an agreeable change from busting filthy drugs gangs in the East End.'

'Yes, no problem, kiddo.' Janet answered. 'Perhaps another woman's opinion of Ben Strange would support my own?'

'Which is?' Lucy raised her eyebrow.

'I'll fill you in when we're alone. Donald already thinks I have a fixation on him.' Janet laughed and pecked his cheek as he looked peeved.

Lucy raised her eyebrows at him and left the office. Donald asked Rosemary to make reservations at The Red Lion and then went on to talk to Tom.

'We're not taking any chances this time, Donald. We go armed. Let's meet John Masters in the armoury and see what he recommends we take with us.'

Forty-five

Seated in the Ford Mondeo's back seat, Janet silently breathed a sigh of relief as the car pulled into the Red Lion's car park. From the driver's mirror, Donald saw her face relax, and he guessed what she'd been thinking. As they reached their overnight bags from the boot, he spoke to her. 'I know what you imagined as we reached here.' Tom moved ahead to register their arrival and collect the room keys.

'I can't help it, Donald. I was half expecting to see *The Crucified Abbot*. I'm already jittery at what we're going to discover on this jaunt.'

He held her shoulders and looked into her eyes. 'We're going to nail this Ben Strange for a start.'

She hesitated. '... I hope so, but even that will bring up many implications. I've been pregnant for nearly three months now and...'

'... don't even think about it. That's our baby you're carrying, Sergeant.' She held him tight, and they laughed.

'Mrs Downing, may I introduce my wife, Janet. She is also a sergeant at Scotland Yard.' Janet smiled as she greeted the hotel owner, seated in reception.

'Excuse me not getting up, Mrs Lawrence, my arthritis is playing me up somewhat terrible this morning.' Janet could see her arm crutches leaning against the counter.

'Oh, I'm sorry to hear that. I don't know how you run such a large hotel.'

'With difficulty, my dear. Of course, now Tessa doesn't turn up for work I've had to resort to a couple of locals to help.'

'Ah, yes, Mrs Downing. Tessa! Could I ask if anyone has been here asking for her? I'm thinking of Ben Strange, particularly?' Donald asked.

'Oh, him! Yes, he has, and he's becoming a nuisance. But I haven't seen him for the past two days...'

'Inquiring about Tessa?'

'Yes and pestering me, asking do I know where she might be.'

'You didn't tell him, did you?'

'Well, I don't know, do I?'

'Good.'

'He also upset old Ted...'

'Ted Baxter?' Janet asked.

'Yes, poor old Ted, he's nearly ninety-three, you know. I heard him sobbing out on the back patio one sunny afternoon last week. I hobbled around there to find him with his head in his hands.'

'That's unlike Ted.' Donald interjected as Tom came down the stairs from putting his bags in his room.

'Very unlike Ted. As you know he's the life and soul of Upper Slaughter, there's not much that disturbs him. Ben Strange had been pestering him to find out where Tessa is. I was unhappy when he told me Ben had threatened him with violence.'

'This man needs stopping.' Tom added. Mrs Downing nodded.

'Is Ted alright now?' Janet asked.

'I think so. He was here yesterday as normal with his son-in-law, drinking his usual tipple of Abbot cider.'

'I'll have a chat with him later.' Janet said.

'Well, you won't have long to wait, it's lunchtime now…'

'… yes, talking of lunch, could we eat, please?' Donald added, rubbing his hands together.

Immediately after lunch, Janet left Tom and Donald chatting at the dining table. At the same time, she proceeded for a stroll in the sunshine. At the rear of the hotel, Janet edged closer to the Abbot Ibáñez yew tree. Her flesh turned to goosebumps as she recalled seeing the murder of Lizzie Cartwright. Two cooing doves high in the top branches diverted her attention. Her senses shuddered as she ran her hands around the gnarled bark but looked across to the patio when a voice disturbed her reverie.

'That old tree is still giving you nightmares, is it, my dear?'

'Hello, Ted,' she called as she rushed over to him. 'It's so lovely to see you again.'

'Ah, my dear, it does my old bones the power o' good that you've come back to The Red Lion,' he wheezed as Janet gave him a firm hug and held him close. They sat down on the wooden slatted bench.

'What have you been doing with yourself…?' Her words were interrupted when a fresh-faced young man brought Ted a pint of cider.

'Here's your pint of Abbot, Mr Baxter,' he said as he carefully placed the glassful of amber coloured cider on the wrought iron table.

'Thank you, young Michael. While you're here can you fetch my nice young lady friend a pint as well?' Michael looked towards Janet as Ted took a huge slurp.

'Yes, please,' she said. 'These two drinks are on me. Can you put them on a slate for me? I've checked in, I'm Sergeant Janet Lawrence of the Metropolitan Police.'

'Hello, I'm Michael Thompson from the village. I'm helping Mrs Downing while she's short-staffed.' He returned to the bar.

'You're a sergeant now, then?' He wiped the white froth from his whiskers.

'Fancy you observing my change in rank, Ted. Yes, I've had a promotion.'

'I remember everything about you, my dear. You're the prettiest woman that's come to The Red Lion in many a year and a brilliant and capable woman by the sound of it, a fully fledged sergeant now.'

'Get off with you, flatterer.' She smiled, but straight away turned more serious. 'I hear from Mrs Downing that you had an upset the other day.'

Ted's demeanour changed, becoming sombre with a more resonant voice as he answered. 'Yes, my dear, that horrible man Ben Strange came here questioning me.' He'd reached for his glass again but replaced it on the table without taking a drink.

'What did he say to you that upset you so much?'

'He wanted to know where Tessa is. I kept trying and trying to tell him I didn't know, but…'

'… he threatened you, so Mrs Downing said.'

'Yes, he dragged a great big knife out of his back pocket. It had a serrated sharp-edged blade, and he held it against my throat. I thought my days sitting here on this bench taking my pleasure of the Abbot cider had ended, I did.' He pulled his handkerchief from his pocket and wiped away a tear. 'He said to me he understood I knew everything that occurred in the village and the wider area and that I knew where Tessa was.' Ted sobbed, and Janet put her arms around him.

'I'm sorry, my dear. When he pulled the blade back, I knew Ben was going to slit my throat, so I had to tell him…'

'… tell him what?'

'… that I knew the whereabouts of Tessa, where she was staying, of course.'

'You told him?'

'Yes, I had to. She's staying with her Uncle Silas, of course, at Brooklands Cottage.'

'What did he do then?'

'He laughed at me. I can stand being laughed at, my dear, but what he did then was unforgivable…'

'What did he do?' Janet was transfixed, wondering what Ted thought was so dreadful.

'Why, my dear? He picked up my glass of cider and tipped it upside down before my very eyes. Can you think of the spiteful thing he did to me? All that lovely cider being wasted over the floor of this crazy paved patio. Sacrilege, that was.'

Janet smiled and relaxed, but then jumped up at once at the realisation that Ben now knew where Tessa was. She dashed across the patio and back to the dining room.

Ted called after her. '… but my dear, you haven't finished your cider.' He looked longingly at the whole glass of the fizzing amber nectar. 'Ah well!' he thought. 'I'd better help the pretty young lady out and not let it go to waste.'

'Donald, Tom!' she called as she rushed into the dining room. They were finishing their cups of coffee. 'I've been talking to old Ted. When Ben was here last, he threatened him with a knife and made him confess where Tessa is staying…'

'… oh my God, Janet!' Donald exclaimed.

Tom jumped up. 'Come on, Donald, I hope we aren't too late?'

The car pulled up with a screech of the brakes outside Silas Jackson's cottage. As they walked down the moss-covered pathway, Tom immediately noticed that the front door was slightly ajar. He held Donald back with his one hand and with the other reached for his Glock handgun. John Masters, the chief armourer at Scotland Yard, had suggested the Glock. With its lightweight polymer frame and 10mm calibre, it was deadly at short range and easily manoeuvrable. Making use of the barrel of the gun, he carefully prodded the door open. He turned to Donald and put his finger to his lips, suggesting they were hushed and careful.

The house was silent. They tiptoed through the hall and peered around a massive vertical oak column into the lounge. Tom could see the window that looked down onto the garden and the flowing stream. He looked left, then right, before continuing further. Donald diverted to investigate a side bedroom. In the lounge, Tom noticed the dishevelled appearance of the room. Curtains were haphazardly drawn aside. Clothes were strewn about the floor, and a cold, uneaten dish of beans on toast remained on a tray by the fireside hearth. Flapping helplessly in a cold mug of tea, a blue-bottle fly spun around and around. He noticed a clicking noise and turned to see a vinyl disc was still going around on the player's turntable. He reached and turned the knob to off. As it stopped, he saw it was entitled 'Crying in the Chapel' by Elvis Presley. He started towards the window but turned abruptly when Donald shrieked.

'Tom! Tom! Oh, my God!' He dashed into the side bedroom and found Donald with his hand to his mouth, looking down at the floor. 'Sweet Jesus, Tom, it's Silas.'

Tom's face twisted with revulsion in unison with Donald's. Bright red arterial blood was still gently seeping from Silas's severed throat. His unseeing eyes stared upwards. Tom bent to feel for a pulse in his neck. There was none. 'He's gone,' he uttered through clenched teeth. 'His flesh is still warm, so I'd guess this has only happened within the last two hours.' Donald lifted his foot as he realised he was standing in Silas's blood, gently soaking into the bedroom carpet. Tom put his Glock in his pocket and exchanged it for his mobile phone. 'Gov, Tom here. There's already been a development here in Staffordshire. We've discovered Silas Jackson's body at his home. I'd say he's had his throat cut within the last two hours and there's no sign of his niece, Tessa… yes, gov… I understand, thanks, gov.' Tom closed the phone.

'Donald, Jack is sending three riot squad officers to help us. One of them is Lucy, so she can support Janet. In the meantime, I think we'll seal this place until forensics can do their job.'

'Do we need to inform our incompetent friends from the Staffordshire force…?'

'Unfortunately, I think we have to. It's on their patch, and we need their Scene of Crime officers and medical team to help with looking after poor old Silas. However, their presence won't prevent us from taking charge and searching for Ben and Tessa ourselves.'

'They could be anywhere.'

'Yes, they could, but we have a clue, don't we?'

'Do we?'

'In Jack's office, when you spoke on the phone with Tessa, didn't she say that she'd seen Ben walking past this cottage a few times…'

'… yes, well, what does that mean?'

'We know he frequented the Red Lion, where he spoke with Mrs Downing and threatened Ted.'

'Yes? Well?'

'Well, if he was walking past this cottage, where would he be going in the opposite direction from The Red Lion?' Donald pointed his finger towards Cannock Chase.

'Yes, towards The Chase. He has to be living somewhere in that direction.'

'Tom, Cannock Chase is fifty square miles of natural heathland and forests…'

'We already know from our last visit here that he's not living in a normal household as he doesn't appear on any register of electors…'

'Do you mean he's living rough…?'

'That's my best guess, Donald. Not rough exactly, but I'd proffer a guess that he has a trailer or caravan, or some other temporary shelter holed up somewhere well off the beaten track.'

'What about Tessa?'

'He's got her with him, and I'd suggest she's probably safe for now until he tires of her…'

'… I hardly think she's safe. Tom…'

'… when I said safe, I mean I don't think he'll do away with her yet, until…'

'… until he's raped her and such like…?'

'… unfortunately, yes, but we can't do anything about that right now.'

Forty-six

'I'm not taking any back-chat or arguments from either you, Sir Bartholomew, or you, Superintendent Naismith. I'm taking charge of this operation with Superintendent Jack Croaker's express authority. Although you both outrank me, I represent the highest police authority in the United Kingdom, which takes precedence over any lesser shire force. I know my Superintendent has previously given you official notice that this case is our jurisdiction now…'

'… this is highly irregular, Inspector Cropper…'

'… that's as may be, Sir Bartholomew, but I'm politely requesting your help. If that's not forthcoming, I'm serving you notice that I'll officially commandeer some of your junior officers to help in the search for Ben Strange and Tessa Jackson.'

Seated around the Red Lion's polished dining table, Janet and Donald watched with awe and respect how confidently Tom was dealing with the Staffordshire constabulary's high-ranking officers. Four other county constables sat in the hotel foyer, straining their ears to listen to what was going on in the adjoining room. They had accompanied Sir Bartholomew and Superintendent Naismith to Upper Slaughter after receiving Tom's telephone call.

'Superintendent, do you remember when you found Lizzie Cartwright's body at Castle Ring?'

'… I may have done,' he replied hesitatingly.

'Are you going to cooperate with us or not?' Responding to Tom's ultimatum, the arrogant senior officer looked towards his gov for approval and consensus. He nodded imperceptibly and reluctantly, with a grimace.

He turned back to Tom. 'Yes, I remember. It was an emotionally unpleasant experience for everyone in the county constabulary…'

'… all murders and discoveries of corpses are distasteful, superintendent, and I assure you we are experienced in dealing with such cases daily in the metropolitan force…'

'… that's your misfortune, Inspector.'

'… our misfortune maybe, but it qualifies us to provide understanding and clarity in dealing with such profound matters. We do so without emotionally finding them distasteful as you so amateurishly described murder and its aftermath.'

'Pick the bones out of that, you snobbish prick,' thought Donald, repressing a smirk.

'When you found Lizzie's body, you had the help of a local countryside ranger, I understand.'

'Yes, both the local and county councils have rangers who provide practical help in managing the myriad of issues that crop up over such a vast area of outstanding natural beauty. Why do you ask?'

'Because I want that same ranger to help us now. Can you contact him and ask him to come here, please?' Roger Naismith turned to his guvnor.

'Wasn't that Phil Chalmers from Brocton village?' he asked quietly.

'Yes, it was. Ask Constable Roberts. He's sitting in the foyer. He has his telephone number.' Sir Bartholomew turned to Tom. 'He only lives three miles away, so it shouldn't take him long to get here.'

While waiting for the ranger to join the meeting, discussions took place for the post-mortem on Silas Jackson's body and how his home was being examined and sealed as a crime scene.

'Incidentally, why do you wish The Chase ranger to be here?' Sir Bartholomew asked.

'I think Ben Strange is living on The Chase in a caravan or other vehicle. This Phil Chalmers, I'm assuming, is the best person to help us. We can't afford to waste time searching Cannock Chase on an ad hoc basis. He might pin down areas where such caravans or vehicles could be concealed.' The conversation was disturbed when a waitress brought pots of tea and sandwiches to the large table. Janet watched the young woman then take a similar tray into the foyer for the other constables.

'Hey, aren't you Linda Forbes?' she heard one constable say when she placed the tray on a low coffee table.

'Yes, I am. Who are you?'

'I'm Constable Mike Derry; I'm originally from Upper Slaughter. You obviously don't remember me, but we used to attend junior school together. Our parents were good friends.'

'Oh, my Lord, yes. I recognise you now. Your family moved to Stafford.'

'Watch him, Miss Forbes. Our Mike is a bit of a charmer on the quiet,' joked one of the other constables.

Mike waved his hand in a dismissive gesture before turning back to Linda. 'You know why we're here, don't you? Tessa Jackson has gone missing. You and she used to be friends, didn't you?'

'Yes, we were. We used to play together all the time, exploring The Chase...' After listening to this part of the conversation, Janet left the meeting and went into the foyer.

'Excuse me, I'm Detective Sergeant Janet Lawrence from Scotland Yard. Did I hear correctly that you used to be friends with Tessa Jackson?' Linda nodded timidly, slightly overawed at receiving attention.

'Perhaps you may help us locate her?' While Janet was speaking, a handsome, well-built man with a weather-beaten face and tousled, auburn hair walked through the foyer. 'He must be the ranger, Phil Chalmers,' she thought, watching him enter the dining room as his hob-nailed walking boots echoed on the wooden floor. His suede jacket was reinforced with leather patches at his shoulders and elbows. His upright bearing suggested to Janet that he'd been a soldier before becoming a ranger.

She turned back to Linda. 'So, you know The Chase well if you used to explore around here with Tessa?'

'Only the area surrounding Upper Slaughter. Our parents didn't allow us to venture any further for fear of getting lost.'

'Your knowledge must be better than any of ours...'

'Perhaps?'

'Would you know the places that a caravan or motorhome could be hidden on The Chase with no one's knowledge?'

'I suppose so, but only close to the village...' Donald interrupted Janet's conversation by calling her.

'Excuse me, Linda, I'm wanted in the dining room. Perhaps we could have a chat later?'

Janet entered the dining room to see everyone bent over a map spread out across the table. 'This is where we are, see, The Red Lion is clearly marked.' Phil, the ranger, was pointing out features on the map he had brought with him. 'You asked about where someone could hide a caravan or motorhome, Inspector?' Tom turned from the plan to glance at him as he explained further. 'To hide either needs vehicular access. To gain such access on Cannock Chase invariably undergrowth needs to be cleared. Bracken can grow to a height of six feet, young saplings can grow up to three feet in one growing season. Inevitably, as most of The Chase is open, high land, it's susceptible to bearing the full brunt of storms. Trees and bushes easily become diseased and succumb to winds. These fall over and block earlier open access quickly. The Chase is an ever-changing landscape. What was yesterday an open trackway, today could become blocked or covered? By tomorrow you wouldn't even notice that it had once been a driveway or the access path. That's where my team and I come into the prime reason our department was created, to maintain and replenish the features of Cannock Chase.'

'So, are you saying that we face an impossible task?' Tom asked. The question brought a smile to Phil's face.

'It may seem an impossible task to outsiders, but to my team and me, no.'

'Before I get to point out where I think we should begin the search, could I explain one vital fact about this part of Cannock Chase. You'll see on this plan the evidence and remnants of the once flourishing coal mining industry. The Chase is littered with old mine shafts and sites of disused collieries. To the uninitiated, it's hazardous to wander through The Chase. You could easily fall down a sinkhole or old mine shaft that has collapsed in on itself.'

'Point taken, Mr Chalmers. So where can we start?' Tom looked at his watch. 'Because of the lateness of the hour, I'm now assuming this will be tomorrow morning.' Most people around the table looked at their wristwatches and agreed.

Phil laid his index finger on his map. 'Here, Inspector, we start here at the western outskirts of Upper Slaughter village.' Everyone looked back to the plan. 'From this point, there are several old trackways that lead in three separate directions. Two of these old tracks were made by colliery companies during the heyday of coal mining. The Forestry Commission made the third track when they brought in heavy earthmoving machinery to create fire breaks in the pine agricultural estates. These tracks all lead us through many coverts and plantations. You'll see tomorrow that all these old tracks are indistinguishable from surrounding flora and trees. The vegetation hides the existence of old tracks, but they are still there. I suggest we split into three groups and follow each track. I have more copies of this plan for each group. It's also vital that we keep in touch by phone…'

'… what do you think our chances are of…?'

'… of finding this Ben Strange and this girl he's kidnapped? All I can say is, Inspector, bring your handcuffs and your heavy, well-built constables. We'll catch him, that's for sure, but not without a considerable struggle. If this is the same man responsible for the death of that lovely girl, Lizzie Cartwright, he must be a powerful bloke. He must have carried her body for several miles to where he attempted to conceal it at Castle Ring.'

As the meeting concluded, Tom, Donald, and Janet continued chatting around the dining table.

'We may as well stay here for dinner now?' Donald suggested.

'You'd better set places for four more Donald,' voiced Lucy as she burst into the dining room.

'Kiddo, you've arrived. I'm glad to see you.' 'Hello, everybody', Janet called to the three riot squad officers with her. She rose from the table and hugged her fellow, newly promoted, colleague.

'Hello, Lucy,' Donald called before going to greet her and the other officers. Tom remained seated as his phone began to ring. It was Jack asking for an update.

'Hello, gov… yes, Lucy and the squaddies have arrived. We'll be starting the search tomorrow morning.'

As Tom was on the telephone, Lucy chatted to Janet. 'Hey, kiddo, where's the infamous yew tree?'

'Let's have a peek. It's around the back of the hotel.' The rear garden was quiet as Janet showed Lucy the tree. Janet looked across to the patio to see two glasses standing on the table and remembered her earlier conversation with Ted. She smiled, seeing the two empty pint glasses, and surmised Ted had drunk them both. Lucy brushed her hands across the coarse bark and felt the iron nails' heads firmly embedded in the tree trunk. Unknowing to them both, a pair of leering eyes were watching them. Ben had left Tessa in his bed, naked and subdued through plying her with constant drugs, and helpless with her hands tied behind her back as insurance should she try to escape.

'So, this is where it all happened, is it, kiddo?' Lucy asked as she walked around the yew tree, looking down to the manicured grass. Noise from within the adjacent woodland caused the turtle doves nestling in the treetop to fly off. Lucy looked up and then in the direction where the noise had come from. To her, it sounded like a twig snapping. Ben had eased his haunches as he crouched behind a thicket of bracken to get a better view of Lucy as he ogled her.

'What was that?' she asked Janet.

'I think you frightened the doves away…?'

'… no, not the doves. There was a noise in the woodland.' Then a tawny owl hooted.

'… it was that owl. You probably disturbed him as well.'

'This place gives me the creeps!' Lucy exclaimed. Just then, a black, spindly, lace web spider dropped onto Lucy's forehead. It had been displaced from the upper branches by the flapping turtle doves. 'Aargh!' Lucy screamed. Seated more comfortably behind bracken fronds, Ben sniggered as she flapped her arms, knocking the spider onto the grass where she stamped on it.

From sitting quietly in the hotel lounge, Donald heard the scream and came dashing onto the patio.

'What's going on, Janet?' he demanded.

'It's Lucy.' She pointed, with a smile, to the yew tree where Lucy continued to tousle her hair in case there were any more spiders.

'I hate spiders!' she yelled, with a red-faced grimace, looking up into the tree. Ben's snigger turned into a faint chuckle. Lucy at once twisted to stare in his direction.

'You can think what you like, kiddo, but there is definitely something or someone in the woodland.' Donald walked over to her.

'Where?' Donald asked.

'Over there in the bushes. I was aware of someone.' Donald brushed away some low spreading branches from the yew tree and ventured into the relative gloom of the woodland. Lucy followed close behind him. Within six yards he entered the dense thickets of bracken and thistle and found a small clearing. He looked down to where the grasses and moss had been flattened. Ben had gone. Donald turned to call Lucy, but she was right behind him. Their faces met. Neither could resist the opportunity, and they kissed in a long, passionate embrace. They didn't notice the turtle doves' cooing nestled with intertwined heads above them, perched on a new branch for the forthcoming night. Neither did they understand the male cicadas, croaking their invitations to their female counterparts to join them on tree trunks for a night of insectivorous passion. Besides recognising the natural world's sounds, Janet's senses recoiled at the silence as she stood on the patio. She looked nervously towards the woodland.

'Oh, Lucy, wouldn't it be wonderful if we could slope off into the forest and find a secluded glade?' Donald whispered.

'Yes, it would, but we can't. Have you forgotten your wife is only a few yards away? She'll be wondering what's happened to us.'

'I suppose so!' Donald agreed reluctantly. 'Anyway, it looks as if you were right. There was somebody here. Look at the flattened grasses. I'd guess that someone has lain here and been watching you.

If you glance back from here through the branches and bushes, you can see the Abbot Ibáñez yew tree.'

'What's happening, Donald?' Janet asked anxiously as she joined them. Lucy and Donald looked up, guilty expressions written on their faces.

'… er… er… Janet! See here! I was pointing out to Lucy, there's been somebody here. Can you see the flattened grasses? Whoever it was, they've been watching you.'

'Yes, I can see that, and I can also see Lucy's lipstick on your cheek.'

'Oh, my God!' Lucy thought with trepidation, looking aghast at him. Donald's reaction was more reasoned. He tried to sound nonchalant as he calmly reached for his handkerchief to wipe it away.

'Oh, that! Lucy bumped into me, didn't you, Lucy, as I was pointing out this area to her?' Donald looked at Lucy for support.

'… er… er… yes, I did, Janet. I nearly knocked him over.' Lucy tried to laugh. Attempting to change the subject, Lucy carried on. 'I can see now why this place has caused you so much upset. It really is so eerie and mysterious.'

Their tenuous explanation didn't convince Janet, but she decided to let it pass and ignored Lucy's comments. 'Okay, we'd better get into the dining room. I heard the dinner gong being sounded. That's what I came to tell you.'

Unknowing to all of them, Ben had merely moved further into the woodland, where he concealed himself again and continued to watch. He'd seen Donald and Lucy's passionate embrace and then witnessed Janet almost discovering them. He sniggered again. 'Well, well, there's a thing. The situations that some people get involved in.' In the pervading gloom, he glided stealthily through the myriad of pathways, back to his humble abode, ambling through The Chase to Tessa who anxiously awaited his arrival.

Forty-seven

Ebenezer Strange had found the old caravan quite by chance as he'd wandered through The Chase, examining the various gin-traps he'd set to ensnare game. The moss-laden trailer lay over two miles as The Chase chough flew from the village of Upper Slaughter. Since well before his parents died, Ben preferred sleeping rough in the forest, living from the fruits of his guile, and using the natural resources that Cannock Chase supplied. He enjoyed building shelters using fallen tree trunks and branches. Bracken fronds made an excellent roof covering that, although changing colour from a bright lime-green to a rusty-brown, lasted from one year to the next. After expertly weaving the fronds together, neither winter storms nor autumn gales failed to dislodge his shelter rooftop. Inside, his animal fur bedding and wicker tabletop remained dry and serviceable.

His lifestyle improved considerably when he'd stumbled upon the old caravan previously occupied by an old hermit named Dick Slee. Legends abound in the locality that the aged recluse had settled on Cannock Chase. Since being made homeless by the Luftwaffe's bombs that had destroyed his terraced house in London's east end in 1940, he'd had nowhere else to go. Ben quickly restored the caravan into a liveable abode. He'd ousted the rock pigeons that had entered through the broken window and had raised several clutches of young. Ben had also swept away the detritus that had built up on the floor by several generations of invasive ants and cockroaches.

He erected a cover over the aluminium caravan that completely concealed it from the outside world. Interwoven branches were supported by stout tree trunks. Bracken and mosses substituted for roof tiles. Soon after that, nature took over. Fallen autumn leaves built up over the bracken. In the spring, blackbirds and thrushes made their nests above where Ben slept. The following year bluebells were followed by kingcups and clovers that bloomed in profusion before new bracken grew again. His home blended into The Chase landscape so thoroughly that even Ben sometimes had difficulty distinguishing the location from any other copse and covert. He'd had a stroke of genius when moving a hollowed-out tree trunk into the Horseylane brook that ran next to the caravan. After that, Ben no longer needed to fetch water using a bottle. He benefited from the luxury of having fresh running water straight to his front door.

As he returned along the many pathways back to Dingle Dell, the name he had given to his home, Tessa had awoken. Her eyes were wide open in fright and apprehension as she was still naked and captive in Ben's hideaway. She wrestled in futile agony at the metal handcuffs that seared her wrists and held her hands behind her back.

'So, you're awake,' he called, as he entered.

'Please take these handcuffs off me, Ben. My arms have gone numb, and my wrists hurt so much.'

'Only if you promise you won't attempt to run away. Turn around.' He inserted a rusted key into the silver anodised handcuffs. Tessa exhaled a sigh of relief and rubbed her wrists.

'Can you see the blood and the cuts on me? You're a sadist and so cruel, Ben.' He passed her a sponge soaked with water and watched as she cleaned her flesh. 'I hate you, Ben Strange. I hope you didn't hurt my Uncle Silas?'

After finding out from old Ted Baxter where Tessa's Uncle Silas lived, Ben had walked past the picturesque cottage several times before deciding to go in. He knew Tessa was there when he'd spotted her peeping at him from behind one of the curtains. Rarely did anybody who lived in Upper Slaughter venture out at 4:30 in a morning. Ben thought this would be the best time to get hold of Tessa when everybody was asleep with the dawn barely breaking. Using a stout forged steel crowbar, he'd smoothly eased the mortice latch from the screws that held it to the doorjamb. Once in the hall, he'd looked up the stairs to where he imagined Tessa would sleep, but noise to his left had diverted him. In a side bedroom, seventy-eight-year-old Silas Jackson slept uneasily. He occasionally suffered from encroaching emphysema and often issued snorts and loud snoring as he slumbered. The nocturnal noises he had emitted were to be his last. Ben had entered the ground floor bedroom without remorse or conscience for his murderous actions and had silently drawn the long, serrated blade of his knife across Silas's heaving throat. A few days earlier he'd threatened Ted Baxter with the same vicious-looking knife at The Red Lion. This time there had been no threats, only callous, cold-blooded murder with no aforethought plan and no postscript regret. Ben left Silas to gasp his last few breaths, and while he'd gone upstairs to look for Tessa, the old man had crawled to the side of his bed where he fell to the floor dead.

Ben had quietly entered Tessa's bedroom and silently guffawed at the sight of her nakedness as she'd lain on top of the bed covers. He'd previously applied some chloroform to a cotton wool pad. Ben had held this over her nose and mouth until she was unconscious. Using a firefighter's lift, he'd carried her over his shoulder out into Upper Slaughter's morning mist, down the woodland pathways, past Stoneyflats covert to Dingle Dell. As Tessa's lifeless form left Brooklands, she had been oblivious to the world and the fact that her Uncle Silas lay bleeding to death inside.

'Methinks you protest too much, Tessa. Shut your mouth if you know what's good for you,' was Ben's reply when she asked about her uncle. 'I'm going outside, so don't abuse my trust in you and get up to any funny business.' Ben closed the door behind him. She heard and felt the judder of a heavy lock turning in the door. Tessa looked around the low-ceilinged caravan for any way of escape. She pulled the curtains aside and saw that the windows were bolted shut. Her senses then recoiled in terror when she saw scratched in the tawdry plastic wall covering, - *Lizzie was here*. She lay back on the bed and pulled the surrounding bed covers to conceal her nakedness. Psychologically Tessa felt that the flimsy covering offered her some sort of protection against Ben. She sobbed, letting the bedclothes soak up the floods of tears.

Forty-eight

As dawn flooded the bedroom with a yellowish light, Donald awoke and looked across at Janet. Sensory organs inside her brain told her she was being watched, and she opened her eyes to see Donald's smile. 'Good morning, darling,' he whispered.

'Good morning, Donald. Have you had a good sleep? I have. Thank goodness we had no more peculiar dreams.'

'Well we aren't at *The Crucified Abbot*, we are at The Red Lion, had you forgotten?'

Janet nodded and gave him a kiss.

'Are you coming with everybody else on the search for Ben today?' he asked soberly.

'I don't know. What do you think? Do you think I should?'

'I'd prefer you to stay here, where it's safe. Your wrist hasn't completely healed yet, and I honestly can't think that your presence would add anything to capturing Ben. What's needed today is brute force. I know once we catch up with him, there's going to be some rough stuff, so I'd rather you stay well clear.'

'What about Lucy?'

'Darling, I'm concerned about you. Whether or not she comes is up to her. Apart from her not having a cut wrist, the same criteria apply to her. Why don't the two of you have a girly day together?'

'A girly day?' Janet laughed.

'Well, I don't know, what do you call it when women have a day together in the absence of men?'

'Who said anything about men being absent from a girly day? We might have a foursome with two hunky brutes from the Chippendales for all you know?' She looked teasingly under her eyelashes at him.

After breakfasting on cereals followed by bacon and eggs, the group of policemen assembled in the hotel's foyer. Along with Tom and Donald, three riot squad officers from Scotland Yard and four constables from the county force pored over Ordnance Survey maps provided by Phil Chalmers, The Chase ranger. Apart from the shire policemen and the countryside officer, they were all armed with handguns. Phil carried his trusted twelve-bore shotgun in a shoulder slip with the barrel hanging down his back and pointing downwards.

A magazine held several red coloured and brass tipped cartridges in an extra leather belt around his waist.

Tom addressed the team. 'I want to remind everybody that we are searching for a murderer. He's extremely dangerous and most probably armed. We know he has already killed two people in cold blood and possibly killed more. I'm assuming when he's cornered, he won't come quietly, so we must all be ready to defend ourselves. For those of you who are armed, you have the express authority of the Metropolitan Police's commissioner to discharge your firearms to protect yourself and the lives of our fellow officers. If that means that Ben Strange gets injured or killed during this operation, that will be an unavoidable consequence. I prefer that outcome to have to visit any of your families to explain to your loved ones how any of you came to lose your life. Is that clear? Of course, I prefer this fugitive to be taken alive and then face justice in the British courts. We all have our phones to keep in close contact.' He paused and looked around the room.

'We'll split into three groups. The first group will be led by Phil, the second by Sergeant Lawrence and the third by me. Phil knows Cannock Chase's terrain like the back of his hand, so we'll all be guided by his local experience. Phil…?' Tom turned the attention of the assembly over to him. Janet and Lucy sat at the back of the room, impressed with Tom's professionalism. Both had faced mortal danger many times in their brief careers with the Metropolitan Police but gave a little shiver at the thought of what risks the officers would meet. Both were also concerned about Donald's safety more than anyone else's.

'As Inspector Cropper has explained, I know this area well and have designated each group a distinct pathway. Wherever possible, adhere to these pathways and don't deviate on your own initiative into uncharted areas of the forest. Cannock Chase is vast and riddled with old mine shafts that could have been infilled properly, but probably weren't. Over time, loose material dumped into these shafts will have settled, leaving great chasms. By now they will have overgrown with vine weed, knotweed and even mature trees growing out of them. If you stumble into one of these chasms, it's likely you won't ever be found. As Chief Ranger, people and animals have gone missing in my short twenty-year tenure without being found or seen again. To recap, so we all know where we are going, I'm taking the pathway into Hare Hills leading to Stoneyflats Covert. Tom is going ahead from the village direct to Sweakham Covert and you, Donald, through Coppice Hills and into Horsepasture Covert. I'm banking on my gut instinct that we'll find this Ben Strange in one of these three areas. As well as the maps, I have a black and white aerial photograph of this part of The Chase. This photo was only taken last year. I want everybody to examine this photograph and submit some of the key features to your memory. God forbid if one of you gets lost or detached from your group, recall this photograph to help you return to the known pathways. Incidentally, on close examination of the photo, no trace of a caravan or motorhome or other building is apparent. That means wherever Ben Strange is living is well concealed both from the ground and the air. If we don't find him today, then there's always tomorrow to try a different area of Cannock Chase. The weather forecast looks as if it is going to be kind to us and remain dry. Combing dense woodland in the pouring rain is no joke, and not for the faint-hearted. Good luck and good hunting. Let's go!'

Janet and Lucy watched the ten men saunter down Gallows Lane towards Upper Slaughter. Before turning the first corner and disappearing from the Red Lion's sight, Donald turned and waved. Both women returned his wave with anxious hearts and retreated into the lounge where they ordered another pot of tea.

'What shall we do today then, kiddo, as the men have excluded us from the action?' Lucy asked. Janet smiled. 'What's funny?'

'Oh, something Donald said this morning about us having a girly day.'

'… a girly day?'

'Yes! I said for all he knows we could entertain two of the Chippendale male strip group?'

'Why not? I'm up for that if you are? Oh, sorry, but you're a married woman.'

'… and should being married to Donald exclude me from that pleasant activity?' Janet laughed.

'Well, it certainly wouldn't exclude me if I were his wife?' Lucy joined in the laughter.

'Well, unfortunately, we aren't. I thought after this cuppa, we could have an amble into the village. Upper Slaughter is very picturesque, apparently. Donald says it portrays a typical English landscape with a duck pond and a village green. There are some fifteenth-century half-timbered black and white cottages too, straight out of a John Constable or a William Hogarth masterpiece.'

226

'I didn't know Donald was a connoisseur of English art?'

'Neither did I.'

'Okay, a walk to the village sounds good to me…'

'… This afternoon, I thought as the weather looks good, we'd take a siesta in the rear garden. Ted will be there…'

'… Ted…? Is he a Chippendale by any chance?' Janet laughed.

'… No, he's not and… yes, you know of him. I've told you about old Ted Baxter. He comes here every afternoon for his tipple of Abbot cider. He's nearly ninety-three and a fascinating bloke. Be prepared for your purse to be lighter because he always contrives a free drink out of anyone he meets. I don't mind, I love listening to his stories of the area and the old days, but before we do anything else…' Lucy looked at her with trepidation, knowing what Janet was going to bring up. Janet put her cup down on the table and looked at Lucy full in the face.

'Lucy, kiddo, we are good friends, aren't we, and I don't want that to change…?'

'… neither do I…' Lucy's interruption didn't stop Janet from carrying on.

'… Whatever traits of personality I have, stupidity isn't one of them. I know you kissed Donald yesterday in the woodland…'

'… but… but…'

'… let me finish. He had your lipstick on his cheek, but knowing you both, and given your history, I can't imagine that your encounter in the bushes remained at only one kiss ...'

'… I did really bump into him…'

'… that's as may be. I believe you, but if I ever discovered that you were having an affair, that would be… well… that would be the end of our friendship and the end of my marriage…'

'… Donald and I are not having an affair, Janet.' Lucy tried to sound abrupt and assertive.

'Okay! There, I've said what I wanted to say, and that's an end to it. Let's enjoy the day, shall we? There haven't been many days in recent times at Scotland Yard where we've been given a day off.' They continued to drink their tea in silence before Lucy spoke.

'I'm going to have a quick shower, kiddo. How about we meet down here in, say… half an hour… and we'll take that stroll into the village?'

The hotel dining room buzzed with boisterous conversation from many passing visitors. Janet and Lucy enjoyed lunching on a smoked salmon salad washed down with two glasses of Chianti. Lucy had ordered a full bottle of the Italian white wine, so it was still half empty as they carried it out onto the rear patio. Ted was already sitting there. A half-full glass of cider sat on the table before him as he dozed face upwards to the hot sunshine. Listening to the slight snoring coming from his heaving chest, they quietly sat down. Lucy sat opposite and Janet beside him. Perhaps their movement caused him to stir, but he coughed a little before issuing another snore. Janet and Lucy silently clinked their glasses together and mouthed 'cheers'. The sound of liquid being swallowed must have stirred his subconscious, and he remembered he hadn't finished his cider. With his eyes half shut, Ted reached for his glass and took a huge slurp. He thought he was still dreaming. His nose twitched at the women's perfume irritating his nose; he looked up at the sunshine and blinked. Dropping his eyes, he saw Lucy's blonde hair and bare shoulders. He further dropped his eyes to her generous bosom and rounded hips, all covered by a flowing flowery printed dress.

Still in a daze, he mumbled to himself. 'Ah! Happy days. The old Abbot nectar never fails me. If only this gorgeous girl I've dreamed up was real, I could give her a right old…'

'… Ahem! Ted!' Janet stopped his reverie before he became obnoxious. 'Ted, it's me, Janet.'

His eyebrows lifted, and he opened his eyes fully. He sat upright and wiped his whiskers.

'Oh, my dearie, it's you. I think I was dozing…'

'… yes, you were. I'm sorry if we disturbed you.'

'How can a pretty young woman like you be disturbing me… we…?' Ted looked inquisitively to Janet.

'I'm here with my colleague, Lucy…' Ted shielded his eyes from the sun and squinted towards Lucy.

'… well, I'm dashed! You're the pretty young lady I've been dreaming about… It's this place you know, it does many funny things to your dreams…'

'Hello, Ted, Janet has told me so much about you…' She held out her hand.

'… am I still dreaming…?' Ted rubbed his eyes before shaking her hand.

'… I assure you, Ted, I'm no dream.' Lucy laughed.

'I can see that, my dearie. You sure are a sight for this old man's eyes.' Ted kept hold of her hand. Lucy gently eased her fingers from his fragile grasp and smiled. He reached forward for his glass and downed the remnants in one swallow. He replaced the glass and watched the few remaining dregs of froth settle to the bottom. After a few seconds of silence, he asked, 'Are you here for Ben?'

'Yes, we are. My husband and other policemen have gone to search for him.'

'I thought that was the case, my dearie. I saw them all tramp past my cottage earlier this morning. The sparking of their hobnail boots on the cobblestones diverted me from my knitting.'

'You do knitting?' Lucy asked. 'That's unusual for a man.' Lucy commented.

'Not really, my dear. Most old codgers like me around here can knit. My eyes aren't what they used to be, so I can't read a book for long. I can do knitting without having to glance at the stitches. It keeps me occupied, and my fingers supple. My old Martha taught me how to knit before she was promoted to glory, of course.' He coughed, turned, and spat out some phlegm.

'Aagh! I'm sorry about that, my dears. The trouble is when you get to my age, I can't talk for long before my throat gets dry.' He looked towards his empty glass.

Janet smiled. She put her glass of wine on the table and stood. 'I can take a hint. What is it? Another pint of Abbot?'

'Oh, my dear, what a lovely kind gesture. Yes, please.' He passed her his empty glass. Lucy smirked and turned away as Janet walked to the bar.

Lucy turned back as Ted spoke. 'Are you married, my dear? Forgive my nosy question, but I can't see a ring on your finger.' Before she could answer, Ted carried on. 'A pretty young woman like you should have a regular fella to keep you warm on the wintry nights, you know if you see what I mean.' He winked before adding. 'No offence meant, my dearie, but you are so lovely. If I were fifty years younger, I'd…'

'… if you were a young sprog again, you'd do what…' Ted and Lucy looked up as a young, tall, well-built man sat where Janet had been sitting.

'… what are you doing here?' Ted growled.

'Now, now, Ted, what sort of greeting is that for an old friend…'

'… You're no friend of mine, as you well know, and you're not welcome here.' Lucy looked on, concerned by the downturn in the conversational tone as Janet returned with Ted's pint of cider.

'What...!' Janet exclaimed.

'Hello, Janet, pull up another chair. You don't mind me joining the gathering, do you?'

'Aren't you going to introduce me to your charming friend?' he asked as Janet sat on another chair and played along with the situation.

'Lucy, this is Ebenezer Strange.' Lucy had extended her arm to shake his hand but retracted it, reacting to what Janet said and eyed him up and down.

'Janet, Janet, my darling, my lovely. It's Ben, only my old Mom used to call me Ebenezer. You were happy to call me Ben when we danced around yonder yew tree.' He hoicked his arm towards the tree. He leaned towards Lucy. 'Janet and I are old friends, you know.' He turned back to Janet. 'We've spent some lovely times under those old branches, haven't we, darling?' Janet looked apprehensively towards Lucy and thought about getting up to leave.

Ben sensed her reluctance to stay. 'Now, now, Janet, don't you think about going. We have a lot of catching up to do, especially as that husband of yours is out of the way…'

'… Um! Er! He's not out of the way. He's taking a shower; he'll be down soon…'

'Tut, tut, Janet, you must do better than that. Do you think I'm having a dreamy day, like this old codger here?' He turned and gestured towards Ted before carrying on. Ted squirmed in his seat.

'Why do you think I'm here? I saw him and the other coppers walking into the woodland. They all think they're going to find me, don't they…?'

'… what have you done with Tessa…?' Janet asked.

'… Tessa!? She's okay. I've left her in my Dingle Dell. I'm confident nobody will find her in my little abode, not even that wimpy ranger, Phil Chalmers. He thinks he knows every blade of grass and piece of bird shit on The Chase, but not as much as I do. I know he could stare at Dingle Dell right now as we speak and not even realise it's my humble abode and where Tessa is.'

'Why are you here?' Janet asked with increasing alarm.

'Why? To come and see you and to meet your lovely blondie here. I knew that stupid husband of yours wouldn't risk you and his girlfriend coming into the woods after me.' He turned to Lucy. 'You are his girlfriend, aren't you, darling? Well, after what I saw in the woods yesterday… they were having a good old snogging session, weren't you, Lucy?' He half-turned to Janet who looked daggers at Lucy.

'Whoops! Oh, dearie me! Me and my big mouth, I'm sorry, have I said something I shouldn't have…?' Ben didn't see it coming. Nobody was taking any notice of Ted listening to the tetchy exchange, he'd been summoning up his courage and opportunity. He carefully reached for his walking stick that he'd left propped by the side of the bench. The stout gnarled bamboo cane was topped by a heavy, cast, solid, silver knob in the shape of a duck's head. The cast silver was a massive lump of metal, as big as his hand. Clutching the steel tip, Ted swung as hard as possible, ensuring the heavy silver duck hit Ben's head above his right ear. As he fell to the side and then down to the crazy paved concrete floor, blood spurted from a gash of flesh that opened in his hair. Ben's face hit the concrete, causing two of his teeth to fall out and more blood spew from his mouth.

The bottle of wine and two glasses toppled from the table and fell around Ben's lifeless form, smashing to pieces. With the benefit of their police training, Janet and Lucy acted instinctively and at once. They knew Ben would only be temporarily stunned. As added insurance to the possibility of Ben immediately coming round, Janet kicked him sharply between his legs as Lucy delivered a kick to his stomach. Ben's body reacted in pain as he involuntarily retracted into a foetal position. Janet knelt on his chest and shouted to Lucy. 'Quick, fetch some handcuffs.' Gasping for breath with excitement, Ted retrieved his stick.

'Shall I give him another clout with my walking stick for good measure, dearie…?' His chest heaved with excitement as he spoke to Janet.

'No, Ted, but stay ready in case he quickly comes round. I think he's only stunned.' Ted menacingly lifted his stick above his head, ready to deliver another blow should it be necessary. They watched Ben's motionless face lying in the encircling mixture of blood and wine. Gasping for breath, Lucy returned with the handcuffs. Janet turned him fully onto his stomach. At once, Lucy clasped his hands behind his back and secured the cuffs by firmly closing the ratchet mechanism digging into Ben's flesh.

'Well done, my dearies, I can see you've done that a few times, haven't you?' Ted reluctantly lowered his stick. 'Ah well, and I was looking forward to giving him another hit for good measure.'

'Well done to you, Ted. That was fantastic.' Janet called.

'I'm rather proud of myself. I've meant no harm to anybody in my life since I fired my rifle at the Bosch in the trenches, but that was in a war.' Ted puffed out his chest before returning to the table for another slurp of cider. 'Ah! The good Lord has decreed that my pint of cider hasn't gone the way of your foreign wine, that's divine providence…' As Ted took a drink, Michael from the bar came running.

'What's going on? I heard the glasses smashing…'

'… Michael! You know we're police officers. This is the man we've come here to apprehend. Have you got a piece of rope that we can use to tie him up with?' They looked down on Ben's lifeless form. Blood was seeping from his head wounds and cuts to his arms from the smashed glasses.

'I sure have. Solid, hemp twisted rope that we lower the barrels of cider into the cellar from the brewery lorry deliveries. Hang on, and I'll find a piece.' As Michael dashed away, Ben moaned. Ted raised his stick again, but Janet held up her arm and knelt on Ben's neck, forcing her weight through her kneecap onto his spine.

'Aargh!' Ben gurgled in his own blood.

'It's alright, Ted. We'll tie him up. I don't think he'll be going anywhere else today.' Janet prodded Ben with more force. 'Will you, Ben?' He groaned again as the seeping blood ran into his eyes.

Michael returned with the rope. Lucy tied Ben's bent legs behind his back to a loop around his neck and then to his ankles. She pulled slowly on the coil of rope as his back arched and his head lifted from the floor. With his stomach pressed into the concrete paving, Ben was helpless. Janet forced her fingers into his mouth to ensure he wouldn't choke on his own blood.

They all sat back on the bench and looked down at him. 'Didn't we do well?' Ted offered and laughed, looking at Janet and Lucy.

'Michael! I think this calls for a drink,' Ted called.

'What? Are you buying, Ted? I've never known that to happen before.'

'Well, maybe you haven't, but this is a special occasion, and I'm going to treat my two good friends here. Two pints of Abbot, my young man. No! Make it three. I think I've deserved another. Wait till my son-in-law, Tom, comes to collect me and hears what I have to tell him.'

Michael walked away muttering. 'The old codger, well I'd never have believed this! From what I know, another pint for Ted will make it he's had three, so he has. His son-in-law is going to have his hands full getting him home today.'

Ted spoke to Lucy, 'Have you tried the Abbot cider before, my dearie? It'll put hairs on your chest.' He looked at Lucy's heaving chest and generously revealed cleavage. 'Oh! Oh! I'm sorry, my dear, women don't have those, do they? No offence meant, my lovely, but as I know I've told Janet in the past, this 'ere amber nectar will make you fruity. Woe betides any young man in your life…' As Michael returned with the drinks, they all took a huge slurp.

'… That's enough of that, Ted. Lucy's already fruity enough.' Janet added icily. A momentary silence ensued between them. Ted looked from Janet to Lucy, sensing the underlying animosity. 'Snogging, eh? With my husband.' Janet accused and arched her eyebrows at her. Lucy tried to appear demure and contrite, but the sense of triumph quickly overcame any accusations and destructive emotion. It was Janet who smiled first, then Ted, followed by Lucy. In unison, they all burst out laughing and clinked their glass together. On the floor, Ben continued to moan. Ted was nearest to him and gave him a violent kick in the chest.

'Shut up, scum of the earth!' he offered with a scowl, as Ben's moaning increased.

'Now, now, Ted, any more of that and I must arrest you for assaulting a prisoner.' Lucy said between laughs.

'I'll come quietly,' replied Ted through intense laughter. 'Have you got any more handcuffs?'

From inside the hotel lounge, Mrs Downing smiled as she listened to the riotous laughter coming from the patio.

Forty-nine

As they left the outskirts of the village, the men split into three groups. Tom and two other officers ambled down an old pathway. The frequent patches of tall grass on the otherwise moss-covered gravel suggested to him that the path hadn't been used for quite a time. Overhanging sycamore trees supplied shade as they walked for about a hundred yards on the muddy, twisting trail that rose and fell through puddles of black and green stagnant water. Barbed wire fences on either side of the pathway suddenly gave way to open fields full of foraging sheep. The three men's sudden appearance disturbed their sedate grazing, and they herded together, watching the men continue towards Sweakham Covert as they chewed the cud. Arriving at the plantation, the transition from the sunny, open landscape to a gloomy, overcast canopy of oak and pine was stark. The forest seemed to clamp in on the policemen as the pathway suddenly disappeared. There was no obvious direction to follow. Tom looked back and tried to keep some guidance and a sense of movement from the earlier straight corridor.

'Let's keep apart a little rather than bunching together, that way one of us at the rear can keep some sort of sense of where we are going. I'll lead. Hopefully, we'll come across something that resembles a shelter?'

It was eerily quiet. The birds had stopped chirping, and the close overhead foliage was devoid of any breeze to ripple the leaves. Years of successive autumn falling oak leaves and pine needles had built up a deep brown covered carpet on the forest floor. Suddenly Tom stumbled. He stepped into a hole that was camouflaged by twigs and leaves. In an instant, he was submerged up to his waist in cold, foul-smelling brackish water.

'Aargh!' he yelled. 'Damn and blast.' The two other officers knelt, reached under his armpits, and tried to pull him out. As they did so, another officer named James slipped and also fell partly in the hole. Gradually, Tom and James extricated themselves and lay back on the dry leaves, cursing their luck. Unfortunately, as Tom spread his hands out, he disturbed an adder's nest. In a flash, the curled female snake, protecting her young, lurched forward in an aggressive swing of its body towards him. Tom jumped up and moved away, avoiding contact with the viper's fangs.

'Bloody hell! It's like we've entered the jungle.' James uttered as he fell backwards into a thick bed of stinging nettles.

Meanwhile, Phil Chalmers and two other Staffordshire officers had made excellent progress over Hare Hills. The pathway they were following was more defined and regular. They entered Stoneyflats Covert, and the atmosphere changed. As Tom had simultaneously discovered, the ambience and environment differed totally from the heady breathable air out on the heathland. Phil likened it to entering a medieval cathedral where the air is still, and everyone involuntarily whispered, looking on in awe and reverence at religious artefacts and solemn monuments. A movement ahead took Phil's attention. A magnificent stag, sporting four-pronged antlers, watching over his three does as he foraged on the forest floor. The deer all moved silently to another hidden copse where they wouldn't be disturbed. Phil held his fingers to his lips and pointed for the others to watch the natural spectacle in a hush. All the time they kept examining every small dell and divot, wondering if this was where Ben had hidden his abode.

Donald and three riot squad officers from Scotland Yard, crossing Coppice Hills, gulped in the clean air that Phil and his PCs had experienced on Hare Hills. Up ahead they looked uneasily at the looming woodland and mysterious dense forest of Horsepasture Covert. From outside looking in, it was oppressively black. It was only when they entered their eyes adjusted to the cloying dimness. Donald and the officers, more adept at patrolling London's asphalted streets, were inexperienced in countryside matters. Their chatter and plodding feet had already alerted several roe deer who scampered away before the policemen could witness them. One sharp-eyed officer pointed out to Donald, several strange, dark brown coloured bats that clung upside down to overhanging branches of Hornbeam trees. He'd walked through layers of whitish droppings that stained the forest floor and sullied his newly polished black boots. The pile of foul-smelling dung caused him to glance up. Everyone stared at the curious sleeping mammals. Donald wondered if they were the same colony of long wing bats he'd seen flying around the Abbot Ibáñez yew tree on his and Janet's first night at *The Crucified Abbot*. 'Phew!' he exclaimed; 'they stink of ammonia!' His voice alerted the bats, and Donald straight away noticed several sparkling black eyes staring down at them. 'Come on, let's move on,' he gestured calmly. Without further incident, they walked for twenty minutes before dropping down a slight slope. The lush carpet of brown leaves and sharp pine needles gave way to clean, washed, small stones and angular gravel. Donald stopped and looked to the left and then the right. The gravel and rocks lay in a channel as far as he could see, disappearing into the gloom. He pulled out his map from his backpack. The officers crowded around.

'I think we are here?' he pointed to the map. 'I think this is Horseylane Brook?'

'… but there's no water, Sergeant.'

'I can see that, constable. That's peculiar, isn't it? I know it's been dry lately, but you'd imagine a stream wouldn't totally lose its flow. Come on, let's carry on.'

'Here's a pathway,' called one officer.

'Wait!' Exclaimed Donald as he turned to the constable. 'You know what the ranger said about the dangers of moving off into the forest.' Donald and the others peered into the gloom where the PC pointed. 'It's not much of a pathway, Jim, more an area of flattened grass. Perhaps this is where some deer have been lying?'

'Bloody hell,' said Campbell, another one officer, 'the forest here is thicker than anywhere else. I wouldn't have thought even any deer could progress beyond this point.'

'Yeah! I think you're right, talk about nature taking over, only a snake could crawl in there.' Donald added. The officers stood alongside him, trying to peer into the blackness. They were completely unaware that they were within seven yards of Tessa as she lay motionless in Dingle Dell. Ben had given her more drugs. Had she been awake, she would have been aware of the policemen and could have called out to them. As it was, their presence close to her was short-lived.

'Come on, let's move on,' Donald commanded.

After another half an hour, they came to a clearing in the forest. The men held their faces up to the blue sky and the welcome sunshine. 'Shall we take a break and have lunch, sarge?' Jim called.

'Yeah, let's stop for a while. My legs are aching,' added Campbell.

After eating and resting for an hour, they struggled for a further hour to the end of the almost impenetrable obscure forest of Horsepasture Covert. The bright sunshine caused their eyes to squint when the trees and undergrowth gave way to the open heathland and the manicured grasses of Beaudesert Old Park. In the distance, they could see the village of Hazelslade. Donald smiled at the familiar vista. He could faintly make out the neighbourhood children's laughter still playing football in the streets. A queue of people stood meandering its slow progress into Frank James's post office. He looked to the left towards Rawnsley village where Ebenezer Strange's aunt lived.

'Looks like we've exhausted the entire possibilities, sarge,' Jim commented. Donald reluctantly nodded in agreement.

'Let's make our way back; we've obviously drawn a blank on this route. I'll phone the ranger and let him know what we're doing.' Donald dialled Phil's number. 'Hi, Phil, Donald here. Just to let you know that we've found nothing and are making our way back to The Red Lion. How are you doing?'

'Nothing on my route either, Donald. It seems I may have underestimated Ben Strange. He's more ingenious than I gave him credit for, but there are loads more areas to explore…'

'… perhaps Inspector Cropper is having better luck?'

'No, he's not, he's contacted me. He's making his way back too. Let's regroup back at The Red Lion, and we can plan another search for tomorrow.'

Donald and the three Scotland Yard PCs turned and retraced their steps back into the shade of the Covert. The downbeat grasses they'd trodden earlier were an easier path to follow. With Donald leading, they walked on in silent procession. Halfway through the covert, Jim commented to Campbell who walked behind him bringing up the rear.

'We're coming up to that pile of bat droppings soon, Campbell. Mind your boots; the smelly crap has taken the shine off mine. It must be acidic too; the leather's gone all dimpled.' Jim carried on, not concerned that Campbell hadn't replied. 'Here we are, phew it doesn't half pong.' Jim turned as he still hadn't commented. There was no one walking behind him. He called out.

'Campbell. Campbell. Where are you?' Donald and the others turned around, hearing Jim's cries.

'What's the matter, Jim?'

'It's Campbell, sarge, there's no sign of him.'

'Campbell, can you hear me?' Donald shouted.

'He's probably only taking a piss somewhere, sarge?' the other officer commented.

'Let's hang on a minute for him to catch up.' Donald said calmly. They stared once again at the colony of drooping bats hanging upside down, watching them.

'Ah! God forbid,' said Jim, 'they're awful creatures. Notice their horrible big fangs.'

'They're like something out of a Dracula movie,' the third officer replied.

'Campbell!' Donald called again. He sensed a movement above him, and he looked up at the black infinity of the bats' eyes watching them. His call had disturbed the colony again.

'I'll backtrack, sarge, and see where he is…'

'… no, Jim, we'll all go. When was the last time you saw him?' Donald commented as they started walking along the trackway.

'Ooh, sarge, I don't remember. I was talking to Campbell a few times as we walked along. Mind you, come to think about it, he didn't reply…'

'He could be quite a way down the track then?'

'Well, he can't have come to any mischief, can he? He's probably taking a crap, and he's constipated.' Jim commented and laughed.

'Knowing Campbell's usual good luck, he's probably met a local pretty young flaxen-haired maiden, and they're lying in a shady glade somewhere?' joked the other squaddie.

They walked for a few minutes, and then Donald pointed out something in the leaves. 'What's that? That's his cap, isn't it? Campbell,' he called as they all stopped. Donald picked up his cap and looked left and right into the side of the forest.

'Campbell.' Donald shouted again.

Everybody else joined in. The loud noise disturbed some birds in the topmost branches of the canopy. As the sound of their flapping wings ceased, the covert went deathly quiet. Donald turned sharply as he noticed a faint noise.

'What's that?' he asked.

'I can't hear anything, sarge,' Jim said.

'Shh! Listen.' Jim rustled his feet in the brittle leaves.

'Shh! Keep still. There it is again.'

'You've got better hearing than me, sarge. I can't hear a bloody thing either.'

'There's definitely something…' they all stood still, straining their ears.

'Aaaw!'

'I heard that, sarge,' Jim whispered.

'Listen!' Donald murmured.

'Aaaw! Help!'

'It's Campbell,' Donald shouted. 'Campbell, where are you?' he called again.

'Down here, sarge,' His voice sounded clearer.

Jim pinpointed the direction of Campbell's voice and started ambling off the track. Then he slipped and almost fell into the void where Campbell had dropped.

'Bloody hell, sarge. What's this? It's a bleedin' great hole in the ground.'

Donald knelt on the floor and carefully searched through the moss and grasses with his groping fingers. He felt the sharp edge of old brickwork. He pulled at the overhanging vegetation before the others joined in and between them they exposed the curved side of a large, bricked opening about twenty feet across.

'Oh, saints preserve us; it's one of those old disused coal mining shafts that Phil warned us about.'

Donald looked down into the black void and shouted. 'Campbell, are you okay?'

'Yes, I'm okay, sarge. A bit battered and bruised. I must have passed out when I hit the bottom of the hole. Thank goodness it's soft ground otherwise I'd be brown bread! In fact, I'm lying in about six inches of water, and it smells something awful.'

'We can't see you, Campbell. Can you tell how far you've fallen?' Donald called into the blackness.

'I can make out a light at the top, sarge. I think I can see you at the edge of what looks like a vertical tunnel. It looks a fucking long way down to me.'

Donald reached for his phone and called Campbell again. 'Hang on, mate, I'm calling the ranger.'

'Oh, there's something you should know, sarge. I've tried to stand, but I can't. I think I've broken my leg. Thank goodness I'm not in much pain…'

'How do you know you've broken your leg?' Donald shouted down.

'Cos, I've had a broken leg before, sarge, in the West End, so I know what it feels like. Also, I can feel the bone sticking through…' Donald's phone burst into life.

'Phil, thank goodness, Donald here. We've got a problem. One of my men has fallen into one of those mine shafts you warned us about… Yes…. He's conscious… yes, Phil… but I think he's broken his leg…'

'… Where are you, Donald?' The others listened to the ranger's sharp voice from the phone.

'How deep is he, can you tell?'

'Hang on!' Donald shouted into the blackness.

'Campbell, can you estimate how far down you are…?'

'… Bloody hell, sarge, it could be fifty feet; it could be a hundred feet. It's hard to tell…' Donald thought his voice sounded fainter.

Donald answered Phil. 'Campbell reckons he's between fifty and a hundred feet down… okay…'

'Tell me where the bloody hell you are, Donald?' Everybody's listened to Phil's sharp voice.

'About halfway through Horsepasture Covert…. Okay, Phil… yes… we'll hang on,' Donald closed his phone. He called Campbell again.

'Hang on, Campbell, help's on the way. Phil and the rangers are coming.' Donald listened, but no sound came from the mine shaft.

'Campbell, Campbell, answer me!' Donald turned to the others, and they all listened.

'It looks to me as if he has passed out. Perhaps the pain from his broken leg has kicked in?' They sat back in the dry leaves and waited.

'How the fuck can anybody get him out?' questioned Jim.

'I'm sure Phil has encountered these sorts of situations before. Let's relax and wait. We can't do anything for Campbell by ourselves.' Donald tried to reassure everybody but remained as equally perplexed as Jim.

Fifty

'What are we going to do with him?' Lucy asked Janet as they finished their drinks. Lucy nodded towards Ben, still lying tied up on the patio like a trussed Christmas turkey ready for the oven. His head wound was now a mass of congealed blood. His left eye had closed because of the considerable swelling of his nose and cheeks.

'Throw him in a cell and chuck away the key,' Ted offered between dozing. The third pint of cider had taken its toll on his sensibility but enhanced his humour. 'All this excitement is keeping me awake, and I can't think of a better way than spending my afternoon with you two sexy beauties.' He laughed and wheezed before belching loudly. 'Oh, pardon me, my dearies. I suppose the wind is better coming up my throat than from anywhere else. I'd be in trouble then, wouldn't I?' He laughed again along with Lucy and Janet.

'I feel a song coming on, my beauties. Come on, join in...' Janet looked askance at Lucy. They were prepared to sing but stopped and listened to him, frequently laughing and slapping their thighs in merriment at not having heard the old war song before. To the tune known as 'Colonel Bogey,' Ted sang at the top of his voice.

'… *Hitler, he only had one ball, Goering had two, but they were small; Himmler had something similar, but poor old Goebbels had no balls at all*… oh no. I can't sing that one can I, it's rude, and I don't want to cause offence to you two lovelies. I know… *Mademoiselle from Armentiéres, parlez-vous? Mademoiselle from Armentiéres, parlez-vous? Mademoiselle from Armentiéres, she hasn't been kissed in forty years, inky pinky parlez-vous. Mademoiselle…*'

'… What the bloody hell is going on here then…?' Ted's son-in-law, Tom, looked on in astonishment as he walked onto the patio.

'… Hello, Tom. We're having a party, aren't we girls? Why don't you come and join in?'

'I can see you're having a party. What's this man doing lying here? What's happened to him? Oh my God, he's covered in blood.'

'There's no problem, sir, we're police officers. We've apprehended this man.'

'Oh, Lucy, you don't know my son-in-law, do you? Tom, this is my excellent friend Lucy. Lucy, this is my…'

'... yes, Pops, I think she gets the gist. How many drinks have you had today...?'

'... Oops, I think I'm in trouble girls, he sounds angry, doesn't he...?' Ted and the women burst into laughter.

Tom could see he wouldn't get any sense out of them, and he sat down and waited for the merriment to subside.

'I suppose you've come to fetch me, have you, Tom?'

'Isn't that what I always fu... bloody well do at this time o' day. Your dinner's ready.'

'Well, for a change, I think I'd sooner stay here, Tom. Have a peek at my two beautiful companions. Have you ever seen such lovely looking women...?'

'... Never mind these two women; Aggie is waiting for you with your dinner...'

'... ooh, Ted, you old goat, are you two-timing us? You have a woman at home waiting for you...' Lucy joked and laughed again.

'... My lovely beauty, Aggie isn't my woman, she's Tom's elder sister...'

'How much has he had to drink, ladies?' Tom asked in exasperation.

'Only three pints, I think.' Lucy answered.

'Is it three, Ted?' she asked, with another laugh.

'Oh, my dearest lovely, yes I think it is three, but...' he whispered quietly to her and held his hand to the side of his mouth. '... How about we have another one together away from here somewhere, only you and me...'

'... That's enough o' that sort of talk, Pops, I think it's time for you to come home?' Tom stood and turned to Janet and Lucy.

'... This is what Ted's like when he's had too much to drink. God only knows what tonight is going to be like. Aggie won't be safe for a start, and I think I'd better watch what I'm doing as well.' Janet and Lucy laughed, but Ted's voice turned sour.

'... Are you suggesting I'm a pooftah...?'

'... no, Pops, I'm not suggesting that. Please, come home now, so these nice young ladies can have a bit of peace and quiet.'

'... alright then, I'll come peaceably... on one condition though.'

'... What's that?'

'... That I can come again tomorrow and hopefully have another enjoyable time with my friends here.'

'Alright, Pops, a day in Upper Slaughter without you coming to the Red Lion wouldn't seem right now, would it? Come on, then.' Tom lifted his father-in-law from the bench. Janet stood and took Ted's other arm and helped him into Tom's car.

'Oh, my God, what a character,' Lucy commented as Janet sat back down on the bench.

'He's lovely, isn't he?'

'Returning to what I asked you half an hour ago, what are we going to do with him?' Lucy motioned to Ben.

'We'll wait to see what Tom has to say when he returns, but I think he comes back with us to Scotland Yard for interrogation. We still haven't found Tessa yet…'

Lucy's face pulled into a smirk. 'What's the joke?' Janet asked.

'… I'm wondering what the gov and the powers that be at the Met will say about today. Ten big strapping blokes armed with guns have been charging across fifty square miles of the countryside after Ben. Here's little ol' you and little ol' me, two frail women police sergeants minding our own business have nabbed the arch-villain from right under our male colleagues' noses.'

'It's going to make for a few interesting conversations back at the Yard, no doubt about that.'

Lucy edged closer to Janet and lowered her voice. 'Incidentally, I see what you mean about him…' She motioned her head towards Ben. 'He's a bit of a hunk and handsome, or what?'

'He certainly is. Although he's had those attractive features rearranged now, especially losing two front teeth. Pity he's such a murderous rotten swine.'

Ben had recovered his sensibilities and had been plotting how he could escape his current incarceration. He'd been listening. He bent his head towards them and murmured. 'You didn't say that to me when we were at *The Crucified Abbot* together.'

Lucy looked aghast to Janet, seeing her change in pallor. Janet's flesh cringed at the sound of Ben's evocative words. She turned to him with an open mouth.

Ben could see her confusion. 'Yes, that *was* me.'

'… But… but… *The Crucified Abbot* isn't real.'

'You and I and that soppy husband of yours know different, don't we? And forgive me if I'm mistaken, but I know about women, and I can sense the change in you since we last enjoyed each other's company. Are you pregnant by any chance…?'

Janet held her hand to her mouth.

'… Don't answer, kiddo. Can't you see he's trying to goad you?' Janet nodded and ignored his words.

'I'm more interested in *The Crucified Abbot*, Ben. How can it exist when The Red Lion stands in its place?' Janet asked.

'I can help you with that question and loads of others you must have, but we can't talk while I'm tethered up like this, a chicken ready for the oven.'

'Well, don't think for a second you're going to be released,' Janet hissed.

Lucy stepped in. 'Never mind the other matters, what have you done with Tessa Jackson?'

'Quid pro quo, ladies. If you help me, I'll help you.'

'We need to have a chat with Tom and Donald,' Janet said to Lucy.

Fifty-one

Forty-five minutes elapsed before Donald and the PCs noticed the sound of fallen brittle leaves being rustled on the forest floor. They got up to see Phil leading three other rangers. Between them they carried ropes and other equipment.

'Where's the mine shaft, Donald?' Phil shouted.

'Over here!' Donald pointed out the extent of the circular shaft. 'Campbell's gone quiet. I think he must have passed out.' Phil didn't seem to listen to Donald's last few words as he and the other rangers huddled into a tight group and then began sorting out their gear. One man tied a stout, twisted nylon rope around a tree trunk opposite the mine shaft. A second ranger tied a similar rope around another tree. Phil took off his overcoat and donned a harness with metal toggles and clips dangling from the leather reins. Another ranger laid out what looked like a car battery on the leaves and attached two wires to a lamp. To each rope they secured a complicated metal frame that had a long handle.

'What are those?' Donald asked.

'Turfers! We call them turfers, but they're winches if you like.' Phil called to him. 'Here's what we're going to do. The lads here are going to lower me down on the turfer on one rope. I'll be carrying the other rope for Campbell. Once I'm down there, I'll attach the rope to him, and he can be winched up. In sync, I'll be winched up on the other rope at the same time. That way I'll make sure Campbell's ascent goes smoothly, and he doesn't get fouled up in tree trunks and such like that are bound to be growing out of the side of the shaft.' Phil turned to his men as he curled the second rope over his shoulder.

'Are we ready, guys? Lower me away.' In an instant, Donald watched as Phil descended into the blackness. The other ranger with the lamp flicked a switch and lowered the lantern on another rope. With the aid of the bright, fluorescent light they could see the slimy red brickwork effusing with black slime and pendulous weeds for the first fifteen feet of its depth. As Phil descended, they watched the taut rope tremble and shake. Another ranger moved the lever backwards and forwards on the turfer that gently lowered Phil on the heavy-duty ratchet. They turned as a short-wave radio held by a ranger bristled with atmospheric noise. Then Phil's voice came through clearly.

'It's as we expected, Noel. Trees and bushes are sticking out everywhere. You must lift carefully once I secure him. Aargh!' They looked concerned at the radio as Phil shouted. Suddenly the air became thick with bats. Donald and the others held their hands over their heads as the mammals flew above them. Donald was at once thankful that the bats weren't the long-haired, sharp-fanged ones they'd seen earlier. He thought they were the common short pipistrelle variety.

'Are you alright, Phil?' implored a ranger.

'Yeah! I'm okay, Noel. I disturbed a colony of bats as I pushed against the wall with my foot. Have they reached you yet?'

'Yes, they have. Be careful, gov, I don't want to have to come and rescue you as well.'

Heeding the radio, they listened and sensed Phil's exertions and heavy breathing before his clear voice came again. 'Stop! I've reached him! What's the reading on the depth gauge on the turfer, Noel?' He looked towards Jonas who worked the winch.

'Thirty-eight and a half metres, Phil. How's the copper?'

'He's unconscious alright and bleeding from his lower left leg… hang on.' Concentrating on the radio, they listened to material being torn and Phil's heavy breathing.

'He's got a compound fracture of the left tibia and fibula. Both bones are protruding from his flesh. I've put a compress on the wound and tied his legs together. Wait a bit while I fix the harness over him.' More heavy breathing preceded his next command. 'Okay, guys, start lifting. Try to do it in synchronisation, the same rate for the invalid copper and me.'

It took fifteen minutes before the unconscious Campbell and Phil were back on the forest floor. The other ranger had assembled the stretcher. The entire party was soon walking through the rest of Horsepasture Covert with Campbell lying immobile on the stretcher. As they passed the concealed Dingle Dell, Tessa had roused into consciousness and thought she heard a noise and expected Ben to return, so she kept quiet. Had she shouted the passing group of policemen and rangers would have become aware of her? As it was, Ben didn't return. The afternoon passed into the evening, and Tessa remained handcuffed, naked, and semi-drugged on the bed. It was going to be a confusing, long, cold, dark night. She couldn't understand why Ben hadn't come back. She was thirsty, hungry, and shivering. Through a combination of drugs, boredom, and fatigue, she eventually slept.

Donald telephoned Tom to keep him informed about what was happening. He asked him to arrange an ambulance to be waiting in Upper Slaughter village to transport Campbell to hospital. As the men left Coppice Hills and approached the hamlet, they could see the ambulance's flashing blue light. As everyone walked through the village back to the Red Lion, the ambulance passed them en route to Staffordshire General Infirmary with Campbell on board.

'I wonder what the surprise is that's waiting for us back at the hotel?' Donald asked his men. 'Tom told me we'll never guess what the girls have done.'

Fifty-two

On the hotel patio, the Scotland Yard police officers looked on in awe as Janet and Lucy explained how, with Ted Baxter's help, they had captured Ben Strange. Tom looked at Ben, still lying tied up on the crazy paved concrete.

'We can't leave him here for the night, much as I'd like him to suffer. Donald can you ask Mrs Downing if there's a locked room in the hotel where we can hold him. Also, ask her for some food and drink for him, I don't want to have a dead prisoner on my record and have to answer awkward questions at an internal inquiry.' He bent down to Ben and spat in his face. Ben blinked as Tom's sputum dripped from his nose. 'If I weren't a decent copper, I'd let you rot.' He turned to Janet and Lucy.

'Can you come with me into the lounge, please? Phil Chalmers is going to de-brief everybody about today's unsuccessful search for Tessa and what the plan is for tomorrow.'

'What about Ben?' Lucy asked.

'He's not going anywhere for the time being, is he?'

'You'll never find Tessa without my help,' Ben gurgled.

'So, she's still alive then?' Tom accused.

'As far as I know, but she won't last much longer without food and drink, and there's only me who knows where she is. The wimpy ranger thinks he can find my Dingle Dell, but nobody will without my help.'

As they strode into the lounge, everybody was poring over the map of The Chase, spread out on the table. Phil had already allocated three more walks for the following day.

'Ah, Tom,' he called. 'Here are the details of your next walk, further from where you finished today into Brereton Hayes Wood… phew Tom! You pong, mate…'

'… I fell into some stagnant water… but before you go on any further, we have Ben Strange tied up at the back…' Donald came into the room.

'… Excuse me, Phil. Tom, yes Mrs Downing has an old pantry in the basement. I've examined the room, and I think it's an ideal lockup for Ben.'

'… Oh, excellent work. Phil's explaining about tomorrow's search, but I was about to suggest that we could try talking to Ben later. He may see reason and decide to tell us where Tessa is?'

'We can hope, but his hideaway is somewhere… I'll find it.' Phil turned to the plan again.

Donald peered at the plan and retraced in his mind where he'd been and where the mine shaft was that Campbell had fallen into.

'It sure is beautiful around there, Phil. Especially Coppice Hills and the transition into Horsepasture Covert.' They looked at the map. Donald screwed up his eyes and held his chin.

'What's the matter, Donald; can't you see where you've been on the map?'

'… Uh? Oh, yes, I can. I'm a little confused trying to trace the course of Horseylane Brook…?'

'Straight through the middle of the covert, it's here on the map.' Phil pointed out.

'I can see where the source is and where it runs down towards Brereton and eventually into the River Trent, but it's not running through the covert as you and the map says it should.'

'What? You're mistaken, Donald, it's there, always has been. Perhaps it's covered with bracken and grass, I'll get one of my blokes to clear it out…'

'… No, Phil. The bed of the stream is there alright…' he turned to ask Jim. 'That's right, isn't it, Jim?'

'… sure is. The bed's all dried up. There are washed pebbles and gravel where the stream used to be but its bone-dry now.' Jim confirmed.

Phil returned to the map. 'That's odd.' He walked into the foyer and asked one of his rangers to come into the lounge. 'Noel, have you been near Horseylane Brook lately?'

'No, gov. Not for a couple of years, as you well know, we've always been too busy for any maintenance work on watercourses. Why?'

'Sergeant Lawrence here reckons the stream is not running through the covert.'

'You must be mistaken, sergeant. The stream has been there since the year dot.' Noel questioned Donald.

Phil stepped in. 'I tell you what; I'll go with Donald as we set out tomorrow and have a peek first before I go on my search. There must be a sensible reason the brook is dry through the covert.'

'Phil, I'm thinking that for good measure we should think about the possibility of taking Ben Strange with us tomorrow.' Tom explained. 'Donald and I are going to interrogate him later.' Donald turned and looked towards Tom, 'hopefully he'll see sense and lead us to Tessa, saving all of us more fruitless searching.'

Janet and Lucy sat at the adjacent table and had been listening to the conversations. Janet noted that Tom and Donald were going to question Ben later. She needed to pick her time because she wanted a private chat with Ben about *The Crucified Abbot.*

After eating dinner in a boisterous dining room full of ebullient police officers, Tom and Donald left Janet and Lucy sharing laughs with their male colleagues. Donald held the key to the old pantry that Mrs Downing had given to him. They found Ben sitting on the chair that had been put in the old pantry for him. He had a water jug, and a plate rested on the table with the remnants and scraps of uneaten food soiling the plate and littered around the floor. Donald undid the one handcuff that secured him to the metal frame of the table. They took him into a quiet corner of the hotel lounge.

'Now, Ben, are you going to lead us to Tessa?' Tom asked him gruffly.

'Why should I? What's in it for me? You've already got me in the frame for Lizzie Cartwright, and Silas Jackson, so what difference will one more murder make?'

'Listen to me. If you show us where you've hidden Tessa, I'll make sure your cooperation will go a long way in the mitigation of your sentence.' Ben looked at Tom from under his bushy black eyebrows. He was well aware that no justification would reduce the life sentences he would receive for having committed two murders in cold blood. Ben's one coherent thought was how he could escape. For all his life he had lived on Cannock Chase, at one with nature. He was a bucolic outdoor man. The thought of spending the rest of his days incarcerated in a prison cell with only a small, barred window to glance at the sky filled him with the utmost trepidation. He knew the best chance he had of escaping his current plight was to play along with the detectives. Once back out on his beloved Chase, he would be in a better position to use the elements he knew best, the nature and flora of the forests. Cooped up in the small seven feet by five feet pantry, he had already agreed to cooperate.

'Alright, I'll show you where Tessa is,' he quietly replied to Tom's question.

'Very well. First thing after breakfast tomorrow morning, we'll come and collect you. I'm warning you; we are armed. Should you try any rough tactics or try to escape, myself, the sergeant here and my officers are ordered to detain you by using our firearms. Don't underestimate our resolve, Ben. Once you have shown us where Tessa is, you'll be treated fairly.' Ben nodded, but Tessa's welfare didn't figure in his reasoning at all.

They took him back downstairs to the old pantry where Donald refastened the handcuffs to the metal table and locked the door. 'Wait a minute, I need the khazi.'

'Donald, get him a bucket, please.' Ben looked stunned at Tom.

'Don't look so shocked. That's all you're going to get and think yourself lucky. You can soil the floor where you are lying down for all I care.'

'Are you alright, darling?' Donald asked Janet as soon as he joined her in the bedroom.

'How did you get on with Ben?'

'Very well. He's coming with us in the morning to show us where Tessa is.' Janet noticed with interest that Donald placed the key to the pantry on his bedside table.

'Oh, that's good. Poor Tessa, she must be terrified of being left alone somewhere in the middle of The Chase.'

Janet waited until she knew Donald was snoring and quietly got dressed. Carefully, she turned the key in the lock on the old pantry door and pressed the light switch. Her senses recoiled as she entered the small room that substituted for Ben's temporary prison cell. The bucket left by her Scotland Yard colleagues as a makeshift toilet for him had been used. The smell of his faeces and urine in the bucket was overpowering. Still, the inconvenience of having to endure such a horrible ambience in the room was the least of her concerns. She wanted answers to the matters that troubled her most, *The Crucified Abbot.*

As Janet entered and sat on a folding chair that had hung behind the door, Ben aroused from his slumber. 'Ah! Hello Janet. I wondered how long it was going to be before you came and chatted to me. Have you missed me?' He rubbed his eyes with his free hand and yawned.

'… No, I haven't missed you…'

'… I'm sorry about the pong…' They spoke simultaneously.

They stared at each other and both reflected upon their earlier encounters. Janet kept her distance from him. She assessed that,

251

although he was manacled to the metal table, he was powerful enough, should he wish to attack her, to bring the table with him as well. Ben saw her apprehension.

'Don't worry darling, you're safe with me; we are lovers.'

'I haven't come to listen to such stupid comments like that. We are not lovers…'

'… well, we were a couple of months ago in *The Crucified Abbot*.'

'That's why I've come to have a chat with you; I want to know how we might have met in an old public house that burnt down over a hundred years ago?'

'Don't you know…?'

'… of course I don't. I wouldn't be here asking you otherwise.' He laughed. His laughter concealed the noise of the creaking staircase. Donald had woken and, at once aware of Janet's absence, he guessed where she'd be and he crept down to the basement. Not wanting to interrupt what he was hearing, he sat on the stairs out of sight of Ben and Janet.

'Well, it's a long story…'

'… I've got the time. You're doing nothing else and you certainly aren't going anywhere.'

'I'm a man of nature, I am. I was born to live the life I do, free and as nature intended on Cannock Chase… I don't pay any taxes or receive any government handouts. I don't bother anyone, and nobody bothers me…'

'… And as a murderer?'

'Lizzie's death was unfortunate. I had no choice…'

'… You know that we have DNA evidence defining her murder on the yew tree. Also, my husband, Donald, and I saw you slit her throat, and how can you justify what you did to Tessa's poor old Uncle Silas?'

'Well, he was there and in the way.'

'If I were recording this conversation, you would have condemned yourself.'

Ben laughed again. 'If you think I'm going to spend the rest of my days locked in some stinking prison cell, you are deluded.' Janet shuddered as she saw his resolve and didn't doubt that, somehow, he was foretelling the outcome for himself.

'Getting back to *The Crucified Abbot*…' Janet whispered.

'You and your soppy husband happened along Gallows Lane at the wrong time, that's all.'

'What do you mean?'

'You may or may not believe what I'm about to tell you, but frankly, I don't give a shit whether or not you do...' He paused.

'... Yes...?' Janet was hanging on his every word.

'The Red Lion and before this hotel, *The Crucified Abbot* stands on unholy, evil soil. You know about the yew tree and Abbot Ibáñez.' Janet nodded. 'Somehow, and don't ask me how, this land around here from time to time reverts to those pagan times. It's as if the land must renew itself, must have some new sacrifice to replenish evil rites and satiate Lucifer's lust for blood. The Abbot Ibáñez was one of the first we know about, but there are probably thousands that perished before him in the mists of time...'

'... and Lizzie?'

'She was merely another on the list. In the wrong place at the wrong time, as you were. Perhaps if Lizzie hadn't been there, it could have been you on that yew tree?'

'Okay, I understand about the pagan rituals and having to produce a sacrifice, but how can *The Crucified Abbot* manifest itself here, in today's twentieth-century modern world?'

'That's something that my father told me about. My Grandfather told him, and the secret's been passed down by generations from one to the next. Of course, you know, it was my ancestors that kept *The Crucified Abbot,* Caleb and Margareta Strange.' Janet nodded. Ben paused again to make himself more comfortable.

'Can't you do something about these handcuffs? They are making my wrist sore.'

'No, I can't, they stay put. Carry on...'

'... Where was I? Yes, from time to time, I get the vibes to visit this place...'

'... why?'

'Because I know that a sort of time warp is about to occur. The air gets thick; I can taste it in the wind. The land gets into a swirl of mixed-up time, and somehow, there it is *The Crucified Abbot.* You and your hubby drove into here, just after I arrived, and we all interacted with the certain events. Of course, Caleb and Margareta help things along by plying everybody with hallucinatory drugs to help the occasion along and get everybody in the right mood.'

'How and when does this phenomenon happen...?'

'... Ooh! Every few months...'

'... as frequent as that!'

'It's not synchronised to a regularised time or run by clockwork, and it doesn't affect everybody. I reckon there's only a certain sort of person who gets drawn into its vortex.'

'So, we could be due another warp soon...?'

'Yes! It's overdue already.'

'Does everybody around here know about this? The villagers in Upper Slaughter, I mean?'

Ben nodded. 'Ted Baxter knows all about this too, doesn't he?'

'Most of them do, but as most are God-fearing people who have been raised in the Christian beliefs, they know they are not welcome in *The Crucified Abbot*. Bad things happen to non-believers of the pagan rites. And as for Ted Baxter, he's a stupid old fool who gets in the way.'

'... hence Lizzie. She was a Christian, wasn't she? She was wearing a cross when you murdered her.'

'That wasn't me who murdered her. Well, it was by my hand, my flesh and blood, but I was controlled by pagan forces, and it didn't happen in today's world.' Janet could see the faraway stare in Ben's eyes as he related his story, as if some unknown force were controlling him.

'I can't believe or understand that, Ben.' She shouted at him that jolted him from his robotic state. 'You murdered Lizzie on that tree. We saw it happen. My husband and I collected the evidence. Also, you weren't controlled by a time warp when you murdered poor Silas.'

'Yes, you gathered the evidence. The time warp can't take everything that happens back with it. Events and people get left behind.'

'... and what about you and me...?' Ben smiled and then chuckled. Seated out on the staircase, Donald became more alert.

'... you and me, what a pair we made.' He whistled. 'We certainly provided some entertainment for those old codger farmers, Jasper and co, didn't we?'

'... so, did we actually...'

'... We certainly did, and I know you received as much enjoyment as I did. Still, as I've said, Margareta made certain you and your husband were both drugged enough for you not to control events. You were merely pawns in the grand scheme of things and not aware of the bigger picture.'

'... yesterday, on the rear patio, you suggested I might be pregnant...?'

'… You didn't need to answer, I know you are.' Janet clutched at her throat and grimaced. On the stairs, Donald held his head in his hands.

'Whether I'm responsible for your belly swelling is in God's hands or, in this case, Lucifer's. But you were on your honeymoon, so your husband is probably the cause.' Janet stared at Ben in disbelief.

'I can see that you are in denial about what I've told you, but as I've said that's up to you and I couldn't care less what you believe.'

'Ted Baxter told my husband and me you are an incubus, a slave of the devil…'

'… I told you he's an old fool. He's had too much of the Abbot cider over the years. He doesn't know if he's on his arse or his elbow. The incubus he's referring to is Caleb and Margareta's son, also called Ben.'

'Well, he's not such an old fool after all, is he? He gave you a whacking with his walking stick, and that's why you're here now.'

'One lucky blow with a walking stick won't change my life, wait and see.'

'There's one other matter that has been puzzling Donald and me…'

'… Yes…?'

'The fire in 1866. Everybody was killed.' Ben looked wistfully to the ceiling.

'That was horrible and unfortunate…!' With his one free hand, he lifted his shirt to reveal a crumpled bluish scar running across his stomach.

'I've seen your scar before, remember?' Ben sneered at the recollection of them being naked together. 'Were you there? Did you get this scar when *The Crucified Abbot* burned down?'

'Yes! This scar is a reminder of that horrendous night. The time warp can't take everything that happens back with it. Events and people get left behind. This scar bears testimony to that fact.'

'How did you get burned?' Ben rubbed his face with his hand, and a strained, haunted expression came over his forehead and eyes.

'It was all my fault. I had another girl from the village with me, Annabelle Cross was her name. Her parents still live in Upper Slaughter. I should have known she would cause trouble. She was Christian too.'

'… and Caleb and Margareta didn't take kindly to her?'

'… nor did anyone else there that night.'

'… why Halloween night in 1866?'

'The time warp doesn't dictate what date we take back to; it's completely random as far as I can tell. Perhaps it was the powerful vibes that were being given off by such a special celebration as All Hallows' Eve.'

'What happened?'

'Nobody liked Annabelle. I only took her because she was my first girlfriend. I think I was truly in love with her, and I wanted to have a good time with her. I told her about *The Crucified Abbot,* and she kept pestering me that when I felt the change in the air, she wanted to come with me...'

'... Does Annabelle still live in the village?'

'... no, she died, but I'll tell you about her afterwards. Let me tell you about the fire. It still haunts me to this day. We all ate Margareta's mushrooms, and we danced and made love around the yew tree as usual. Still, they all noticed the crucifix that Annabelle wore on a chain around her neck...'

'... Like Lizzie.'

'... when I took Lizzie, I made sure that she took it off before we arrived at the yew tree, but unbeknown to me she put it back on because she became frightened. With Annabelle, Jasper and the others became angry. I wouldn't let anything happen to her, so I carried her from the tree inside...'

'... How come you could help Annabelle, but you murdered poor Lizzie?'

'That was happenstance! I don't think I ate as many mushrooms that night, or perhaps they weren't as potent? Anyway, with Lizzie, I think Margareta must have made certain I was well under the influence...'

'What happened inside *The Crucified Abbot?*'

'Things got out of hand. They turned into a mob demanding Annabelle was crucified on the yew tree. They wanted to take her out into the moonlight and pin her to the tree to copy the old Abbot Ibáñez. I wouldn't let that happen. I think it was Jasper, but it may have been David, but anyway they tried to grab Annabelle from me. I pushed them back. Simon, one farmer, fell backwards into Margareta, carrying a tilly lamp full of oil in the lounge. The lamp fell onto the couch, the red hot oil dripped to the floor, and within seconds the whole place was alight. We all tried to put out the flames, but the place was tinder dry and old and dusty. People were screaming, shouting, and running around in a blind panic. I pulled Annabelle out of the melee, and we edged our way into the foyer and through the front door. I left her on the rear patio and returned to rescue some old codgers. What I saw was horrible. Margareta's crinoline dress was ablaze. She was panicking and howling in pain, thrashing around the lounge spreading the flames even further. Then the old thatch caught alight, and the game was over. I got these scars when one window blew out, showering me with red hot shards of glass. Annabelle and I stood out under the yew tree watching *The Crucified Abbot* being gradually reduced to a pile of ash.'

Ben stared at the blank wall, reliving the horrendous Halloween night of 1866.

'You said you'd tell me what happened with Annabelle.'

Ben spoke quietly. 'Afterwards, Annabelle never seemed quite the same. Her zest for life was diminished as she retreated into herself. Apathy led to depression, and this became her normal state of mind…'

'… why was that? Were you cruel to her as you were to Lizzie and now to Tessa?'

'No, I wasn't, quite the opposite. I loved Annabelle and cared for her, despite her parents not liking me.'

'As with most things where you're concerned, we must try to believe you. Based on your track record, you must admit that engendering trust requires a great leap of faith and imagination.'

'Annabelle seemed to give up and fade away. She stopped eating and lost weight. Towards the end, she was a virtual living skeleton. Old Doctor Skilton, the village quack, reckoned she had cancer of the stomach. Still, I think at that awful experience on Halloween night she was cursed. Margareta was good at that sort of thing. It was simply good fortune on your part that she seemed to take to you and your husband; otherwise, both of you could have developed an affliction of some sort?'

From the grandfather clock standing in the hotel foyer, they heard four chimes. 'It's four o'clock in the morning, I'm going back to bed,' Janet said. 'Hopefully, I can make more sense of the things you've told me after getting some sleep?' She folded the chair and hung it back on the door.

Ben looked at her, askance. 'As I said to you earlier, I don't give a shit whether or not you believe me. However, as I know, you and your husband have experienced *The Crucified Abbot,* the same as I have; you know it to be true. You also have an added reason to believe me, don't you…?'

'… which is…?'

'… You and I made love. You know what it feels like to have me inside you. That could only have happened while you and I were at *The Crucified Abbot* together under the yew tree.'

Janet turned and stared at him in the abject realisation of the unalterable truth. She turned off the light switch and locked the door. She saw Donald sitting on the stairs and shouted out.

'Oh my God, Donald. It's you. You frightened me.' She sauntered to him and held his hands. She could see he seemed shaken and pensive. 'How long have you been sitting here?'

'Long enough!'

'I'm sorry, Donald.'

'Not half as much as I am.'

'What are we going to do?' He shook his head and continued looking at the stark wooden staircase.

'Come on, let's go back to bed.' She whispered.

Fifty-three

Throughout breakfast the following morning, Donald remained reflective and brooding. Janet tried to break his mood and stay cheerful. Still, she too couldn't dislodge the awful truth that she could be carrying Ebenezer Strange's child.

The intervention of Phil Chalmers did what Janet couldn't. He interrupted their breakfast by reminding Donald the rest of the team were ready to search Cannock Chase again. Donald perked up, reached over and pecked Janet on her cheek. 'I'll see you later, darling, have a good day,' he offered tersely.

Once again, the weather was kind. A significant difference to the previous day was only two teams set out to explore the area of The Chase to the west of Upper Slaughter. The larger group included Tom, Donald, Phil and three other Scotland Yard squaddies. Phil's ranger colleagues led the other team. Two of the squaddies took close order in charge of Ben Strange as he walked along, handcuffed and tied with ropes to a Scotland Yard officer, bringing up the rear of the convoy. They re-trod the route Donald and his men had walked the day before, over Coppice Hills and towards Horsepasture Covert. Throughout every step and hop over obstacles en route, Ben had only one aim, and that was to escape. He had planned in his mind what he considered to be his best chance of success. Unlike any of the personnel walking with him, including Phil, the head ranger, he knew Cannock Chase intimately. He understood every copse and covert's characteristics and knew where every disused mine shaft was. Ben had no intention of leading them towards Dingle Dell and Tessa Jackson. He was going to guide the procession of men to another location inside Horsepasture Covert called Fairoak Dell. In 1893, the Fairoak Colliery Company suffered a major catastrophe that made headline news throughout the Victorian society of the United Kingdom. The coal mining venture was inundated with an inrush of water from the Triassic rock measures overlying the coal seams. Fifty-eight coal miners that lived in the surrounding villages, including Upper Slaughter, drowned when torrents of water, previously trapped like a sponge inside the overbearing rocks, rushed along tunnels and passageways. The men had no means of escape and were trapped inside the mine where their bodies still lie several hundred feet below the surface. The newly bankrupt coal mining company subsequently sealed and infilled the two vertical shafts. As with most of the old mine shafts on Cannock Chase, the infill material gradually settled over time, leaving massive voids.

The previous day, Campbell had discovered to his misfortune this unalterable fact. Ben, however, was to use this geological phenomenon to his advantage. He knew the Fairoak Colliery mine shafts. Ben had descended both mine shafts that were two hundred and sixty feet in-depth to where the infill material of silt and rocks had settled. He also knew that the brickwork shaft lining was irregular and contained voids and massive holes. One such fissure about ten feet down the western-most shaft was positioned below an overhanging tree branch and behind dangling bushes and ferns that concealed its existence. Ben's ingenious plan was to stage-manage an accidental fall down this shaft and hide in the hole. It was common knowledge to anyone who knew The Chase, the depth of these shafts. They would have to admit, reluctantly, that anyone who had the misfortune to fall into these Fairoak Colliery shafts was lost and gone forever. There was no chance of them being recovered, having suffered death because of the colossal depth. Phil Chalmers and his colleagues knew the characteristics of the shafts. They would calculate that, having watched Ben fall into the void, would naturally assume that he was dead and his body irrecoverable.

Other than Michael, the hotel worker, no one had paid much attention to Ben at breakfast that morning. Michael had taken a tray of food down to Ben; he had been supervised by a police officer while he took the tray into him. It was a simple task for Ben to conceal a knife in his clothes.

Within the gloom of the covert, from the rear of the convoy of men, Ben shouted to Phil at the front. 'Hi, ranger, Dingle Dell is off to the right.' Phil looked back and then turned to Tom.

'We'd better have him up at the front to lead us to Tessa.' Tom looked back and motioned for the Scotland Yard squaddie to bring Ben to the front.

Ben led the others through thickets of thistle, gorse and patches of bracken that were four feet deep. The thrashing men's boots disturbed swarms of horseflies enjoying recent droppings of deer dung. It was a much warmer day, evident from the sweat that ran down the men's brows. The rampant horseflies sensed another tasty source of nourishment and honed in on the sticky human labour and endeavour.

Struggling to dislodge the buzzing horseflies' stings and reacting to several bites and nettle stings, the policemen's attention was elsewhere and not keeping a close eye on Ben. Ben knew the Fairoak mine shaft was nearby. He saw his opportunity and, using the knife concealed up his sleeve, severed the rope tying him to the squaddie. Ben then brought into play a useful technique he'd employed before during his life. He dislocated his thumb joint, causing the handcuff to fall away from that wrist. With a loud shout, he feigned alarm at falling into the shaft. He possessed sufficient movement and strength to grasp at the overhanging tree branch as he fell into the void. Using the bough as a fulcrum and gaining momentum, he swung his body into the black hole of dislodged brickwork and at once lay still and quiet.

The first to call out was the squaddie. 'Oh, bloody hell, he's slipped his handcuffs, and he's gone.' Everyone looked around at his loud retort.

'Oh, my good Lord,' Phil shouted. 'Ben has fallen into the Fairoak mine shaft.'

The others peered over the edge into the blackness. 'Careful everybody, this shaft is over two hundred and sixty feet deep.'

'Ben!' Donald called out.

'He won't hear you, Donald. He'll be dead.'

'Dead?'

'Nobody could survive a fall of that depth onto the hard rock at the bottom.'

'Ben! Ben!' Donald carried on shouting as Tom joined in too.

'It's no use,' repeated Phil.

Concealed in the void a few feet below them, Ben had difficulty repressing a snigger.

'Well, can't you get him out, as you did with Campbell, yesterday?'

'Not a chance, it's too deep. We don't have equipment that could penetrate that sort of depth. The turfers are only useful for shorter depths. We must face it, gentlemen, Ben has escaped British justice, but not justice that's meted out from on high. Even by a miracle that he somehow could have survived the fall, his body will be smashed and broken. To even attempt to move him would sever arteries and organs.'

'There must be some sort of equipment available somewhere that could retrieve him?' Tom pleaded.

'The only potential source for such equipment is coastal rescue helicopters and abseiling marines. Even those brave military wouldn't have ever descended a depth such as this into complete blackness. There is no visible access for a helicopter to hover overhead. Lastly, it would take a few hours for such a trained team to get here. As I warned everybody at the start of this operation, anyone who has the misfortune to fall down these disused mine shafts has to be considered lost.'

'He's had some bad luck, hasn't he?' Tom added as he stared into the black hole. 'One second he'd escaped our clutches only to fall immediately into this hellhole. I for one won't lament his passing, neither should anyone else…'

'… aren't you forgetting something, Tom?' Donald added soberly. 'Ben was the only person who could lead us to Tessa. His unfortunate death also seals Tessa's fate.'

Tom looked stunned at him, as he had momentarily overlooked Tessa. His immediate thoughts were explaining to the gov how Ben had escaped justice.

'We'll find her.' Phil insisted, 'maybe not today or tomorrow, but she's on this part of Cannock Chase somewhere, we'll find her. Perhaps we could enlist more bobbies to help?' He looked inquiringly at Tom. He nodded, still looking down the vast chasm.

'The only thing is, Phil, later today, tomorrow, or the day after may be too late?' Donald muttered. 'Tessa's been concealed on The Chase somewhere for days now. Ben has more than likely tied her up and even drugged her. She will have had no food or water. We have to find her today, or I fear it will be too late.'

Tom came over and put his hand on Donald's shoulders and whispered. 'Donald, we have to face it, Ben's been killed. You can't be too broken-hearted about that in the circumstances, can you?' Donald stared at him, knowing that they both understood Donald's personal reasons that supported Tom's assertion. Donald nodded, and they both resignedly gazed down, knowing they couldn't see anything, but both mentally conceding defeat.

'I can accept that no one could survive a fall like that, Tom, but all the same, my mind can't be entirely put to rest until I see his body.'

'Well, from what Phil has explained, I don't think anyone is ever going to see his body? We're looking at Ebenezer Strange's grave. We accept that.'

Phil took command. 'Let's work our way back through the covert. That clearing we passed is only a few minutes away. Let's pause, regroup, and try to work out how to proceed.'

Ben sighed and relaxed in the foxhole as he listened to them leave the area before attending to his thumb. He reached for a small hard stick from the overhanging branch, put it across his tongue and bit down hard. Applying the hard metal of the handcuffs that remained chained to his other hand, he pushed hard; with a well placed push, he eased the joint back into place. The stick stifled all but a minimum of noise caused by Ben's cry of pain.

Back at the clearing, sitting in the soft grasses, Phil and the rangers were poring over their maps trying to work out where to extend the search. Donald sat with the squaddie who had been holding Ben.

'I'm sorry, gov. I feel bad about what happened. I can't work out how he got himself free.' Donald placed his hand on his shoulder. 'Don't fret lad, he's done himself no favours, has he?'

'Here's the rope that held him, it's still attached to my belt, and it looks like it's been cut.'

Donald looked at the neat edge at the end of the nylon rope. 'Yes, it looks like he must have had a knife.'

Phil stood and announced the next search area. 'We're making our way back through Horsepasture Covert then, before crossing over Coppice Hills, bear left and head towards Hare Hills where we trekked yesterday. Let's go.'

'Marching through the covert for five minutes, Jim, the Scotland Yard squaddie, sidled up to Donald. Gov, to our right is where we found the dried up Horseylane Brook.'

'Thanks, Jim, with all the drama about Ben being killed, I'd forgotten all about that.' Donald shouted to Phil, twenty yards ahead.

'Phil, can you come back here?' He paused and turned, looking annoyed at being diverted from his objective.

'What, Donald, we need all the daylight hours there is if we are going to have any success today…'

'… yes, but you said you wanted to examine the course of Horseylane Brook.'

Phil tutted and raised his eyes in frustration. 'Perhaps we should do that another day? As you've said, our primary concern is Tessa now…'

'… well, we're here now, it's right here.'

'… oh, alright, Donald.' He stomped back in irritation that he was being compromised. He was used to giving out orders, not receiving them. 'Bloody coppers coming here from the smoke telling us what to do,' he muttered under his breath.

'Where is it?' he asked brusquely. Donald didn't like his manner and confronted him.

'See here, Chalmers. Don't get all uppity with me. It was you who said you wanted to see the brook. Surely if we came back another day, that would be an even bigger waste of time than stopping for a few minutes now. There again, I'm only a Detective Sergeant from the Metropolitan Police at New Scotland Yard in London, used to stomping around streets rather than trekking through heaps of stinging nettles and deer shit. Still, that assessment makes better sense to me.' He looked Phil squarely in the face. Tom couldn't help but issue a soft chortle how Donald had asserted his authority over their civilian colleague.

Phil totally ignored Donald's witty riposte and looked to the ground.

'I can see what you meant yesterday. This has been dried up for quite a considerable period. Let's walk up the stream bed to see what the problem is.' Donald followed, but not before Tom gave him a winning smile and a thumbs-up gesture.

They walked for a hundred yards when Phil called out. 'Well, I'm bowled over. Donald, Tom.' They walked up to where Phil was standing. 'Therefore, the Horseylane Brook is not flowing where it should be, it's been diverted.' He turned to Noel, his second in command. 'Do you know anything about this, Noel?' Noel also walked to where they were looking down at the dry stream bed.

'Gov, as I told you yesterday it's been a couple of... who on earth would want to divert the stream like this...?'

'... it's probably the local kids that have been messing about. Tom and I have experienced what the kids are like in Hazel Slade...'

'... no, Donald, it would take more strength than kids have got to insert a massive hollowed-out tree trunk like this into the stream.' Phil prodded the ground with his walking stick. 'See here, the tree trunk is well embedded in the ground below the waterline. This has been constructed properly meaning much soil and gravel being moved. No, this is beyond what the local kids could have done.'

'More to the point, gov,' Noel added, '*why* would somebody want to do this?'

'Let's follow the brook's new course.' They walked along the elevated bank, running alongside the alternative course. 'I apologise for sounding off at you, Donald,' Phil offered quietly to him as they walked together.

'No problem, Phil.' Donald smiled.

Tom was leading and became perplexed when the brook's course suddenly seemed to end, and they couldn't walk any further. 'What!' he exclaimed. 'What's this?'

They faced a firm wall of vegetation with the water disappearing underneath.

Phil walked to join Tom and prodded the obstacle that barred their way with his stick. Much to his complete astonishment, his stout stick disappeared into the barrier. 'Curious or what?' he muttered. He reached forward and touched the bracken, nettles and kingcups that were growing on what everyone thought was an unyielding earth embankment. His fingers intruded into the growth of vegetation. He retracted his hand and pulled with it a fine-meshed net interwoven with every type of flora that grew on The Chase. 'Wow! This is a net.'

Tom and Noel joined in with Phil, and they grabbed a handful of bracken and pulled the net. A complete wall of netting wavered and rippled as they pulled, then it collapsed into the running water as they tugged harder.

'Oh, my good Lord!' Phil gasped.

'Bloody hell,' echoed Tom.

'I think we've found Dingle Dell,' Donald wheezed.

They followed the watercourse and then saw the moss-covered caravan entirely enclosed by other vegetation.

'We'd never have found this if you hadn't insisted on looking at Horseylane Brook,' Noel said back to Donald. 'See the intricate roof covering and camouflaged walls. It's like a living construction blended into the forest…'

'No wonder this has never been discovered before, or why it doesn't show up on the aerial photos.' Phil muttered. 'This has been cleverly put together.'

'… let's see if Tessa's in here. Tessa!' Tom shouted.

Phil and Noel joined in, calling her name. 'Listen,' Donald shouted.

'Help!' a faint voice from inside called out.

'Oh, thank God, she's alive,' Donald hissed. He approached the door and saw the heavy-duty padlocked bars. 'Tessa,' he shouted, 'it's me, Donald.'

From a little way off, secluded behind some clumps of dense bracken, Ben watched the destruction of Dingle Dell. After the police had left the edge of the Fairoak Colliery mine shaft, Ben had climbed out and carefully followed them.

'Donald!' Tessa shouted, 'Help me!' Phil tugged at the door.

'This is securely locked. We can't force this without a crowbar or a metal jemmy?'

'How about we break a window?' Noel suggested. He picked up a stout log of wood that was stored under the caravan. 'Stand clear, everybody.' He rammed the end of the wood against the glass, which immediately shattered into a spider's web formation. With his gloved hand, he carefully picked away at the shards of glass. He pulled the curtains aside, and his eyes widened, seeing Tessa's lying naked on the bed. 'Oh, sorry, miss, but we're so glad to see you alive,' he called to her. He turned to Donald. 'She's starkers in there.'

Tom walked up to the window. 'Donald, come on, you know Tessa better than we do. I'll give you a leg up. Go in and put some clothes on her.'

Once inside, he saw she was handcuffed. 'Is there a key for these?' he asked her.

'Oh, Donald, I'm so relieved you've found me.' She swallowed hard. Her throat was dry and inflamed from lack of water. She was shivering and deathly pale. 'Ben keeps the keys over by the other window on the sideboard,' she croaked. Within seconds he freed her constricted wrists. Tessa's first action was to throw her arms around his neck, and then she wept copiously into his shoulder. 'I thought I was going to die,' she uttered between sobs.

'Where are your clothes?'

'I don't have any here. Ben brought me here naked.'

'I see. Does Ben have any clothes here?'

'Yes, in the wardrobe.' She nodded to the end section of the caravan.

'Donald, I feel ever so faint. I'm dying for some water.'

Donald poked his head out of the window and shouted. 'Does anyone have a bottle of water?'

A squaddie stepped forward and handed him a bottle of Buxton spring water. She didn't stop gulping until it was emptied. 'Ah! That's better,' she gasped.

'I bet you're hungry too, aren't you?' Donald asked as he threw some of Ben's clothing to her.

Donald looked away as she pulled on a pair of underpants and a tee shirt. She saw him avert his eyes. 'That's sweet of you, Donald, but there's no need, you've seen…'

'… shh!' Donald held his fingers to his lips. 'My gov is outside.' Tessa smiled impishly.

'Come on, let's get you back home. I bet your mom and dad are worried sick…'

'… and my Uncle Silas.' He looked agonisingly at her.

'What's the matter?'

'Tessa, um! Er!'

'What is it? Has something happened to my parents?'

'… no, it's Silas…'

'… oh no! Uncle Silas…' Still only clad in Ben's underpants and tee shirt, she held her hands to her face. Tears flowed through her fingers.

'How? Was it Ben…?'

'… I'm sorry to say it was.'

Outside, everyone could hear her crying. Agonised looks passed between them, feeling sorry for her pain.

'… The rotten bastard!' She called out. 'I hope you catch him and put him away for good. First Lizzie and now my Uncle Silas…'

'Ben is dead!'

Her eyes widened in surprise, then relief. 'How?'

Donald told her how he'd fallen down the mine shaft.

'Good riddance! Oh, my poor Uncle Silas,' she sobbed.

Fifty-four

After watching the tearful reunion with Tessa's parents, Donald and Tom walked back through Upper Slaughter. Phil, the rangers, and the other policemen had gone on ahead. 'You'd have thought her mom and dad would have offered some thanks to us, wouldn't you?' Donald muttered to Tom.

'Don't worry about it, Donald. We meet all sorts in our line of work. Though I didn't like their attitude when we first visited them.'

Janet and Lucy were waiting in the hotel foyer when they returned. Donald went up to Janet, and before he could say hello, she commented.

'He's dead then!'

'So, the others have told you?'

'Yes. Down a mine shaft? It's probably the best outcome…'

'… for us, yes, it is, for Ben obviously not.'

'… I don't know. You knew what Ben said, he could never spend the rest of his life in a prison cell. He has his ultimate resting place where he's lived all his life…'

'… and what about justice for Lizzie and Silas…?'

Lucy joined in the conversation. 'Well, at least Tessa is safe and sound.'

Donald looked at her and smiled. 'She's fine, a little hungry, but nothing a good hearty dinner wouldn't put right. We left her with her parents.'

Tom joined them. 'Well, it looks as if we are done here.' He looked at his watch. 'It's late to be getting back to the smoke today. How about we stay one more night and leave in the morning?'

Donald looked at Janet, who nodded.

'Right then, folks, I'm going for a shower before dinner.' Lucy said and walked upstairs.

Tom also made his apologies and followed Lucy, leaving Janet and Donald to mull over the implications of Ben's demise. 'Shall we go out on the patio; we can tell Ted all about…?' Donald asked.

'… Oh, you don't know, do you? Ted's not here today. He's got a tummy upset, apparently.'

'More like his son-in-law has barred him from coming after his revelries with you two yesterday.' Janet nodded and smiled. 'So, with no Ted to talk to, what have you both been doing with yourselves?'

Janet was still reflective about Donald and Lucy being familiar with each other, so it was easy for her to be flippant and tease him. 'Oh, not much. Oh, yes, Mark and Stephen from the Chippendales came; you know the two blokes who always strip themselves naked at the end of the group's performances, like in the movie, The Full Monty. Lucy knows them, so she gave them a ring. They suggested we all took a walk into The Chase. There are some lovely, secluded walks and glades around here, aren't there? Away from prying eyes. If you lived around here and were having an affair, you certainly wouldn't have to book a hotel room.'

Donald was already staring at her. Janet lifted her eyes and returned his stare. Their expressions remained blank and unrevealing. 'Oh, Christ almighty,' he thought, 'how much does she know about Tessa and me?'

'Let him chew the fat on that,' Janet pondered, 'if the cap fits him, let him wear it, and I hope it weighs heavy.' Donald released the tension between them by forcing a laugh.

'It sounds as if you've had a good day then?'

'Oh yes we have, and old Ted is right, isn't he?'

'Is he? What about?'

'The Abbot cider making you fruity!' Donald didn't feel like extending the theme any further and sat looking glum-faced. He knew Janet was teasing him, but the implications of what she had said severely disturbed his conscience. For all they had been through together, he regretted that his earlier flippant attitude in their marriage had caused her to hurt.

They sat on the bench looking towards the Abbot Ibáñez yew tree. Janet was holding a book she'd been reading.

'What are you reading?' he asked, looking down at the title, 'All Hallows' Eve?'

'Yes, I found it on a bookshelf in the lounge. You know what Ben was telling us about Halloween, where such a special day gives off peculiar vibes…'

'… yes, well?'

'… yes, well, what's today's date?'

Donald reached into his pocket, pulled out his phone and looked at the calendar. 'Bloody hell, it's October 30th. It's Halloween tomorrow night.'

'I'm glad we'll be left here before then. Oooh, darling, I'm having tummy pains.'

'Shall I get you some pills?'

'No, I'm okay for now, it will pass.'

'Oh, come on, Janet, what's going to happen tomorrow? It's merely another day...'

'... well, this book may change your opinion about that. Here, have a read, I'm going up for a shower, as well.' She gave him a kiss and left, leaving the book on the bench by his side. He looked at the tree; as the breeze bent the branches, little sprigs of newly grown yew fronds parachuted onto the grass. His hand felt for the book; he randomly opened the stiff, brown cover and read...

'... originated as a pagan holiday honouring the dead. On All Hallows' Eve, the veil between the world of the living and the deceased is thin. It allows the souls of the dead to come back to earth and walk among the living. Christians believe the holiday is associated with Satanism or paganism, so are against celebrating it.'

'Samhain' is a particular type of demon called an incubus. When he walks amongst us on earth, Christians keep their children indoors and wear masks to hide from him. Believers of his cult place pumpkins at their front doors to worship him and leave sweetmeats to appease him. In this way, 'Samhain', the incubus, is the modern-day originator of Halloween...'...

Donald slammed the book shut. 'Bloody stuff and nonsense,' he said aloud and followed Janet.

From his concealed viewpoint in the forest, Ben watched Donald leave. Ben could have gone anywhere. He had a new lease of life now. Anyone who knew him believed him to be dead. Whatever he did from now on couldn't be attributed to him, but he didn't go anywhere else; Ben came back to The Red Lion as if drawn by a fatalistic resignation. He was aware of the year's autumnal season and knew a time warp was about to happen. Ben felt the vibes and the gathering vortex of judders in the breeze. The dichotomy of absconding to new freedom and the dawning time warp left him helpless for any definite decision. He had to remain close to The Red Lion that he knew in his bones would soon revert to *The Crucified Abbot.*

The next morning the yellow sunshine and pink skies woke Donald early at 6:30. He stepped out of bed and went to the window. He squinted at the sun before letting his eyes fall to the yew tree and then down to the branches, but he couldn't see them. The grey morning mist was still evident on the ground and extended up the trunk of Abbot Ibáñez's final resting place. He turned, visited the bathroom, and returned to snuggle next to his wife. His concern was aroused when he saw sweat resting on her forehead. The situation mounted when he felt her flushed cheeks. She felt hot. He watched her while she still slept, her head moving from side to side. 'Perhaps she's experiencing a bad dream?' he thought. He reached for her book from the bedside table and continued reading for the next hour and a half.

He had dozed back to sleep when the sound of Janet vomiting in the bathroom woke him. 'Darling, what's the matter?' he asked with added concern, as he tapped on the locked bathroom door.

'I feel bloody awful,' came her muffled reply between retching.

'Do you have a tummy upset?'

'I don't know, Donald. It feels more than that. I think I have a fever, I'm shaking, vomiting; I have diarrhoea, a vile headache and yes, awful tummy pains. Arrgghh!'

'Well, it can't be the roast venison we had for dinner last evening. I had the same as you and I'm okay.'

'Can you go to breakfast by yourself? I can't face any food this morning, and we have a hundred miles to travel to return to London. I don't want to throw up in the car.'

'Okay, if you're sure, darling. I'll pass on your apologies to the others. Hopefully, when I come back, you'll be feeling better.' His last words were drowned out by Janet's continual retching.

He enjoyed a pleasant breakfast sitting opposite Lucy and, for the moment, temporarily forgot about Janet's plight upstairs. His thoughts for Janet were clouded further when Lucy reminded him they still had to celebrate her promotion to sergeant when they returned to London.

'Where shall we go?' she asked. 'La Ultima Puccini, like the old days, or La Vista, or...?'

'Definitely not La Vista, unless you want to bump into Robbie, the plumber, again?' She laughed.

'… what was the other option you were about to say?'

'… *or* you could come back to my place, and…'

'... definitely the third choice. I'm not sure how I can wangle a reason to have a night out, but I'll think of something... perhaps I'll be needed on an all-night stakeout watching out for more drug gangs?'

'... a whole night?' Donald nodded. 'In that case, here's to more stakeouts.' They clinked their cups of tea together. Then, as if a dark cloud appeared overhead, he knew at that moment that he wouldn't be fabricating any fictitious stakeouts and spending a night away from Janet. His thoughts diverted back to how his wife was lying poorly upstairs. He wouldn't cause her any more hurt. Lucy noticed his change in demeanour and expression. She was about to ask him what was the matter, but Tom interrupted.

'Stakeouts? What's happening then?' Tom came up to their table. Lucy answered quickly.

'Oh, I was just saying to Donald, it will be good to get back to The Yard. I left some stakeout assignments on my desk...'

'Yes, it will be great to return to some routine work again, I don't think I'm cut out to be a country chap. Phew, I'm sure I can still smell that brackish water on my skin, and I've had three showers since then...'

'... yes, now you come to mention it, I wondered what that peculiar smell was...' Lucy shared a laugh with him.

'I'll see you both down here in reception in half an hour. I hope Janet's fit enough to travel?' he motioned to Donald. The mention of Janet's plight brought him back to reality. Lucy looked at him, knowing he was thinking about Janet, and rose from the table.

'I'll see you later too, Donald,' and left with Tom.

When he returned to the bedroom, he found Janet no better than before breakfast. She had a high temperature and was partly delirious, rambling on about *The Crucified Abbot* and pagan rites. Her nausea had ceased, and he assessed she needed to sleep and rest to bring her temperature down. He gave her a drink of water and some paracetamol tablets and walked to Tom's room.

He explained Janet's condition and suggested that he and Lucy and the other squaddies return to London without them. They would follow later that day or tomorrow when Janet's situation had improved.

'Yes, I agree with you, Donald. Make sure she gets well, and I'll give your regards to the gov.'

Fifty-five

Donald returned to the bedroom and sat in the chair reading Janet's book, watching her while she slept soundly. From time to time, he thought she looked and sounded better. He must have dozed off because he was woken by her shaking his arm. 'Donald, Donald, wake up…'

'Yes? What's the matter?' He roused with a start. 'Wow! I've been fast asleep.'

While they had slept, the imminent time warp vortex that Ben knew was arriving had occurred. At that moment Donald and Janet were unaware that, once again, they had slept in the Honeymoon bedroom at *The Crucified Abbot,* once occupied by King Henry VIII and Anne Boleyn. They hadn't witnessed the mists that Donald had seen swirling around the Abbot Ibáñez yew tree that morning had gradually enveloped The Red Lion. As Tom and Lucy drove from Gallows Lane, they didn't glance around, or they would have seen the dense grey fog rolling out of Gallows Lane and completely engulfing The Red Lion.

'Can you see the time, it's nearly mid-day. What about returning to London?' Janet asked him in frustration.

'Oh, thank goodness you're feeling better.'

'Where are Tom and Lucy? I've been onto the landing, and their bedrooms are empty.'

'That's because they've returned to London.'

'… without us?'

'… everybody left after breakfast. You weren't in a fit state to travel.'

'Well, how are we going to get back?'

'I've thought of that. We can get a taxi to Stafford railway station and from there a train down to London Euston, or I could hire a car.'

'Okay, well, I'm ready when you are. I don't want to stay a minute longer than we have to; you know what date it is today…'

'… I know. October 31st, All Hallows' Eve.' Donald replied in exasperation.

'Yes, it is, and I have an awful sense of foreboding in my stomach that we need to leave now. Now, Donald! Please get a move on and let's pack our stuff and leave.'

Janet and Donald were aware it was the 31st of October, All Hallows' Eve, and indeed it was, but the year was 1866. The time warp had returned the pagan site once more to the fateful day when *The Crucified Abbot* would burn down.

They sauntered down the staircase carrying their overnight cases. Donald at once thought the hotel smelled different. There was a different ambience. They reached the bottom of the stairs, and with a start, he dropped his suitcase. He could see the old sepia parchment scroll of *The Crucified Abbot's* deeds in a swept, embossed picture frame on the wall of the foyer. In the same instant, his senses reeled at Margareta Strange's voice. Tingles travelled the length of his spine, and he turned.

'Oh, hello, Donald, where are you going? Hello, Mrs Lawrence; how nice to see you both again.'

'Aarrggh!' Janet screamed, dropped her bag, and stumbled back to the bedroom. Donald turned around and watched her scamper up the stairs.

Margareta's voice caused him to turn again. 'I'm so glad you've returned; we have an exceptional occasion here today. In the year of our Lord and master 1866, Jasper, the farmer, has spit-roasted a wild boar he shot on The Chase to celebrate All Hallows' Eve. It's a wonder you haven't smelled the wondrous aromas coming from the back garden. I have some lovely birch boletes from Horsepasture Covert, I picked them myself. Caleb has also gathered some hazel truffles from Beaudesert Glade; you know the one in the dappled field before entering the village. I know we're all going to have a wonderful time. I'm short-handed now trying to get everything ready; you could give Jasper a hand in the rear garden. I know Ben is also helping him. If you glance out of your window, you'll see Ben turning the spit. Jasper's getting on a bit these days, so he and Ben are taking turns spinning the handle.'

Donald was transfixed. Involuntarily he picked up Janet's case and walked back upstairs. Donald found her lying in bed completely covered by the bedclothes. He lifted the top sheet to see her lying with her knees bent up in a foetal position. Her eyes were scurrying from side to side, displaying the awful contradictions she experienced that outwardly manifested themselves in her shivering flesh.

She stuttered. 'Oh, Donald, I'm so frightened. Why has this happened to us again?'

He held her tightly. 'I don't know, darling. I'm frightened too. Margareta has told me they're having a special celebration today as it's All Hallows' Eve in the year 1866 and you know what that means...'

Janet felt her nerves fusing together in one colossal tremor that racked through her body. '… Oh, my Lord. The day *The Crucified Abbot* burned down. We must get away from here, Donald.'

As they lay hugging each other, Donald was aware of someone shouting. He turned his head towards the window. Janet looked to see what Donald had sensed.

'What's the matter, Donald, what is it?'

'I think somebody's shouting… there it is again.'

'Donald, it sounds like a man calling our names…' Donald got up and walked to the window; he gasped and had to sit down on the nearby chair as his knees buckled beneath him. He looked again in bewilderment out of the window.

'What can you see out there, Donald?' Janet asked, not really wanting to know why he had suddenly gone so ashen.

'… it's… it's… Ben!' he stuttered, before looking again to make sure. 'But how can that be?' he murmured to himself.

'What! You told me he was dead. That he'd fallen down a mine shaft.' Donald turned to Janet as she started to get off the bed.

'I saw him myself, darling. I watched him disappear into the blackness of the disused colliery…' Janet joined him at the window. Together they watched Ben turning the handle of the spit, roasting a whole wild boar. Jasper stood to the side, avoiding the grey smoke that was wafted by the breeze into the forest from the pile of blazing pine logs. He reached forward with a giant, silver ladle and dipped it into the juices from the dish below. He carefully basted the golden skin of the boar as a burst of flames consumed the flesh.

Ben saw them standing at the window and waved. 'Janet, Donald,' he called. Jasper also turned and waved. Ben started shouting louder, but his words were indistinct, so Donald lifted the sash on the window. His unmistakable voice now penetrated their bedroom.

'Janet, Donald, come on down. We're going to have a special celebration today.' Jasper joined in.

'Hello, my dear Janet. How are you? It's so nice to see you again. I hope you're feeling well enough to join in our dancing later. David and Simon will be here later too. I know you'll want to dance with us all again after the wonderful time we shared when we last cavorted together.'

Janet shuddered and sat on the bed. Her thoughts returned to the dreams she'd had of them all dancing in the nude and being intimate with each other. Remembering what Ben had told her, Janet now knew they weren't dreams, and the events had actually happened. Her body trembled, accepting the realisation that three lewd, old farmers who were practising satanic worshippers had been on intimate terms with her and she with them. She sobbed and held her head in her hands, remembering that, despite the awful implications, she had derived pleasure from it. 'Close the window, Donald,' she shouted. Donald dropped the sliding sash with a bang.

'I can't go through any of it again, Donald' Her cries intensified. They listened to Ben and Jasper's raucous laughter coming from the garden. She imagined they were discussing her and held her arms across her chest in shame. She envisioned Ben explaining to Jasper on the merits or otherwise of the pleasure he'd obtained from making love to her as if she were his plaything.

'Donald, come on, we have to leave here now.' Janet stood but felt the discomfort in her stomach and sat down again. 'Ooh, Donald, I'm still having terrible stomach pains.'

'Come on; lie down in bed for a while.'

'Ooh, Donald, I think I'll have to. I'm having real cramps.' Donald could see her wild eyes.

'… but Donald, we have to get away from here. I'll crawl out of the door if I have to…'

'… I'll get you a drink of water.' He rushed into the bathroom to fetch her a drink. When he returned, his worries grew. She was sweating again, and her complexion was deep pink. He felt her rapid pulse. She clutched at her stomach and shouted out.

'Oh, Donald, what's happening to me?' They watched the lower part of her nightie suddenly become soaked. 'Oh, darling, I'm sorry, I can't control my own plumbing, I've wet myself.'

'Darling, I think I ought to send for a doctor…'

Janet was gasping in pain. '… how the bloody hell can we send for a doctor? We're cocooned in a hotel that's suspended in a time bubble in 1866?'

'Well, even in 1866, they had doctors. I'll ask Margareta…'

'… no, Donald, I don't want any local pagan believer quack friend of Margareta looking at me. This will pass. Are there any more paracetamol tablets?'

'We only have six left. Here, take a couple now with this water.' Janet took the tablets, swallowed the water, and after cleaning herself in the bathroom, she got back into bed.

Donald sat back in the chair by the window, looking across at her. He reached for his phone and, as before, there was no signal reception. Donald thought of telephoning Tom and asking him to return to collect them, but that wasn't a possibility now. He looked back to Janet with increasing concern and recognised the deep trauma and anxiety she was suffering. His thoughts returned to her pregnancy. He remembered what Doctor Pritchard had said to him in Saint Thomas's Hospital in London. *'Try to keep your wife calm, avoid stress and anxiety.'*

'Avoid stress and anxiety? Some hope! Here I am with my eleven-week pregnant wife suffering more stress and anxiety that would tax a hundred sane people at once.' He sat watching her, and she seemed to doze peacefully. He turned to peer over The Chase and watch high clouds meander overhead. But, after half an hour, Janet moaned and roused.

'Donald! Oh, my God, Donald, fetch me a towel from the bathroom.' He dashed to fetch a large white bath towel. He watched her reach down and place the cloth between her legs.

'What's going on, darling?'

'I hate to consider what might happen, but I suspect I may be going to have a miscarriage? Something isn't right. I can feel it…? Earlier, I didn't wet myself, it was the waters surrounding the baby in my womb?'

'… you mean the pain…?'

'… yes, a little pain, but more than that. I don't know, a feeling that it wasn't meant to be… aargh!' Janet's body doubled up in pain. She brought her knees up to her chest as she lay trembling in a foetal position. Her mounting distress blanked out anything else that was happening around her.

Janet's cries and gasps of pain jolted him into a panic. He felt helpless. 'Oh, my God, Janet, what should I do…?'

Through her tremendous distress, she falteringly answered. 'There's… nothing… you… can… do,' she gasped, 'there's nothing… anybody can do… not even a doctor if he was here… now.'

'Did you want the towel because you think you're going to bleed?'

'I'm… bleeding… now… Donald. Arrgghh!'

'Oh, my Goodness, Janet.' He saw the tears falling from her cheeks.

'Aargh!'

'Janet!'

'When… the pain… comes, I… know… I'm… bleeding.' Donald noticed she was breathing heavily, gasping for breath.

'Aargh!' Janet cried out again.

'… we need a doctor, Janet. I'm going…'

'… no… Donald… stay. I'm… losing… our baby, I'd… sooner you… were… with… me… as… I… know… you'd… be… with me… if I was… giving… birth… after nine months…'

'… darling, after what Ben said, do you still think it's *our* baby?' Through a reddish mist, Janet gazed at her husband but couldn't answer him. Donald knew in his heart at that moment she thought the father was Ben, and his wife's impassioned stare cemented his own thoughts and fears. 'Perhaps this is for the best?' he thought. Donald hated seeing the trauma and pain she was going through. He tried to envisage the rest of their lives together; he didn't relish the thought of forever looking at their child, knowing Ben was the father.

Janet cried out again and tried to peek down into the towel. Donald leaned forward to see what she was staring at. There were large, deep red clots of blood interspersed with yellowish-brown fluid discharge. Between the lumps, there was a more massive clump of clots and mucus about the size of a golf ball. The tiny baby was about an inch and a half long. Its head was more significant than the rest of its body, which had diminutive legs and arms. He marvelled at how he could see spidery arteries running between wafer-thin bones. Its eyelids were closed. He acknowledged its eyes would never see the world; its fingers and toes separating from a web-like pale skin would never touch or feel. Its earbuds would never listen to his mother telling him of her love; and from the indistinct lump between its tiny legs, Donald confirmed it would have been a boy. Donald sobbed, his chest heaved, and he hugged his wife, who felt anaesthetised by the pain and loss of her child. Donald held Janet close to him, and they both wept.

After a while and their tears had dried, he lifted his head from her heaving bosom. She held his cheeks and whispered in bursts. 'Oh, Donald… I think it's for the best… I know in my heart it wasn't *our* baby…' Donald nodded in agreement and accepted what had happened was meant to be. He gathered up the towel, placing it in the bathroom, and passed another one to Janet.

'Stay in bed, darling, and rest for a while. I'm going to get us a pot of tea from Margareta.' He saw the fervent plea in her eyes. 'Don't worry; I won't tell anybody.'

Resting alone in the room's stillness, Janet reflected on the cycle of events that had overtaken her in the last three months. It was here at *The Crucified Abbot* that her pregnancy had begun, and it seemed fitting that it should end here. She thought of what Ben had said in the basement pantry. *The time warp can't take everything that happens back with it. Events and people get left behind.* His prophetic words reinforced what she was feeling. In this case, it seemed entirely right that her foetus child should stay behind at *The Crucified Abbot* after they left. Whether she fell asleep, she wasn't sure. Still, her senses were aroused when another discharge of fluid and mucus flooded the bedclothes as her body discharged the placenta.

Donald returned with a pot of tea and some biscuits. 'Here we are, darling, have a cuppa and try to get some of your strength back.'

'I don't think I have any energy left… to do anything else… but we *must* leave, Donald.' Janet's fatigue caused her to gasp between uttering her words.

'I know we must, but I've been thinking. Didn't Ben say that the fire was started by Margareta's tilly lamp?' Bathed in a sauna-like sweat, Janet nodded. 'Well, that suggests it was getting dark when it happened, so I'd guess we have until later this afternoon before we need to leave. That will give you a few hours to rest and recuperate. Are you still bleeding?'

She nodded. 'Yes, more blood. Can… you clean me up, please? I think it was… the placenta coming away… from me.' She drank some tea and nibbled at a biscuit. 'Did you… see anyone, other than… Margareta, I mean?'

'Yes, quite a few others are coming into the hotel, but I didn't get involved. They looked at me suspiciously at first. I noticed after they'd chatted to Margareta, they seemed friendlier. I suppose she told them who I am. How are you feeling?'

'Weak and empty, but the… cramps and pain… have gone.'

'Lie down now and try to sleep. I'll make sure we have plenty of time to leave this accursed place before anything is going to happen.'

Fifty-six

Donald waited until Janet was deeply asleep before he ventured out. He wanted to have a chat with Ben. Donald ambled to the rear of the hotel where Ben was still attending to the roast boar on the spit. He noticed Jasper was fast asleep on the bench, usually occupied by Ted. Ben saw him approaching as he ladled some more juices over the crackling flesh.

'I told you it was going to happen, didn't I? Well, here we are together again at *The Crucified Abbot*.'

'How did you escape from the mine shaft?' Donald asked him bluntly.

'Easy. I told you I know The Chase better than anybody. I also tried to tell you about Phil, the ranger. He thinks he's the bee's knees and knows everything there is to know but, once again, I've proved him wrong, haven't I? He didn't know what I knew. When they built that old shaft, the mining engineers placed metal step rungs at five feet intervals in a spiral pattern to the bottom. From where I'd concealed myself, climbing out was easier than walking up some stairs. Discovering Dingle Dell and Tessa was even down to you. Phil was even ready to ignore the only telltale sign that gave it away, Horseylane Brook. How is Tessa, by the way?'

'She's fine now and back with her parents. No thanks to you. She would have died if we hadn't broken into your caravan…'

'… I wouldn't have let Tessa die…'

'… why, so you could rape her again, before disposing of her…' Ben looked daggers at him. '… and why did you kill old Silas? He'd done nothing to you. Whatever other foul deed you've done in your miserable life, slitting the throat of an old, helpless man comes as low as it can get. You deserve to swing on a hangman's noose and suffer for hours while the rope tightens and chokes the breath from your miserable body.'

'… now, now, Donald. You can't do anything like that to a man that's already dead. Don't you realise I'm free and easy now? Even if I wanted to abduct Tessa and slit *her* throat, you are helpless to pin a conviction on me. How many witnesses were there that watched me fall into that shaft…?'

He grabbed Ben by his shirt collar. 'If ever I hear that any harm befalls Tessa, even though I'm a law-abiding police sergeant, I'd make it my life's mission to hunt you down and string you up myself. Preferably on your beloved Chase somewhere, leaving your body to rot and be scavenged by the fowls of the air.'

'Tut, tut, Donald. There, there, that's no way to talk to the real daddy of your child, is it? The baby growing in your wife's belly *is* mine, you know. For the rest of your life, you'll be merely a stepdad. You must stand aside once a fortnight when I come knocking at your door to claim my visitation rights over my son. You'll become a distraction to him as I make sure that he knows his true heritage, *The Crucified Abbot* and the Strange family. Enjoying and taking part in the legacy of being able to take part in the pagan rituals that this land demands.'

Donald sneered at him. 'Not anymore, it's not. You have no hold over us anymore.' Ben's face dropped. 'Nature has discarded something that shouldn't have happened in the first place.'

'Oh, that's a shame, but never mind; perhaps we can rectify that when we all dance around yon yew tree this evening. I know Janet will look forward to renewing an acquaintance with me once again if you know what I mean.' It was Ben's turn to sneer and snigger.

Their confrontation was disturbed by Margareta as she walked towards them. Donald immediately noticed she'd discarded her apron and cardigan. Her flowing dress hung precariously from her shoulders, revealing a substantial part of her heaving breasts. She was carrying two large glasses of Abbot's cider.

'I can hear you two arguing from the kitchen. Here we are, have a drink of cider together and bury your differences.' She passed a glass to Donald.

'No, thank you, Margareta, I don't drink with scumbags.' He walked away, leaving them staring at each other.

Ben watched him go back into the hotel before speaking to her. He knew what she was already thinking. 'I think we have a problem that needs sorting, Margareta.' She nodded thoughtfully. 'It seems Donald and Janet are no longer any use to us here… she's got rid of the child.'

'Has she? Well, that puts a different viewpoint on the situation now. What shall we do? Now there's no child to consider, they're expendable…'

'Leave it with me, I'll think of something…' Ben gawked into the flaming pine logs. '… I have the perfect solution. Our celebrations will be extra special this evening. Our Lord and master can be appeased by having two sacrifices. One crucified on either side of the trunk...' Margareta laughed aloud with a hideous cackle. For an instant, her face transformed into an evil looking skull full of deep wrinkles and living maggots slowly devouring her flesh.

She held his leering face. 'An excellent solution and the perfect ending to our special festivities. I was thinking of the same result.' Margareta and Ben turned to stare up at Donald and Janet's bedroom window.

Donald returned to Janet. He relaxed a little, seeing her deeply asleep. Gazing at his watch, he estimated they had three hours before the light would fade. He sat in the chair by the window and for something to do and to pass the time he read some more of Janet's book. Donald hoped she would be fit enough to leave by having a few extra hours' rest and sleep. He envisaged them merely walking away from *The Crucified Abbot* and not looking back.

Donald became bored with the book and fell asleep. He was slouched in the chair and gently snoring when he was woken by Janet shouting at him.

'Donald, wake up! Look at the time! It's... after seven-thirty... and it's dark... outside.'

He jumped up straight away and exclaimed. 'Oh, Lordie, Janet. I'm so sorry, I've been asleep. I meant to wake you at four o'clock! How do you feel now?'

'A little... better than... earlier. My pains... and cramps... have gone, but I feel so weak and helpless, but even if... I wasn't, we must... leave. I told you I'd... crawl out of... here if I... had to... I'm still... bleeding... but nothing like earlier.'

'Would you like to take a shower before we leave...?'

'... no, Donald, we're... going now. I don't have the energy... to stand in thc... shower, anyway.'

Donald was alarmed to see how weak Janet was but equally buoyed by her determination. He placed an overcoat over her soiled nightie and helped her into her shoes.

'Okay, come on, let's try.' Donald left their bags, supported Janet, hobbled onto the landing and struggled down the stairs.

Before they reached the bottom, they gasped at what faced them. Holding Donald and Janet up in the foyer were Caleb and Margareta, with Ben and all the other visitors. They were there to celebrate the special All Hallows' Eve.

'Where are you two going?' Margareta asked with an evil leer.

'We're leaving, please stand aside…' Donald said forcibly.

'… Before you go, why don't you join us in the garden for a barbecue and celebration?' Ben said with a threatening voice.

'No, I don't think so, out of the way and let us through…' Donald pleaded. They reached the bottom of the stairs where Caleb held up his hands.

'You're not going anywhere. We've gone to all this trouble, haven't we…?' Caleb turned to gain everyone else's agreement. They all shouted 'yes' and 'why don't you stay?'

Donald stared in horror when he saw Ben was holding his hefty, serrated knife that had slit Lizzie and Silas's throat. Standing to the side, Jasper, David, and Simon were holding pitchforks. The crowd pushed and forced Donald and Janet towards the door that led onto the patio. They had no choice but to edge slowly backwards. Janet cried out a little when she saw Jasper come to the front, pointing his pitchfork at her. In her weakened state, she stared and gasped at the horror mounting before them.

'Oh, Donald… what can… we do?' She wheezed into his neck as he supported her.

'Unfortunately, Tom and the lads took all the firearms back to Scotland Yard with them; otherwise, I wouldn't think twice about shooting the lot of them. There's not much we can do except fight with our bare hands if we have to.'

'There, there, Donald, that's not a nice thing to say about us all. We've given you and your nice lady wife so much of our hospitality. Is that a kind thing to express and is that how you would repay our kindness by shooting us?' Margareta threatened.

David and Simon joined Jasper with their three-pronged pitchforks, beckoning them to move backwards and out onto the patio. They kept pushing the prongs forward, forcing Donald and Janet back. At one instance, Jasper's fork penetrated Donald's trouser leg, causing him to cry out. He felt the blood running down his thigh. Janet uttered another cry when she heard a woman's voice from the rear shout, 'Crucify them!' Janet was filled with dread and ensuing panic. Donald couldn't see how they could escape. He tried to hold Janet behind him as they shuffled over the crazy paving, walking backwards.

Ben came to the fore, holding his knife, as a conjoined chorus of disapproval all demanded that they be crucified. 'Crucify them;

crucify them together on the tree. Let Samhain be appeased by the infidels' blood.'

Ben encouraged the mob by shouting, 'can you see everybody, she has murdered my child, the one who was to become our saviour.' The group of revellers became a frenzied mob, demanding their death.

Donald and Janet edged further backwards. They were being forced towards Abbot Ibáñez's yew tree. Donald suddenly felt the heat on his back from the barbecue spit roast that still blazed in the garden. He edged Janet around the fire. They were only a few yards from the tree. The mob was closing in on them. What Donald and Janet saw added to their dismay. Caleb and Margareta held a hammer and nails. The crowd were shouting and waving their arms. The three farmers were advancing with their pitchforks; Ben was ready to slit their throats with his knife. Suddenly Janet cried out, 'I love you… Donald, I've… always… loved you…'

'… I love you too, my darling Janet, but don't give up, we're not done yet.' He spotted the only thing that he could defend themselves with. Quickly placing Janet by the trunk of the yew tree he turned to face the murderous throng. He reached forward towards the flames of the barbecue spit roast and grasped the dry end of a pine log incandescent with bright flashes at the other end from burning in the fire. Shouting and wincing in pain, he burned his fingers. Donald raised the flaming log above his head and threw it towards Jasper, who was nearest. It struck him on his chest, and he dropped his pitchfork in shock. He saw Caleb and Margareta drop the hammer and nails, raising their arms in alarm.

'What…?' Jasper screamed as his dry clothes caught alight and flames quickly seared up his body. In a second, his bushy white hair was a mass of glowing embers, and he thrashed around, trying in vain to douse the blaze. The heat overcame him, and he fell backwards, causing two more men standing behind to catch fire.

'Get them,' Margareta screamed at Ben as he looked across in horror at Jasper's burning body. It was the last words she would ever utter as she clutched at Caleb in fear and despair.

'More logs, we need more logs…' Donald shouted desperately as if someone else could help him.

Despite being horrified by the intense agony he'd already caused, Donald at once realised the barbecue fire was their only salvation. He picked up other flaming logs and threw them forward too. Despite suffering severe burns to his hands, in increasing blind panic, he threw more and more without looking where they were going. Suddenly, Donald realised there were no more logs available to be grasped as the fire was consuming the rest of the fuel in a white heat. He edged backwards to the yew tree, expecting to be crucified and resigned to their fate. He glanced down at Janet, who lay on the grass with her head slumped against the gnarled trunk. Donald and Janet heard the shouts, the horrible screams, the shrieking, and screeches and gazed up. What had been an angry mob intent on murder was now a mass of orange flame, inside an intense inferno. They watched Ben, burning from head to foot, running back into the hotel, flailing his arms, and roaring with unbearable agony, crying, and squealing. Janet noticed in fatal fascination the flesh of his once handsome features being melted away to reveal his blackened skull. One by one, his remaining teeth fell out into the mounting ash pile. Donald saw Simon lying in the white-hot embers, curled up in an embryonic position. His hands covering what was left of his face were powerless to prevent the complete incineration of his body. Janet's face twisted with revulsion as she watched David's flesh disintegrate like melting ice-cream on a warm summer's day. Caleb and Margareta, already thrashing about in bewilderment and excruciating pain, fell inside the foyer entrance. In a blind panic, the others had trampled them underfoot as they tried to evade the airborne flaming logs before falling over themselves. The en massed howling and baying reached an intense fever pitch before gradually diminishing, and then it grew quieter. Donald and Janet looked above the burning smouldering rabble and noticed the old, thatched roof was also alight. In Donald's blind desperation, one of the blazing logs he'd thrown had landed on the tinder dry thatch.

The scorched cinders from the burning thatch added to the inferno as it trickled down like red hot lava running from a fissure in a volcano onto the already burning throng. Watching in fascinated horror and revulsion, Donald and Janet witnessed flesh melting off human features and torsos, revealing blackened bones and bubbling tissue. Donald's future nightmares would recall the sight of a blackened cranium trying to whimper as the fleshless jawbone fell away. It dropped into a mounting pyre of incandescent ash that was the incinerated remains of the rest of his body. The burning corpses then joined Caleb, Ben, and Margareta on the hotel foyer floor transformed into a communal crematorium where one anonymous crumbling luminous body merged with another. Donald and Janet edged further back against the yew tree trunk and couldn't go any further. He sank to the ground, clutching Janet, thankful for their deliverance. His hands were burned and blackened; his hair singed. They held each other and watched *The Crucified Abbot* gradually reduced to cinders and ash. In the darkness of Cannock Chase on All Hallows' Eve, the ancient hostelry slumped into a pile of shimmering ash with yellow sparks and flashes leaping sporadically into the dark evening. For most of the night, Donald and Janet lay comforting each other under the spreading branches of Abbot Ibáñez's yew tree. From time to time they looked towards the fire that gradually turned from white to a bright yellow, to orange and dimming to a dull mauve purple amid the mounting pile of grey ash. From sheer fatigue and relief from a gathering sense of deliverance, they eventually slept.

The new dawn signalled the Christian festival of All Saints' Day. The sun illuminated the morning mackerel sky. Donald and Janet awoke and peered through the retreating morning mist towards *The Crucified Abbot.* They saw, to their immense relief and delight, the familiar red brickwork and clay tiles of The Red Lion. They smiled, looking towards the slatted wooden bench, expecting old Ted Baxter to come along carrying his pint of Abbot cider. The orange sunshine reflected from their bedroom window. The sense of joy they felt was tempered and diverted by the pains from Donald's scorched hands and arms and Janet's intense fatigue.

They turned and hugged each other so tightly they momentarily couldn't breathe. Loosening their embrace, their kiss was deep, long, and full of a love they hadn't previously experienced in their brief marriage. Releasing from the kiss, they smiled and gave a short laugh. 'We've come through this, darling,' Donald purred.

'It's almost poetic that fire being the downfall and destruction of *The Crucified Abbot*, in the end, came to our rescue.' Janet hummed back at him. 'Ouch!' he shouted and looked at his blistered and cracked fingers and scorched hands and arms. They hugged again as the glowing orange ball of sunshine gradually illuminated their faces.

'Donald,' Janet spoke tenderly. He looked at her and smiled. 'Donald, you know when we were near the end, and our last hope had gone…'

'… you said you loved me and had always loved me…'

'… and you said you loved me…' He smiled and nodded.

'Let that be the renewal of our vows to each other. Let that be the new beginning of our marriage, to the mutual exclusion of all others. Who else could survive the horrors that we've been through…?'

Donald carefully placed his blackened finger on her lips and whispered.

'… and it's those horrors that have shown us what genuine love is and what really matters is having each other and being true to one another. We are all the stronger for it, but we'll never forget *The Crucified Abbot.*'

Fifty-seven

Six months had passed. Donald and Janet were immersed in other cases at Scotland Yard. Rarely in their waking hours did they think of the traumatic events at Cannock Chase. *The Crucified Abbot* only seldom made appearances in their dreams. One bright, sunny, spring morning on Westminster's embankment, Donald gazed out of his window. The leaves of the plane trees rippled in the gentle, warm breeze as he opened his post. Donald savoured the familiar hoot of barges on the Thames. He was about to go to a meeting but stopped when he saw the postage frank on one letter was marked, Stafford. Discarding the other memos, he noticed with interest it was a handwritten letter from Mrs Downing at The Red Lion. She explained that in ten days, it will be Ted Baxter's ninety-third birthday. He and Janet were invited to attend a small celebration that she was putting on for him at the hotel.

Later that evening, he discussed it with Janet. 'Shall we go?' he asked with expectant eyes.

'I can see you'd like to,' she replied as she served their meal. 'Let me think about it.'

'Cheers,' they exchanged. They clinked their glasses of rioja as they finished eating and retired to the cosy settee where they both immersed themselves in their own reading. Janet's book was a romantic novel. Donald studied a boring departmental resumé expounding how to economise and affect efficiency in the workplace.

'We're due a break. We haven't had a day off for months,' Janet blurted, putting her book down and holding her finger against the line of words she'd reached, not wanting to lose her place. He stopped theorising on saving money for the Yard and looked at her, eagerly.

'You mean you'd like to go?'

'It would make a pleasant change, wouldn't it? We could stay for a night and have a longer view of the area before we head back.' He reached over and kissed her. She let the novel drop to the floor, no longer caring where she'd got to with the fictitious romance but returned Donald's very real eager and fiery embrace.

'Great! I'll book a hire car tomorrow and get Rosemary to book us a room. First, I need to talk to the gov to see which days will be convenient for us to have off.'

Donald and Janet strolled into the foyer of The Red Lion. It was a warm, sunny day and the windows of the conservatory dining room were wide open. They smiled at the decorative garlands and bunting hung around the hotel declaring *Happy birthday, Ted, 93 years young.*

'Hello Mr and Mrs Lawrence, I'm so glad you could come.' Mrs Downing came from behind the reception desk to greet them. 'Your usual room is all ready for you.'

'Hello, Mrs Downing. Wow! You're walking much better…?'

'… yes, it's a miracle. Since all that nasty business with Ben Strange was over and done with, I'm delighted to say my arthritis has gone into remission,' she laughed. 'Of course, my doctor would say it's down to the new steroids I'm taking. Still, since Ben is no longer about, the whole place has become a new and happier environment…'

'… Donald, Janet!' They turned as Tessa came from the lounge. 'I heard your voices. I'm so glad to see you both.'

'How are you, Tessa?'

'I'm fine, thank you…'

'… she's more than fine, aren't you, Tessa? Aren't you going to tell them your news?'

Tessa looked demurely under her eyelashes. 'I'm engaged to be married.'

'Oh, that's wonderful news.' Janet enthused.

'Who's the lucky chap?' Donald asked.

'You remember Michael, Michael Thompson from the village…'

'… yes, I do,' Janet turned and prompted Donald. 'Don't you remember? He helped us get some rope to tie Ben up on the patio.'

'Of course. Michael's a nice chap. I hope you'll be happy, Tessa...' Donald added.

Mrs Downing joined in, '… and since you were last here, of course, Tessa started working here again and… well… I don't know what I'd have done without them both. So, I've promoted them to joint managers of The Red Lion. Now I don't have the stress of the day to day management of the place, and I think that's also helped my arthritis improve?'

'When's the big day then, Tessa?' Janet asked.

'In June, you both must come, I insist. What's also so wonderful is that dear old Uncle Silas left me Brooklands Cottage.'

Later that afternoon, The Red Lion bustled with the joyous occasion of celebrating Ted's birthday. His family joined his many friends and the villagers from Upper Slaughter to add their congratulations to this happy milestone in his life. Donald and Janet met Aggie. Tom had already warned Ted about drinking too much Abbot cider but knew his edict would fall on deaf ears. Appreciating the special event, for once he wouldn't condemn his father-in-law's overindulgence.

As the afternoon wore on, Ted became weary and left the party to seek a little quietness on the patio in the sunshine. He carried with him a partly consumed pint of cider that he placed on the table. Simultaneously, Donald and Janet ambled towards the patio.

'Ah! My old friends come and join me away from the bustle and noise. They won't miss us, will they?' Ted laughed with them as they sat alongside.

'We wish you our own personal congratulations, Ted,' purred Janet and kissed him.

'I'm sorry you lost your baby,' Ted offered with a sombre tone. Janet looked at Donald before replying and decided not to divulge that it had been Ben's child.

'That's alright, Ted. We're fine, aren't we?' Janet reached for Donald's hand.

'It's nice to see everyone so happy, isn't it, my dear?' Ted wheezed before taking a slurp of cider. 'It hasn't always been the case around here, has it?'

'We were only saying that earlier,' Donald replied. 'In fact, the whole of The Red Lion and the villagers seem different somehow. I know everyone is celebrating your birthday, but there doesn't seem to be those scowls, those questioning, suspecting eyes from everybody…'

'… That's because Ben isn't here anymore…'

'… do you believe that Ted?' Janet asked.

'I know it to be a fact, my dear. Can't you sense it? Why, even yon Abbot Ibáñez yew tree has lost its foreboding, mysterious air…'

'… all because of Ben?' Donald questioned.

'That man was the very embodiment of evil, he was. I genuinely believe… well, I know… he was the catalyst that brought so much malevolence to this place. When I look back over the years, the bad things that have happened in the area must have mostly been attributed to the Strange family and *The Crucified Abbot*. Thinking about it, why, even the German Luftwaffe pilot flying his Heinkel bomber over us in 1940 seems a peculiar coincidence. His target was Coventry, so how come he dropped his bombs here in Upper

Slaughter? I reckon he got lost alright, but as he flew over he came under the evil influence of *The Crucified Abbot*. He was compelled to drop his bombs on the priory.'

'When we were last here, Ted, Ben told us you and the villagers all knew about the time vortex that came and transformed The Red Lion back into *The Crucified Abbot...*'

'… yes, we all knew, well, most of us. That's why we always tried to stay away from here when we knew it was coming…'

'… but the yew tree is still here with the nails still embedded in its trunk. The same land…'

'… and the same evil past, but the incentive to coalesce all that evil has gone. Oh, but it still tries. On a few mornings, I've sensed the tingle in the air and the vibrations that used to bring about Caleb and Margareta Strange back from their fiery death. I glance out of my window, along Gallows Lane, up towards here and The Red Lion. I can see the grey mists, and I can feel them wanting to turn and whip up a vortex, but they wither and go away. For they have nothing to focus on anymore. Ben, and his wicked ancestors before him, mind, were the causes of so much misery in Upper Slaughter. Ben has his grave at the bottom of the Fairoak Colliery shaft. You did us all such a great big favour when, in your company, he fell down that deep mine shaft…' Donald looked at Janet.

'What?' Ted noticed the querying looks on their faces.

'Shall I tell him, darling?' She nodded. So, Donald explained to Ted what had happened before they left The Red Lion when they were last here. Ted's eyes widened and relaxed as Donald spoke. He exclaimed a few 'ooh's!' and 'oh my!' as Donald told him how Ben had really died.

'That explains the red sores on your hands. I noticed them when you arrived.'

'Oh, yes. I'm mostly healed up now, aren't I, darling?' Janet nodded.

'Well, I'm dashed!' he exclaimed when Donald had finished. 'What a story! Why, my old son, that's even better for us around here, the villagers and The Chase. Already folks hereabouts were having phobias about the Fairoak mine shaft. People avoid walking around that part of The Chase anymore for fear of evil vibes rising from his grave. Wait until I tell them that Ben isn't there. So, he perished right here with all the others.' Donald and Janet nodded and smiled.

'Doesn't all this talking make your mouth dry, my old fella, my lad?' Ted wheezed with a smile.

'It sure does, Ted. Come on let's go inside and I'll buy us another pint of Abbot.' Donald lifted him off the bench and arm in arm they walked across the patio. Donald stopped and turned. 'Are you coming, darling?'

'No, you go ahead; I'll be along in a moment,' Janet replied with equally wide a smile. She lifted her face to the sunshine and breathed the fresh, country air. She smelled sweet, wild hyacinth, the tang of the pine plantations and aromatic wild garlic growing on the forest floor.

After a short while, her head turned as she noticed a slight noise. It was coming from the yew tree. It sounded like a creaking, dry sound. With increasing fascination, her eyes focused on the trunk. Her keen eyes noticed an infinitesimal movement. Slowly, imperceptibly, the two remaining wrought iron nails that had crucified Abbot Ibáñez were being ejected from the rustic bark. It had only taken two thousand years, but there were no more evil, obnoxious influences on the pagan plot of land. The old tree had at last spewed out the last remaining relics of its satanic past.

Janet watched in wonderment as the old nails dropped onto the grass. The Abbot Ibáñez yew tree was whole again, and *The Crucified Abbot* was consigned to history.

Introducing the author's previous riveting novel, published by New Generation Publishing

PEOPLE GO MISSING FROM TIME TO TIME, SOME ARE FOUND AND RETURNED TO THEIR FAMILIES, SOME ARE NEVER FOUND, SOME TURN UP DEAD.

When amateur mudlarks discover body parts on the Thames' beaches, the Metropolitan Police start investigating. They determine that some of the body parts belong to missing people.

A newly formed team of detectives in the Metropolitan Police commence enquiries to discover where the body parts originate. Their investigations unearth scenes of horror that are beyond what any reasonable person could imagine existing in modern London.

A lonely old Church on the Thames quays at Rotherhithe in South London that supplies food and shelter for homeless itinerants attracts their attention.

Complicated love affairs between three of the young detectives interact with evil criminals who commit gruesome murders.

One homeless itinerant manages to escape the clutches of the criminals and provides retribution for herself and justice for the thousands of people who have been murdered and mutilated.

ISBN 978-1-80031-780-2

9 781800 317802

90000

New Generation Publishing

294

About the Author

Alan was born in a coal mining village called Chase Terrace, Cannock Chase, Staffordshire, in the English Midlands. He continued his father and grandfather's legacy, working underground in the local coal mine before qualifying as a land and mining surveyor. Alan later became a lecturer and a Master of Philosophy at Birmingham University. Before becoming an author, he achieved chief examiner posts with several United Kingdom examination boards.

Apart from writing, his passion is playing the euphonium on the unique English brass band scene. From humble beginnings as a boy in a colliery band, Alan has performed in various musical ensembles across Europe.

He's written and published eight non-fiction books on the history of Cannock Chase in Staffordshire. '*The Crucified Abbot*' is his fourth published fictional novel.

After living at a watermill in the Loire Valley in France, he now shares his time between his homes in Cannock, Staffordshire, and San Miguel, a coastal village on southern Spain's Costa Blanca.

Other publications by Alan Brookes

Technical and professional
1991   The Calibration of Electronic Surveying Instruments
*   Published by The University of Birmingham*
1993   Electronic Creep in Theodolites
*   Published by The Institution of Civil Engineering*

Autobiographical
2001   Arising from Coal Dust Published by The Merault Press
2006   The History of the Cannock Chase Colliery Brass Band
*   Published by The Merault Press*

Biographical
2005   The Life of Doctor John Pooley Published by The Merault
*   Press*
2007   The Few of Cannock Chase Published by The Merault Press

Historical novels
2003   Tales of Cannock Chase Published by The Merault Press
2004   Black Nuggets of Cannock Chase Published by The Merault
*   Press*

Fictional novels
2016   Bellesauvage Published by Authorhouse
2019   The Bellesauvage Redemption Published by Authorhouse
2020   Mudlarks Published by New Generation
2021   The Crucified Abbot Published by New Generation

Lightning Source UK Ltd.
Milton Keynes UK
UKHW041947260421
382669UK00001B/31